Clare Dowling was born in Kilkenny. She trained as an actress and began her writing career as a playwright with the independent theatre company Glasshouse Productions of which she was a founder member. She has written short films, children's books, drama for teenagers and is currently a scriptwriter for Ireland's top soap *Fair City*. She lives in Dublin and is married with a son. She is expecting her second child in the autumn.

Praise for EXPECTING EMILY:

'The wry voice, confident plotting and the upbeat mood . . . elevate this to a very satisfying read'

Marian Keyes

'Very funny and original'   Cathy Kelly

'What sets this apart is the quality of the writing. It is great fun, a great read'   RTÉ

Also by Clare Dowling

Fast Forward

Expecting Emily

Clare Dowling

headline

First published in 2002
by HEADLINE BOOK PUBLISHING

10 9 8 7 6 5 4 3 2 1

ISBN 0 7553 0362 8

Typeset in Palatino by
Letterpart Limited, Reigate, Surrey

Printed and bound in Great Britain by
Clays Ltd, St Ives plc

HEADLINE BOOK PUBLISHING
A division of Hodder Headline
338 Euston Road
LONDON NW1 3BH

www.headline.co.uk
www.hodderheadline.com

For my parents

Acknowledgements

Thanks to Gaye Shortland, Paula Campbell and all at Poolbeg. Thanks to Betty Moore for sharing her medical knowledge. Thanks to Margaret, Pamela and my mother for those Sunday morning brainstorming sessions. Thanks again to Siân and Caroline for reading it. Thanks to Stewart for all his overtime at the weekends and to Sean for helping me with the research.

Part One

The day started well enough for Emily except that she was late.

'Excuse me, excuse me, thank you, excuse me. Oh! You're very kind!'

She beamed at two men who whipped open the double doors of the clinic for her and rushed past, not seeing the look of fear on their faces. It was the huge, tent-like denim maternity trousers that did it, and the way her belly swung wildly from side to side like an uncontrolled missile.

Now. Floor three. Emily paused by the lift. It said 400kgs only. She hadn't been weighed since last week but just to be on the safe side she headed for the stairs. It would be unfair to put the other lift occupants at risk.

'You're late,' Mr Chapman's receptionist said with a little sigh. Her hair looked nailed on. Emily admired it. She'd left half of hers on the pillow that morning. Conor said that soon they would have enough to stuff a duvet.

'Sorry,' Emily said. The thirty-mile drive from

Paulstown to Cork City always took longer than she anticipated.

'I'll see if Mr Chapman can squeeze you in.'

'He did the last time I was late. Squeezed me in. Or should that be squez?'

The receptionist didn't crack a smile. She never did. Oh well. She was probably only on 15k a year and couldn't afford to smile.

'Are you feeling all right?' she asked instead, looking at Emily.

'Fine. Well, maybe a little dizzy.' Big black dots were bouncing before Emily's eyes. Next time she would definitely take the lift.

'Dizziness tends to happen.' The receptionist nodded sagely. 'You know, when you're pregnant.'

This was rich from a girl who Emily guessed had been on the pill since she was twelve and still double-bagged everything. Emily stealthily reached behind and unzipped her 'roomy' maternity pants. The relief was instant and enormous, and the black dots disappeared.

'Why don't you take a seat,' the receptionist said. 'But as you've missed your appointment, I should warn you that you could have a bit of a wait.'

'That's fine,' Emily said quickly, inching away, but the receptionist had long experience of dealing with the likes of Emily. A long, pale hand shot out over the reception desk.

'Your sample.'

'I forgot it,' Emily admitted.

Behind her, she could feel the rest of the women in the waiting-room startle into awareness. Imagine forgetting to bring a sample! When they had probably been up since dawn drinking gallons of mineral water and decaff tea to generate that perfect, precious 10 ml. Some of them had probably used a tea-strainer in an effort at quality control.

The receptionist gave another little sigh.

'Mr Chapman needs a sample from you every week.'

Emily looked at her. 'Why, can't he produce his own?'

'No, no, he needs yours for the tests, you see . . . oh! You're joking. Um, aren't you?'

'I am,' Emily said patiently. Sometimes she wondered why she bothered. But then a tiny snigger escaped the receptionist, before she guiltily covered her mouth with her hand. Nobody laughed at Mr Chapman, the most eminent obstetrician in the whole of the southwest. Some women planned their pregnancies around his holidays.

The receptionist produced a spare plastic sample jar and leaned in. They were co-conspirators now. 'The bathroom's down to your right, Emily.'

'Thanks, ah . . .?'

'Sandra.'

The tiny plastic container defied all reason. Emily did her best but her efforts were as usual more miss than hit. She dried up the bathroom floor with wads of toilet paper and hoped that nobody would notice her damp shoe.

'My God!' A bloated, pasty face suddenly confronted her. 'Oh, it's only me,' she noted sadly, looking quickly away from the bathroom mirror. Once upon a time she had been quite nice-looking.

She carefully washed her hands. Her wedding ring wouldn't budge, she noticed, the skin around it pinched and red. She should have taken it off before it was too late. Now they'd probably have to cut it off.

Still, Conor would buy her an eternity ring, wouldn't he? Wasn't that what men bought their wives on production of the first heir? A little well-done-love, smashing-job – mind you, I'd have done it ten times better myself if I'd had a pair of ovaries.

'Excuse me . . . sorry . . . excuse me.' It was extraordinary how much of her life Emily seemed to spend excusing herself. She squeezed into a corner in the waiting-room and picked through the same tired selection of magazines. All the good ones were gone of course; *Gardener's Monthly* and 1998's copy of *Newsweek* had already been snapped up. Emily opened up *House & Home* and immediately wished she hadn't. The baby's room was only half-painted. She and Conor had spent an hour last night trying to assemble the easy-to-assemble cot. Conor had given up in a near tantrum, vowing to write to the manufacturers. Emily didn't know what that would achieve apart from causing a fuss. Conor had retorted that there would be a greater fuss if the baby fell through the bottom and broke its neck. 'Jesus, Conor!' Emily's knees had snapped together in case the baby might fall through her own bottom. Conor had lugged the cot into the garage. There were sounds of sawing. He'd reappeared, triumphant. 'It's assembled.'

The waiting-room was silent save for the sounds of magazine pages furiously turning. Not that anybody was reading, Emily included. She was watching the woman in the red trouser suit out of the corner of her eye. The woman in the red trouser suit was watching your woman in the baggy jumper. *She* was watching Emily and Trouser Suit simultaneously. And the one in the flowery frock was watching them all, or at least their midriffs. The air of competition was intense. Who had the biggest belly? Who wore the nicest maternity clothes? Whose ankles were the least swollen? And occasionally a smug sense of reassurance – thank God *my* baby won't have a hooter like that.

It had been the same in antenatal classes. Everyone watching each other in a kind of guarded way. And the men were worse! Strutting about, giving each other I've-got-a-functioning-willy looks. It was nonsense really. Surely they were all in this together?

Emily lowered her magazine and leaned in to the woman in the trouser suit. The woman started a bit, her hands flying protectively to her belly.

'How many weeks are you?' Emily enquired politely.
'Thirty-two.'

'Me too.' Emily smiled. 'I'm due the tenth of May.'

'I'm the eleventh!' Trouser Suit was delighted now.

'No!'

'Have you had any Braxton Hicks yet?' Trouser Suit asked eagerly.

Emily looked at her blankly. 'What?'

'You know, the preparatory contractions?'

'Um, no.'

'Oh.'

Emily was losing Trouser Suit – it was happening before her very eyes. 'But I'm hoping for one any minute now.'

'I'm getting quite a few of them,' the girl in the baggy jumper offered shyly.

Trouser Suit's defection was complete. She turned her back on Emily. 'Thank God! I thought I was the only one!'

'They woke me up the other night,' Baggy Jumper confided. 'I thought I was going into labour!'

The woman in the flowery frock just couldn't keep out of it. 'You've a lovely little bump,' she told Baggy Jumper.

'Oh stop! I'm like an elephant!'

'*I'm* like an elephant!' Flowery Frock cried. 'And I'm only twenty-eight weeks!'

'God, I thought you were nearly full-term,' Trouser Suit said.

Flowery Frock was sorry she'd opened her mouth now. Emily saw her chance to get back into the fray, but Baggy Jumper beat her to it.

'Mr Chapman thinks I'm not putting on enough

weight,' she murmured nervously even though every-one could see she was delighted. 'I've to eat more.'

'I ate a whole sliced pan last night,' Trouser Suit sighed.

Emily leaned forward eagerly. 'That's nothing! I had three Aeros and a Galaxy ice cream!'

Baggy Jumper, Trouser Suit and Flowery Frock looked at her in silence.

'Um, all that sugar and additives . . . it mightn't be good for the baby . . .' Baggy Jumper eventually offered.

Emily felt like she had been slapped across the face. She retreated behind her magazine, raging with herself. Why hadn't she said something about the sliced pan? All that gluten! Not to mention the pound of butter that had probably gone with it. But the moment was gone. The women had moved on to various discharges now, discussing colours and textures with glee. And she after starting the bloody conversation too!

She gave her bump a quick, loving pat. At least you won't have ears like hers, she reassured it.

The baby kicked her roundly in the kidneys. You little shit, she thought dispassionately.

Here came the husbands now into the packed waiting-room, having been despatched to park cars, buy mineral water and phone the office. There was much confusion as each tried to get as close as possible to the mother of their child without upsetting the mother of anybody else's child.

'I can scoot over . . .'

'No, no, you're the one who's pregnant.' A nervous laugh.

'I'm not that big.' More laughter.

'Jerry, there's a space over here.'

'Oh right. Excuse me . . . sorry . . .'

Jerry slid in beside Baggy Jumper, relieved, and took her hand as though she were made of bone china. He was no sooner settled before the glass plate at reception flew back.

'Michelle? Jerry? Mr Chapman's ready for you now.'

Baggy Jumper and Jerry exchanged a secret smile before walking down the corridor and into the inner sanctum, him steering her with a firm hand on the small of her back, as though by being pregnant she had also lost her sense of direction.

There was no more chatter in the waiting-room. It was all very well to confide in your womenfolk about eating sliced pans, but not in front of the men. It would have been as tasteless and embarrassing as discussing period pains.

The door opened again and Conor breezed in. Sensibly, he had bought a copy of the *Irish Times* in the shop next door.

He didn't try to squeeze in anywhere. He simply stood by the door, looked at Emily and nodded around easily at everybody.

Emily felt she should speak to him, claim him or something. 'Did you manage to get parking?'

'Yes,' he said. Of course he had. Everybody else had

driven around the clinic in circles for half an hour but car parks seemed to swell and open up for Conor.

They had driven down separately. Conor would be working in Cork tonight and figured he would pass the afternoon shopping, rather than making the sixty-mile round trip home and back again.

'Did you?' he asked. 'Get parking?' He had a great interest in these things.

'Oh yes,' Emily said breezily. She had ended up parking in the consultants' car park. She had stuck a note to the windscreen saying 'On a delivery'. She had been quite pleased with that.

'We're going to have a bit of a wait,' she told him. 'Sandra told me.'

Conor's eyebrows jumped up at the cosy reference to Sandra. So, Emily had finally broken down the hard-faced bitch. Conor himself didn't waste his energy on people like that.

'Well, we'll see about that,' he said, throwing a grim look towards reception.

'Conor, please don't make a fuss.' Emily was embarrassed. She hoped he wouldn't trot out his argument in front of everyone – that they paid handsomely for Mr Chapman's time and that it wasn't right to make pregnant women wait around like this.

Thankfully, he didn't. He merely shrugged and opened his paper.

Emily sat back, closed her eyes, and concentrated on the movement in her tummy. The baby was turning over. She still wasn't quite used to it after all these months. In fact, it was very odd sometimes when she was lying quite still to see her belly bulge and flop over entirely of its own accord. She thought she knew exactly how Sigourney Weaver had felt in *Alien*. Or was it *Alien 2*?

She had confided this to her sister Liz once. Liz had five boys and liked to be consulted for advice.

'My God, Emily, you're not very maternal, are you? Robbie! Get out of that puddle this instant or I'll murder you!'

Emily had felt guilty afterwards. Maybe there was something wrong with her. Surely her maternal instincts, whatever they were supposed to be, would come to the fore once the baby was born? Or was it possible that she was one of those freak mothers who took one look at their new infant and demanded that it be taken away and reared by apes or something?

The baby had gone very still now. Probably frightened out of its wits. Or else, of course, it had just gone to sleep.

Mr Chapman, as usual, wanted to palpate her.

'Conor, there's no reason why you shouldn't see this,' he said generously.

Emily found herself lying on the examining table with Mr Chapman on one side and Conor on the other. They looked at her as though waiting for her to perform a trick. Emily vaguely resented them; she was growing a baby inside her, wasn't that enough?

'If you could just ease up your top,' Mr Chapman prompted clinically. 'Great. And loosen your trousers . . . oh, they're already loose.'

Telling herself there was nothing to be embarrassed about, Emily peeled down her trousers, embarrassed. Her underwear came into view.

Conor winked at her. Emily shot him a stony glance.

They had discussed knickers the night before (just before the cot incident). Emily had been hand-washing a roomy white pair with a pink trim especially for today. She had three pairs that she rotated for this weekly visit, all new and white and granny-like with different coloured trims. The trims were important – that way Mr Chapman would know that she had actually changed them.

Emily had tried to explain to Conor why she could never wear her black lacy ones in here, for example. Well, the mere idea of sex at these examinations seemed obscene or something. But sex had led to her condition in the first place, Conor said reasonably. Of course it had, Emily said, wanting him to understand. But she didn't want Mr Chapman . . . well, to get a fright. Supposing he thought she was coming on to him?

Conor laughed. Chapman's a professional, he said. He's sick of the sight of women's bums. He probably turns his back on his wife in bed at night with the words, 'Sorry, darling, but if I see another one today . . .'

Emily, perversely, took umbrage. What was wrong

with her bum anyway? No, no, she understood perfectly! It's all very well to say that pregnant women are gloriously sexy, but when push comes to shove, it's only lip-service!

Conor said that she sweated the small stuff. It had sounded like an insult. Emily opened the first of the three Aeros in a dignified silence. Conor enquired carefully whether they were having a row over knickers. The way he said it made her laugh. She dropped the subject. She hadn't thought it was a row. She had thought it was a lively discussion. Still, no sense in letting it spoil the cot assembly. Conor had already studied the instructions for ages in anticipation.

Mr Chapman, of course, never once looked in the direction of her knickers. He just palpated, pressed and pinged her naked stomach, a detached smile on his face.

'The head's starting to engage,' he announced.

Having maintained a respectful distance thus far, Conor now stepped up close to Emily's belly proprietarily.

'Is that good?'

'It just means that the baby's head is working down towards the birth canal.'

'So he's in the vertex position?'

'Exactly!' Mr Chapman was delighted to be speaking to a man, having spent most of his life dealing with women. And a man with knowledge to boot. 'He's head-down which saves us a lot of bother when it comes time to get him out.'

Conor nodded vigorously. He had read *The Pregnant Father*. It's a manual, he had patiently explained when Emily had roared laughing; you wouldn't take a new computer out of its packaging without first reading the manual, would you? Emily would and had. Conor had persisted with his reading and could now fling around words like 'haemolytic jaundice' and 'tainted meconium' as though he were a chronic sufferer himself. He wasn't so hot on the practical aspects; when the book had gone on about voice recognition, he had laid his head on Emily's naked tummy that night and directed a rather stiff monologue at her belly-button, starting with 'Um, this is your father here.' Emily had said that if the baby didn't recognise his voice when it got out, at least it would know all about how the lawnmower was acting up. She had only been joking. But he hadn't done it again after that.

'He's lying side-on at the moment,' Mr Chapman said, digging his fingers into Emily's pelvis. It hurt.

'Or she,' Emily said, as loudly as she dared. Mr Chapman could be very intimidating. He reminded her of Magnus Magnusson in his three-piece suit. His chosen subject was pregnancy, naturally. But today Emily felt brave with Conor beside her.

Mr Chapman smiled in a detached way. 'Are you hoping for a girl?'

'We don't mind so long as it's healthy,' Conor said strongly.

'Sensible attitude,' Mr Chapman said just as strongly.

Any minute now Emily expected them to excuse themselves and go off for a round of golf together.

'Are we done here?' she asked, wondering how she had managed to become superfluous to the entire proceedings.

'Not quite.' Mr Chapman was indulgent now as he picked up a stethoscope. 'Let's listen to the heartbeat, shall we?'

It was the part of the visit that everybody liked best. Emily shivered a little as Mr Chapman applied cold gel to her belly. Then he laid the stethoscope gently on her skin, moving it around, his brow furrowed as he listened.

'Ah!' He reached over and dramatically flicked a switch over Emily's head. Immediately, the baby's muffled heartbeat filled the room. Mr Chapman stood back to watch Emily and Conor's faces. This was his moment, the time when he modestly felt like the giver of life.

'It's so fast!' Emily said, more because it was expected than anything else. She lived with this baby twenty-four hours a day, felt its every hiccup and kick. That was enough.

No, let Conor have this one, she magnanimously thought, peeking at him. His wonder was there for all the world to see – well, for Emily anyway, who over the years had learned to spot those subtle signs of emotion. He blinked more than usual, for example, and his chin would occasionally dip in a violent bob.

She knew that he would go into Mothercare that afternoon, arriving home with baby ski boots or a car-seat neck-support or some high-tech toy that would confound adults, never mind a newborn. Emily would put it away in the baby's room along with all the other ridiculous stuff he'd bought. She never said anything. She could afford to indulge him. And it made her feel a bit superior in a way.

Back at his desk, Mr Chapman made cryptic notes on Emily's chart. He caught Emily looking and shielded the notes with his hand; lest she discover something about her own condition.

'It's a fine big baby,' he pronounced eventually, as though it were all his own doing.

Emily felt a nervous twinge in her nether regions. Conor sat a little taller.

'And doing quite well from what I can see,' Mr Chapman concluded.

'Great,' Emily said with feeling.

There didn't seem to be a lot else to say. Emily decided that she would take the initiative and dismiss herself.

She stood airily. 'Cheerio then! Same time next week I suppose?'

'Not so fast,' Mr Chapman said.

Emily sat down again clumsily. He peered at her over his bifocals.

'We need to talk about your blood pressure.'

'What about it?'

'It's up a little.'

'How much?'

'Nothing to be too worried about,' Mr Chapman assured her. He hadn't answered her question. 'High blood pressure is a common complaint in late pregnancy. We just need to keep an eye on it.'

Emily's eyes flew to Conor. He gave her a measured look that said 'don't panic'.

'I'm also a bit concerned about your weight gain,' Mr Chapman added.

Jesus Christ, why did everything come back to weight in this world?

'It's due to water retention,' Mr Chapman clarified. 'Surely you've noticed a bit of puffiness?'

'Yes,' she admitted. She had been hoping he would not mention it.

'Nothing to be too worried about,' Mr Chapman said again, tactlessly. 'But I'd like to see you the day after tomorrow all the same. Sandra will fit you in.'

It rained all the way back from Cork. Conor was forced to drive in the end because Emily's car had been towed. When they'd rescued it from the car pound, the battery went flat because she'd left the lights on and the jump leads had mysteriously gone missing from the boot of the car. They'd left it on the side of the road. Conor would have to get Billy Middlemiss to help out tonight.

She felt him looking at her from time to time. But

mostly he kept his eyes on the road. At least he hadn't given out about the car. That was some indication that he knew how upset she was. And his index finger was twitching for a cigarette, an indication of how upset he was. Any minute now he would say something momentous, something so sweet and comforting and insightful that all Emily's worries would be blown away.

'Look at that joker! No brake lights! It's a good thing I'm not a plain-clothes garda.'

Conor had missed his calling. Every single trip he wished he were a plain-clothes garda. And he would have been very good at it too, Emily often thought. She could just imagine him whipping out his notebook and leaning in a car window, stern yet compassionate. 'Do you realise you're doing forty in a thirty-mile zone, madam?' And he would write a ticket in his clear, strong handwriting. If the driver were elderly or infirm, he would let them off with a caution.

Conor had a robust appetite for law and order in all areas of life. Which made it all the odder that he was, in fact, a professional pianist. But that too had its own order, Emily supposed, as she thought of him doing his scales on the piano on Saturday mornings, his long brown fingers belting methodically up and down the keys, head cocked slightly towards the piano as though he suspected it were trying to catch him out. But then, when she had left the room, she would hear him launch into Chopin's Revolutionary Study. Peeking in the door, she would see his head flying backwards, his body coiled with a peculiar, passionate energy. His eyes would squint up and become very far away. Emily would sometimes have the sensation that he was a total stranger. Which was ridiculous. When the piece was over, he would straighten up and he was just Conor again, and he would go and put the rubbish out.

Emily's hands smoothed her belly. The baby hadn't moved since they'd left the clinic. Typical. It would probably torture her all day with its stillness, and then break into a samba just when she was trying to go to sleep. But she wouldn't mind, not this time.

The weight of this new worry settled down on her shoulders, adding to all the other worries Emily seemed to pick up so effortlessly. Please God, she prayed, let nothing go wrong. Oh, and sorry I haven't been to Mass since 1996.

'Look, Emily, it's a bit of high blood pressure, that's all.' Finally, he said something.

'And water retention,' she pointed out.

'It's a common complaint in late pregnancy. Chapman said so. There's nothing to worry about.'

He roundly pipped the driver in front as they overtook.

'Conor?'

He knew what she was going to say and he swiftly headed her off at the pass. 'Nothing is going to happen to this baby.'

'How do you know?'

'Nothing is going to happen.' He just didn't want to hear it.

'Do you think I'm doing something wrong?' Emily asked. She knew this was ridiculous, but you had to be clever with Conor, you had to find little ways of drawing him out. Sometimes she thought a lot of their conversations only came about because of her increasingly imaginative ploys to get him to talk.

'Maybe,' he said, flooring her.

'What?' She twisted in her seat, hotly defensive. 'What a stupid thing to say!'

'But you asked!' He was confused.

She hadn't meant for him to agree. Didn't he know anything?

'And what exactly am I doing wrong, Mr Expert?'

'I don't know . . .'

'Don't try and backtrack!'

He shrugged. 'Maybe you're working too hard.'

'Well!' It was difficult to argue with him. Crawley Dunne & O'Reilly, solicitors, demanded forty-eight hours a week of her time, plus the odd weekend. But everybody worked the same hours. It wasn't just her!

'What am I supposed to do, take it a bit easier because I'm pregnant?'

'That would be an option,' he said mildly.

'I can't do that! They've been very understanding so far,' she said loyally. 'Letting me off for appointments and hospital visits and everything!'

'They're obliged to by law. Being solicitors, I'm sure they're well clued up on their obligations.'

She detected that familiar faint note of contempt in

his voice and was insulted on Crawley Dunne & O'Reilly's behalf. They had given Emily her first big break! They gave her a pay rise without fail on June 1st of every year, and regular bonuses too. Crawley Dunne & O'Reilly knew how to reward their workers. And now Conor expected her to turn around and admit that she couldn't hack it just because she was pregnant? Five other women in the office had had babies in the past two years, and not a single one of them had taken so much as a day off before their official leave. So what if Emily didn't feel so hot some mornings? There were standards to be upheld, expectations to be met. She was well aware of them.

'I don't know what you have against them,' she said stoutly. 'They pay our mortgage.'

'I contribute too.'

'Yes, yes, of course you do, I didn't mean . . .' She moved on swiftly. 'And then there's the partnership.'

He looked at her blankly – as if she hadn't been talking about it for weeks now!

'Oh yes,' he eventually said. Doubtfully?

'The meeting's today.' She checked her watch. 'In five minutes to be exact. I was hoping to make it back to talk to Mr Crawley.'

They were only in Fermoy. Another eleven miles to go.

'What difference would it make?' Conor enquired carefully. 'They're either going to give it to you or they're not.'

'Well, yes, but there's no harm in stating my case.'

He impatiently slowed at a roundabout. 'Surely you've proved your case, Emily? After giving those guys six years of your life? I'd think the bloody least they could do is give you a partnership.'

'Yes, well, it'll happen today,' she said, sitting back.

He had taken the good out of it somehow. She had put a bottle of champagne and everything in the fridge for a little celebration later. One glass only, mind. But not now. And especially not after Mr Chapman's news.

Emily suddenly wondered how they had ended up talking about work, instead of her worries. Conor had that knack, though. Last week she had been putting baby things into a box that would go in the attic. Conor had come upstairs and somehow or other they had ended up discussing Mrs Conlon-next-door's application for planning permission to extend her kitchen. Right into Emily and Conor's back garden, as it transpired. They had hurried to the back window to assess the potential damage, the box forgotten.

He surprised her now by reaching over and squeezing her hand.

'This baby is thirty-four weeks old. Fully formed. If it were born this minute it'd have a good chance. Look at the statistics.'

He was in his plain-clothes garda mode again, breaking her down with facts and figures. And it was working because she wanted it to.

'You're right, I suppose.'

'Of course I am.'

They drove in silence for a while, Emily looking out the window. The landscape grew more and more familiar. And here now was Paulstown, population two thousand.

Conor checked his watch. 'That meeting will have started. Why don't we just go home?'

She thought of the stack of work waiting for her in the office. They might cheerfully let her off for her appointments but it was sort of on the understanding that she caught up in her own time. She should delegate, really, but those law-student ninnies on work experience never got it right, which meant more work for her in the end. Besides, she wanted to have her desk cleared before she went on maternity leave in two weeks' time. That too was sort of expected of her.

But this business of the high blood pressure was bothering her. If she took it easy today, then that might sort things out. She owed it to the baby. Anyway, she could always work at home.

'You know, I think I'll take the rest of the day off,' she said loudly. 'They can ring me if they want me.'

Conor's eyebrows disappeared into his hairline. 'Good God, are you sure about this, Emily? Let's not do anything rash here.'

'Shut up,' she snapped. It was easy for him to laugh, with no commitments all day long except for three hours' work tonight.

He was repentant now. 'I'll make you a cup of my special cappuccino.'

Emily was pleased. Conor hardly ever made cappuccinos these days. It seemed to take too long. When they married six years ago, making cappuccinos was an altogether quicker business and they had drunk it morning, noon and night.

Still, there were other compensations, Emily was sure, for the froth of cappuccinos.

She looked over at Conor now, fondly. He reminded her of that Beamish ad – consistency in a world gone mad. And there was a lot to be said for that, wasn't there?

Crawley Dunne & O'Reilly was the biggest solicitors' firm in Paulstown. In fact, it was the only one. It did a brisk trade in farm auctions, period house sales and occasionally drew up wills for the more well-heeled locals. Business was so good that they had recently refurbished the entire reception area in glass and chrome. This deterred some of the more undesirable elements in the town who took their minor legal worries elsewhere, leaving Crawley Dunne & O'Reilly to the business of selling vast tracts of farmland for a hefty two percent of the sale price. The last time they had set foot in an actual court of law was to defend Mr Crawley's nephew who had been up on drunk-and-disorderly charges two years ago. It had been a distasteful and unprofitable experience for everyone concerned and they had gratefully returned to selling land. They were auctioneers by any other name but would have been highly insulted at the accusation.

Crawley Dunne & O'Reilly were not only rich but also shrewd; they watched *Ally McBeal* and knew that bright young things helped to shift properties much faster than ponderous old farts, and so they actively headhunted solicitors from the bigger firms in Cork City. One of the brightest of these bright young things was Neasa Martin who right now was studiously applying herself to her computer in the open-plan office. She heard the squeak of new leather shoes approaching. Here came Creepy Crawley. She quickly closed the poker game on her computer screen and brought up a contract instead.

'Neasa?'

He stood as close to her as he dared. She smelled mouthwash and Joop! He was a man desperately fighting Old Spice and middle age.

'Yes, Mr Crawley?'

'Is Emily back yet?'

'No, she must have been delayed. You know she had an appointment with her obstetrician?'

'Yes, yes,' he said quickly. For all his put-on panache, Charles Crawley had led a sheltered life. Pregnancy to him was still that horrid picture in that book his father had forced on him at the age of twelve; after all his talk of graceful white storks, too. It had been a desperate betrayal. For seven months now, Charles Crawley had been unable to look Emily Collins in the stomach.

Neasa smiled innocently. 'Or maybe she's dropping it

right this minute.' She enjoyed his blush.

'Oh! Well! Let's hope not!'

'Absolutely,' Neasa agreed. 'With the partners' meeting and everything. I know she was anxious to talk to you before it starts.'

'Yes, I was hoping to talk to her too,' Crawley said with a regretful nod.

He was lying. Neasa just knew it.

'Still, I suppose she'll be in later this afternoon. To hear all the news, you know . . .?'

She offered him one of her wide-eyed, inquisitive looks. Usually this induced an erection and he would babble on in an effort to distract her while it subsided. But Crawley's trousers remained resolutely flat today and his lip buttoned.

'We won't be finished before the close of business,' he said, clipped. 'By the way, Gary is waiting for that contract on The Paddocks sale. He's meeting with their people this afternoon.'

'He's about to get it now,' Neasa told him sweetly.

'Good.' Crawley's eyes lingered on her shiny black, clean, clean hair. Sometimes at night he dreamed that she was waiting for him when he got out of the shower and she would offer him her mane of black hair to dry himself with. He had fantasies of telling her about this some day and her nodding understandingly.

'Carry on,' he said, thickly.

His shoes squeaked across the plush carpet and down the corridor into the boardroom where the other partners, Daphne Dunne and Ewan O'Reilly, waited. The door shut firmly as they went into session.

Neasa picked up the phone and dialled. At the other end of the open-plan office, she saw Gary look over before picking up.

'What!'

'I have that contract you need.'

'About bloody time.'

'Yes, I'm sorry. Would you like to go over it?'

'I think I should. The last one was littered with mistakes.'

'Will I come down to your desk?'

'I can't concentrate with all the noise in here!'

'I think Emily's office is free . . .'

'Fine. Now.'

He hung up on her. Regina looked over, her eyebrows jumping up. That pig Gary seemed to have it in for Neasa. Neasa rolled her eyes in silent agreement, picked up the contract, and walked into Emily's office.

The smell of Emily's citrus air freshener hit her. The desk was completely bare except for a neatly folded document. Oops. Emily was slipping up on her filing again.

Gary was lolling in Emily's swivel-chair. He had his penis out.

'Oh goody,' Neasa sighed, locking the door, hitching up her skirt and leaping on him. The swivel-chair went flying backwards, violently colliding with Emily's cheese plant. The leaves bobbled merrily for five minutes as they went at it hard.

Neasa eventually flung herself away. 'My thighs. They're killing me.'

'No problem,' said Gary, flipping her over in a daring manoeuvre. There was nothing wrong with his thighs, honed and fine-tuned by ten years of amateur rugby. The cheese plant wilted under a fresh assault.

'How are you doing?' Gary eventually enquired, his eyes glazed.

'Just keep going,' Neasa panted.

'Are you sure you don't want me to slap you or anything?'

He was so sweet.

'No, I think I'll be all right.'

Through the wall, they heard Mr Crawley's voice as the partner's meeting began. It was enough for both of them.

'Ohohoh,' Gary said.

Neasa simply broke a fingernail on his back.

Then they were tidying up quickly, straightening Emily's chair, sellotaping the cheese plant. They gave each other little aren't-we-so-daring looks, thrilled with themselves and each other.

'I am so in love with you, Neasa Martin,' Gary said sincerely. He was big and butch enough looking to carry this off.

'I know,' Neasa agreed smugly. 'Me too.'

She had washed her hair every single day since she'd got it together with Gary. If that wasn't love, she didn't know what was.

'Better get back,' he said.

'Absolutely. I think Regina might be starting to twig.'

Not that it mattered really. Office romances weren't forbidden here – only heavily frowned upon and greatly discouraged. But Neasa and Gary had talked seriously about it and felt that what they had was so precious that they didn't want to expose it to tawdry office intrigue and, well, gossip. Besides, they would no longer be able to nip into empty offices for quick sex. They found it desperately exciting. Also, it was the sort of thing you only read about in very trendy magazines and both of them were rapidly pushing thirty.

Gary's penis was growing big again.

'Wow!' he said cheerfully. 'Are you wearing new perfume or something?'

'No,' Neasa said, fascinated. She would love a new spring coat in just that shade of purple.

'Oh, well! I'll put it away now,' Gary said efficiently.

'Don't! Let's just watch for a minute.' It was enormous now. How could he manage it again so soon?

'Maybe it's that kinky underwear of yours,' Gary said, embarrassed.

'You've seen it before,' Neasa reminded him, suspicious now. He was trying to stuff the penis back into his pants. He bent it this way and that, but it escaped and waved its bulbous head merrily.

'What the hell is going on?' Neasa said accusingly. 'I've never had this effect before!'

'Oh all right!' Gary shouted. 'I've got the partnership, okay!'

Neasa blinked. 'What?'

'Creepy Crawley came up to me before the meeting. He more or less said I had it in the bag.'

'Fantastic!' Neasa spat sarcastically.

'It's not my fault, Neasa! I didn't go canvassing!'

'Turn it down!'

'I can't turn it down! Jesus Christ, I've waited six years for this! Six years of selling boggy bits of fucking land!'

'Don't curse.'

'Sorry.'

'I mean, fucking hell, Gary!'

'I deserve it! Come on, Neasa, I feel just terrible about all this!' His erection pointed gloriously towards the ceiling.

'For God's sake put it away!' she snapped.

He did so in silence. She found that she was trembling. She couldn't believe that they were having their First Fight. And it was only this morning that Gary had told her that he actually thought she looked better without make-up.

The silence stretched. They were on dangerous territory now. Neasa knew she would have to handle this one very carefully.

'They're pigging bastards,' she said eventually.

Gary looked up warily. 'I suppose.'

'They suck the blood out of you.'

'Shamelessly,' Gary agreed more robustly.

'It just makes me sick to have to work here!'

'Me too! God, I hate this place! If it wasn't for my two mortgages, I'd . . . I'd . . .'

'Quit!'

'Well. That's a bit drastic.'

They smiled crookedly at each other. Whew. That was a close one. Neasa didn't feel she had given in by deflecting the anger onto Crawley Dunne & O'Reilly. It was just that if they were going to have a Big Row, then she would at least like to be a main player in it, as opposed to an interested third party.

'Emily's my best friend,' she said. 'What kind of person would I be if I didn't feel bad for her?'

'I know,' Gary groaned. 'I feel bloody awful too. I mean, I wouldn't have minded beating Phil or Tony.'

He'd have had an erection for a week.

'But Emily . . . she works so hard.' He added hurriedly, 'not that I don't work hard too.'

'You're a total dosser.'

'Well, yes . . .'

'And you fiddle your expenses.'

'Naturally, I . . .'

'You're always calling in sick.'

'Can we stick to the important things here? I close the sales, Neasa.'

And that was it, really. He was known around the office as Jaws. He was sent in by Crawley Dunne & O'Reilly to all the biggest sales, where he would bite lumps out of potential vendors until, bleeding and legless, they coughed up the asking price plus twenty grand more.

What hope had Emily against him, ploughing away at her desk behind the scenes, running the entire office with unseen strokes?

'When are they going to announce it?'

'In the morning.'

At least she would get a chance to tell Emily tonight. She would bring a bottle of wine and they would eff and blind Crawley Dunne & O'Reilly out of it. Neasa would even threaten to hand in her notice at this latest piece of debauchery from them. She would be half-serious too. She had no intention of hanging around six years to be made partner in this backwater firm. But they had offered so much money when they had poached her from a proper solicitors' office in Cork, and Neasa had her priorities right. Still, she had an itch to practise real law again, and figured she would soon move back to a young, exciting firm in Cork. She too watched *Ally McBeal*.

'Aren't you pleased for me at all?' Gary asked in a small voice.

'Of course, Gary, amn't I mad about you!' Oh, the treachery.

'This could be a future for us,' Gary said meaningfully.

Cork suddenly receded at a dizzying pace. The 'future' had not been discussed thus far. They were too busy having sex in any case.

'Let's not jump the gun,' she said with admirable coolness. She flicked her long black dyed hair over her shoulder and left, secure in the knowledge that Gary was watching with his tongue hanging out.

'Yoo-hoo! Anybody home?'

'Isn't the car parked outside and the key in the door?' Conor said mildly, as he reached for milk to make the two cappuccinos into three.

'She's probably just passing.' Emily always felt she had to make excuses for her family, even though she no more wanted to see Liz than Conor did. She had a pain in her back and the start of a headache. Also, there was a nasty, buzzing sensation down there somewhere, as though she were sitting on an electric fence. *The Pregnant Father* had nothing to offer about this. Conor had already checked it.

The kitchen door burst open and Liz barged in, dragging Tommy, Robbie, Mikey and Bobby by various bits of their clothing. Willy was strapped to her front in a baby carrier. At least Emily assumed it was Willy. His face was sandwiched between Liz's breasts and he didn't appear to be breathing.

'Not disturbing you or anything?' Liz's colour was a bit high. But then again she was always rushing somewhere.

'Not at all,' Emily said.

Conor grunted something.

'And you've brought all the boys!' she added, feeling

she had to compensate for him.

'Say hello to your Auntie Emily and your Uncle Conor,' Liz commanded automatically.

'Hello,' they chorused glumly.

'Hi there!' Emily said, smiling her big, bright Auntie Smile. 'How's everyone?'

Tommy looked at the floor. Robbie and Mikey sniggered as though she had made a joke. Bobby was looking at her tummy in fascination.

'You're getting very fat,' he said happily.

'Bobby!' Liz was mortified.

'No, really, Liz, it's all right . . .'

Bobby knew he had said something wrong but he wasn't sure what.

'Apologise right now,' Liz ordered.

'Honestly, Liz . . .'

'Sorry,' Bobby said miserably. 'You're not fat at all.'

Conor miraculously produced a plate of biscuits. Not mean old fig rolls or boring digestives, but lovely big Chocolate Kimberlys in their own individual wrappings. Tommy, Robbie, Mikey and Bobby fell on them like a pack of starving dogs, before belatedly looking up at their mother for permission.

'Oh, go on then!' Liz looked at Emily rather accusingly. 'They won't eat their dinner, you know.'

'Why don't I give them a run around in the back?' Conor offered. 'They can burn it off.'

Liz looked suspicious that anybody would want to spend time with her sons. 'They can be very rough.'

'I'm sure I can handle them.'

'I suppose it'll be a bit of practice for you,' Liz said, with a nudge-nudge look at Emily.

'Yes,' Conor said evenly. 'Boys, would you like to go and feed the dogs?'

This sounded safe enough. The boys, though not exactly thrilled, were glad of the opportunity to get away from their mother. 'Yes.'

'Yes, please,' Liz said automatically.

The boys traipsed out.

Conor deposited two cappuccinos on the table. 'You two relax and have a chat.'

He dutifully followed the boys out the door.

'Isn't he lovely?' Liz said, sitting down with a sigh. She always sighed when she sat down, but today it seemed to have more resonance than usual.

'Lovely,' Emily agreed. Conor always found some reason to get out of the room when Liz arrived. He was so good at it that nobody ever suspected anything, including Emily herself until recently.

'Anyway,' Liz said, 'I just called in to see how you got on with your consultant.'

'Oh, right. We're just back actually.'

'That drive must kill you,' Liz said. 'All the way to Cork and back every week!'

'It's only thirty miles away, Liz.'

'I couldn't have done it,' Liz declared. 'Not with the rest of them in the back of the car. They'd have murdered each other by Fermoy.'

'Well, of course, you couldn't—'

'No, I was just as glad to go to Martha's. It's only down the road, so handy, and the Outpatients' there is terrific.'

St Martha's General Hospital was five miles away in Mitchelstown.

'You see the same consultants, you know. Whether you go private or public,' Liz added.

'Yes, I know that.'

'Not that we could have afforded a "private consult-ant".' She put this in rather scornful inverted commas, before nodding violently after the boys. 'That lot go through five packets of cornflakes a week. And Robbie's shoulder popped out again yesterday. Another twenty quid to the doctor. Eamon says that next time he'll try and bang it back in himself.'

Eamon would, too. He was the local builder. He had laid the patio for Conor and Emily last year, because they hadn't the nerve to go to anybody else. He had done them a special price because they were family.

'Threw in a dead body and everything,' he'd winked.

'Money down the drain, on private consultants,' Liz finished.

'Yes, well, we just decided to go private,' Emily said, gritting her teeth. 'It's probably silly, but we just felt safer.'

She could see Conor through the window. He was still standing, which was a good sign.

'Safer! Shur what could possibly happen to you down

in that big hospital in Cork? With all their new equipment and private rooms and Indian doctors coming out of the woodwork? Tommy! If I have to come out to you . . .'

Emily carefully lifted her cappuccino. It was easier to have something to do with her hands when talking to Liz. Sometimes she came perilously close to belting her.

'We didn't actually get to choose the hospital, Liz, believe it or not. I'd have had the baby in St Martha's except that it's closing down.'

Liz was sent scurrying in another direction. 'It's a disgrace, that's what it is. The memories I have of that place! All five born there, right down to little Willie.'

She gave the bundle on her chest a vague pat. Emily had forgotten all about Willy. He still hadn't moved. But she didn't dare ask if he were okay. The last time she had expressed concern about Robbie, whose nose was bleeding violently, Liz had got terribly defensive.

'It's the politicians, of course,' Liz said. 'They don't care so long as they have Blackrock Clinic.'

'They don't actually deliver babies there,' Emily felt she had to point out.

'Well, Vincent's Private then.'

'They don't deliver babies there either.'

'You're so difficult, Emily. Anyway, they've got a petition going and everything to stop the hospital closing. I've signed it. I don't suppose you have.'

Oh just leave, Emily wanted to shout. But Liz would be appalled, uncomprehending. Their mother would be informed, their mother with the weak heart. She would be on the phone asking Emily why she couldn't see fit to be nice to poor Liz who had five children swinging out of her, six if you included Eamon; Liz who had only called around out of the goodness of her heart to find out how Emily was getting on. A huge family rift would develop and it would be all over the place. That was because Eamon knew everybody right down to the outskirts of Cork and possibly into Cork City itself. Emily might as well move country.

'I haven't signed the petition yet because I haven't actually seen it,' she said with great care, 'but you can rest assured that I will.'

'Not that it'll do any good,' Liz said. 'Those politicians will close it down anyway. And we'll all have to drive thirty miles to Cork in the throes of labour.'

'Thinking of going again?' Emily enquired.

'Jesus Christ, are you mad? No, we were going to hold out for the girl but, to be honest, I don't think Eamon's sperm has got what it takes. The sex is determined by the father, you know. We were thinking of having it tested or something, but he's not keen on the idea of going into one of those cubicles with a magazine.'

She was joking, surely. Eamon, who went around with a copy of the *Sun* glued to his armpit?

'Oh well,' Emily said, because there wasn't really anything else to say to that.

'I suppose you'll have a girl,' Liz said.

'It's a fifty-fifty chance, isn't it?'

'Oh, you will.' She sounded very depressed.

'Don't you want to know how I got on with Mr Chapman?' Emily enquired coolly.

'Of course. How did it go?'

'He said my blood pressure is up.'

'By much?'

'He didn't say.'

'They never do. It's like some kind of state secret, isn't it?'

'And he thinks I'm a bit puffy.'

'Well, maybe a bit. But I was puffy too. With all of them. Like a balloon.' Liz threw her eyes to heaven and smiled. She was great when she was like this. Not exactly sisterly, but definitely friendly. But then things seemed to rub her up the wrong way again. Or maybe it was just Emily.

'I'm kind of worried, Liz. You know, after everything.'

Liz was sympathetic. 'I know. But Emily, you're thirty-four weeks gone, you're nearly there.'

'That's what Conor said.'

'Of course he did,' Liz said, as though any words that came from Conor's mouth should be set in doctrine.

'I'm thinking of giving up work sooner than planned.' She wasn't really, but she wanted to sound Liz out on it. She immediately regretted it.

'Didn't I work until the day I dropped Tommy? And on my feet, too, not like you. Standing behind that counter handing out Lemsips and Vicks Cough Syrup to people who don't even know what it's like to be sick!'

Liz had wanted to study pharmacy. She had believed that it would be glamorous and rewarding, and had been impressed by the white coat. What she'd really wanted to do was get a job in Boots in London, where medicine and make-up seemed to blend seamlessly. But then Eamon Clancy set his sights on her and college was somehow put on the back burner for a year. Then they got married, and Liz had taken a part-time job as an assistant in Roche's pharmacy in Paulstown to keep her hand in, where the only make-up was a cheap line of American cosmetics on a white plastic stand inside the door. Not that the customers were interested in make-up. Mostly they came in to confide in Liz about their irregular bowel movements, and peculiar patches of hair that had sprung up in odd places overnight. After having Tommy, Liz's maternity leave from Roche's was up the week she discovered she was pregnant again. She hadn't worked since. In the meantime, Eamon had expanded his business and was apparently doing well.

Emily sometimes wondered if Liz minded giving up her ambitions, but Liz never said anything, contenting herself with the odd dig about Emily's job, which she and Eamon regarded as a very cushy number. 'Fallen on your feet there,' Eamon was fond of saying, as though it were merely a matter of luck. 'Oh, who knows what way it might all have turned out,' Conor would nod vigorously in agreement and Eamon would look at him suspiciously. But then again, Conor was one of those arty types, playing pianos for a living. A nice enough fellow but not the sort you'd play darts with in the pub on a Saturday night.

'You're lucky being able to work,' Liz said glumly. 'Try staying at home all day with five children.'

'Go back to work so,' Emily asked impatiently. 'What's stopping you?'

'If you need to ask that . . . childcare, of course! I'd be paying out more than I'd be earning! And those children—'

'They go through five packets of cornflakes a week, yes, I know.'

Liz was hurt at her tone. 'Honestly, Emily, I don't know what's got into you today.'

Emily took a long, deep breath. Her headache was there in all its glory now, throbbing nicely just behind her eyes. 'I'm tired, Liz, okay? I'm as big as a whale, my back is killing me and I want to put my feet up.'

Anybody else might have offered a smidgen of sympathy. Liz merely sprang up from the table. 'Oh, well, sorry! I'll just get the boys and go.'

'Stop, Liz! Just sit down and drink your coffee.'

'I'm not that keen on cappuccino. Well, I usually only have it when I'm out.'

'You are out.' Jesus, Mary and Holy Saint Joseph. 'But never mind, because guess what! We have Maxwell House as well, the good old pulpy stuff that we keep especially for visitors!' She got up noisily to refill the kettle. Behind her, Liz started to cry.

'Liz?' Emily swung around, her heart beating fast.

Liz was hunched over in her chair, her head in her hands. She didn't seem to notice the baby strapped to her front. Emily could see only two tiny blue-tinged feet sticking out either side of Liz's heaving ribcage.

'Liz, please, what's the matter?' Emily was frightened. Liz never cried. She shouted and roared and cursed, but she didn't cry. It was alarming. Surely to God she wasn't that upset about the coffee dig? Suffused with guilt, Emily leaned over. She put out her hand to touch Liz, but drew back. They weren't a touchy family.

Liz eventually straightened, her nose streaming. Emily ran for a tissue, wondering whether she should call Conor. But no. That would mean Tommy, Robbie, Mikey and Bobby too, and they might be too traumatised by the sight of their mother in this state. But Emily was worried about Willy. His feet were definitely blue. She wanted to offer to take him from Liz but didn't want to upset her further.

'The bank is foreclosing on the mortgage,' Liz said, her voice thick with tears.

'What?'

'I know, it was news to me too. Eamon's been hiding the post. But he went out early on a job this morning and I opened the letter. Apparently we've made no repayments since last August.'

'But that's six months.'

'Seven,' Liz said grimly. 'He's been hiding it from me for seven months!'

Emily felt dread. 'Maybe it was a clerical error . . .'

'No. I went through all the files, the ones he keeps hidden away. And the business is gone to the wall, Emily. He's been borrowing like mad, hasn't made a tax return in three years and the Revenue are looking for twenty thousand.'

'Oh my God,' Emily said.

'And now we're going to be thrown out onto the street with five kids!'

'How could this have happened, Liz?' This time Emily actually did touch Liz. Liz drew away jerkily and sat up a bit straighter.

'Oh, he lost the Gannon contract last year. Or his mother's nursing home fees have gone up. Or the kids are bleeding him dry. Or I'm bleeding him dry, who knows? But he'll find someone to blame, you can be sure of that.'

'Oh, Liz,' Emily said again. She was raging – that big stupid lump of an Eamon! And sad, too, for her belligerent, harassed sister with her work-worn hands and her flabby stomach that wasn't back into shape after Willy yet. She kept the whole shebang together. And this was the thanks she got?

'Can I use your bathroom?' Liz asked. She always asked, like she was in a hotel or something. In anyone else's house, it was just, 'I'm running to the loo.'

'Of course.'

'Hold Willy for me, will you?'

She popped the baby out of the sling with a speed born of long practice and Emily found him thrust onto her lap. Or more precisely, onto her big belly.

'Liz . . .'

Emily was terrified that the child was dead and that, when Liz got back from the toilet, she would get the blame for that too. But Liz was gone down the hall, her thin, angular body held with an awkward kind of pride. The bathroom door slammed.

Willy lay precariously on Emily's bump, quite still, his eyes closed. He was so small that Emily was afraid she would break him. She had held him before, of course, but always under Liz's eagle eye and constant instruction; 'You have to support his neck, Emily!' or 'Don't bounce him like that, he'll puke.'

Now Emily gingerly lifted Willy up so that his head was nestled comfortably on her arm and he was more or less balancing on her bump. She looked worriedly at his chest for signs of motion, but there was none. On the plus side, he was quite warm, but that could just have come from Liz.

'Willy?' Emily said gently. Nothing. His blue-veined lids seemed glued together. And why were his feet now so white? Conor, she decided. Conor would know what to do.

Willy's eyes opened and looked directly into hers.

'Oh!'

Unfortunately he had Eamon's eyes, but Emily ignored that. She smiled tentatively at him. 'I'm your Auntie Emily.' She always introduced herself. Just because three-month-old babies had the memory span of a goldfish was no reason to dispense with courtesy.

Willy looked steadfastly at her. It was gratifying. And oh, how lovely it was to have him all to herself, with no one watching and judging. Emily lifted him higher and gave him a little kiss. Yummy smooth white skin. And he still had that newborn baby smell, although Liz maintained that she only threw him into the sink in the kitchen for a wash once a fortnight. She managed to get the dishes done at the same time.

Emily pressed her finger into his palm now, and watched his little fingers curl around hers strongly. She cocked an ear and heard water running. Good. Liz was still busy.

'Buh buh buh buh,' she said to the baby, feeling a bit ridiculous. But in Liz's presence, she'd always had to suppress her urge to talk nonsense to Willy. Liz said it was unhealthy to indulge in 'baby-speak' and that one should just talk normally to children.

But Willy was mad for it. His little fists pounded the air and his feet kicked out robustly. What with his four brothers, he hadn't had so much attention since he was born.

'You're lying on your cousin,' Emily whispered.

She cuddled Willy's floppy form into her. Might as well take advantage of the opportunity for a dry run.

Imagine, in two months' time, she could be holding her own baby. All going well. Which it would, please God, I'll do anything. She didn't mention about Mass again. Best not to remind him.

'A smile!' He was definitely smiling at her.

'Wind,' Liz said, having arrived back in the kitchen. Her hair was freshly scraped back. 'But I think he likes you,' she conceded. Well, that was something. None of the others seemed to.

'I'd better get going,' she said, efficiently scooping up Willy and stuffing him back into the carrier.

'Look, why don't you stay here for the evening? We could all have dinner together or something. The boys would love it.'

'I can still manage to feed them, you know,' Liz said stiffly.

Emily tried again. 'Maybe Conor could have a word with Eamon or something.'

Liz gave a high-pitched half-laugh. 'And what would that achieve?'

'I don't know,' Emily said unhappily. 'But Conor's quite good about all that tax stuff.'

'I don't think so,' Liz said, tight-lipped.

'You're right,' Emily said. 'It's up to you two. Maybe you can work something out with the bank or something.'

Liz's eyes flashed a bit. 'Emily, I know you're trying to wave your magic wand and make everything all right.'

Emily was annoyed. 'You're my sister. I'm just trying to help.'

'Just be thankful that Conor hasn't taken the roof from over your head.'

Well. There was no arguing with that.

Liz looked a bit bitter now. 'Conor would never let you down. You're very lucky, you know.'

There was that luck thing again, as though Emily and Liz had been dealt their entire lives in a random hand of cards. Emily didn't tell Liz that she felt exhausted and depressed sometimes too, that she was riddled with worry over this baby, that she felt her entire life was out of control on her most of the time, that Conor was great but increasingly silent. It would look like childish griping compared to the demands of raising five boys, and Eamon Clancy's gargantuan capacity for financial folly.

'Maybe I should cancel,' Conor said.

Emily was irritated. She was lying on the sofa with her feet on a cushion. Her headache had developed into a migraine. But she had risked taking one aspirin and expected it to work very soon. The box had promised as much.

'I'm fine.' Creepy Crawley hadn't rung. The meeting was over by now. At the very least, would he not be wondering where she had been the entire afternoon? It was all very ominous.

'I know, but all the same . . .' He looked at her. She

knew he was waiting for her to make the decision for him. He was playing in the Cork Opera House tonight with the orchestra, a performance of *The Nutcracker Suite*, and needed to be there for a warm-up at six o'clock. But he had to rescue her car from the side of the road first.

'How can you cancel, Conor?'

'I could pick up the phone and just cancel!' he said stalwartly.

He couldn't, that was the thing. It wasn't as though the double-bassist could cover for him.

'Neasa's coming round after work.'

'Is she?'

'Yes.'

'Well, in that case . . .' He was already reaching for his sheet music.

Emily smiled fondly, remembering Liz's words. 'At least you'd never let me down.'

He went a bit still. 'Sorry?'

'Eamon, Conor?'

'Oh. Yeh. Eamon.'

I give up, Emily thought. She had told him the whole sorry saga the minute Liz was out the door and now he was acting like he'd forgotten all about it. Something as big as that! Or, more likely, it just wasn't important to him. His reaction had been predictably downbeat. He'd contented himself with a few murmurings of 'Bad situation, that,' and had refused to get involved in any bitching about Eamon.

'Haven't we enough problems of our own?' he'd said rather ominously.

Sometimes Emily wished that she'd married a right little gossip, someone who would indulge in all kinds of bad-mouthing and speculation with her. It wasn't half as satisfying doing it on one's own, and she just ended up feeling mean.

'Are you sure?' Conor asked again, edging towards the door.

'Go, Conor. You're off the hook!' If he stayed, he would just be watching her all the time and looking up that book of his and asking her all kinds of stupid questions about her perineum.

'Just say the word and I'll stay,' he said coolly. 'It's my baby too.'

It was hardly Eamon Clancy's.

'Yes yes yes,' Emily said, trying to smile nicely. She didn't want to row with him before he left. If he got killed on the drive down she would never forgive herself. Mind you, when Conor was annoyed he tended to drive slower.

'I'll be home at midnight,' he promised. 'But don't wait up if you're tired.'

'Good luck tonight.'

He kissed her and left. Emily plumped up the cushions under her feet. The headache was receding. She would do a bit of work before Neasa arrived.

She reached for a file and patted her bump. 'And I don't want to hear another word out of you.'

★ ★ ★

'I'm really sorry, Emily.'

'No, don't be, Neasa, no, no, that's ridiculous, no . . .'

'I feel terrible.'

'No, no, it's nothing to do with you, no, no, no . . .'
She was trapped in a vicious cycle of no's. She had to
break it.

'Yes,' she said.

'Yes what?'

'Yes, they've passed me over, yes, they're pigging
bastards, yes, yes, yes . . .' It was happening again. She
decided to stop speaking altogether.

Neasa was watching her carefully for signs of
unhingement. 'Would you like a drink?'

This required a yes or a no answer. She wasn't going
down that road again.

'Maybe.'

'I've brought a bottle of wine. And some snacky
things. Are you hungry?'

Another trick question. 'Possibly.'

Neasa efficiently unpeeled a miniature bottle opener
from her heavy, jangling key-ring. Her key-ring also
held a miniature pair of scissors and nail-clippers.
Nothing remotely useful such as an actual key, which
she always put in her pocket. She got two tumblers
from the sideboard, poured wine, then dumped a
packet of salt and vinegar crisps into a clean ashtray.

'There *are* bowls in the kitchen, Neasa. And proper
wine glasses.'

49

'You can't be left alone at a time like this. And if you can't think of yourself, at least think of the baby. Cheers.'

Neasa drank her wine. Emily looked at the crisps. Ten years of friendship and not a word to say. That's what happened when boyfriends complicated the picture.

What Emily really wanted to do was ring Conor's mobile just as he was tuning up with the orchestra and cry lustily down the phone to him.

'Gary didn't want to take it from you, Emily.'

Like this was somehow to his credit.

'But he did,' Emily said a bit spitefully. God Almighty, she was allowed a bit of spite at a time like this, surely? Neasa seemed to think so too. She bowed her head in acknowledgement.

'You deserved it. Everyone knows that. Gary does too.'

He had probably heard the news in Emily's office. Emily knew very well that the pair of them went at it like knives the minute she vacated her swivel-chair. She had found a pubic hair there once the exact shade of blond as Gary's large head. And the cheese plant was haemorrhaging leaves. How the partners would love to know that their most recent addition was lifting his leg all over the office furniture!

'Are you over the shock?' Neasa asked eventually.

'I can't seem to feel anything below my hips.'

'That's par for the course,' Neasa said knowledge-ably. 'Remember when my grandmother died?'

'God yes,' Emily said. 'Your legs gave way at the graveside.'

'They didn't even ring you, did they?'

'No.'

'The pigging bastards.' Neasa thought this might be a good time to threaten to hand in her notice. Emily was so white. And she hadn't even given out about Gary, which was very nice of her. Neasa had even been prepared to join in, a little bit.

'You could sue,' she suggested instead. 'Discrimination against pregnant women.'

'Or just sexual discrimination.'

'Get them on both counts. And Crawley on sexual harassment.'

'He doesn't sexually harass me.'

'Oh, of course, you're pregnant.'

Emily didn't seem that enthusiastic about suing. Neasa was relieved. Gary would have a fit.

'I mean, it's not as though he said to me "You're going to get the partnership",' Emily gulped. Crawley's words were 'you could be in line for it', if her memory was correct. And the year before, it had been 'you never know', or something equally vague. In fact, he had never really promised her anything at all. Everything was just a distant possibility. If she put in the required work, of course.

Her face felt a little hot. 'Why do you think I didn't get it, Neasa?'

'They're a law unto themselves, those bastards,'

Neasa spat. 'You wouldn't know.'

'But why do *you* think I didn't get it?'

Neasa shifted indignantly. 'Well, this is the thing, isn't it! You work so hard! In at nine every morning, you drag the secretaries out of the bathroom, set up the Internet server for everyone, chase up the bad payers – my God, you even re-organised the entire filing system last year!' She gave a delicate shudder. 'Nobody else could have done that! You even make the coffee!'

'I also sell land,' Emily said quietly.

Neasa realised what she'd implied. 'Of course you do! Acres and acres of it! That goes without saying! I just meant that you do that on top of everything else. In addition.'

'Has Gary ever made the coffee? No, no, it's not an accusation. I'm just wondering.'

'To my knowledge,' Neasa said slowly, 'he has not. He certainly might have at some time in the past but I've, ah, never actually witnessed it.'

They were speaking like solicitors. It was terrible, like they were on different sides of a courtroom – not that either of them had ever been in a courtroom. But they had got their law degrees together, meeting that very first day in college, Emily sick with nerves and Neasa sick with a hangover. It was unthinkable that a man should come between them now.

'Oh fuck them all anyway,' Neasa said in a rush.

It unleashed something in Emily. Two fat tears slid

down her face. 'I really wanted this!'

'I know,' said Neasa, crying now too. She could never watch anybody crying, even on the telly, without joining in. 'It's very unfair, isn't it?'

'It's the lack of respect, Neasa. They didn't even bother to let me know!'

'I know, I know!' Neasa bawled. 'They're so spineless!'

'There's lawnmower petrol in the garage – will we go and burn Crawley's house down?'

'We could,' Neasa gulped, doubtfully.

'I know. I wouldn't normally. It's my hormones. They're all over the place. Did you know that my hair is falling out?'

Neasa's hands flew protectively to check that her own was still in situ. If it ever fell out she might as well commit suicide.

'You'd never notice, the way you comb it over like that,' she said loyally.

Emily cried harder. 'Thank you. And have you seen my ankles?'

Neasa tried to lie again but her natural brutality got the better of her. 'I know. They're huge,' she sobbed.

'Thank you! And Eamon's after bankrupting himself and Liz too.'

Neasa had to think for a minute. Oh yes, that horrible, jolly builder married to shrewish Liz. Neasa stopped crying. Otherwise she'd be puffy for two days.

'More wine,' she pressed.

'I can't. I've already had one glass and I'm not really supposed to be drinking at all according to Conor's book.'

'Shut your face, Emily, and have a half glass. The baby won't die.' She saw Emily's expression. 'Jesus Christ, sorry. I've an awfully big mouth.'

'You haven't. It's all right. Don't be silly.'

'Emily, why do you always say everything is all right when it's bloody not?'

Emily blinked. Somehow this conversation had sneakily mutated into an entirely different conversation. This always seemed to happen to her. Well, this time she would retaliate. She would fight her corner fair and square.

'Oh, leave me alone. I'm pregnant!'

Neasa didn't push it. There was a fine line with Emily, not that you'd think it to look at her. Anyway, Neasa was a bit drunk. Her natural honesty tended to flourish under the influence of alcohol and there was no telling what she might say. All her deepest thoughts and feelings about herself and, unfortunately, others tended to come out.

'I might get pregnant,' she said airily. This took her as much by surprise as Emily. Obviously the thought had been festering all day.

'You?'

'What's so odd about that?'

'No, it's just that, well, you don't particularly like children.'

'Other people's children,' Neasa said haughtily. 'It'll be different with our own.'

'Our?'

'Me and Gary, of course. He's talking about a future.'

She looked at Emily fiercely, defying her to say something mean and nasty about Gary.

'Well, if that's what you want,' Emily said.

'Why wouldn't I want it?' Neasa challenged.

'Then I say good luck to you,' Emily said sincerely.

Neasa deflated a bit. You'd think that Emily might at least be a little bit anti-Gary after the partnership and all that. She was just so fair and nice. It wasn't natural.

'Can I have a feel?' Neasa asked politely.

Emily had a strict policy about people feeling her bump. It was amazing the liberties friends and even total strangers took. Once, a woman had planted her hand on Emily's midriff in the supermarket, clucking and benign, as though Emily were public property.

'Just to see what I might be in for,' Neasa added.

'Of course you can.' Emily generously hitched up her baggy t-shirt. Neasa bent over to have a good look.

'Your belly-button's gone sideways.'

'I know. It's weird, isn't it?'

'And look at all those veins!'

'Conor said if you look closely, you can actually see a map of Munster.'

Neasa was rapidly having second thoughts. She didn't say anything about the stretch marks. It was like an army of slugs had marched drunkenly across Emily's belly.

'My hands might be cold,' she said, trying to get out of it now.

'Oh go on.'

Neasa put her hand down squeamishly. Emily's belly was as hard as a rock, not at all nice and squishy and soft. Then Neasa felt something poking through the hardness right under her hand.

'That's the baby's bum,' Emily told her.

That was enough for Neasa. She snatched back her hand. 'Obviously, it's something Gary and I will have to talk about.'

He would be at home now, maybe even cooking a nice romantic dinner. Neasa, in the throes of drink, had a wild urge to be with him. Still. She mustn't let on. She was here for Emily.

'Oh go home, Neasa. You're dying to.'

'I am not! Well, if you're sure you'll be all right.'

'Yes.' There was no lawnmower petrol left anyway, now that Emily thought about it. Not that burning Crawley's house down had been a remote possibility. She had only said it really to sound dangerous and exciting. Because surely a blow like this demanded some kind of drastic action? Instead of just crying and bitching around the house, which was all she would end up doing. Before going meekly in to work tomorrow, of course.

'Well, I just won't!'

'Won't what?' Neasa was looking anxiously at the door.

'I won't go in to work tomorrow. That'll show them!'

'It would,' Neasa said dubiously.

'Decided then,' Emily said, wondering how long she would be able to stick it out in the morning, looking at the clock every ten minutes, before finally giving up and going in. She wished her parents had been members of any other cult but the good, loyal, hard-working Catholic Church. And Emily had never perfected the art of rebellion.

Emily's mother Pauline was very fond of saying that one should count one's blessings. She had applied this maxim to the instance when the chimney had caught fire one Christmas. 'At least it didn't spread to the roof.' Then it had. 'At least the whole house didn't go up.' Then it had. 'At least nobody was hurt!' she'd shouted, daring somebody to fall down dead.

The blessings thing went naturally hand in hand with the need to be grateful for what one had. This could be liberally applied to any situation, and was. The time Liz had decided to cut Emily's hair, for instance. By the time she was finished, Emily looked as though she had been through extensive chemotherapy. 'Be grateful she didn't cut off your ear,' Pauline had said, kindly.

Situations that defied blessings and gratitude generally fell into the 'expect not and you won't be disappointed' category, a kind of useful, catch-all phrase. Emily was very familiar with this from the time she had been studying for her Leaving Certificate.

In fairness, her Trojan work had been noted, encouraged and praised. But all the good had somehow been wiped away by the advice not to expect seven A's, that way she would be spared disappointment. In the event, she got only six.

Sometimes, harassed, Pauline would get confused and mix up the three. 'Be grateful that your blessings are not disappointed!' she would shout. 'At least your expectations won't be grateful for what they have!'

The household was routinely weighed down under blessings, gratitude and disappointment. Everybody else seemed happy enough with this state of affairs. But it seemed to Emily that it kind of quenched any hope, ambition or hand in one's own fate. Once she had voiced this.

'Can we not expect anything?'

'What?' Pauline was startled.

'This disappointment thing – I was just thinking that maybe a bit of disappointment is okay. It means that at least you've tried for something.'

'What are you talking about, Emily?' Pauline was busy dishing up dinner from seven different pots and pans and it required considerable concentration.

'She's off,' Liz said, as though Emily routinely upset dinnertime with philosophical discussions, which she didn't.

'I'm just wondering, that's all.'

A piece of pink, wet ham landed on her plate.

'It's just a saying, Emily.'

'But why do people say it?'

Pauline was impatient. 'I don't know! It wouldn't be a saying if it didn't have truth in it!'

And they had all looked at Emily as though she were being very unreasonable. She had kept any other thoughts on disappointment and ambition to herself.

She hadn't told her mother or Liz or indeed any of the family about the potential partnership. She was fiercely glad now. She would have proved the thesis that anybody who dared to aspire higher would be brutally and swiftly squashed. Proper order, too.

At least I know before Crawley tells everyone tomorrow, she thought – oh Christ. She was doing it. She had said At Least.

Furious, she dragged herself off the sofa before she started naming Conor and the baby amongst her blessings. Upstairs, she went through her wardrobe. It was divided neatly into 'Before Pregnancy' and 'Pregnancy'. She shunned the flowing, suitable, sensible maternity dresses and trousers she usually wore in to the office. From the other section, she took a skin-tight red lycra dress and laid it on the bed. She would go in to the office tomorrow (after making them sweat for a few hours first, of course) in all her red glory, her belly sticking into Crawley's face. She would wear matching violent lipstick and high heels. And she would refuse to make the coffee. She would do nothing except what was required of her and she would be sure that everyone saw her reading the 'Situations Vacant' at tea break.

She mightn't even wear a bra!

The phone by the bed rang. Ten past seven – Conor, checking to see how she was before he went on stage. He wouldn't expect her to put on a front for him. She snatched up the phone, already crying a bit in anticipation.

'I didn't get the fucking partnership!'

It was Mr Chapman.

'Oh! Sorry, I thought you were . . .' Just move on. 'You certainly work late!'

Mr Chapman hadn't time for chitchat. He'd been given two tickets to a performance of *The Nutcracker Suite* in the Cork Opera House that night by a grateful patient whose triplets he had delivered, and he was greatly looking forward to it. He informed Emily that he'd had her urine sample double-checked in the lab and that there were indications of uric acid in it. Protein, in other words. It was a cause for concern.

'How, exactly?'

He went on a bit about her raised blood pressure again, and her water retention and then he said the word 'pre-eclampsia'. Now, pre-eclampsia was a condition—

'I know what pre-eclampsia is,' Emily said, who wasn't all that sure. 'But I feel absolutely fine.'

Yes, par for the course, usually the sufferers didn't experience any physical discomfort—

'No, really, I'm about to start ironing.'

Mr Chapman advised her not to do that. Instead she

was to pack a small overnight bag and go to the hospital. No panic, just for observation. He would see her in the morning.

Emily could think of nothing except the obvious. 'I don't have any car. It was towed, you see.'

A small silence. Mr Chapman wasn't used to dealing with patients' travel problems.

Could she prevail upon a friend? A relative?

Neasa was probably under Gary at this very moment. And to ask Liz to come over with the five boys? Deirdre and Jackie lived in Cork. Michael and Brian, Emily's two brothers, lived in Australia.

Into the lengthening silence, Mr Chapman suggested a taxi.

'They'll never take me to Cork,' Emily said. 'They don't even like going too far out the Cork Road.'

Mr Chapman was nonplussed now. Short of coming to get her himself, the only thing he could suggest was an ambulance.

'An ambulance?' Emily had visions of being borne down the High Street of Paulstown, sirens wailing and lights flashing, drinkers in Milo's pub coming to the door to see what was happening. She would die of mortification.

Mr Chapman told her he would organise the ambulance and got off the phone before she complicated matters further.

Emily's brain went into a peculiar, very practical mode. Should she ring Conor? No, what was the point?

He was about to go on stage. It would only worry him. Best to pack and get there and ring him later. He would be in the same city anyway; he could just nip by when the performance was over.

Emily's hospital bag and the bag for the baby were already packed in readiness for the big day. It would be easiest to just take those. But she wouldn't. It would be like admitting that everything was going wrong. And it wasn't. It wasn't. Chapman had said just to pack for overnight. She would do that.

Two nightdresses and a pair of pyjamas just in case. Her huge old bunny slippers, because the new ones were already packed away. Underwear, toothbrush, toothpaste. A towel. Even her anti-wrinkle cream.

The suitcase on top of the wardrobe was much too big. It would look like she was going on holidays. Should she just empty her hospital bag? Too much hassle. She dragged Conor's bag from under the bed and shook off the dust.

Unfortunately it had Manchester United emblazoned across it. It had been a freebie. Stickers for Germany, Italy and France were plastered on the sides, relics from his tour with the orchestra last year. They would probably think in the hospital that Emily was a football hooligan who followed the team all over the world.

She began to pack, removing a pair of Conor's forgotten socks first. Rancid. She threw them in the laundry bin. When she was finished, she zipped up the bag and went downstairs. She switched off the TV and all the lights, and took her house keys. Then she sat on the chair by the front door, the bag on her knees. It all seemed very unreal.

The doorbell rang, startling her. There had been no lights or sirens or anything. In the darkness, Emily felt her way up the door towards the latch. She had to put the bag down first. It took a while. The doorbell rang again.

'Could have a stiff in here, Joe,' one of the ambulance men said outside.

'Easier really,' Joe said.

Emily flung open the door and loomed out of the darkness, giving them a fright.

'Emily Collins?' Joe asked.

'Yes.'

'Hop in.'

Joe was very kind as it turned out.

'All right, love?'

'Great, thank you,' Emily said. She was perched on the little bench at the side. Far from screaming down the town, the ambulance chugged along at a leisurely thirty miles an hour. The driver was called Liam, she learned, and he was eating egg sandwiches in the front. She could smell them. Occasionally the radio crackled and she heard him mumble incomprehensibly into it.

'And how's the babby?' Joe wanted to know.

'Oh, kicking away.'

'Good, good,' Joe said, his brown eyes crinkling. 'That's the way to have him.'

'They think I have pre-eclampsia,' Emily found herself saying.

Joe clucked and shook his head. 'Do they now?'

'But I feel fine,' she insisted to him.

'Most people we pick up do,' Joe said sagely. 'They ring 999, all hysterical, saying they're having a heart attack or a brain haemorrhage or they can't breathe or they're unconscious. We rush to the scene and find them sitting up having a cup of tea, telling you that it was only wind. But we have to bring them in all the same.'

'I didn't ring,' Emily quickly clarified.

'Oh I know. Some consultant did. They think we're a taxi service.' He banged on the partition. 'Don't they, Liam?'

'What?'

'Taxi service.'

'Oh, yeh.'

Emily looked at the wires and tubes and masks hanging from the ambulance ceiling. It all looked very clinical and menacing and she felt frightened now.

'Don't mind that stuff, love,' Joe told her. 'That's only for the serious cases.'

'What'll they do to me down there?' she blurted.

Joe scratched his head. 'I don't honestly know. Our job stops at the front door.''

'Of course, sorry,' Emily said. She thought that this was a shame. Joe seemed much more human than Mr Chapman.

'But the girls are very nice down there,' Joe assured her. 'Fiona, she's the Head Nurse in Maternity, she's a real cracker – isn't she, Liam?'

'Smashing,' Liam shouted.

'They're all very nice,' Joe repeated. 'Most of them have babbies themselves. They'll take good care of you. And the food's great, for a hospital. Chips and everything.'

Emily nodded vigorously. She fixed her gaze on a plastic mask dangling near her nose.

'My wife had one four weeks ago,' Joe said shyly.

'Sorry?'

'A baby.'

'Did she?'

'A girl. Eight pounds four ounces.'

'Oh! That's a great weight.'

'It is,' Joe said proudly. 'We named her Tamzin.'

'Tamzin?'

'I know, I wasn't that keen on it to be honest, but the wife is a terrible *EastEnders* fan. That blonde one in it, she's called Tamzin. In real life, mind – I can't remember what she's called on the telly.'

'Melanie,' Emily said faintly, vowing never to watch it again.

'That's it! Anyway, I couldn't get me tongue around this Tamzin business at all in the beginning, but funny, the baby, she seems to have grown into it.' He pondered this for a moment. 'But the point is that the wife had her in the same place you're going to now.'

'I'm not having it now, though,' Emily clarified quickly. 'I'm only in for observation. It's not due for weeks and weeks yet.'

'Sure,' Joe said easily. 'This your first?'

'Yes,' Emily said, eventually.

They sat in silence for a while. Emily thought of Conor who was probably ringing the house at this very minute before he went on stage. Would he be worried when he got no reply? Probably not, sensibly assuming that she had gone out to the dogs or something. Emily herself always got slightly panicked when Conor was unreachable by phone for any length of time. She always imagined that something nasty had happened or, if he was driving, that he'd been in a crash. Conor, home safe and sound, would listen to these fantasies with a faint amusement. He would ruffle her hair and tell her she was a dreadful worrier. Once, she told herself, just once, she would like to see him harried and hassled. It wasn't that she wished him discomfort; she would just like to share with him occasionally, that was all.

She jumped as the black glass partition separating the driver flew back. She was presented with the back of Liam's head. He was replacing the radio mike. He spoke over his shoulder.

'Car crash down by Finnerty's Cross. Three vehicles, one a truck.' He cast a look at Emily, and said carefully, 'Fairly bad. They're sending two units up from Cork, but they'll be at least forty minutes. We have to divert.'

Emily swallowed hard. She didn't know if she was up to a bad car crash at the moment. And what if there wasn't room enough in the ambulance for everybody? Emily's problems might look fairly tame compared to some poor soul who had lost limbs, or worse. Would she have to get out and walk? But what about her baby? If it were just Emily, she wouldn't mind. She was going to say something to Joe about it when he jumped to his feet.

'Are you strapped in properly there?' he said.

'I think so. Why?'

The siren exploded on the top of the ambulance. Strobe lighting flashed on the tinted windows. The ambulance shot off at speed and Emily bounced from side to side.

Joe – nice, slow Joe – mutated into a person of extreme efficiency. Balancing expertly in the careering ambulance, he checked tubes and wires and opened little cupboards that Emily hadn't noticed before. He took out big pouches of clear-coloured liquid, rolls of white gauze, syringes, more tubes. Things must be very bad down at Finnerty's Cross.

'Do you want me to do anything?' Emily asked loudly over the roar of the ambulance.

'What?'

'If it's bad. I did a first-aid course last year.'

Joe looked at her.

'It was quite advanced,' she added.

'Thanks, anyway, but sure you'll be getting out.'

'What?'

'We're here.'

Emily looked out and saw lights – shops, a petrol station. They were coming into Mitchelstown, just five miles from home. And now here was St Martha's coming up on the left. Joe was apologetic.

'Don't worry. They'll transfer you to Cork in the morning.'

The ambulance screeched to a halt, lights still flashing. Joe flung the doors open and held out a hand to Emily. She stepped out to see a porter and a nurse rushing out the front door at all the commotion. The nurse was pulling on plastic gloves.

The pair stopped just short of Emily, taken aback to find her on her feet and clutching a Manchester United bag. Suspiciously, they looked around her person for signs of blood or broken limbs or indeed any injury at all which would merit such a noisy and dramatic entrance.

'Diversion,' Joe explained. 'She was due to go to Cork. Pre-eclampsia.'

'Oh,' the nurse said, deflating. The porter sighed and went back in.

Emily looked around for Joe but he was springing back into the ambulance.

'Good luck,' he said to her, and the doors closed. The ambulance screeched off, leaving Emily feeling bereft.

The nurse looked at Emily. Her badge said V Mooney. 'Pre-eclampsia then?'

'I don't know,' Emily said unhappily. 'That's just what Mr Chapman thinks.'

'Mr Chapman. I see.' Her mouth went a bit tight. She reached over and took Emily's bag, her last object of safety and comfort in a world gone insane. 'Right, let's get you inside then.'

She was put in a ward with three other pregnant women. A television blared high in a corner. Despite this, one patient appeared to be soundly asleep, her hair all over her face. The woman in the bed next to Emily had so many visitors that they were perched on any available piece of furniture, including Emily's bed.

Nurse V Mooney shooed them off. 'Don't tire Maggie out now,' she said mildly. Maggie, the patient, was sitting up in the bed like a queen and eating oranges.

Emily nodded politely at her and got a big beam back but Nurse V Mooney whipped around the curtain, cutting Maggie off.

'You can get undressed and into bed,' she told Emily. 'I'll be back to take your blood pressure and all that.'

'This pre-eclampsia—'

'We don't know if it's that yet. I'll have to find out what instructions Mr Chapman left, which means I'll have to phone Cork.' She sighed as though she personally shouldered the phone bill.

Emily was left alone. She unzipped her bag and neatly stowed her belongings in the battered metal locker. The catch on it wouldn't close properly and the door kept swinging open to reveal her knickers and socks to anyone who cared to look. In the end she unfolded her towel and tucked it in around her things. Now it just looked as though she were hiding a stash of vodka.

She had forgotten to bring a book, of course, or a magazine. It hadn't been high on her list of priorities. But she couldn't face an evening of making small talk with the other women. She was too upset. And the thing on the telly was in Irish, of all languages. At the bottom of the Manchester United bag was a copy of Conor's concert programme from his tour last year. It was better than nothing.

It felt silly to be getting into her nightie at a quarter past eight in the evening. The bed was old-fashioned and high and she had to give a little hop to get into it. She tried to pull up the stiff sheets but, as in all hospitals, they seemed to be welded to the bed some-where around hip region. Short of stripping the bed and re-making it properly, which she suspected wouldn't go down too well with that nurse, she would just have to put up with it. Also she didn't want the other women to think she had some kind of fetish. When the lights went out later she would sort it out.

The din from the visitors in the next cubicle was deafening as more people arrived – Maggie's husband Tiernan, his two sisters and a brother, a couple of second cousins and someone from Boston. It was unclear whether they'd flown over especially to see

Maggie. Emily's curtain bulged as they squeezed in. It must be a special occasion. Probably Maggie's birthday or something.

'Okay.' Nurse V Mooney was back, carrying all kinds of equipment and a chart. She proceeded to fill in details with a pen that she had to give a good shake to every now and again.

'Everything in this blasted place is falling apart,' she said, to herself more than Emily. 'Now. If you could hold out your arm.'

Emily did so obediently and a pressure cuff was put on it. She felt it tighten unpleasantly. Nurse V Mooney didn't meet her eyes.

'Well,' she said, looking at the pressure gauge.

'Is it bad?'

'One eighty over one ten.' She glanced up. 'It's high but I've seen worse.'

Emily bet she had. Nurse V Mooney now sat down on the bed. Emily had to move her feet.

'Any nausea?'

'No.'

'Vomiting?'

'No.'

'Flashing lights?'

'Apart from the ambulance.' Joke, woman, joke!

The nurse didn't smile. 'Any pain in the abdomen?'

'No.'

'Any bleeding, irregular discharge, discomfort?'

'No, no, no.'

The nurse shot Emily a look as though she were making fun of her.

'Any headache?'

'Yes. Well, not now. But earlier. I took an aspirin.'

The nurse hadn't much interest in this. 'Right, good.' She flipped a page in the chart. 'Well, we've certainly caught it in time.'

'The pre-eclampsia?'

'We don't know if it's that yet,' the nurse insisted, as though it were all a fuss about nothing. 'But if it is, it hasn't developed into eclampsia.'

'That's bad, isn't it?' Emily remembered reading up on the condition, but there were so many things that could go wrong during pregnancy that she couldn't remember the exact details.

The nurse seemed to cheer up for the first time. 'Oh yes. Convulsions and a coma, usually.'

Oh, how Emily wished she were in Cork, in a nice bright hospital with low beds and lockers that worked, away from this mean, cheerless cow.

Nurse Mooney was nearly finished with the chart now.

'Have you any other children?'

'No.'

'Is this your first pregnancy?'

'No.'

The nurse looked up at her. 'What was the history of that, please?'

'I had a miscarriage at twelve weeks,' Emily said. She

had been due to come to Martha's for the first scan on that Thursday.

The nurse filled this in carefully. 'Any complications or problems after that?'

'No.' Just one of those things.

The nurse snapped the top back on her pen loudly and stood. 'I'll get one of the girls to bring you up a cup of tea.'

'That'd be nice.'

'Mr Chapman appears not to have left any notes for you in Cork, or at least the staff down there can't find them,' the nurse said, that tightening of her mouth back again. 'They're going to page him and ring me back.'

'Thank you.'

'He'll probably just prescribe bed-rest, which is usual in a case like this. In the meantime, if you'd do a sample for me' – she slapped a plastic container down on the table at the bottom of the bed – 'we'll check it for signs of uric acid. But a house doctor will be around later anyway to examine you.'

She looked at Emily's chart one last time then back at Emily.

'You're not by any chance Liz Clancy's sister? You look very alike.'

'I am!' Emily was delighted that they had finally found common ground. 'She had all her five boys here.'

'Yes. I was here for every single one,' the nurse said grimly and left.

★ ★ ★

Emily rang Conor's mobile three times from her own mobile, even though there were stern signs up all over the place not to use mobile phones. Maybe it wasn't so bad if it were mobile to mobile, she reasoned. Anyhow, the concert must be running over because all she got was the answering service. She didn't want to leave a message. No matter what way she worded it, it would sound like a panic situation.

The house doctor had been around and had told her more or less what the nurse had. Bed-rest, sleep, and monitoring of her blood pressure and urine. Mr Chapman apparently had ordered the same. They had found his notes. Emily would be transferred to Cork in the morning and she would see him then.

The curtains were still pulled over. Relatives kept coming and going in the next cubicle at a steady pace, paying no heed at all to the hours set for visiting time. The telly blared some American sitcom and canned laughter exploded into the ward from time to time, jarring Emily's nerves. She lay in bed on her left side, as the doctor had advised. Apparently it helped the flow of blood to the placenta.

Nobody knew she was here. Not a single soul. She was tempted to use her mobile again, but what was the point? It was nearly half past ten – what could Liz or Neasa or her mother do? Anyway, she didn't really want to see any of them.

She rubbed her tummy and wanted nobody but Conor. He always made her feel safe. He would stroke her hair and tell her that Chapman was only covering his ass in case she sued, that it was all a storm in a teacup. She'd be out tomorrow, just wait and see.

She turned over in the bed carefully and picked up Conor's concert programme. There would be a photo of him in it; they always printed little photos of the orchestra.

There he was, page seven, his hair a bit longer maybe, but otherwise looking exactly like a plain-clothes garda, stern but compassionate. Billy Middlemiss, the fat cellist, was on one side of him; Ffion Rivera, the first violinist, on the other. That was her stage name, of course. Everybody else just called her Mary Murphy.

Mary had her violin in the picture. And Billy Middlemiss was holding his cello. You could see the top of it. Conor had obviously been playing the piano when the photo was taken because his arms were held out from his body. But they hadn't been able to fit the piano in the picture so he looked like he was levitating.

Emily smiled fondly. Her eye travelled down to the tour dates. Italy. Then France, before going over to Germany for the final weekend, the 3rd and 4th of September it said here. She had driven up to Dublin airport to collect him when he'd arrived back from Germany on that Sunday night. It would have been the 5th. But no. The 3rd was a Thursday. It said so here. And the 4th was a Friday, the last concert date. She must have collected him on Saturday.

She hadn't. She'd had the whole weekend to herself, she remembered it. Indeed, she would never forget it. She'd gone for a pregnancy test in the Well Women Clinic in Cork on Friday and it was positive. She didn't want to tell Conor on the phone; the news was too precious, especially after the miscarriage. Saturday and Sunday had crawled by until six o'clock on Sunday evening when his flight came in.

The programme was wrong. Probably a misprint.

She had a sudden memory of Conor coming through arrivals on his own. No Billy Middlemiss dragging his cello, none of the other thirty members of the orchestra.

No one, in fact, except Ffion Rivera. She had waved quickly over at Emily and gone out another way. She hadn't waved at Conor, nor he at her. She hadn't looked at him at all.

Emily carefully put the programme down and lay quietly on her left side. Maggie's visitors eventually left. The woman across the way asked if anybody minded whether she turned the television off. Emily didn't reply. Her mind was in a different place.

Her mobile rang, startling her. It was Conor, sounding the same as always.

'Where are you? I've been phoning home all evening. Emily?'

'Yes, yes. You see, there's been a bit of a development.'

'Well, what?' He was a bit impatient. Emily knew that he expected her to say that Liz had called in the throes of some new crisis and that Emily had dutifully gone over.

'I'm actually in hospital.'

'What?'

She told him about Mr Chapman, the pre-eclampsia, St Martha's.

'Jesus Christ. Are you all right?'

'Fine, fine.'

'You sound a bit funny.'

'Do I? I'm in a ward. It's hard to talk.'

'I'll be there in forty-five minutes,' Conor promised.

'No, it's too late. And you'll be tired after the drive up.' Emily wanted to go to sleep too. She felt exhausted.

'I'm coming in.'

'They won't let you, Conor. It's a quarter to eleven.'

He was silent. 'In the morning then. First thing.'

'Sure, fine.'

'Emily?' She heard his concern over the phone, his love for her. 'Just . . . sleep well.'

'Yes,' she said. 'You too.'

Nurse V Mooney came by, pushing a drugs trolley. Emily wondered whether she ran the place single-handed.

'Everybody all right here?' she called.

'Have you got any sleeping tablets?' Emily asked. She wasn't able to drop off; it was the strangest bed and the worry about the baby.

'I'm sorry. You're not down for sleeping tablets. You'll have to consult Mr Chapman in the morning.'

'Oh.'

The nurse looked cannily at Emily and came over. Emily tensed for another invasion of some part of her. But the nurse just switched the light off over the bed and poured a glass of water from the jug on the locker.

'Listen,' she said quietly, 'it's perfectly natural to be worried about something like this. But you'll be absolutely fine. Bed-rest and sleep. That'll sort you out.'

She pulled up the covers over Emily as though she were a baby herself and tucked her in.

Hospital wards are the natural enemies of bed-rest and sleep. The whole night long people came and went in Emily's ward, toilets flushed, babies bawled in the distance, phones rang, nurses talked at the tops of their voices and at one point someone, somewhere, screamed. Emily had bolted up wildly in the bed, wondering if it had been her.

It had all taken on a rather surreal air sometime around half past four. Visions in white would appear at the bottom of Emily's bed and loom over her. They had Mary Murphy's face and one of them even started playing the violin. Quite well, too. Emily surfaced only to find yet another nurse checking her chart.

Emily got up quietly and negotiated the leap from the bed to the floor. The nurses at the station outside were eating Roses from five different boxes. 'He's such a fucking pisshead and he's not even a real DJ, did you know that? Oh, Emily, are you feeling all right?'

'Terrific, thanks.' She went on her way, moving through the dim warm corridors in her bare feet, aimless and dislocated. The wards were dark and quiet on either side of her, but she could see shapes moving around inside slowly: someone picking up a baby, someone else just drifting up and down. It was all like some kind of benign horror movie.

She moved on slowly, past doors that said Staff Only, Kitchen Staff Only, Private, No Entry. She looked in vain for one that said Okay, Come On In. But there was no refuge for Emily tonight.

'Make way, please!'

Emily whirled around to see a wheelchair coming towards her at speed out of the darkness. A woman lay prostrate in it, her huge belly heaving. Her eyes were closed and her skin white. She looked to Emily like she was dying.

A porter pushed the wheelchair. A midwife ran beside it.

'Breathe, Martina. That's it!' she shouted enthusiastically, as though she were an Olympic swimming coach. 'I didn't hear you breathe!'

Emily saw the whites of Martina's eyes as the wheelchair flashed past and through big double doors at the bottom of the corridor: Delivery Ward – Authorised Personnel Only.

Emily, stricken, hurried down and pressed her nose to the glass at the top of the door. It was bright inside, fluorescent lights everywhere. There was no sign of poor, pitiful Martina. Something had obviously gone terribly wrong for her. Emily made sure to stand to one side because surgeons, consultants and possibly resuscitation staff were bound to be on the scene in seconds.

But nobody came. And inside the delivery ward, midwives and doctors hung around in small, cheerful clumps. There was no panic. A doctor said something and everybody laughed.

Emily was confused. What about Martina? What right had they to go on laughing and behaving normally at a time like this? Didn't they realise that there was a woman not thirty yards from them on another planet with pain? Did they not care?

Emily, ludicrously, found that she was crying bitter tears for Martina. She wanted to march in there and take Martina's hand, protect her, curl up on the bed beside her and tell her that everything would be all right. God Almighty, what kind of a sick world was it when the woman didn't even have a friend or relative or anybody at all who understood her at a time like this? And where was the wretched husband or boyfriend? Probably conveniently fainted back in the ward.

The air in the delivery ward was thick and warm and quiet. Nobody was around now except for a nurse at the station and she was busy filling in notes. Emily drifted past as though she had every right to be there. The nurse didn't look up.

The first two cubicled delivery rooms were empty. In the third, a woman and a man walked up and down slowly, him rubbing her back. They looked very intense. Emily felt a bit like a voyeur as she stood on tiptoes to look over the glass at them. She moved on.

The door to the next delivery room was shut tight. The glass on this one was too high to see over. Voices came from inside, low and calm. Emily heard moans: Martina. Her heart constricted in sympathy. She put her hand on the door.

'Hello?' The nurse from the station was bearing down on Emily, curious and wary.

'I'm looking for Martina,' Emily told her politely.

'This is a restricted area.'

'Yes, but I'm looking for Martina.'

The nurse cocked her head to one side. 'Why?'

'I'm a friend of hers,' Emily informed her. 'And she's in there all on her own.'

'She's not, you know. There's plenty of people in there with her.'

'Will she be all right?'

'I'm afraid I can't discuss patient information.'

Emily was surer than ever now that something had gone terribly wrong for Martina. Fresh tears cascaded down her face.

'I'm very sorry,' she said.

'That's all right.' The nurse must think that Emily was a very close friend indeed of Martina's. They might even have planned their pregnancies together. 'I'll tell her you called by okay?' she assured Emily. 'Now I'm going to have to ask you to go back to your own ward.'

She kindly escorted Emily to the double doors and went back to her station. Emily half expected her to whip out a walkie-talkie and murmur, 'Psycho in Delivery, can we have security please?' But the nurse just took a chocolate from a box of Roses and went back to her notes. The wonder of it was that none of the staff was fat. It must be something to do with night shifts and botched-up metabolism. It would be interesting to see whether any of the day staff was fat. There could be a whole new diet book in this one, Emily thought. Eat all you like between the hours of midnight and 6am.

'You've certainly cheered up.' Nurse V Mooney swished by. 'Now, back to bed with you.'

'I'll go in my own good time,' Emily said pleasantly and turned a corner.

Back down the dim, warm corridors. Emily bit back more tears and felt very unsure about everything. She didn't even know how to get back to her own ward from here. She felt she was halfway between normality and utter insanity and feared that if her mind went down a particular road then the balance might just be tipped. Best not to think at all, just keep on walking. Eventually morning would be here.

At last she approached a door that was open. Bright, welcoming light spilled out, and spirited chatter, along with the unmistakable stench of cigarette smoke.

Emily went in and sat down. Two women in their dressing-gowns were perched on hard plastic seats, both puffing furiously.

'Couldn't sleep either?' the one in pink said sympathetically.

'No. It's very noisy.'

'It's desperate, isn't it?' the one in the blue said. She was heavily pregnant. 'Get your hubby to bring in some earplugs. Want a cigarette?'

'I don't smoke,' Emily said regretfully.

The woman tensed, expecting Emily to look at her judgmentally. Emily couldn't give a hoot if she jumped off the top of the building. Now they were wondering what the hell she was doing in the smokers' room. *Their* room. Emily sat there defiantly and tried not to breathe in.

'When are you due?' she politely asked the woman in pink, eyeing her big belly.

The woman looked at her. 'I had my baby yesterday.'

Just when Emily thought that nothing else could happen that day. But then the woman threw back her big head and guffawed. 'Jesus Christ! And there was me thinking that I was tiny!'

The woman in blue laughed too. So did Emily, after a moment. She laughed harder and harder. Then she was the only one laughing. She screeched to a silence, her mouth still open in a silent bray.

'Are you all right?'

'Oh yes,' Emily said vigorously. 'I'm in for pre-eclampsia. I was passed over for a partnership in work today and I've just discovered my husband might have been unfaithful. Maybe he still is, who knows.'

The woman in pink looked at the woman in blue.

'She's a ticket, isn't she?' And they both guffawed heartily again. They liked her now, her supposed humour had broken down that difficult barrier between smokers and non-smokers, and she was one of theirs.

'Cathy,' said the one in blue.

'Petra,' said the one in pink.

'I'm Emily,' Emily said, not at all sure.

'Seriously, girl, what are you in for? You're not due, are you?'

'No, no. Just observation.'

'Who is it, O'Mara? Dunphy?'

'Chapman,' Emily said, feeling a bit irreverent at dropping the 'Mr'.

'Chapman!' Cathy said. 'Don't get me started.' Before Emily could, she was off. 'He had my sister in and out to Cork three times on her last one! He won't come up and see you here, you know. Too far a journey for him in his big Mercedes.'

It felt very bad to be discussing Mr Chapman like this, and Emily leaned in eagerly for more. It was a kind of escape.

'He heads up the maternity unit down in Cork. Did you know that?' Petra hissed.

'I didn't.'

'Oh yes. He can't wait for this place to close so that he can get his hands on even more women. Some people say that he was one of those lobbying hard for the closure. For his private practice, you see. We'll all end up paying him instead of O'Mara or Dunphy.'

'No!' Emily was amazed at her capacity to still feel shock.

'I'll tell you, it beats the hell out of brown envelopes.' Petra stubbed out her cigarette authoritatively and reached for another. 'I have O'Mara this time. He's very good, except that his hands are always cold.'

'I've got Dunphy,' Cathy confided to Emily. 'He's great with a needle. Stitch you up good as new.'

Emily was feeling a bit light-headed. Either it was tiredness or the second-hand smoke. 'I think I might go back to bed, see if I can sleep.'

'Good idea,' Cathy said. 'Although you won't have much chance of that. The kitchen girls are setting up for breakfast now. They bang around a good bit, don't they, Petra?'

'They do,' Petra agreed. 'Did you order an egg?'

'What?' Emily was mystified.

'You'll only get Weetabix and brown bread so. Take my advice, fill in the menu forms as a matter of priority. Otherwise they'll just give you whatever's handy.'

'Okay, thanks.' Emily stood. 'I'll see you around.'

'You will, girl,' Cathy said. 'And come up and see the baby tomorrow. I'm in Elizabeth's Ward – I'll let you look after her for a few minutes.'

Who was looking after the baby now was unclear. Emily nodded and smiled some more and left.

Her own ward seemed oddly familiar and safe. She

got back into bed and pulled the covers up tight around her and listened to the snoring, the crashing of breakfast utensils, the nurses' chatter outside.

'Are you all right?' someone whispered.

It was Maggie, peering in the side of the curtain.

'Fine, thanks,' Emily whispered back.

'I've got half a sleeping tablet left – I could slip it to you and they'd never know.'

'You're very good, but I'm not allowed.'

Maggie nodded and smiled and let the curtain drop back. Emily fell asleep instantly and dreamlessly.

Neasa heard the news the next morning. Conor had phoned at the crack of dawn, after first trying Neasa's house. But Neasa had stayed in Gary's overnight, as she did every Monday, Wednesday and Friday night. Gary stayed at hers on Tuesday, Thursday and Saturday nights. It was only fair, they assured each other. Equal. Sunday was a day of rest, which they were both secretly grateful for.

'Isn't that just the worse luck?' Neasa said to Gary. 'She must be in bits. After losing the partnership too.'

Gary shifted uneasily. He wasn't used to this feeling of guilt. 'But it's just for observation.'

'All the same, I'll go in. Tell them in work that I'm taking the morning off,' Neasa ordered.

'Right . . . are you sure you can take off just like that, honey?'

Neasa observed that a new note of loyalty had crept

into Gary's voice when it came to Crawley Dunne & O'Reilly.

'You're a partner now. You can okay it,' she said, sweetly.

'Of course,' he said quickly. 'Not that you'll be taking any liberties now that I'm a partner.'

'Will I heck,' she said. 'You're as good as a sick note from the doctor.'

She left Gary at the breakfast table looking slightly worried. She wouldn't rush straight over to Martha's, of course. Eleven o'clock would be a perfectly acceptable hour to be by Emily's bedside. She had time to get her roots touched up at the hairdressers' first, and see if they had any decent make-up in the chemist. It was very high maintenance being in love, she had discovered over the years. You constantly had to be on your guard against underarm hair and wayward cuticles, not to mention bikini lines. Expensive too: all the new clothes and underwear, romantic meals out and little spur-of-the-moment presents. It would nearly be a relief to slide into domestic cosiness where chipped nail varnish was just that, not some indication of a slovenly and weak character. She might actually be able to save some money, too.

Immediately she regretted her thoughts. Imagine turning into Emily and Conor, for example! Lovely, lovely people, God knows. But like two old comfortable boots at the end of the day. Finishing each other's sentences and forgetting to kiss each other every time they left the room! How could they have let themselves slide like that? They had been married six years, true, but that was no excuse.

Neasa and Gary had made love on the kitchen table the night before. Then they had opened a third bottle of wine and taken it into the living-room where they had talked and talked. Neasa couldn't remember for the life of her now what they had talked about, but it had all been very deep and meaningful. Gary had actually cried at one point. Naturally, so had Neasa. Then he had puked. Neasa hadn't been a bit offended; in fact, she had felt very tender and maternal, unusual for her, and had cradled his smelly head as he bent over the toilet.

Neasa herself never puked. She had a very strong constitution that way, even if the head was falling off her this morning. They really must buy better wine next time – you couldn't drink three bottles of that Spanish stuff without some ill-effects. More expense.

'Do you think I should call by Conor on the way to work?' Gary enquired, having followed Neasa into the bathroom. He looked a bit green.

'What for?'

'I don't know, to offer a bit of support or something.'

'He's probably on his way to the hospital now,' Neasa said.

Gary was relieved. Conor didn't like him. He never gave the slightest indication of this, but Gary just knew. He seemed to irritate him or something. And all the effort Gary made too, just because Emily was Neasa's friend! He was just trying to be nice, for heaven's sake. Asking Conor what it was like being a pianist and all that and even asking to see Conor's piano. Conor had dutifully shown it to him and had pointed out the difference between the black and white keys. You'd think he was taking the mick except that he looked so serious. Gary had then tried to talk about football to him, a sure fire safe bet. But Conor had no interest in football. He wasn't normal in that respect. Gary secretly thought of Conor as a bit snotty and removed, content to stand on the sidelines and observe other people, and looking as though he were enjoying some private joke.

He sometimes wondered what Conor was like in bed. Oh, nothing sexual, you understand. Gary was a man's man only in the pub, nowhere else, and anybody who suggested otherwise would get a black eye, all right? No, Gary only wondered about Conor in bed because he'd love to see him out of control for once. Abandoned and lustful and roaring, 'Come get it, baby!' Gary tittered.

'What?' Neasa said.

'Nothing, sweetness.' He was applying Neasa's cover-stick to a spot on his chin. All this drinking with Neasa was taking its toll. But apparently copious amounts of red wine went hand in hand with romance. 'Just thinking how lucky we are, that's all.'

'I know, I've never met anyone like you,' Neasa said fervently.

'Would a touch of powder over this be too much?' Gary wondered.

'Not at all,' Neasa said tenderly. 'Although, really, you're gorgeous enough.'

'You're just saying that.'

'Am not!'

'Awww.' He kissed the back of her neck. Neasa sighed in bliss. She must not let this one slip through her fingers like all the others had. Not that it had been her fault, of course. None of them had turned out to be what she thought they were. Take Fintan, for example, the nicest, sweetest, most romantic man you could ever hope to meet. That had lasted four heady months, until Fintan had revealed himself to be a chat-room junkie on the Internet. Then there was Michael, the secret cross-dresser. Neasa had thought that she could live with it until he confided that he would like to walk down the street just once in one of her dresses. He'd swiftly been dumped on the refuse heap along with Darren the sexist and Neil the guy who didn't believe in washing. There had been others too, whose infractions had been less dramatic but none the less unpalatable. She always seemed to go for men who let her down in some fundamental or deeply embarrassing way.

Gary was blissfully normal. The others had started out normal too, but the cracks had appeared much sooner. Neasa had six months with Gary under her belt and it was looking good. In fact, it had never looked better. She hated to say it, because she had said it so often in the past, but this time she knew she was right: Gary was The One.

'Got to go, baby,' she said.

'All right, chicken. See you for lunch?'

'Great. Crawley's office?'

'I suppose. Although we could just go for something to eat.'

Something to eat? They always had sex in Crawley's office on a Wednesday because he took a half-day. 'We could,' she said slowly.

Gary saw that he had displeased her but wasn't sure why. 'Crawley's office it is,' he said easily. 'I'll buy two Mars bars.'

Neasa beamed at him. Everything was great.

Nurse V Mooney woke Emily at a quarter to eight.

'Do you work here all the time?' Emily asked. She wondered what the V stood for.

'Eight to eight, the night shift,' the nurse informed her crisply. 'Now, let's see how the blood pressure is this morning.'

It wasn't much better from the look on her face.

'The urine came back, by the way. It's clear.'

Some good news at last.

'So I won't have to go to Cork?'

'No use asking me. Nobody tells us anything.' She added notes to Emily's chart. 'Mr Chapman will make the final decision. But he's not a man to take risks with other people's health.' She made this sound like a bit of an insult. 'Now, up you get and have some breakfast. Oh, and there's a man out there who says he's your husband.'

'Right.'

'He's been here since seven.' The nurse didn't look at her. 'But I thought you needed your sleep.'

She was gone before Emily could thank her. Emily got out of bed and put on her dressing gown. Then she brushed her hair back rigidly and found herself hunting for her powder to take the vulnerable shine off her nose.

She leaned against the bed heavily. What was she doing, armouring herself against her own husband? Against Conor, her plain-clothes garda, the man who couldn't even bring himself to double-park? The very idea of Conor and Ffion, Conor and Mary, seemed ludicrous in the cold bright light of the morning.

Emily was embarrassed at her conjecture now, mortified by her emotion last night. She wouldn't even tell Conor about this. He would be outraged by her suspicion. She would be if he thought the same about her.

But the heavy feeling in the pit of her stomach wouldn't go away, like she had opened some Pandora's box and would be sorry ever after.

She stepped out past the curtain and into the ward. The two other women and Maggie were sitting at a small table under the television, munching their way through Weetabix and boiled eggs. Emily hadn't even introduced herself to them yet, and she didn't now either. She slipped out into the corridor and found Conor sitting stiffly on a hard chair by the nurses' station, his feet sharply drawn in for fear of tripping up anybody.

'Hi.'

'Hi yourself,' Emily said, trying out a smile.

He looked at her belly. 'How are you feeling?'

'Okay, I suppose. Tired. It's hard to sleep in here.'

He nodded. He hadn't had much sleep either from the look of him. And he hadn't shaved either. He came over and awkwardly embraced her. It was very public here – nurses were everywhere as the shift changed over.

'Can we go somewhere?'

Emily thought of the smokers' room. 'Not really. Just back to my bed, I suppose.'

The other women didn't even look up as Conor arrived in. Like Emily, they had been poked and prodded and palpated throughout their pregnancies and were past embarrassment at being seen in their nighties by strange men. They'd been seen in a lot less.

Emily pulled the curtain tight around them again. It gave some small illusion of privacy.

'You have the chair,' she said.

'No, no, you must be sick of the bed, you sit in the chair.'

'Conor, take the blasted chair!'

She didn't know who was more surprised, her or Conor.

'Sorry. This is all a bit odd. Being here, I mean.'

'I know. You should have rung me, left a message or something. Remember, we agreed that I'd check the answering service at the interval?'

'I know, I know.' Emily felt as though she had broken the rules.

'I'd have come straight up.'

'I didn't want to worry you.'

'Oh Emily. I don't know why you do this. Try and take everything on by yourself.'

'I know,' Emily agreed. 'I should be shot really.' Oops. There she went again. She breezed on quickly. 'How did the concert go?'

'What? Oh, fine, fine. Look, have you talked to Chapman?'

'No. They might be transferring me to Cork. I don't know yet. Nobody tells the nurses here anything.'

'Neasa will be in later.'

'Why did you have to go ringing her?'

'What? She's your friend. I thought you'd like some company, that's all.'

He was feeling under attack. This was pointless and silly, Emily knew. And very unfair.

'I didn't get the partnership, Conor,' she said.

'Ah.' This explained everything. He looked very sympathetic. 'I'm sorry, Emily.'

'Yes. Gary got it instead.'

'Gary?' Conor's face said it all. 'Well. They'll be sorry.'

'Maybe.' Emily was unable to shake the feeling that she was making conversation.

Conor produced a plastic bag that she hadn't noticed before.

'I brought you some supplies. You know, 7UP and stuff. And some magazines.'

He must have stopped by the Spar that stayed open all night. A bunch of flowers stuck out the top of the bag, the ones you see in buckets outside garages.

'It was all they had,' he said apologetically. 'But I wanted you to have something nice to look at in this place.'

'Oh, Conor.' She took the bag and held it tight to her chest as though it were some kind of shield, and looked at his square, handsome, confused face.

'I do love you, you know,' she said.

He looked a bit embarrassed. 'Ah, I know. And I love you too.'

He got up and sat on the bed beside her and stroked her tummy, their baby. Emily laid her head on his shoulder and they sat for a while like that.

'It's just a precaution, Emily. Chapman's covering his ass. They're all terrified of litigation these days.'

Emily tried to find solace in his predictability but couldn't.

'You'll be out today, I bet you anything. And I'll take you home and everything will be like normal.'

'I suppose.' Reluctantly, she lifted her head off his shoulder. 'Conor, I have to eat breakfast now. Then the house doctor will be around again and they'll have to see about transferring me to Cork and all that.' She didn't look at him. 'Maybe you should go on home and get some rest.'

'I'm staying here.'

'There's nothing you can do. I'll ring you as soon as I know anything. I promise.'

Conor wasn't happy at all about this. 'I can just sit quietly in that chair – I won't be in anybody's way.'

'You'll be more use at home.' Emily appealed to his practical side. 'I might need more clothes and things for Cork and I'll need you to get them for me. And people will be ringing. Someone should be at home to tell everybody that there's no panic.'

Conor looked at her for a moment. 'Okay. If that's what you want.'

'It is,' she quickly assured him, adding brightly, 'and who knows, I might be ringing in an hour's time to ask you to come and drive me home!'

She wasn't fooling him. She knew by the twitch of his left eyebrow, a dead giveaway.

'Ring me anyway,' he asked.

'Of course I will!'

He stood and bent to kiss her. She turned her head slightly so that he kissed her cheek.

'Take care,' he said.

'You too.'

It was all a bit awkward and formal. Part of Emily hated sending him away like this; it seemed very heartless when he was probably as worried as she. But she was afraid of what she might say if he stayed any longer.

She gave a little wave as he went out into the corridor, but he didn't look back and she let her hand fall.

Her stomach rumbled, surprising her. She'd had no dinner last night, she remembered. The thought of Weetabix revolted her, but the baby would start eating itself if she didn't feed it soon.

For the first time since she'd arrived, she pulled back the curtain around her bed all the way to the wall. The breakfasting women looked up in surprise; they'd been having a whispered argument as to whether Emily was very sick or just plain rude. Only Maggie smiled.

Emily was weary. She would have to be civilised because they would all turn out to be related in some distant way to her neighbours in Paulstown, don't you know, and she wouldn't give any of them another excuse to think that she was getting above herself.

Neasa didn't like hospitals. It was to do with her grandmother dying three years before. Mrs Martin had been in and out of hospitals for eighteen months before somebody had finally said the word 'terminal' to her. She had looked at them, upset. 'What do you mean, terminate?' For weeks afterwards, in her drugged haze, she had been convinced that there was some plot afoot to carry out euthanasia on her, and wasn't happy unless Neasa was there to protect her. 'She's a solicitor,' she would ominously remind the doctors every now and then.

Towards the end, Neasa had taken a week's compassionate leave from work and had spent it by her grandmother's bedside, leaving it only for a quick shower and a change of clothes. It had been a slow, miserable, painful death. Neasa had gone on a bender for three days. If there was one lesson to be learned from it all, it was to enjoy life while one could, because the odds were that there was no happy ending in store.

And so she strode down the corridors of Martha's carrying a big red helium balloon and a six-pack of Guinness. Emily wasn't sick, thank God, and there was no point in pretending she was.

Neasa found her chatting with three other women as though they had known each other all their lives.

'Oh, hi, Neasa! This is Trish. She's overdue by two weeks. They might have to induce. And this is Siobhan, a false alarm. She'll be out today. And Maggie, of course. Maggie was going to try for a water birth, but they don't do it here, apparently.'

'I'm going to ask for a birthing chair instead,' Maggie told Neasa earnestly.

'Oh, yeh, I saw one of those in Habitat,' Neasa said, and roared laughing.

Maggie and the rest looked at her blankly. Shit. They were serious.

Neasa looked around for a window to open. She wished now that she wasn't so hungover.

'You've had your roots done,' Emily observed.

Neasa was embarrassed. Nobody in the world knew that her hair wasn't naturally black except for Emily, and that was only because a pack of Clairol Midnight Black had fallen out of Neasa's bag one day.

'It's all right. We're all women here,' Emily said, seeing her face.

All pregnant women who didn't have to worry about their appearance. Neasa wasn't part of their club, thank you very much.

'This your bed?' Neasa asked. It was dressed differently to all the others: the covers were brought right up to the pillow and folded under neatly. She dumped the Guinness on the end of it and sat down.

'See you later,' Emily said cheerily to the others, and pulled the curtain around herself and Neasa. A bit unnecessary, Neasa thought.

'So,' she demanded, 'what's the diagnosis? They're not going to do a caesarean section or anything like that, are they?'

'No, no,' Emily said vaguely. 'I'm not even being moved to Cork. No beds available, apparently. I'll probably be out tomorrow.'

'Great! They were all asking for you in work, you know. Gary rang. And Creepy Crawley is mooching around the place looking sick as a parrot. He told the cleaner this morning that he thinks he might have brought it all on you. When I go in this afternoon, I'm going to tell him that his name is down on your chart as a possible cause.'

She had expected Emily to laugh. Come on. It was a little bit funny, wasn't it?

'I want you to do something for me,' Emily said. She looked very intense.

'What?' Neasa asked warily. She hoped that this wasn't something to do with delivery wards and birthing partners and all that. Maybe Conor had bottled out. Neasa would just die.

'I want you to ring a hotel in Germany. You'll have to look up the number in directory enquiries. That's the name of it.' She pressed a piece of paper into Neasa's hand. Or, rather, a square of hospital toilet roll, the stuff that looked like greaseproof paper. The pen had run out halfway, before starting again with a big blob of blue.

'You're not thinking of taking a holiday, surely?' Neasa asked, confused.

'I'm not.'

Neasa looked from the piece of paper to Emily's too-bright eyes. 'What then?'

'Well, you see, it's all very silly, really,' Emily said lightly, and stopped.

'How silly?' Neasa enquired.

'Probably extremely silly.' Emily bit her lip. 'But I need you to check some dates for me.'

'I see.'

'I need to know when the orchestra stayed there last

year when they were on tour. What nights.'

Neasa looked at the piece of paper again.

'The entire orchestra?' she asked eventually. 'The whole thirty-one of them?'

'Thirty-two,' Emily corrected. 'You see, I think most of them might have left at the one time. But some of them might have stayed on. Two of them.'

Neasa nodded slowly. 'Wouldn't that kind of information be . . . privileged, so to speak?'

'You might have to be clever about it,' Emily agreed.

Neasa said nothing for a little while, then, 'Is this urgent?'

'Not urgent, no.'

'Maybe you should wait until you're out of hospital.'

'Maybe. But I can't.'

'Emily,' Neasa said, 'of course I'll do it for you if you really want me to. And I'm a great one for rushing in there myself.' As her last nine boyfriends would testify. 'But you've got a baby to think about. And your own health. You've only two months to go, you know. Maybe you should just concentrate on that and tackle everything else afterwards.'

Emily looked at her, closed. 'Will you do this for me or not?'

Neasa folded the piece of toilet paper and put it efficiently into her bag.

'So, how's Gary getting on as a new partner?' Emily enquired, as though Germany had never been mentioned at all.

'Oh, terrible,' Neasa said cheerfully. 'Already he's been put in charge of the timesheets for everyone – you know, making sure people are there when they say they are. Which means, of course, that Gary has to be there himself, which is an awful pain.'

'Forgive me if I don't have much sympathy.'

'Neither do I,' Neasa agreed. 'And listen to this – Daphne Dunne has announced a crackdown on people fiddling expenses and has asked Gary to root out the perpetrators.'

'Which is himself.'

'And Phil,' Neasa felt she had to point out. 'He taught Gary how to do it in the first place. Gary's told me that I'm not allowed to put in a claim for make-up any more either. Imagine!'

'Terrible,' Emily said.

'If they expect us to wear make-up in to the office then they should pay for it,' Neasa complained. 'But Gary's said no. He doesn't want to show favouritism in case anyone suspects.'

'Why don't you just tell people you're an item?' Emily said impatiently. They all knew anyway.

'Because we have to keep it more of a secret now than ever! He's a partner – he can't be seen to be humping the staff!'

'I don't see why not,' Emily said. 'Unless he's going to stop humping you, is he?'

'Well, no.' Emily was being difficult today, which was very unlike her. Still, you couldn't expect too much of her, given the circumstances. 'Listen, Gary said that this isn't common knowledge, but Creepy Crawley and the rest are writing you a letter officially informing you that you didn't get the partnership. Apparently it's a very nice letter, full of praise for you and all that, and saying that they value you very much in the company. Plus giving you a big pay rise. Can you believe that?'

'I can,' Emily said, grimly.

'I'd write a letter straight back telling them they're right fuckers. And I'd threaten to go to the Revenue Commissioners on them too. Gary said that from what he saw of the accounts this morning, they're fiddling tax right left and centre. I'm sure I could get you details if you want.'

Emily just gave a tired shrug.

Maybe it wasn't a good idea to be going on too much about Crawley Dunne & O'Reilly in the present circumstances, Neasa thought. Certainly she wouldn't be telling her now or ever what Crawley had told Gary about Emily this morning in his office. The partners had considered Emily to be too soft for the top job, too malleable and eager to please. Didn't have that necessary aggression and elusive go-get-'em mentality. A fine, fine worker though. In fact, Crawley had confided, the best they'd ever had.

'How are you feeling? Really?' Neasa asked quietly.

'How do I look?'

'Like shite.'

'I don't know, Neasa. It's all a bit strange. Like

everything is happening to someone else. Do you ever get that feeling?'

'No,' Neasa admitted. She had never understood this thing of being 'outside' yourself, looking in. Except when she had smoked cannabis for the first time at college. That had been very odd, and she had stuck to drink ever since. At least you knew where you were with alcohol.

'But the doctors say there's no cause for alarm.' Emily seemed determined to stick to the practical. 'They just don't want it developing into eclampsia. That's when your placenta starts packing up.'

'How exactly?'

'Clots start forming and that kind of thing.'

'Oooh. Sounds nasty.' Neasa was all interest.

'The baby doesn't get vital nutrients and stuff, and maybe even oxygen.'

'Does it make a break for freedom?'

'Sometimes. Other times they do a section.' A caesarean section was now a 'section'. Emily was talking the talk after only twelve hours in hospital.

'But the baby's not ready for that yet,' Neasa said. 'It might still only have one ear or something.'

'No, no, the baby has been fully formed since it was twelve weeks, Neasa. Remember I showed you the picture of the scan?'

'You couldn't tell anything from that,' Neasa declared. 'It looked like a tadpole. And I certainly didn't see any ears.'

'Anyway, the point is, it's the lungs they'd be worried about. They're the last to mature.'

'Well, Conor's a smoker,' Neasa said, more to test the waters than anything.

But Emily didn't react. 'He doesn't smoke in the house, Neasa. And it's nothing to do with cigarettes. Every baby's lungs are the same.'

'The poor blighters,' Neasa said. 'If I were to be born prematurely, I'd rather have only one ear than one lung.'

'They're not actually missing a lung . . . oh, it doesn't matter. The thing is, it's not going to happen. Everything seems to be all right.'

'Apart from the high blood pressure, the water retention and the presence of uric acid in your wee,' Neasa said helpfully.

'Well, yes.'

'And what has Mr Chapman to say about any of it?'

'I haven't seen him. I would have if I were in Cork. Still, they're taking good care of me here.'

'But you're paying him.'

'He delivered four babies this morning in Cork, Neasa. I can pay him all I want but he can't be in two places at the one time.'

Neasa just shrugged. She had dragged a doctor from his holidays in Kerry to come look at her grandmother. And she hadn't even been paying him.

'I wish I'd paid more attention in antenatal classes when they were going on about this,' Emily said. 'But I suppose I always thought these things happened to someone else.'

'We always do.' Neasa paused slightly. 'I suppose Conor's been in?'

Emily nodded. 'Oh yes. This morning. Brought me flowers and all.'

'Good, good.'

Neasa was confused. From Emily's expression, there didn't seem anything too wrong in that department. What was with all this Germany business so? Neasa had a very strong urge to wrestle Emily to the bed and drag the information out of her. But Emily seemed too fragile this morning, everything about her too tenuous. Neasa was forced to go for the subtler approach instead, which she had no confidence in. She always ended up sounding like some tit from a B movie.

'Emily,' she said awkwardly, 'you would tell me if anything was wrong, wouldn't you?'

'Of course I would.'

'Because, you know, a problem halved and all that?'

'Yes, I know.'

'And I always tell you when things are going wrong for me, don't I? Remember when I caught Gary going through my underwear drawer a couple of months ago?'

'I do,' said Emily, quickly.

'And I was upset because I thought, oh fuck, here's another cross-dresser – I mean, what is it about me? But you said no, calm down, that you bet he was just checking for my size. And, hey presto, he comes home with a dinky little number from one of those basement shops in Cork and everything was fine!'

'Glad to be of service,' Emily murmured.

'So, like . . . I'm here, just so you know that.'

'Thanks, Neasa.' But she wasn't going to say anything more, that much was clear. Neasa, in a bit of a huff, collected her bits and pieces.

'I'd better get in to work. Gary's told me that my timesheets are particularly bad. I hope he's not going to be a pain in the arse about this.'

'Thanks for the Guinness.'

'No problem. And that Maggie woman has blackcurrant cordial on her locker – you might be able to score some if you give her a can.'

When Neasa's grandmother had been in hospital, the patients had swapped all kinds of things. The items most hotly coveted had been alcohol and cigarettes and Neasa had been able to procure for her grandmother the TV remote control in exchange for a hundred Major and a bottle of vodka.

Emily walked with her to the corridor. 'Neasa – let me know, won't you?'

'Yes.'

At Emily's pointed, anxious face, Neasa felt so moved that she gave her a quick, hard hug. It felt awkward. They weren't kissy-kissy friends.

'You'll be grand, girl.'

'Oh, I know. Out tomorrow.'

'Out tomorrow!'

Neasa went off down the corridor, the piece of toilet paper lying in her bag like a stick of dynamite. It must be big, she thought grimly, if Emily hadn't told her.

Mr Gerald Chapman was at that moment delivering his fifth baby of the morning.

'I can see the head, Maeve – why don't you give one more push,' he told the mother.

'I can't,' she sobbed. 'I'm dying.'

Mr Chapman smiled sympathetically. Out of the side of his mouth, he said to the midwife, 'Pain relief?'

'Insisted on a natural birth,' she murmured back. 'Until it was too late.'

Epidurals were not usually given once labour had passed a certain stage. It slowed things up.

Mr Chapman sighed inwardly. He had no truck with the way natural childbirth had become a sort of a badge with some women, something to boast about to their weaker sisters who had epidurals. 'I was in labour twenty-seven hours without so much as gas!' And the bloody hospitals were worse, promoting pain like it was some kind of lifestyle choice. Tell that to this poor young one here who was beside herself with anguish.

He looked at her frightened face and spoke in the trademark calm tones he prided himself on. To everyone else he sounded bored stiff. 'You are not dying, Maeve. Believe me. But I can't get this baby out unless you help me. Let's give another push, shall we?'

She didn't argue. She hadn't the breath in any case. Besides, he was the expert in the white coat. Nobody had argued with him in years.

'There's a contraction coming now,' a trainee midwife said, watching the monitor.

'Right. Have the vacuum ready just in case.' But Mr Chapman thought he'd be able to manage without vacuum suction, which usually temporarily distorted the soft bones of the baby's head. The parents always got a fright when their baby came out looking like an extra from Star Trek. 'Okay, let's give her some help.'

Everyone scurried around him. Maeve braced herself, holding on tight to her husband's hand. He hadn't said a word in ten minutes and his face was ashen. That was another thing that Mr Chapman had no truck with. Half the men didn't want to be in the delivery room in the first place and, in his experience, half the women didn't want them there either. They'd have been much more comfortable with another woman. But the men came because they had been told it was their rightful place, that their presence was necessary to make the event meaningful. Next thing, people would be encouraged to bring in any other children to witness the wonderful event, maybe even a couple of close relatives and the family dog.

It was all in danger of going too far, Mr Chapman sometimes thought. Not that he ever voiced these opinions. He would look like a dinosaur. Instead, he contented himself with banishing videocams from any of his deliveries, and only allowing photographs to be taken at the end. You wouldn't believe what some people tried to photograph for the album.

'Oh, Christ,' Maeve moaned as the contraction swept over her.

'Let's do it this time,' Mr Chapman said.

Helen, the chief midwife, went into action. She knew her stuff. She watched the monitor all the time as the contraction slowly peaked.

'Don't push don't push don't push, Maeve, wait wait wait wait wait . . . okay, here we go, push push push, come on Maeve girl, PUSH PUSH PUSH!'

Everyone was screaming push, even the husband.

It was merely background noise to Mr Chapman, who had the baby's head out. Now a shoulder, which popped out wetly. Mr Chapman eased the baby sideways and got the other shoulder free just as Maeve ran out of steam. But it was okay. A little gentle manoeuvring, a little pull, and the rest of the baby was in his hands. He held it up for Maeve to see. It started to cry – a thin, outraged wail at the brutality of it all, and Mr Chapman felt compassionate.

'A boy,' he said.

Maeve burst into tears. Her husband resisted, thank God.

Mr Chapman handed over the child to Helen, and quickly cut the cord. He never offered to let the father do this, as some doctors did. Ridiculous. They weren't opening supermarkets. And what if something went wrong? What if the father mis-aimed and inadvertently stabbed his wife? You see! Those doctors never thought about that, did they?

Mr Chapman did. Most of his more sensible colleagues did. Some of them had been on the receiving end of solicitors' letters for a lot less. Caution and accountability were the order of the day. It would strangle them all yet, Mr Chapman often thought sourly, this entire compensation culture. Oh, people expected them to work miracles, but they were not allowed to make a mistake. As if medicine were an exact science where nothing could ever go wrong.

Now he had the placenta out and had put two neat stitches into Maeve. She was oblivious to Mr Chapman, cradling her baby.

'Let's have a look at the little fellow,' Mr Chapman said, preparing to leave. Maeve shyly held out the bundle, all gratitude now. The father was bursting with pride.

'He's grand,' Mr Chapman said, looking at their shiny, smiling faces.

Little did they know what was ahead of them. Mr Chapman's own three teenage sons should have been drowned at birth. Drinking and taking drugs and crashing cars, then coming to him looking for money. After all their fine education too, and all their mother's hard work in trying to put manners on them. When they were twenty-one, he would buy each of them an apartment very far away and tell them to pack their bags.

It might have been different had they had girls, they often consoled themselves. But some said that girls were worse, far more devious than boys. They sucked up to you, smiled at you, gave you a hug before they went to bed. Next thing you know they've shinned down a drainpipe and are shagging the gardener. This had actually happened to a colleague of Mr Chapman's.

And even if by some miracle your children turned out to be a credit to you, what kind of a world awaited them? One ruled by greed and jealousy, internal squabbling and political back-stabbing, Mr Chapman thought gloomily. Life was an endurance test until you amassed enough for a very comfortable retirement split between West Cork and a villa in Spain. And then you were too old and fat to enjoy it.

Mr Chapman had had plans when he was young. He was going to dedicate his career to groundbreaking research into birth defects, holed up in a laboratory paid for by meagre grants. Somehow the plan had changed. He couldn't remember now how or when.

'Mr Chapman?'

'What?' he hurled over his shoulder as he briskly left the delivery ward. Nurses, doctors and interns reverentially stepped out of his way, like the Red Sea parting. Dr Doolan, a junior doctor, eventually caught up with him, a commendable feat given that he hadn't slept since Monday.

'Two of yours have been admitted,' he panted. 'One's just started; the other looks like a false alarm.'

'Right. Don't discharge the false alarm till I look at her.'

He hurried on. He had a lunch appointment with a member of the hospital board. He had issues about the closure of Martha's to discuss with her. Like, how to pile more people into an already overloaded public healthcare system; how to manufacture extra beds where there was no staff to administer them. His sinus headache began to throb nicely behind his eyes.

Dr Doolan caught up with Mr Chapman again, like a terrier on its last legs.

'What about Emily Collins?'

'Emily Collins Emily Collins . . .'

'In Martha's.'

'Oh. Yes. Emily Collins.' The threatened pre-eclampsia. He had meant to ring Martha's this morning but had been caught in delivery for the past three hours.

'How's she doing?'

'BP is still up.'

Mr Chapman sighed again. He had hoped to be able to tell them to discharge her.

'Haven't we any bed here for her?' he said impatiently.

'We did an hour ago, but now . . .'

'God almighty!' This didn't bode well. Everybody had assured each other for the past two years that Martha's could be seamlessly devoured by Cork. He would have to bring this up with the board. Again.

And he would have to drive up and see Emily Collins. He wouldn't be satisfied otherwise. This meant that everything this afternoon would be pushed back. Another late night. Hannah would go mad. There was a golf do on at the club. She would just have to go on her own.

'Tell them I'll be up around four.'

Dr Doolan looked very far away. He was in fact asleep.

'Dr Doolan,' Mr Chapman said sharply. 'Go home.'

'Did you put a birthing chair down on your birth plan?' Maggie wanted to know.

'Not yet,' Emily conceded. She didn't want to tell Maggie that she had yet to draw up a birth plan. Maggie's seemed very elaborate, running to five pages of dense handwriting with two diagrams thrown in lest anything be open to confusion or question. She was making a change now with Tipp-Ex and a red pen.

'I'm going to put down that if there's no birthing chair available, I want extra pillows,' she confided. 'Oh, hello, Auntie Paula!'

Auntie Paula was followed by several more relatives. Apparently the influx of Maggie's relatives happened all day every day, according to Trish, who now took out a pack of cards and started playing by herself, very concentrated. Siobhan packed to go home. Emily put on her dressing gown and took to the corridors again.

There was a visitors' room at the end of the floor; a dark, cheerless room with shabby chairs and a big poster on the wall that warned, Don't Wait! Vaccinate! Someone had added a moustache to the pink-faced baby on the poster, and two rotten teeth.

Emily wondered why people felt the need to destroy things, to ruin them on an impulse.

She closed the door behind her and sat down. It was the first time she had been truly alone since she'd arrived here.

'Hello, baby,' she said, patting her belly. She liked to have conversations with the baby every now and then but not in front of other people. 'It's all a bit mad in here, isn't it?'

The baby lay quietly, listening.

'Mr Chapman's on his way,' she said. 'He might let us out soon. Wouldn't that be nice?'

She heard her own voice, false and forced, and wondered how she had become such a sham.

There must have been some definable point at which she had made a decision not to notice what was going on in her marriage. But these things were subconscious, weren't they? Surely she didn't consciously ignore the signs that Conor was having an affair? What did that say about her, after all?

Either way she was not coming to this fresh. There wasn't the sharp, horrifying shock of a first discovery, no wordless trauma as though she had unexpectedly been hit a stunning blow. Hers was a feeling of dull realisation as the full impact of something coming for a while now hit her at last.

It was more painful in a way. She had colluded with it by her silence and her stark refusal to notice. In some ways she had gone along with her own betrayal, and in typical Emily fashion, had hoped that if she left well enough alone, it would all go away.

Not that Conor gave much away, in fairness to her. He was too careful, too considerate to leave any tawdry clues around that might hurt her. To come home with lipstick on his collar would be so ludicrous and crass. No credit-card receipts for Ann Summers in his pocket either. The mere notion!

No, what Emily had ignored was much subtler in some ways and more obvious in others. His increased preoccupation, for example, hard to spot in one so preoccupied anyway. His reluctance to just bloody talk about things that mattered. And her own vague unhappiness and loneliness, feelings that she assumed most married people took for granted once the first flush was over.

They had joked about these things in the beginning, those silly jokes that people make in their newly married smugness, and that lie there like time bombs to explode years later. 'Don't go kissing any boys now,' Conor would say when she left for a night on the tiles with Neasa. 'And don't you go filling Mrs Conlon's sugar cup while I'm gone,' she would deliver as a riposte. Mrs Conlon-next-door was always coming round to borrow something. She was sixty if she was a day, and they had both thought this great gas. It wasn't funny at all now.

Emily sat there in the dark visitors' room in her long-buried knowledge, frozen and numb. She was denied those initial hot feelings of disbelief and anger. It would be very false of her to shout and scream hysterically, and throw things across the room. There wasn't anything to throw anyway, except for the ancient television and she'd probably be billed for breaking that. She remembered now all those crappy late-night movies on the telly where the blissfully ignorant wife suddenly discovered a used condom in the back seat of the family saloon and had predictably gone ballistic, setting fire to the car before going after the wayward husband with a shotgun. Emily felt very jealous of these women now. But she suspected there were many more like her who, for a billion reasons, had known all along but had ruthlessly convinced themselves that there was nothing wrong.

Part of her wished fiercely that she hadn't seen that concert programme. She might even have got away with it. They both would have. And that was the honest-to-God truth.

But it was the first and last piece of stark evidence – how she hated that word – that she simply couldn't ignore. Not even her.

She thought about herself and her baby and her marriage, the safe existence she had painstakingly built for herself, the energy and commitment she had invested in everything, like a hard-working squirrel hoarding nuts for a comfortable winter. She even included the dogs in this scenario, and the house and the cappuccino-maker in the kitchen. She thought about all her hopes and dreams and expectations, and she felt the first stab of real rage at Conor for making her entire life seem so fake and contrived now, so worthless. As if he were God or something, free to dabble as he pleased. He had no consideration! That to Emily was a terrible sin.

She took a deep breath, looking at the grey walls of the visitors' room. She supposed that this was where it would all happen later – the confrontation, the angst, the anger. It was, she thought, a wearying prospect. And it wasn't as though there would be something nice at the end of it all, a little reward for putting them through the mill. No well done, let's move on now even better than before. She didn't know what was going to happen but none of it would be nice.

She supposed she should at least wait until Neasa rang with confirmation, and that's all it would be. Perhaps she shouldn't have involved Neasa in her sleuthing. Perhaps she should just have asked him straight out. But Emily was too precise, too hungry for order in her facts to do that. There was still that slim chance she was wrong and she would not accuse him in the wrong.

Also, she was terribly afraid that he would lie to her

face. And that would somehow be worse. That would be unforgivable.

No, she wouldn't play any cat-and-mouse games. They weren't that kind of people. She didn't even feel bad about snooping around behind his back, checking up on him. Honesty had already been a casualty in their marriage, long before any affair had reared its head.

He was at home on his own now, probably worrying and waiting for her to phone. She didn't want to talk to him. But neither did she want to worry him. After all, this baby was fifty percent his.

Cold dread crept over her at this thought of 'percentages', like she was already mentally dividing things up. He had become separate from her already.

The baby had hiccups. Emily crossed her arms over her belly as far as they would go and knew that she had to be very careful about everything. She could not afford to be self-indulgent, neither of them could. It wasn't just about them.

It was strange, she thought, how events had a way of outdoing each other. The loss of the partnership had paled into insignificance when the pre-eclampsia had reared its head. Now the affair had overridden that in a different way. What would it take to outdo the affair? Maybe if Conor dropped dead.

'Look at you! Sitting up grinning! I thought you were sick.' Liz had found her.

'Hello, Liz.' Emily tried to look welcoming. 'You

shouldn't have come in – I told Conor to tell everyone that there was no panic.'

Her voice sounded perfectly normal. And she hadn't even paused before she'd said Conor's name.

'Of course I had to come in! Mammy's very worried.' Oh, it was for their mother then.

'Tell her I'm fine.'

'Obviously.' Liz looked her up and down. 'I thought it was pre-eclampsia?'

'They're not really sure yet.' Emily felt like she had been repeating this piece of information all her life.

'Oh.' Liz looked even more like it was all a storm in a teacup.

'Where's the gang then?'

'I left them with Eamon except for Willy here,' Liz said stoutly. 'It'll serve him right. And I gave them all a can of Coke before I left so they'll be climbing the walls with caffeine.'

'And how's Mammy?' Emily said, when it became obvious that her own health wasn't going to be enquired after any time soon.

Liz sighed. 'She had more palpitations this morning.'

'I think it's that new postman.'

'You can be so facetious sometimes about really serious things, Emily. Poor Mammy might be on the way out for all we know.'

'We're all on the way out, Liz. Even little Willy there.'

Liz hugged Willy to her. 'That's a horrible thing to say!'

Emily didn't see why. 'He'll have seventy good years first.'

'Maybe ninety,' Liz declared. 'If he takes after Eamon's father.'

'Let's hope he doesn't take after ours.'

Their father had died of a sudden heart attack ten years ago at the age of fifty-two. 'It could have been worse,' their mother had said bravely.

Liz looked at Emily suspiciously. 'Have they put you on drugs?'

'No, no.'

'They should. You don't look well at all, now that I get a good look at you.'

'I'm afraid, Liz. After the last time,' Emily said.

Liz was a bit discomfited at this show of honesty. 'Well, of course. But lots of women have miscarriages. And go on to have a clatter of kids, thank God. Too many in some cases. Look at Myra Byrne. She could open her own crèche.'

It could have been their mother speaking, combating any hint of complaint with her mish-mash of religious clichés and good, old-fashioned Irish insistence that there were always others worse off than themselves.

It was just another aspect of the endless denial that Emily had bought into too. Emily didn't pursue it. There was no sense in forcing Liz to see the light. Emily was only starting to see it herself.

'Have you talked to Eamon?'

'I phoned the Revenue this morning from Mammy's,'

Liz confided. 'They were quite sympathetic, if you can believe that. I'm going to start paying off bits of the tax bill straightaway. I'll have to use the Children's Allowance.'

'So you didn't talk to him then?'

Liz sensed criticism. 'And when would I talk to him? He was working till midnight last night. And this morning I had to take Tommy to school, then Willy here to the doctor for his vaccinations, and now I'm visiting you.'

'Okay, Liz—'

'It's not like your house, Emily, nobody to worry about except yourselves, nothing to do any day except talk.'

They talked all right. Emily did most of it, with Conor chipping in occasionally. They discussed endless things in depth, such as Mrs Conlon's kitchen extension, the latest news from Crawley Dunne & O'Reilly, Conor's efforts to find a replacement key for the piano at home. Oh, there was plenty of communication in the Collins' household. And they went to bed at night secure in the knowledge that the TV had not been on while they ate dinner, like they had passed some kind of test.

Emily looked at Liz and for a brief moment considered confiding in her. Surely they might find some common bond in all this? Maybe even be some kind of support to each other?

But Emily would only be telling Liz so that Liz wouldn't feel that her own problems were so bad. Liz would sympathise but she would be thinking that whatever Eamon might be, at least he wasn't a cheat. If their situations were reversed, Liz would think that at least Eamon didn't plunge them into financial chaos.

'And I have to fill out some kind of form for the bank,' Liz said, rummaging in her bag. 'To change the joint savings account into just my name, so that Eamon can't go buying a new hydraulic drill or something stupid. Can you look at it for me, Emily? You're good at these things.'

Emily's expertise as a solicitor was often called upon by members of her family who routinely got confused by ESB demands, bank forms, insurance policies and other standard day-to-day documentation. Institutions had always been held in a kind of fear and awe in their household. It had irritated Emily, but the sight of a brown envelope through the door had always been greeted with great caution by her parents, and examined at length before any decision was taken.

'You just fill in the details of your bank account number, Liz. That's all. And sign there where there's an X.'

'Thanks, Emily.' Liz gratefully signed her name.

'You need Eamon's signature too. You can't change the account into your own name without his consent.'

'I know. I have to trick him.'

'What?'

'I'll have to tell him it's something else and trick him.'

Emily was astounded and disbelieving, until she

thought of the trickery she had just put Neasa up to. Was this what relationships had come to, after all the movements and revolutions and the joyous dawning of an age where there was at last meaningful communication and understanding? Wives filling in bank forms and checking hotels behind their husband's backs, suspicious and conniving. Husbands reneging on mortgages and merrily chasing other women, while their wives gave birth and reared numerous children. Somewhere along the way the plot had been lost, she thought.

Liz saw her face. 'Look, he won't admit how bad it is, Emily. I was trying to tell him we should go and work something out with the mortgage people, but he won't hear of it. Do you know what his solution is? Borrow more! Throw good money after bad! Now, if it means I have to trick him in order to pay last month's ESB bill so that they don't cut us off too, then I will.'

Emily acknowledged this. 'Liz, don't be insulted, but if you need money—'

'No.'

'It would just be a loan – you could pay me back.'

'No. Thanks anyway, Emily,' Liz said stiffly. 'This is our mess. Oh, and you won't say anything about it, will you? To Mammy.'

'God, Liz. Of course I won't.'

There wasn't even any sisterhood any more.

'And she said for you to ring her, by the way. Put her mind at rest.'

There was no question of their mother ringing Emily. She always claimed that she didn't know how to work mobile phones. You're not working one; you're just ringing one from your own phone in the hall, Emily had tried to explain. But their mother cleverly refused to get the hang of the 'new technology', as she called it. Instead she sat at home, raging that nobody ever thought to ring her and put her mind at rest.

Liz rummaged some more in her bag. 'They dropped that petition into the chemist. You know, to stop this place closing. I brought it in.'

'Oh, right. Give me that pen.'

'No, I meant I was going to leave it with you. You could get loads of signatures in here.'

'Sorry?'

'You could go around a few wards, couldn't you? Haven't you plenty of free time?'

'After I ring Mammy and put her mind at rest, and do that form for you for the bank, of course. And see Mr Chapman about my condition.'

'Just whenever you have a minute,' Liz agreed.

She was perfectly serious. Never mind that Emily should probably be on the flat of her back. Never mind that her career and marriage had hit the rocks. But Liz didn't know that, Emily found herself rationalising. But still, she didn't want to do this, why should she?

'Oh, okay! But just my ward,' she said grudgingly.

Willy stirred and started to cry. Liz lowered the sling, hiked up her shirt and stuffed a breast into his mouth.

'At least I don't have to fork out for formula,' she said bravely.

Gary was a bit put out when Neasa abruptly changed their lunchtime plans.

'I have a condom on and all,' he complained.

'Well, take it off,' she said a bit snappily. 'I have work to do.'

'What work?' He peered over her shoulder at her computer screen.

'Creepy Crawley's asked me to touch up the contract for the sale of Tilbury House,' Neasa lied easily.

'That contract went out this morning.'

Gary, through no fault of his own, had done more work in three hours this morning than he'd managed all month. The pace was killing him and he had hoped to let off a little steam with Neasa in Crawley's office.

'I meant Tamworth House.'

'That's gone too,' Gary said self-righteously.

'Oh, all right! I'm doing some personal work, okay? It's not a crime. It's in my lunch break.'

'What personal work?'

'Just bits and pieces,' Neasa said vaguely.

Gary was hurt that she wasn't confiding in him. He told her absolutely everything. She even knew how much he had in his savings account, which was considerable.

'I'll leave you to it so,' he muttered, hoping that she would stop him. She didn't.

'Yeh.'

Out of spite, Gary went off to Milo's with the laddish element in the office and had three pints of Smithwicks. And actually, it turned out to be exactly the right thing to do, because he was able to reassure them that he was still a lad even though he was now a partner, and everybody had a great time.

Alone in the office, Neasa procured the number of the German hotel from the relevant directory enquiries. Now, how to worm the information out of them? What if they didn't speak English on the reception desk? The only German Neasa knew was from the old war films her father was fond of watching and most of it translated into 'Die, you English pig.'

In the end she plucked up the phone, dialled, and just went for it.

'Hello,' she said clearly and slowly. 'Do you speak English?'

'Very well, thank you,' she was told.

Well, if they were going to be *shirty* about it . . .

'This is Crawley Dunne & O'Reilly,' Neasa said in a very threatening tone. 'International solicitors.' Well, there were rumours that a branch would open in Kinnegad. 'We're acting on behalf of some clients who stayed in your establishment last year. There appears to be a discrepancy about the bill.'

A silence at the other end. Feel the fear, Neasa thought nastily.

'I need the details please.'

Neasa told the woman what she knew. 'That would be sometime in early September. We're concerned that a couple of members of the orchestra were billed for some extra nights after that.'

She heard rapid computer clicks on the other end of the phone. The Germans really were very efficient, she thought admiringly. If only Mandy at reception here could work a keyboard like that.

'There was a group booking for the 3rd and 4th of September. Two members of the party stayed on after that,' the receptionist eventually informed her.

'Two?' Neasa barked. 'I'm afraid I have no record of that.'

God, she was hot today.

'They paid for the room themselves.'

Ah-ha. Now they were getting to the crux of the matter.

'And these people, their names . . .?'

'May I ask whether you are acting on behalf of these two individuals also?'

Oooh. The receptionist was hot too. Time to change tack.

'You see, this is the thing,' Neasa murmured discreetly. 'Basically, this pair are trying to claim expenses to which they are not entitled. A little holiday paid for by someone else, you understand?'

The receptionist did, and warmed up immensely. Nobody of any nationality liked to see other people getting away with a fast one.

'I can fax you their account,' she offered immediately.

'That would be lovely,' Neasa gushed, giving her the work fax number. 'Au revoir.'

She hung up triumphantly, buzzing with adrenaline. Wow! How great for a change to actually put into practice everything she had learned in law school – lying, bending facts, bullying and threatening lawsuits at the drop of a hat. She had missed it more than she'd thought. Her New Year's Resolution this year would be to ditch this kip and go back to Cork.

But Crawley Dunne & O'Reilly were very clever. They didn't give bonuses before Christmas, knowing that half the employees wouldn't show up in January. No, they held off until the end of January, when any New Year's Resolutions had gone out the window. And in case there was still some ambition lingering amongst the hardened dissidents, Crawley Dunne & O'Reilly hit people with another bonus at Easter. 'Jesus Christ!' people would moan as they looked at their bank accounts, 'Another fucking bonus!' It was the same in summer. Everyone would gather in Milo's, grim-faced, and try to form a pressure group to stop the bonuses. But the bonuses kept coming and so people kept staying. Neasa personally knew two people who had been trying to leave for fifteen years but had given up and bought holiday homes instead.

Sometimes Neasa woke at night, wet with sweat and screaming, having dreamt that she was still selling boggy land at forty.

'It's all right,' Gary would murmur. 'I get those dreams too. Everybody in the office does. But it's pay day tomorrow.'

And Neasa would happily go back to sleep.

But lately the lack of mental stimulation was getting to her, and she was annoyed with herself. Most people were bored senseless in their jobs; what was wrong with her? And it wasn't as though she had chosen law for any reason other than the money and the fact that she got to wear her own clothes.

Now she had Gary complicating the picture too. It was unlikely he would be open to any suggestions about moving to Cork, now that he was part of the establishment. Was it possible that the 'future' he had talked about meant a detached home with a double garage out on the Cork Road?

It was all becoming very complicated, Neasa thought. Maybe she and Gary should have a chat. But then again, she didn't want him thinking she was putting pressure on him. Neither did she want him thinking that she was happy to put her career on the back burner and gaze adoringly at his star rising higher in Crawley Dunne & O'Reilly.

Neasa jumped as the fax machine over by Mandy's desk chugged, whirred, and spat a piece of paper onto the ground. It lay there, its corners curling incriminatingly.

Neasa walked over slowly and picked it up. Her eye caught Conor's name and she looked away in distaste.

Please God may the other name be Billy Middlemiss or someone. But hang on, wouldn't that be worse?

It was Ffion Rivera. They hadn't even bothered with the pretence of separate rooms. They'd shacked up in Room 134. Room service detailed a bottle of champagne, dinner for two, followed by breakfast the next morning. There was also an international phone call, to Emily and Conor's home number. He'd probably called Emily while Ffion was washing the smell of sex off herself in the shower.

Neasa was generally unshockable and was shocked to find that she was shocked. Wonders will never cease, she thought darkly, as she thought of Conor rolling buck naked on Mary Murphy, pages of sheet music scattered across the bed with abandon. Had they hummed little arias to each other as the pace hotted up?

She tried to do some work, but couldn't. Instead she sat at her desk for ages and ages, her eye constantly straying to the fax.

She heard footsteps on the corridor outside and quickly folded the fax and put it in her pocket. She would decide what to do with it later.

'Hi!' It was Gary, red-faced and slightly foolish with Smithwicks. 'You missed a great session in the pub. Did you get what you wanted to do done?'

'I did.' This came out as extremely bitter and twisted. 'I did!' she said again, happily.

Gary, pissed, nuzzled into her neck. 'I almost told Phil about you and me.'

'What?' Neasa was aghast.

'We have to come clean at some point.'

'Why?'

'I want to legitimise our union, Neasa.' This mightn't have sounded so pretentious if he hadn't slurred it.

'Why is it so important that Creepy Crawley and the rest give us the thumbs-up?'

Neasa knew that Creepy would be sniffing around her even more if he knew she was definitely having sex with someone.

Gary looked at her coolly. 'You know, I'm starting to think that you're a bit embarrassed to be seen with me.'

'I'm not going to dignify that with a reply.'

'She replied.'

Gary was going into Jaws mode, his chin jutting out and his eyes getting smaller. His incisors even seemed to come forward in his mouth. Neasa had never been on the receiving end of this before and wasn't about to start now.

'Gary, can we just leave this? I have other things on my mind.'

'In that case, don't let me intrude.'

He stomped off to his desk at the top of the office. They had offered him his own office years ago, of course, but he hadn't taken them up on it. Not in the interests of team spirit, he had declared sincerely. There'd be no crack at all to be had on his own, and he wouldn't get sent all those jokes and dirty pictures over the internal email. But now he thought that maybe he should reconsider their offer. There was one free room near the back of the building. Unfortunately it was right beside the toilets and some people didn't flush as often as they should. Hardly fitting for a man in his new position, he thought gloomily. Still, he supposed he could always use Emily's office – just while she was on maternity leave. He would mention it to Charles Crawley this afternoon. He had decided to dispense with the 'Creepy' business, it was very childish and immature. And, really, Charles was quite nice once you got to know him.

Vera Mooney should have been in bed hours ago with a cup of cocoa and watching last night's videotaped episode of *Horizon* on the telly in her bedroom. Lay people always thought that nurses watched nothing except *ER* and *Peak Practice*. Those kinds of programmes made Vera Mooney's blood boil. Collectively they were responsible for luring hundreds of naïve girls and boys into a world they believed to be full of glamour and intrigue and revealing pink uniforms, and where George Clooney would spring out at you from every corner. Oh, the hurt and bewilderment on their faces when they were confronted with the reality of bedpans and piles, bullying consultants and chronic staff shortages. Vera would take the worst cases under her wing, feed them sweetened tea in the canteen and advise them on how to sew little tucks into the waistline of their uniform so that it sat a bit better on the hips. She would murmur about the altruistic rewards of looking after sick folk, the wonder of delivering babies. She pointed up the subsidised canteen and played down the vicious hours. Then she would send them back out onto the firing line, looking a little less beaten. Occasionally she would come across a hopeless case and would quietly advise a change of career. The army, maybe. *Soldier Soldier* was a lot more realistic in the portrayal of its profession, in her view.

Anyhow: Vera Mooney should have been in bed, but was in fact still in the staff room along with the rest of the night shift who had given up their sleep to fight the cause. The cause, of course, had been irretrievably lost a year ago, but Vera Mooney wasn't the type to go quietly.

She took a sheaf of application forms from her satchel and slapped them on the table, which rocked violently due to its missing leg.

'Ennis General. Limerick. Athlone.' She looked around at them all. 'And there's always Dublin, of course, but if people are interested then maybe they would contact those hospitals themselves.'

Karen and Suzanne reached for Limerick. Vera nodded approvingly. She was going there herself, even though it would entail her changing her car. Her 93 Clio had a hundred and twenty thousand miles on the clock and the weekly journeys to Limerick and back would add three hundred and fifty more.

Darren took a form for Ennis General. 'My girl-friend's going there,' he mumbled.

'Aw. So sweet.'

'Ooooooh, lurve.'

'Thank you, girls,' Vera said crisply. 'Now. Christine. How about you?'

Nurse Christine Clarke looked up, her blonde curls bouncing. She had already changed out of her uniform and put on fresh make-up.

'I haven't decided yet.'

Vera looked at her. Christine had been one of her very worst cases and had taken a lot of counselling in the canteen. 'But on the telly all that blood is never real,' she had cried, traumatised. 'I know,' Vera had soothed. 'But maybe you could pretend here that it's just ketchup. How about that?' It had worked miracles. Christine now enjoyed blood so much that she was thinking of training to work in theatre.

'Why don't you take application forms for them all and think about it?' Vera said.

'Okay,' Christine said.

Karen shot her a filthy glance. 'Don't waste the paper.'

'Sorry?'

'You heard her, you two-faced little cow,' Suzanne muttered.

'What the hell are you talking about?'

'Don't bounce your curls at me!'

'What's going on here?' Vera enquired politely.

'She's after applying for a transfer to Cork,' Darren chimed in, disgusted.

'I have not!' Christine said indignantly.

'How come you've got an appointment down there next Tuesday?' Karen shot triumphantly.

'Were you eavesdropping on my telephone conversations?' Christine demanded, her curls about to take off.

'Yes!'

'I don't want to move to the back of beyond just because this place is closing! Why should I?'

'Solidarity, you thick eejit.'

Christine looked like she was going to cry. 'But they have Top Shop in Cork.'

'Forget it.'

'And Wallis. And Principles.'

'Big swing.'

'Wallis?' Suzanne said with a slight catch in her voice. She was five-foot nothing and Wallis did a lovely little line in petite wear.

'What the hell is going on here!' Karen said viciously. 'I thought we all agreed to boycott Cork! I thought we all said that they could offer us a million pounds a year and we still wouldn't take a transfer down there!'

'Half a million. We said half a million,' Christine pointed out quickly.

'What difference does it make? Nobody is going to Cork! That's what we agreed!'

Vera cleared her throat. As always, it had the effect of shutting everybody up. Vera had once cleared her throat during a delivery, entirely accidentally, and even the newborn baby had screeched to a silence and looked at her.

'What we agreed at that meeting was that if people felt strongly enough, then they should boycott Cork. But it wasn't an order. People can go where they want. Of course they can.' She looked at Christine without any judgement or malice. 'It's absolutely your preroga-tive to go to Cork. And nobody here will say another word about it. Isn't that right, girls?'

Karen and Suzanne shifted indignantly, but kept their mouths shut. Christine found herself unable to look Vera in the eye. Vera, who had brought her through her first difficult months as a trainee nurse, Vera who had subtly warned her off Doctor Keating with just one word, 'married'.

'Okay! I won't bloody go!' she shouted.

'Go if you want,' Vera encouraged her. 'You might like it in Cork.'

'I wouldn't! How could I spend a single pay cheque in Wallis knowing that I was a turncoat!' Christine was raging now at being forced by her own hand to do the right thing.

'Well, if that's how you feel, then we're all delighted,' Vera soothed, resolving to take her for a cup of tea in the canteen that night and point up the benefits of Limerick. They had Wallis there too, silly girl, and all kinds of wonderful places to spend pay cheques. She must also mention that some of the more attractive doctors from the general wards had already gone to Limerick.

'Okay, well, everyone should start applying immediately. Time is running out.'

St Martha's would close in exactly five weeks' time. Most of the general wards had already been closed. Martha's was really only open for business in Casualty and Maternity.

'I can't bear it,' Karen suddenly said, her lip quivering. 'I know this place is an awful kip, but I don't want to go.'

'I know,' Vera said. 'But we must be brave, girls.' She nodded at Darren. 'And boys.'

Vera herself was very unsentimental about the whole thing. It wasn't that she didn't like Martha's; she loved Martha's with a passion. She had worked there for fifteen years, she'd had her own two girls there; she personally knew nearly every patient who came through the door.

But what use was it to anybody to get all emotional and upset about it? Vera had taken the practical approach of making submissions to the Board of Management. She'd solicited meetings with the Health Board. Then there were the local TDs and Councillors, all of whom she had personally canvassed. She had even written to the Minister for Health and had all the staff do so too.

It had all been in vain. Martha's was caught up in the unstoppable forces of rationalisation and modernisation and, more crucially, staff shortages of crisis proportions. Martha's could no longer attract specialised theatre staff to carry out operations. What junior doctors were still coming into the system went to Dublin or Cork or Limerick or Galway. Nurses couldn't be found for love nor money.

They could have thrown resources and financial support at the place. They could have paid people better to come and work in it. But they didn't, of course. They decided to close it. Their main reason was that it was servicing a decreasing rural population that could be better facilitated by Cork.

Hogwash, Vera often thought. Still. She didn't get involved in the politics of it all. She was just angry for the sake of her job, and everybody else who worked in the hospital. But there are plenty of jobs, they had told her – God knows, aren't they crying out for nurses! Yes, if they relocated or else drove their cars and themselves into the ground.

Vera would commute for as long as she could. But she would no longer be home after a night shift to see the girls before they went to school. She would have to leave every evening before they'd even had dinner together, for God's sake. And what about driving them to ballet lessons and taking them to parties? She would be stuck in her car – albeit a new car – in a bloody traffic jam. For two pins now she would strangle Chapman and O'Reilly and every other goddamn consultant who had sunk this ship, either intentionally or by their silence.

'There's a petition going around again,' Karen said. 'I saw it in one of the wards earlier.'

'Is there?' Vera said, with no interest. There had been many such petitions over the past year.

'With plenty of signatures.'

'Karen, let the patients fight for themselves.'

This sounded a bit harsher than Vera Mooney actually felt. She was not unsympathetic to the cause of the locals, who now had to travel to Cork sick or in labour. People were very angry and upset about it, but it hadn't really translated into action. True, some of them had turned up at the meetings Vera had organised. But the problem was that most healthy people never thought that they would end up in hospital. Cancer, heart attacks and long-term illnesses always happened to someone else. They were emotionally removed from the fight, and that was no good at all. In fact, the people most upset about it were the pregnant women, the ones who knew that in three or four or six months' time they would definitely need the services of a hospital. Those, and elderly people to whom hospital was a future reality rather than an unlikely possibility.

Vera felt very tired and disillusioned now. It was difficult leading a revolt when the revolutionaries weren't that pushed in the first place. But then she saw the faces of Karen, Darren, Suzanne. They had come this far with her and she owed it to them to finish this thing.

'Right. Will we go pound the pavements?'

Today was the start of the next phase: marching up and down outside with placards. The day shift would take it in turns to join them for an hour.

'Can we have a cup of tea first?' Christine begged. She wanted to touch up her lipstick too.

'Of course we can,' Vera said. 'And a nice salad or something.'

They always had salads in the canteen. It was all the blasted Roses. They tried to give them away to porters, ambulance drivers, the cleaning staff. But those sly cows in Delivery always got there before them, and you couldn't even off-load the smallest box. Once someone had given them Quality Street because the shop next door had run out of Roses, and there had been great excitement for a week.

They all traipsed out, faces pasty from lack of sleep. Emily Collins drifted past them in the corridor, eyes very far away. With her huge belly, massive bunny slippers and thin little legs, she looked like a cartoon figure. The woman never seemed to be where she was supposed to be, which was in bed.

Vera was going to say something, then stopped herself. She was not on duty. If she said something, she felt like she would be getting involved. And one of the first things she had learned as a nurse fifteen years ago was never to get personally involved with the patients.

Emily couldn't bear the waiting game any longer. She had already brought up her lunch, what little she'd eaten. She rang Conor and told him that Mr Chapman was coming in in an hour.

'I'll be there,' he said, sounding glad that something was finally happening.

'Come in early,' she said.

'I'll set off now.'

She wanted to ask him to bring in her deodorant which she'd forgotten but the request seemed too cosy and domestic. But she needed it; she was sweating. When Maggie went to the loo, Emily helped herself to two quick blasts of the Sure on her locker, but felt no surer. Guiltily, she checked the contents on the canister. She had read a frightening article once on how breast milk can be poisoned with more than two hundred different chemicals from the products that mothers used, anything from hairspray to the can of Coke you treated yourself to. You might as well be feeding your baby a bottle of Domestos.

Then other articles rubbished this, maintaining that breast milk was the best food for your child until they were well into their teens. But who were you to believe any more? Sometimes Emily thought that there was a conspiracy out there to confuse, addle and bewilder those who simply tried to do their best. Those who didn't bother reading this stuff were able to enjoy guilt-free spraying and a much drier lifestyle. It made Emily feel gullible and annoyed.

'Anybody for a game of bridge?' Trish enquired across the way. She was now fifteen days in Martha's and had started an inter-ward bridge league. Elizabeth's Ward was currently winning and Trish was taking it all very badly.

'Count me in,' Maggie said happily, back in from the loo.

Trish wasn't a bit pleased. Maggie had only learned how to play bridge in the past week and was worse than useless. But she always wanted to play, damn her.

'Emily, will you be my partner?' Maggie pleaded.

Emily pretended not hear. She slipped out of the ward and wandered until she found herself outside the main doors of the hospital. As with every other health institution in the country, hordes of people were standing on the front steps smoking. Emily watched them as they collectively inhaled and exhaled fiercely and wondered who was in the hospital belonging to them. A wife? Sister? Father? Martina, even? Who knew what stories they all had? Who was to say that her own was any more interesting or tragic than theirs?

The elderly man with rheumy eyes and a stooped, beaten back particularly touched Emily. He held his cigarette as though it were the only thing keeping him going right now. He reminded Emily of her own father.

'They're very good in there,' she said, trying to give him some solace, 'the doctors and nurses.'

The man looked up, surprised. 'I'm sure they are.'

'Just, you know, if you were worried.'

He looked at her and put out his cigarette. 'You're a very kind girl.'

'No problem,' she said, embarrassed.

He pulled open the front door and poked his head in. 'Taxi for Tynan?'

She dived into the band of smokers, mortified. She never seemed to learn. Time and again she went right on in there, investing herself in situations and people that never gave her back a thing. Crawley Dunne & O'Reilly. Liz. Her mother. Martina, a woman she'd never even met, for heaven's sake! But she never, ever thought she'd be adding Conor to that list.

His red Peugeot drove into the car park. He didn't go and park in the empty spaces at the back, of course, but came right up towards the hospital. Lo and behold, another car conveniently vacated a position just thirty yards from the front doors, and Conor eased in.

Emily found that her heart was beating fast, and she was thrown back to those days when Conor used to come and pick her up for their dates. She'd hear his car crunching on the gravel outside and she would feel her cheeks reddening and her heart banging away and she would rush to the front door to open it. With previous boyfriends, she would pretend that she hadn't heard the car, and she would make them get out and ring the doorbell. Sometimes twice. She had never tried that with Conor – it simply hadn't occurred to her. He would have seen right through it anyway, and he would have thought less of her. He was always so straight, Conor. That was one of the biggest shocks of this whole thing. She felt that he had irredeemably diminished himself in her eyes.

'Excuse me . . . excuse me . . . oh, get out of my way.'

Emily elbowed her way through the smokers and went fast down the hospital steps. Conor was just taking off his seat belt when she slid into the passenger seat of his car.

'What are you doing?' he said.

'Getting in.'

'It's cold out here. Are you mad?'

'No. Just sick of the hospital.'

He didn't kiss her. The look on her face didn't invite him to.

'They're walking up and down on the road with placards,' he said eventually. 'I nearly knocked one of them down.'

She felt very sad as she turned to him. 'Conor. I know about Germany.'

His whole body seemed to sag a little. Emily had a funny feeling inside, like something was breaking.

'It's over,' he said.

This was no great news or consolation to Emily. She guessed that her pregnancy announcement had probably put paid to it.

'Did you love her?' she asked.

'No.'

It was hard to know whether this was more insulting.

'It was Mary, right? Correct me if I'm wrong.'

'It was Mary.'

His knuckles were white on the steering wheel, but

he didn't say anything more. He offered no bluster or excuses. And he didn't look relieved that it was finally out in the open, either. She'd have slapped his face for him if he had.

They sat like that for a while. Emily was dry-eyed, cold. Somehow she had thought that it would be different. She had anticipated some emotional release, a catharsis of sorts. Not this dry, barren silence that was more frightening.

'Conor, have you nothing at all to say?' she said at last. 'Am I to sit here and drag it out of you bit by bit? Like I always bloody do?'

'Sorry.' He seemed at a loss. 'I just figured the gory details wouldn't make you feel any better.'

She looked at him, askance. 'Don't you dare try to tell me how I feel.'

'What do you want me to do? Sit here and fling platitudes at you, Emily?'

'Platitudes would be something! Platitudes would be a start!'

He sat up a big straighter. 'I can tell you that it wasn't an important relationship, which it wasn't. I can tell you that I'm desperately sorry, which I am. I can assure you that it won't happen again, which it won't.' He looked at her. 'But I figured those were easy words to say right now, Emily.'

His rationale made Emily angrier than she had ever been in her life. 'So you just thought you'd say nothing at all?'

He buried his face in his hands. 'Look, I know how much I've hurt you.'

'You don't. By God, you don't.'

'I'm sorry, Emily. I'm so sorry.'

'So why did you do it?'

'I don't know.'

'You don't know? It just happened? One of those things?'

'No, of course not . . .'

'I'm sorry if this analysis is upsetting you, Conor. I know how much you hate unnecessary chatter, but I find it quite important.'

She stopped. It was just the same old pattern endlessly repeating itself, even with the topic and the emotions involved spiced up a bit. They might as well have been discussing Mrs Conlon-next-door's kitchen extension. 'But they won't pass it in planning permission, will they, Conor?' 'I don't know, Emily.' 'But she can't build in our garden, Conor!' 'Let's just wait and see.' And on and on and on.

The taxi driver got into the car next to theirs. He nodded and waved enthusiastically at Emily. She tried to ignore him.

'Who's he?' Conor asked.

'It doesn't matter.'

The taxi driver reversed out. Emily looked at Conor, her face detached. It wasn't a show. She felt right now that the two of them were so far from understanding each other that they might as well be on different planets.

'I'm worried about the baby,' she said.

'I am too. I'm sorry you had to find out now. It doesn't help.'

'Indeed.' She looked at the dashboard. Had Mary been in this car? Of course she had. She must have been. 'I'd like to keep the upset to a minimum. For my own sake too.'

'Of course.'

'So . . . there isn't anything more I should know, is there?'

'No.'

'Mary Murphy's not pregnant too, by any chance?'

'Emily. Please.'

'Well, let's be thankful for small mercies. It would just be too ironic if you had to visit two wards at the same time. Not to mention the maintenance payments.'

Conor shifted unhappily. Now that she had her pound of flesh, Emily decided to call it a day.

'I think you should go home now, Conor, before we both say things we'd regret. I'll ring you, of course, and let you know what Mr Chapman says.'

'Do you want me to move out?' he asked quietly.

'Why?'

She saw that she had surprised him, perhaps for the first time in years. Oh dear. Things were worse than she'd thought.

'Well, I suppose because you couldn't bear the sight of me,' he offered.

'Not right now,' she agreed. 'But I don't have to look at you, do I? I'm in here.'

'But you might be out today. What'll we do then?'

Emily felt pressure bearing down on her hard. This hadn't figured in her confrontation scenario either. Who would have thought it was all so practical and domestic, with decisions needing to be made immediately? Decisions that somehow seemed to come down to her? Didn't the offending party have to do *anything* except say they were sorry and look guilty?

'Whatever you want, I'll do it,' he said fervently, compounding the injustice of the situation.

'Oh, do what you like, Conor!'

A car eased into the space the taxi driver had vacated. She looked over and locked eyes with Mr Chapman. She rolled down her window.

'Be in in a minute!'

She rolled the window back up quickly before he could say anything.

'By the way, Neasa is on to you,' she told Conor.

'What? How . . .?'

'It doesn't matter,' she said quickly. 'But just be prepared.'

He gave a small sigh. 'Right. Thanks.'

'I'll try and keep her away from the house, but you know what she's like with drink on her.'

'I'll leave the dogs out.'

She adjusted her bunny slippers for the trip back into the hospital, and retrieved a packet of mints she

149

had left in the glove compartment.

'Goodbye then,' she said formally.

He didn't want to leave it now. He wanted to talk. Wasn't that just typical?

'Emily, we've had six years together. We have a baby on the way. Don't write it all off.'

'Let's not paper over the cracks either.'

She saw that she had shaken him to the very core with this. Herself too. Neither of them had really entered into this discussion believing that parting was a real possibility.

Emily got out of the car quickly and walked fast towards the front doors. She bent her head so that the smokers didn't see her face, and slipped into the lift as Mr Chapman started to climb the stairs.

Conor sat in the car, staring at the grey pebbledash wall in front of him until the car fogged up so much that he was looking at his own breath. He wanted to smoke but wouldn't let himself.

Emily had left the glove compartment open. He reached over and shut it carefully, because he had to, because he wanted to finish off an action she had started.

She could not have meant it, could she? About it being over? Emily often threatened things in Conor's experience, but her innate good sense and conservatism usually won out. She sometimes threatened to drown the dogs, for instance, when they dug up one of her plants in the garden. Conor had never been unduly worried for their safety. Sure enough, ten minutes later she would be cuddling them and talking about buying them water bowls with their names on them.

But her face had been different this time. Emily was one of those people who wore their feelings on their face. You could nearly tell what she'd had for breakfast just by looking at her. There was something hard about her today, like an animal who had been kicked one time too many and had made its mind up to run away.

He wouldn't let her. He just wouldn't.

He shut his eyes tight now, trying to blank out the image of her face: that terrible, wounded look, the white pinched skin around her mouth. The shock and revulsion in her eyes. For a moment he thought he was going to be sick.

He did not know how she had found out. Not that it mattered. He had pictured this moment for months and months now; had lived in dread of it, even though he had done his best to cover his tracks. But that was the awful thing about betrayal – you can never be sure that it will not catch up on you. And you do not realise this until long after the affair is over, when the guilt and fear of discovery do not abate but only grow stronger with each passing week. Conor felt that he had been living with a terminal illness since the day he and Ffion had broken up.

He wondered how he had ever thought at the time that the affair was worth it, because he must have thought that. He must have weighed up the illicit excitement against the awful feelings of guilt and betrayal, and gone ahead anyway. At some point, he must have faced the possibility that Emily would find out. Or that he would tell her, which he very much wanted to do afterwards.

But that would only have been selfish. In the end, there was nothing he could do except bury it and hope that it went away. It hadn't and now she was talking about leaving.

Stupid. *Stupid*.

Conor did not fear being on his own. He had always been on his own anyway. He feared being on his own without Emily. He saw no contradiction in this. Without her he would be scratching about on the outskirts of civilisation with no one to help him step in.

He remembered that day all those years ago, the very first day they'd met at a mutual friend's wedding. He had misplaced his date for reasons he could not even remember now, and had ended up hanging around the bar on his own like the proverbial spare part. A big boisterous group had rolled in, the kind of people who always made Conor feel grey and dull. He had noticed Emily immediately, small and darkly pretty, and chatting animatedly to a big handsome fellow with a ruddy face – her own date. She hadn't noticed Conor at all, of course, until her date had collapsed with suspected food poisoning and was carted off. Conor had approached her with the help of seven pints of Guinness. She had invited him to join her group at the bar, and he had felt like he was coming home.

Even back then, she had talked and he had been content to listen, delighted and charmed by her, and quite unable to believe his luck. It wasn't that no other woman fancied him. They did, lots of them, because he was good-looking, and intelligent, and his career seemed very glamorous. But he felt he didn't have to try with Emily. There wasn't that awful forced falseness of early dates, all that careful questioning about background and family, as though each were attempting to eliminate a psycho or hopeless case from their enquiries. Emily took him to her heart straightaway like she did every other eejit, and it all felt so right. Or maybe so easy.

They were different, of course. They wore jokey badges: she was the expressive one, whereas he would intellectualise things. He had felt that it worked very well, in the beginning at least. They had been fond of saying that it was a classic case of opposites attracting.

But he often thought back to that wedding in Paulstown, and the big handsome fellow with the loud laugh. He wondered what would have happened had the egg mayonnaise not been off that day. Would Emily have ended up marrying him instead?

He wondered about these things because sometimes it seemed to him that Emily had come to him purely by virtue of luck. Luck, and his own perseverance. He was the one who had done the chasing; he was the one who had put himself on offer. She'd only had to say 'yes' or 'no'.

In his more insecure moments, he would wonder whether she regretted her decision. It was the way she would look at him sometimes. Oddly. With disappointment?

She never said anything. But as the years went by, those looks became more pointed and he became more defensive and guarded. She had become less bubbly anyway, and more critical in a sort of irritated way.

He listened to her chatter less. It was just married life.

He believed they would have trundled on like this, content enough, had not two things happened. Firstly, Emily had the miscarriage and everything fell apart at the seams.

Secondly, Ffion Rivera, with whom he had become friendly, was suddenly plunged into marital difficulties of her own. Everything that followed seemed inevitable.

The affair had not lasted long. A matter of weeks only. Conor had tried to treat it as a brief lapse, a minor fall from the straight and narrow. He blamed his own weakness rather than his own unhappiness. And with Emily pregnant again, he was gripped by a great need to make things work the second time around. He had to. He and Emily were going to be parents.

Well, Emily was, anyway. For all his determination to become involved, his function seemed to be almost entirely to support her, the person really having the baby, if everything he had read and learned in antenatal classes was to be believed. He was forced to laugh at 'hilarious' jokes about men being confounded by the sight of a dirty nappy, and endure that stupid Liz's remarks about him nipping to the pub while Emily gave birth. This wonderful opportunity to forge something new between them, to make amends to Emily for his behaviour, was whipped from him by doctors and nurses and medical books and hospitals, all of whom seemed to have a great deal more to contribute than him. Even Emily herself sought to exclude him, poking fun at his efforts to educate himself. As if he hadn't felt foolish enough talking to the baby through her belly button.

He went through her pregnancy feeling like this, resentful and jealous and inadequate. And the guilt was always there, poking and prodding away at him. These were not feelings he could admit to Emily. Or to any-one. He had tried once to talk to his brother Mark about impending fatherhood. Mark had two kids himself. But Mark had only seemed embarrassed. They did not talk about feelings in their family. They never had.

Conor reached for the key now and started the car. But why would he go home? His wife and baby were right here – if indeed either of them belonged to him in any sense any more.

He turned off the engine anyway and sat.

The whisper started at the general reception desk on the ground floor.

'He's here.'

'Where? Here?'

'No, he's going up to Brenda's Ward. Emily Whatser-name.'

'The bunny slippers?'

'Her. Tommy-the-porter saw him arrive. In a brand new car.'

'They always have brand new cars, don't they?'

'A convertible.'

'What, in this weather?'

'You know Tommy, it's probably just got a sunroof. But he swears it's new.'

'Well! What's he doing, a tour of the place before it closes?' This was said very bitterly.

'No, no. It's just to see her.'

'What is she, a blue-blood or something?'

'No bed for her in Cork apparently. Tommy saw them talking in the car park.'

'What was she doing in the car park?'

'Chatting away with him – her and the husband. Parked side-by-side, very friendly.'

'So he knows them?'

'I'd say she must be a relative or something. I'd better go see if the girls up in Bernadette's know.'

They didn't.

'A *cabriolet*. He must have had it imported. Probably from Japan or somewhere.'

'He asked Tommy to park it.'

'He didn't!'

'How else would Tommy know that it was a Japanese import with automatic gear stick and a sunroof?'

'Must have cost a fortune.'

'They can afford it, those consultants. I suppose she's loaded as well. Emily.'

'Of course she is. Look at those slippers and that tatty dressing-gown. Only the very rich dress like that. They don't need to bother, you see.'

'Is she from his wife's side?'

'I don't know. I think she looks a bit like Chapman himself.'

'What, have you seen him?'

'No, just his picture in the medical magazines. But she's the spit.'

'The girls in Brenda's say that she never sleeps. Just walks the corridors all the time.'

'Weird.'

'And as for the husband . . .'

'What about him?'

'Someone said that they saw him in the Cork Opera House last night.'

'He dropped her here and went off to a concert?'

'No, no, he was on stage.'

'He's an opera singer?'

'I suppose. Didn't bother his barney showing up last night at all. Highly strung.'

'Not as highly strung as her by the sounds of it.' A beat. 'Did anybody tell them in Brenda's that he's coming up to them?'

Nobody had. The girls in St Jude's Ward volunteered to pass on the information. By the time Mr Chapman arrived at his destination, he was the proud new owner of a stretch sports car with a retractable roof, bonnet and wheels, which did a hundred and ten miles to the gallon and which his Japanese chauffeur drove. Emily Collins was his rich eccentric niece who had ended up in Martha's after a fight with the ambulance men, Joe and Liam, and whose opera singer husband was recording an album and was too busy to visit.

Mr Chapman quickly poured cold water on most of the conjecture by going straight over to Trish and saying, 'Hello, Emily.'

'I'm over here,' Emily said.

Emily knew of white people who thought that all black people looked the same, and vice versa. It seemed that this could be extended to pregnant women. But then she saw that Trish was asleep with her hair all over her face and gave Mr Chapman the benefit of the doubt.

Also, she was secretly glad of the extra few seconds to prepare herself after her sprint down the corridor. She smoothed down her hair and wiped her nose with a tissue. She hoped that he wouldn't be able to tell that she had been crying.

But he didn't really look at her as he crossed the ward and stood at the foot of her bed. Two nurses, a doctor and an intern trooped after him like a gaggle of geishas. One of them reverently pressed Emily's chart into his hands like she was giving him Holy Communion.

'So! How are we this morning?' he asked the chart.

Nobody was looking at Emily. Not the nurses, the doctor or the intern. Emily knew that the world roughly divided into two kinds of people: those who looked, and those who were looked at. Emily had always fitted firmly into the first camp. She had never been the kind of person other people looked at. It was a charisma thing and she believed that there was nothing that could be done about it. But, bloody hell, did courtesy have to go out the window for her kind too? And respect?

'Why don't *you* tell me how I am?' she said, quite loudly.

Mr Chapman looked up, surprised. The nurses, doctor and intern stiffened a bit. Was she giving lip to Mr Chapman? Still, everyone knew that she was a bit off her rocker. Look at those eyes! Kind of sunken and burning, like something you'd read about in a Stephen King novel.

'Your blood pressure is still up,' Mr Chapman said, straight to her face this time.

'I know,' she agreed.

'Nothing too alarming, but we really do have to keep an eye on it.'

He looked again at her chart, peering over his bifocals. He never seemed to actually look through them. Was it possible that they were just for effect?

The thought made her braver still and she struggled to sit up a bit more in the bed. No one could sound forceful on the flat of their backs.

'Is it pre-eclampsia or not?' she enquired politely. 'Because nobody seems to know.'

Another small silence fell at the implied criticism. But thankfully Mr Chapman was used to dealing with all sorts and took this one on the chin.

'It can be difficult to identify,' he intoned pleasantly. 'A woman with high blood pressure alone may not have pre-eclampsia. Or, indeed, with fluid retention alone. It's the combination of factors that lead one to believe that the condition may be present.'

His voice was hypnotically boring and one of the nurses behind started to sway on her feet. Emily fought down her natural urge to smile and nod, her body and face contorted into an apology. Where had nodding and smiling ever got her?

'So it is pre-eclampsia then?'

Mr Chapman found himself forced into that position which every doctor tries to avoid – actually having to commit himself.

'Possibly,' he said, trying to work around it.

Emily was back in the car with Conor again, using all her wiles to extract information from him. Did people see her as some kind of fool who shouldn't be told things for her own good?

'When will you know for sure?' she asked, her voice distinctly frosty.

'That depends,' he said, again trying to shake her off.

'On what?'

Mr Chapman was very aware of the nurses, the doctor and the intern behind him, breathing down his neck.

'On four-hour monitoring of your blood pressure, daily urine checks, and the presence of swelling,' he said, sounding much less bored than usual. 'But from what we've seen so far, I believe it is pre-eclampsia.'

'Thank you,' Emily said quietly. 'I just wanted to know.'

The nurses, doctor and intern relaxed a bit. Mr Chapman took a moment to regroup behind Emily Collins' chart, rattled. The Emily Collins he remembered from the weekly visits at his clinic had been quiet and polite, sometimes forgot to bring in her sample but that was about the size of it. Nothing like this one in the bed here. Was it possible he was mixing her up with someone else? Still, he saw so many women – surely it was only natural that he got confused every now and then?

A small sliver of dread stabbed at Mr Chapman's insides. He was forty-eight next week. But his hands were rock steady still, he reassured himself fiercely. He had years in him yet. Years and years.

Emily was wondering whether it was wise to have ruffled Mr Chapman's feathers. He was looking after her baby, she didn't want to go annoying him. It could all backfire horribly at delivery. Did he have the power to deny her an epidural?

When Mr Chapman and Emily eventually looked at

each other again, it was with guarded eyes.

'I'm afraid I'm going to have to keep you in.'

'Keep me in?'

'Yes. For observation. I can't take any chances until your blood pressure is down. Also, I'd like to prescribe some diuretics, see if we can get rid of some of the fluid retention. Just a mild dose.'

The doctor behind furiously made a note of this.

'I'm going to hold off prescribing anything for the blood pressure. We'll see if it'll sort itself out.'

'Right,' Emily said carefully. 'And how long do you think I'll be kept in?'

Mr Chapman sighed inwardly. She would be difficult about this as well. Where were all the nice patients these days? 'Indefinitely, I'm afraid.'

Emily was relieved. At least one decision had been taken from her. She could stay in here safe and sound for the moment, away from Conor until she had sorted some things out.

'Great,' she said with feeling.

Mr Chapman looked at her even more warily. 'We could be talking a couple of weeks,' he said slowly, sure that she hadn't understood.

'Lovely,' Emily said, beaming at him.

Mr Chapman stopped worrying about his memory loss and started fretting about his ability to interpret patient-doctor situations. Suddenly he felt vulnerable and old and he wanted to leave Martha's very quickly.

'Right,' he said, thrusting the chart into the intern's

hand. 'I'll see you again in a couple of days.'

'But I'll be transferred to Cork, won't I?' Emily enquired.

Cork would be even better. She felt a huge need to put as much space between herself and Conor as possible.

'Yes,' Mr Chapman said gravely. 'I'm sorry.'

He waited for her disappointment.

'Great!' Emily said again.

Mr Chapman was astounded when she threw back the covers energetically, grabbed a Manchester United bag and started to pack. He had never seen a pregnant woman move so fast.

'Um, not right now,' he said, rattled.

'Oh. When then?'

Mr Chapman thought he saw one of the nurses smile. Things were getting out of hand.

'Soon,' he said loudly. 'You're fine here for the moment.'

Emily Collins was not good for his health, he decided. Best to keep her in Martha's for the moment – he could probably discharge her next week anyway. Besides, he had quite enjoyed the drive up here this morning. It had been a refreshing break from the bureaucracy in which he was currently mired.

'Right. Good.' He turned to leave, the nurses, the doctor and the intern trooping after him.

'Mr Chapman?'

He swung back suspiciously. 'Yes?'

'Just thanks for coming all the way up to see me,'

Emily said earnestly. 'I appreciate it.'

Mr Chapman felt colour flood his cheeks. Somehow this was shifting from the impersonal to the personal.

'Um, you're welcome,' he stuttered and strode out of the ward so fast that his entourage were hard-pressed to keep up.

'You were great with him,' Maggie said through the curtain. She'd been listening to every word. 'Mr Dunphy frightens the life out of me. I've put down on my birth plan, quite nicely, that I don't want him to intimidate me during labour if he can help it at all.'

'Oh, you just have to know how to handle them,' Emily bluffed.

Old Chapman wasn't so bad really, she thought. It was funny how she had been so put off by him. Why? Because he wore a suit and accessorised bifocals? But it was difficult to be bolshy with someone who held your health in his hands. And she just wasn't a confrontational person. Emily wondered whether it was a gene thing or the fact that she had been raised in a house where fear had its own place at the table.

She remembered her father now, who had had pains in his chest for weeks before his heart attack. Dr Leahy had prescribed large doses of Milk of Magnesia and told him to stop eating big meals at night. The poor man had watched everyone else tucking into egg and chips at teatime, and would then spend most of his evenings on the toilet. Emily had suggested going back to Dr Leahy. But there was no question of that. A man of medicine! He knew indigestion when he saw it.

After the funeral, Dr Leahy had tucked into ham sandwiches back at the house. Their mother had plied him with whiskey. She should have thrown him out into the rain and filed a lawsuit. The man shouldn't have been practising medicine at all. Emily had felt angry about it for years.

She was angry with her father now. For nodding and smiling, and for taking no responsibility for his own health. And at herself for not insisting at the time. But there was safety in numbers and she had let her dissent be swallowed up.

She was on her own now and it hit her like a slap. For six years she had enjoyed the security of being in a couple. There was always someone there to make the decisions with or, indeed, to take no action at all. Almost every aspect of life was approached with someone else in mind. There was, of course, the odd defiant strike at independence. Going to London on the piss with Neasa, and let Conor cook for himself! Choosing a new car purely on the basis of its nice blue colour, and let Conor laugh! But these were feeble things, and always indulged by the other. No real difference of opinion had existed.

Everything had changed now. She felt the aloneness wrap itself around her like cold fingers, and found that she was shaking. It was like half of her had been brutally hacked off.

She curled up tightly on the bed and wondered how

Conor could have done this to her. How could he tell her he loved her and still do this to her? She thought of his square, handsome face, and she very badly wanted to damage him, to hurt him as much as he had hurt her. The dogs he had nurtured since they were puppies, she wanted to boil them in a pot on the cooker. She wanted to tamper with his car brakes so that he would have an horrific accident that would leave him wheelchair-bound, and she would enjoy the look on his face when she waltzed in on her own two legs with their child for his visitation rights. Or his fingers – she wanted to break them one by one so that he never played the piano again, unless he learned to play with his elbows.

She lay there and fiercely wished that the baby inside her would die. That would hurt him the most. I'm sorry, I'm sorry, she told the baby, weeping now.

The catering girls were very nice in Martha's. Maureen especially, who firmly believed that half the drugs the doctors prescribed to these women were totally unnecessary. In her experience, a nice cup of sweet tea usually did the trick.

'I don't want it,' Emily said thickly.

'Nonsense, of course you do,' Maureen said, expertly balancing the cup and saucer in one hand and fixing pillows, covers and the sliding tray with the other. 'Up you sit,' she said.

Emily had no choice but to do so.

'Thank you,' she said, taking a small sip of the tea. It was sickeningly sweet but strangely nice.

'No problem,' Maureen said, watching as the colour came back into Emily's face. Maybe this one would remember the kitchen staff when it came time to leave. It was always the blasted nurses and midwives who got all the Roses. It wasn't fair.

'Do you want to have sex?' Gary grudgingly asked. He was still in a bit of a snit from earlier but hadn't the energy to go around with a puss on him all night. He was exhausted after all his work today. And Creepy Crawley wanted him in for a meeting at nine in the morning. Nine! Gary had quickly reverted to 'Creepy' as the afternoon had progressed.

Neasa looked at him vaguely. 'No, but thanks anyway. I think I might go to the hospital.'

But she made no move to get her coat. How did you break this kind of news to your best friend? And she banged up in hospital? What Neasa really wanted to do was get tanked up and go over to Conor's. Alcohol would give her the verbosity to sort him out. She would buy two pork chops on the way. That bastard would leave the dogs out. They were well known for their propensity to attack anything that came through the front gate.

'Dinner, then,' Gary offered. He was anxious now to get things back on an even keel. Neasa wasn't paying any attention to his sulking and he was getting rattled.

'No, but you go ahead.' Neasa considered lying to Emily. This went against every fibre of her being, but she was trying to do the best thing. The fax in her pocket would send Emily's blood pressure through the ceiling. It could even bring on labour! Neasa did not want to spend the rest of her life apologising to a child who was born with only one lung.

'A drink? Wine? Gin and tonic?' Gary was getting desperate now.

'No,' Neasa said again, shocking him. Neasa never refused drink. There must be something awfully big bothering her. The blond hair on the back of Gary's thick neck rose slightly. Was it possible that she was going off him?

'Is it me?' he blurted.

'What?'

'Whatever's upsetting you.'

Neasa looked at his big, meaty, open face and felt terribly tender. 'Of course not, sweetness – sure don't I love you?'

Gary beamed back. 'Great.'

She went back to looking terribly vague. Now that he wasn't the problem, Gary's mind travelled in a different direction.

'Will I put the kettle on for a cup of tea?' he asked rather quietly.

'Yes, yes,' she murmured.

'And a biscuit?'

'Yes, fine.'

'Will we tell people in the office that we're seeing each other?'

'Yes, sure, whatever.'

'Great!'

Neasa shook herself. 'What?'

'Now that I'm a partner, it's unseemly to be sneaking around behind people's backs,' Gary said piously.

'No. It's none of their business.'

'But you just said yes.'

'I wasn't listening.'

'Doesn't matter. A verbal agreement is binding.'

'You're such a fucking solicitor,' Neasa said. This was the most vicious insult anybody at Crawley Dunne & O'Reilly could throw at each other.

'We could take a few of them out for a pint and break the news. I'll pay,' Gary offered. He still had some fiddled expenses in his post-office account. It was the same post-office account he had opened when he'd made his First Communion. Neasa didn't know about it. There were some savings accounts Gary didn't tell her about.

'No,' Neasa said.

Gary was annoyed now. What was her problem? Was it because they wouldn't get to have sex in empty offices any more? Secretly Gary wished they could do it in the bed once in a while. It mightn't be as exciting, but it would be a hell of a lot more comfortable – and safe. The last time they'd had sex in Crawley's office Gary had impaled himself on a thumb tack.

'Conor is having an affair,' Neasa said very fast. She hadn't wanted to tell Gary – it seemed disloyal to Emily somehow – but she needed to talk to him about what to do.

Gary laughed. 'You're a gas, woman.'

'I wouldn't joke about something like this. He's shagging someone else.'

'What?' Gary's pale eyes popped.

'And I have to tell Emily,' Neasa wailed.

'Well, well,' Gary said slowly, his mind still on Conor shagging. Who would have thought it? Mr Superior, Mr Cultural, getting down and dirty with the best of them.

'Who?' he asked.

'What?'

'Who is Conor having the affair with?'

Neasa didn't know why this mattered. 'Ffion Rivera. The first violinist.'

'Well, well,' Gary said again. Mary Murphy with the long legs and the short, shiny hair. Trust Conor to go for a classy bird. It would be beneath him to go for the barmaid in Milo's. Gary wondered where they had done it.

'How am I going to tell Emily?' Neasa said a bit tearfully.

'I know. Poor Emily,' Gary said quickly. 'Isn't he a right bastard?'

'Totally.'

Gary was cheering up immensely. 'For all his airs and graces. He's a right fucker.'

'Yes, yes,' Neasa said. 'But what about Emily?'

Gary shook his head in a great show of disgust. 'I know.'

'I think she knows already,' Neasa said. She was feeling better now. Gary was a great comfort. Well, the important thing was to share. 'But I found out that the pair of them stayed in a hotel in Germany and I'm supposed to confirm it to her.'

Well, well, Gary thought to himself, stuck in a groove now. No seedy B & Bs for Conor Collins. A hotel in Germany, no less. He must have been very anxious to keep it quiet.

'What do you think I should do?' Neasa prompted. 'She's seven months pregnant, Gary.'

Gary reluctantly stopped thinking about Conor and Mary and schnitzel, and moved on to the problem of Emily. He wondered why it was that Emily Collins, whom he'd blithely ignored for years, seemed to rouse all kinds of uncomfortable feelings in him these days.

'Can you lie?' he said bluntly.

'No!'

'Don't look at me like that. You know you've thought about it.'

'It doesn't mean I've entertained it!' Neasa looked disgusted.

'Then you're going to have to tell her.'

'What kind of a solution is that?'

Gary sat up a bit straighter, the way he did at meetings where sales were being closed. 'Look at it like this. If I were having an affair on you, and Emily found out, would you like to know?'

171

Neasa didn't like the way this argument was progressing. 'But you're not.'

'If I were.'

Neasa thought of the cross-dresser and the sexist and the chat-room junkie. This was a bit too close to the bone.

'I don't know . . .'

'Would you like to know the truth about me?' Gary insisted.

Jesus Christ, was he going to drop some kind of bomb on her? Was he going to reveal that not only was he having an affair, he had also been born a woman?

Not another wacko, please God, Neasa implored. She really liked this one. 'Yes! Yes, I would like to know!'

'Even if it meant that it was over?'

Her throat felt a bit tight. 'Even if it meant it was over. I would still like to know the truth about you.'

Gary nodded slowly. Then he slapped the table energetically. 'There you go. Tell her.'

Neasa took her first breath in minutes. Gary hadn't been about to reveal anything unsavoury about himself after all. It was just her imagination.

'Are you all right?' he asked.

'Yes, yes,' she said, relieved. 'I suppose something like this makes you think, that's all. About your own relationship.'

'It does,' Gary said, who hadn't been thinking anything of the sort.

'I mean, Conor and Emily . . . they seemed so stable

and happy, didn't they? You couldn't imagine anything going wrong between them.'

'You never know what goes on behind closed doors, do you,' he said sagely, putting his big, bear-like arm around her.

She nestled into him, hating this treacherous feeling of relief that everything was great with her own relationship. But sometimes it took someone else's unhappiness to make you appreciate what you had.

'Let's have that gin and tonic,' she said fervently. 'Make mine a double.'

'Can we not just hug for a minute?'

'Of course we can.' She laid her head on his shoulder sadly. 'I suppose it's over now. The marriage.'

'Well, you don't know that,' Gary said.

'He cheated on her, Gary. God Almighty! You don't expect her to take him back, do you?'

'Well, obviously it's something they'll have to talk about. And now with the baby . . .'

Neasa drew away a bit. 'I wouldn't forgive something like that.'

Gary laughed and kissed her hair. 'That's because you're a tough old bird, Neasa.'

'What?'

'Look, what Conor did was awful, I totally agree. But, come on, at the end of the day, it was probably a roll in the hay.'

'So it's not that serious?'

'It's an affair, Neasa. Unfortunately it happens quite a

lot. But people don't throw everything away because of it.'

'We'll have to agree to differ, won't we?' Neasa said lightly. What was she getting so uptight about? People were entitled to their opinions, weren't they? It wasn't as though Gary had had the affair. 'You'd never do something like that, would you?'

'On you?' Gary said. 'Never! I wouldn't dare.'

He had been joking. But Neasa looked terribly serious. 'You wouldn't want to.' Then she snuggled in again. 'Anyway, I believe you because you're perfect.'

The trouble was, Gary was not. And he knew it, and he was worried.

Emily rang Conor after tea. She kept the curtains pulled back so that everyone could see her. She did not want to risk getting angry. And she wanted to deny him the courtesy of talking to him in private.

'Emily.' He picked up on the second ring.

She did not say hello. She just told him what Mr Chapman had said in even, rehearsed tones.

'He's keeping me in indefinitely.'

'Right. Well, I suppose he's the doctor.' You couldn't tell anything from his voice either. He must be able to hear the television in the background and know that she was ringing from the ward.

'So, there you have it,' Emily said, trying to make her side sound normal to anyone who cared to listen.

'Can I come in and see you?' he asked.

'No.'

'Please, Emily.'

'No.' She hoped he wouldn't ask again, because it was difficult to keep saying 'no' in this high, breezy voice.

'Charles Crawley called around this evening,' he said eventually. 'To see how you are.'

Emily didn't reply. It would be dangerous to start discussing trivia. Before you knew it, you were involved in entire conversations. Conor had learned that much from her, the sneaky, sly bastard.

'I have to go now,' she said instead. 'Goodnight.'

He spoke fast. 'Emily. I've resigned from the orchestra. Just so you know that.'

He hung up without putting her through the charade of a public reaction.

Emily put her mobile away and tried to sort through the confusion of her emotions. He was making her a gesture. He would not be consorting with Mary Murphy even in a professional capacity. It was a clear and forthright effort to lay the groundwork for trust again.

She could not fail to see what this had cost him. People were hardly crying out for professional pianists. He'd given up a steady job, some good colleagues, the buzz of performing in large venues. He'd probably have to go back to playing in restaurants where he would compete for attention with pan-fried trout.

It was too much. And too soon. Emily felt over-whelmed. She needed things to stand still for a while.

Conor had lived with this much longer than she; he was at a different stage. It wasn't fair of him to pressure her like this.

At the same time she was desperately glad that Mary Murphy had gone from their lives. Mary Murphy, that long streak of misery, with her peculiar, starey eyes and bleached moustache.

This wasn't really true. Some people found her eyes quite intense, and you'd have to look closely to see the moustache. Strangely, Emily found that she had no heart for denigrating Mary Murphy. And it seemed rather fruitless to compare Mary's physical attributes with her own – as though the affair had started purely on the basis that Mary had bigger breasts than Emily. Which she did. And longer legs. But Emily had a much better bottom and a neat little waist when she wasn't pregnant. No, all in all, Emily did not feel inferior to Mary Murphy in that way.

In fact she found that she did not care about Mary Murphy at all. Mary Murphy had not made Emily promises and broken them. It wasn't Mary Murphy, Ffion Rivera or whatever the hell she liked to call herself, who had let Emily down. Stand up, Conor, and take a bow.

Emily felt that she would never stop being angry with him. She couldn't imagine it fading, like other emotions did eventually. But then again, when they had married she had felt that she would never stop being totally engrossed in him to the point of grinning foolishly every time he walked into the room. She tried to think now how long that had lasted. A good while. But you couldn't keep that up, for heaven's sake – all the touching and kissing and having showers with each other. You could never get the shampoo out of your hair properly in any case. No, the time naturally came to pass when they took separate showers and did not eat off each other's forks.

Emily felt she had been realistic on the romance front. She had assumed that it would make way for something deeper, a greater knowledge and understanding of each other. And she had believed that it had in a way. She thought she knew Conor to his predictable core.

And now he had done this. Emily forgot about her hurt for a moment. She thought of those Saturday mornings when he played the piano, lost in some secret, passionate world from which she was excluded, and she wondered whether she had ever really known him at all.

Obviously not. Obviously there was some part of Conor not fulfilled by their marriage. By her. Otherwise why would he have turned to Ffion Rivera? To her shock and hurt, Emily added a layer of self-doubt and defensiveness.

Trish ambled in. She smelled of the takeaway curry her husband had brought in and which she'd just eaten in the visitors' room.

'Any joy?' Emily asked sympathetically.

'No. And it was a vindaloo and everything. It

brought on my youngest two.'

The vindaloo was a last resort. They were going to induce her in the morning.

'I suppose I'd better shave my legs,' she said, going to her locker. 'It'll take ages. They've not been done since the last one.'

'It'll all be worth it in the end,' Emily said consolingly.

'Oh, I don't know,' Trish said with a sigh. 'It was a mistake, you know. A burst condom. Blew out like a tyre.'

Emily was mildly shocked. She wouldn't dream of sharing such a personal detail with a stranger. Her heart always went out to those poor souls who were lured onto Jerry Springer-type shows and informed that their boyfriend was in fact their biological father. Emily fretted now as she thought about Conor's affair getting out. She could not bear to have her personal business dissected by the staff of Crawley Dunne & O'Reilly down in Milo's of a Friday night, or doing the rounds of the weekend dinner parties, every hushed sentence prefixed by the words 'Poor Emily'. But these things had a way of getting out. They always did.

She wanted to strangle Conor now for violating her privacy.

Trish went off as Maggie arrived in, her husband Tiernan in tow. Maggie handed Emily two sheets of grubby paper stapled together.

'I got some signatures for you,' she said.

'Me too,' Tiernan added fervently.

'What?'

'The petition,' Maggie explained. 'I saw it on the end of your bed. I went around Jude's Ward. They all signed.'

'And I got a few people as they were coming in,' Tiernan said. 'At least somebody's doing something.'

And they looked at her expectantly, confidently. This was because Maggie had discovered during conversation that Emily was a solicitor. Further probing had revealed that Emily had sold Maggie's brother's house for him last year. Apparently her brother spoke very highly of Emily. 'She didn't treat us like idiots,' he had declared warmly.

Emily looked at the petition. She didn't need this. 'It's not mine. I mean, it wasn't my idea.'

'I know, but you'll get things done,' Maggie said confidently. 'Right, I've to go practise my breathing. Well, it's for Tiernan, really. He always goes much too fast, don't you, Tiernan?'

'I do,' he said cheerfully, pulling the curtain around Maggie's bed.

Emily looked at the petition with its handful of signatures. Even total strangers had her marked down as the kind of person who would get the grunt work done. 'Conscientious', 'Hard-working', 'Disciplined' were words that had routinely appeared on her school reports. Once, her English teacher had run out of superlatives and had simply put down, 'Emily is a Good Girl.'

It sounded vaguely insulting now.

Emily lunged over in the bed and scrabbled in her locker. She took out a can of Neasa's Guinness and cracked it open. It tasted foul, warm and yeasty, but she took another slug anyway. And that was how her mother found her.

'Hello, Mam,' she said defiantly.

'Well, love,' Pauline Ryan said, plonking herself down on the chair, the three crucifixes around her neck rattling. 'I used to drink Guinness too when I was expecting. A can every night.'

Emily deflated and put down the Guinness.

'How are you, Mam?' she said before she could help it.

'All right,' Pauline said, doubtfully.

'Liz said you had palpitations yesterday morning.'

'I did,' Pauline confirmed. 'Liz told me that you thought it was the new postman.'

Thank you, Liz.

'What's this you have then?' Pauline enquired.

'Pre-eclampsia.'

'We didn't have that in my day,' Pauline declared. 'The big worry was high blood pressure and water retention. Oh, and protein or something in your waters.'

'That *is* pre-eclampsia.'

'Well, now, you learn something new every day,' Pauline said, delighted at being able to use another of her favourite phrases.

Emily looked at her mother, finding it hard to believe

that she was only sixty. She always thought of her as an old, old woman. Would Emily's own child look upon Emily the same way, with a mixture of curiosity and pity? The thought was so hurtful that she sat up straighter and tried to look at her mother with new eyes.

'What was it like for you, Mam? When you were pregnant?'

'What?'

'You know, did you feel tired and puffy and did the waiting kill you?'

'I suppose.' Pauline looked unsure. 'It's such a long time ago.'

'I know, but you must remember something. You remembered the Guinness for example.'

'That's true,' Pauline agreed with more spirit.

Emily was eager now. 'And what about childbirth? Don't people say you never forget the pain of that?'

'We didn't have epidurals in those days, that's for sure.'

'Did it last long? Each labour? Was it awful?'

Pauline looked adrift again. 'I honestly can't remember, Emily . . . I think Liz was the longest, but she was the first. You should ask her, you know. If you need to know anything. She'll be able to tell you.'

'I know, but I'm interested to know what it was like for you.'

But Pauline just looked hunted. 'Oh, Emily. Do you have to make such a song and dance about things?'

Emily was terribly hurt. 'Mam! When do I ever make a song and dance about things?'

'Such a chatterbox as a child,' Pauline said with relish. 'Now that I do remember. Always wanting to know things, to talk endlessly about things. Like, where did birds go to die!' She laughed.

Emily looked at her, wondering was she finally going senile.

'And what happened to snake's skins when they shed them? As if you'd ever seen a snake!'

Definitely there was something loose. Emily could not remember this person she was talking about.

'You had us driven demented,' Pauline finished.

'And did I ever find out?' Emily enquired. 'Where birds went to die?'

'Oh, we knocked sense into you in the end,' her mother said, smiling with the satisfaction of having squashed an annoying bug.

Emily vowed fiercely that if her child wanted to know where birds went to die, then Emily would take him or her to the woods where they would camp out in a tent for as long as it took for a bird to pop its clogs. They would go to the jungle in South America and wait for a boa constrictor to shed its skin and see what happened to it. She would, of course, organise all the necessary vaccinations first.

'Mam, I don't want you to stay too late, not if you're feeling a bit under the weather.'

She was finding Pauline hard work. She always

did. 'And you don't like driving in the dark,' she added.

Pauline drove at twenty miles an hour in the dark and pulled over to the side of the road for every oncoming car. If it were a truck, she would go halfway up the ditch.

'Better be safe than sorry,' she would mutter under her breath.

Emily knew now that there was no guarantee at all that if you practised safety you would not get sorrow.

'That's true,' Pauline said. 'And I want to catch eight o'clock Mass.'

This was unprecedented. Pauline went to Mass on Sundays, naturally, and every first Monday of the month. Then there were the Stations of the Cross, of course, and she usually went every morning during Advent. She never let a funeral pass either, and always turned up for the remembrance Masses. But on a Wednesday night?

'Has somebody died?' Emily enquired.

'No, no. I thought I'd go for you, Emily.'

This was Pauline's way of supporting her.

'I'm not that sick.'

'Still. Every little helps.'

'Oh, Mam, sign this for me before you go.' Emily reluctantly reached for the petition. Maggie was probably listening expectantly.

Pauline didn't like this. For no reason at all she didn't like it.

'It's just to stop the hospital closing,' Emily said impatiently.

'But it's going to close anyway,' Pauline said.

'Well, yes, but there's no harm in trying, is there? There's no bloody law against making the effort!'

Pauline fretted as she looked at the form. 'I won't get sent any unsolicited material, will I?'

'No, Mam. I can assure you of that,' Emily said grimly.

There had been a very embarrassing incident last year involving unsolicited material. A monthly magazine had got Pauline's name and address from somewhere and had sent her details of a prize draw. All she had to do was sign and send it back. Each month, more material would arrive from this crowd, breathlessly informing Pauline that she had been selected to go through to the next round, and the next. Pauline's natural antipathy of forms had been overcome by the promise of big money, and she had signed and sent them all back, telling no one. Then a sample cheque had arrived from the magazine people for a quarter of a million pounds, made out in Pauline's name. Pauline hadn't noticed the 'sample only' stamp on the top of the cheque and had tried to cash it in the bank in Paulstown, whispering to the bank manager that she was going to give some of it to Emily and Liz, and the rest to the church fund for a new roof. She had even generously urged him to keep a tenner for himself. The bank manager had discreetly called Emily in. Emily had sent a stiff solicitors' letter to the magazine crowd, warning them never to darken her mother's doorstep again.

Pauline had been very embarrassed and upset about it, and Emily had felt more sad than anything. For the first time in her life her mother had sensed real independence, only for it to be whipped from her because she wasn't sharp or cynical enough for this world.

Emily felt a greater connection with her now as Pauline laboriously signed and handed back the form.

'Thanks, Mam.'

'Who will you give it to?'

'What?'

'The petition?'

'Well, I don't know,' Emily said unhappily. She hadn't thought about this.

'I don't see why you bother half the time, Emily.' This was said with no rancour, just genuine puzzlement, and Emily felt annoyed again.

'It'd be a fine old world if nobody bothered, Mam.'

Pauline just shrugged and stood. 'I'll leave a shepherd's pie over to Conor in the morning.'

'He can cook. He has nothing else to do all day long,' Emily said sharply.

'It's no trouble,' Pauline said, gathering her bits and pieces. It seemed to take ages, as she took keys from her big bag, put her umbrella back in, changed her reading glasses to her driving glasses, checked her keys again.

Emily hadn't noticed her doing any of these things when she'd arrived.

Then she reached in and took Emily's hand. Emily was so touched that she felt tearful, but only until she realised that Pauline had pressed a wad of ten-pound notes into her fist.

'Mam? What's this?'

'For the baby. Best that you choose something yourselves. I wouldn't know what to be getting.'

You'd never think she'd had four children herself.

'But Mam . . . this is too much.' There was at least a couple of hundred pounds there.

Pauline stiffened with pride. 'It's not for you, Emily. It's for the baby. I did the same for all of Liz's.'

'Sorry, Mam . . . thanks. I'll buy something nice.'

Pauline nodded and left, buttoning up her thick coat and pulling on gloves as though she were stepping out into the Antarctic.

Emily put the money away carefully in the little zippered pocket inside her washbag. It was the first present she'd got for the baby. Most people had the tact to wait until the child was actually born alive and in one piece. But it hadn't occurred to Pauline that Emily had had a miscarriage and might be a bit sensitive. To Pauline it had been nature's way of dealing with defects, and had consoled Emily with the words that she could always have another one, and 'lightning never strikes twice'.

Emily wasn't at all sure about this. What about cleft

palates and heart defects, congenital abnormalities and haemolytic jaundice? This was in addition to the big worries of spina bifida and Down's syndrome, which Emily had spent many hours convincing herself the baby would have. Eventually she had stopped reading pregnancy books altogether, because they always seemed to fall open at some new disease or disorder that you'd never heard of before but would immediately start fretting about. It was the deodorant premise again; the more information you had, the more you worried. And the more you worried, the more likely you were to end up in hospital with stress-related pre-eclampsia. It was a vicious circle, Emily thought darkly, and she would very much like to meet the person who had started it all in the first place.

Conor's car was in the driveway, so Gary knew he was home. Gary was delighted with his suggestion to go over and talk to Conor. For one thing, it had earned him untold brownie points with Neasa. 'Oh Gary, would you? Because if I go I'll only wring his neck. You might be able to talk some sense into him.'

Also, Neasa had finally made up her mind to go in to the hospital, and it would be no fun without her at home. He supposed he could have rung up someone to go out for a few jars in Milo's, but then he realised that he didn't have any friends. Not any bosom buddies anyway, he quickly corrected. He had a very wide-ranging circle of laddish acquaintances all right, mostly the guys from work and the boyfriends of Neasa's friends. But he didn't have best friends like Neasa did. It seemed an awful lot of work, all the phone calls and the popping around to each other's houses, the dinner dates made weeks in advance. Sometimes Gary did make dinner dates, of course. He didn't want Neasa to think that he had no friends.

He stepped out of his BMW, grabbing six bottles of exotic beer he'd bought in the off-licence. They would need much more as the night progressed but Conor was bound to have some in the house.

He rang the doorbell with a confidence he'd never had on Conor's turf before, and fixed a suitably empathetic expression on his face.

The two dogs came galloping around the corner, barking viciously.

'Bollocks,' Gary said. Neasa had warned him. But he'd been so busy anticipating Conor's confession that he'd forgotten to buy two pork chops.

Conor came to the door in the nick of time.

'Get down,' he told the dogs quietly and they turned and slunk away.

Conor didn't look unshaven or drunk or red-eyed, as Gary had expected, and he faltered a bit.

'Ah, hello. I was in the neighbourhood.'

Conor looked at him, and Gary had the same uncomfortable feeling he'd had back in school when his science teacher had found him pulling the legs off a live bluebottle.

'I suppose you'd better come in,' Conor said.

The living-room was devoid of leftover TV dinners, whiskey bottles or damp tissues. Was the man human at all? Then Gary got the whiff of cigarette smoke. Ah-ha. Conor had been smoking inside the house. A crack in the armour.

'Neasa not with you?' Conor enquired, looking over Gary's shoulder just to be certain.

'No. She's gone to the hospital,' Gary said softly, as though he were talking to the recently bereaved.

Conor didn't react. Instead he offered tea or coffee.

'I brought some beer,' Gary said unnecessarily.

'You go ahead,' Conor said. 'I'll stick with tea.'

Gary was starting to regret ever coming around. You couldn't have any kind of a bonding session on tea.

In the kitchen, Conor emptied the kettle of hot water and refilled it with cold. It would take longer to boil. He wondered had Neasa sent Gary around in one of her ham-fisted attempts to get even on Emily's behalf. Conor was aware of Gary's reputation as Jaws in the office and wearily anticipated that at some point it would get physical.

When he eventually went back into the living-room, Gary was plonked comfortably on the sofa as though he intended to stay there for the night.

'Would you like a glass with that beer?' Conor asked politely.

'No, no, I drink it by the neck.' And he demonstrated this by twisting off the top and throwing half of it into his big mouth.

Conor sat down in the armchair opposite and tried to think of something to say. Gary didn't seem bothered at all by the silence; he just leaned back and lifted one ankle to rest on the other knee. Conor had tried to sit like that once, it looked so casual and relaxed, but he had just had this awful feeling that he was exposing his genitals. Which, actually, Gary was doing, if you looked closely enough. Those jeans were welded to him. It was almost obscene, and the sort of thing only very confident men could carry off. Conor wondered what it took to become that confident in your own skin.

'What's the beer like?'

'Oh, lovely. Mexican, you know? Lovely little bite to it. Go on, have one.'

'No, really—'

'One won't kill you.'

Conor took the bottle Gary held out. It was quite pleasant actually. Conor felt it was his turn again to say something.

'Manchester United won 2–1. I saw it on the news.'

Gary looked very surprised at this. 'Did they now? Well, well.'

Conor hoped that he wouldn't ask him who had scored, because he didn't have a clue. The appeal of football had always eluded Conor. Everybody else seemed to love it, women too. It was a kind of social grace now to have a favourite team. Conor, rudely, had never had one. He did have a Manchester United bag, though.

'2–1,' Gary repeated, his brow furrowing furiously. Conor was taking the mick again. Just when you thought he was loosening up, just when he'd lowered himself to have a beer. 'I'm not a Manchester United fan,' Gary said loudly, just to let him know that he was on to him.

'Oh,' Conor said. He had even picked the wrong fucking team to talk about. He had thought that Manchester United were perennial favourites. If Emily could hear him now, she would laugh her head off. Talking about football and beer, giving himself airs and graces.

He grappled around for something else acceptable to say. That was the trouble with him, none of it came easily.

'Mind you, they're the cup favourites. Again,' Gary said.

You see, Conor thought, Gary was in the know. Gary had his finger on the pulse of what was normal social interaction. No situation confounded him or left him lost for words. Most of what he said was absolute shite, in Conor's opinion, but that didn't matter. People loved it. Emily too. She'd laughed all night long the last time they'd had Gary and Neasa over for dinner. When they had finally left, the house had seemed empty and devoid of energy and Conor had felt very defensive.

Gary threw more beer into his mouth and decided to cut to the chase. 'So, Neasa was telling me. You know, about yourself and Emily having a bit of trouble. I was

just wondering if there was anything I could do at all.'
Gary had rehearsed this on the way over and had
thought it perfect. But on reflection it sounded like he
was offering to take over the shagging of Mary Murphy
or something.

Conor was very surprised. Gary sounded sympathetic and Conor had not expected this. Sympathy was
something usually reserved for the hurt spouse. The
most the offending party could expect was a dose of
vilification and the possible destruction of personal
property.

'Thanks,' he muttered. He had not talked about the
affair to anybody. Who would he talk to? Mark would
wilt with embarrassment. Certainly he couldn't confide
in any of his friends in the orchestra. Billy Middlemiss
would look at him with such utter disappointment that
Conor would die. Most of his other friends were shared
with Emily and all would be very firmly on her side.
How could they not be?

'Ffion, wasn't it?' Gary prompted, leaning forward.
Best to call her by her proper name. It sounded much
more sexy and mistress-like than Mary.

'Ah, yes,' Conor agreed.

Both of them had known it wouldn't go anywhere,
and neither of them had wanted it to. It wasn't some
great passion that had been bubbling for years and
years under the surface. It was more a recognition that
the other found life wanting. Ffion's husband had been
made redundant and was suffocating her with his

listless presence in the house all day. Conor was suffocating under Emily's disappointed looks at home. It started with Ffion joking about Conor being the strong, silent type. He had found it reassuring at first. Then he had found it necessary. It was like the beginning of his relationship with Emily, when everything was perfect, before he had been found out.

The sex wasn't particularly great. Ffion loved the secrecy and the excitement and the stolen moments. That was her kick. He hated all that – he lived in mortal dread of letting something slip and Emily finding out. But in those evenings and nights with Ffion, he told himself he felt worthwhile and desirable again. She wasn't demanding that he be things he wasn't. There was a curious release in that.

Gary was itching to ask about the details. Like most folk, he had an intense curiosity about other people's lives. If some salacious and forbidden act had taken place, all the better. Gary's desire was all the more acute because of his intense preoccupation with comparing and contrasting his life with that of others, and making sure that he was doing and experiencing all the right things.

'So, ah, is it over?'

'Of course it is,' Conor said testily. Jesus Christ, did he think that Mary was up in the bedroom at this very moment?

Emily's announcement that she was pregnant again had been like a bucket of cold water over the affair.

Conor and Mary had looked at each other as though stepping out of a dream. There had been no discussion about the matter really. Mary, mildly embarrassed, had taken an unscheduled holiday with her husband, who was delighted.

Conor had returned to Emily, whom he had never really left. In his more optimistic moments, he thought that perhaps his self-esteem might be in better shape now and that he might have more to contribute to the marriage. The naiveté of this still astounded him.

Gary had the tops twisted off two more bottles of beer.

'No, one is enough for me, thanks,' Conor said. It had already gone to his head.

'You've had two,' Gary pointed out.

Conor saw that he had. Gary pressed the third into his hand.

'Get that down you,' He said with the authority of a man who dealt with broken marriages all the time.

Conor obediently took it. He found that he was glad now that Gary was here. He really was all right, if you looked past all the shite.

'She won't let me go in and see her,' he blurted.

'I know,' Gary said sympathetically.

'You know?' Emily must be giving Neasa a blow-by-blow account on the mobile.

'No, I mean I don't know, I *didn't* know, I'm just . . .' Jesus, even with alcohol on him, Conor was sharp. 'I suppose you're going to have to play by her ball.' Shit.

Play by her rules? Play ball? This Mexican beer was strong.

'What would you do, Gary?'

Gary was astounded. Conor had never once asked his advice on anything. Not even legal stuff. The only time Gary's 'friends' seemed to ring him up was to get free legal advice.

'Talk to her, Conor,' he said in his most serious voice. This was what everybody recommended. Communication. Openness.

'How can I talk to her if she won't let me in to see her?'

Gary was at a loss. He'd only come around to find out if Mary Murphy had any kinky little tricks involving foodstuffs.

He pictured himself at his desk in the office and he immediately felt better. 'That seems to me to be very unfair, Conor. Especially as she's carrying your baby.'

'Well, it's hers too,' Conor felt he had to point out.

'Yes, but even if she doesn't want to see you, does that give her the right to deny you access to your unborn child?'

Conor blinked rapidly a few times. He wasn't at all sure what Gary was on about. But Gary sounded very confident and certain about things, which was more than Conor was right now.

'I love her, you know. Desperately,' he announced without any embarrassment. 'I've always loved her. I could never love anybody else.'

Gary wasn't embarrassed either. He was half-shot. Neither of them had eaten.

'Yes, yes,' he said soothingly. 'But let's get back to the visitation rights. I'm not sure where the law stands in this when it comes to unborn children, but I could find out.'

'I just want to see her, ' Conor said. 'I want to talk to her. I can talk too, you know. Look at me, I'm talking now!'

'Of course you are!' Gary said staunchly. He was damned sure that there was no law existing regarding visitation rights over unborn children. Was it possible that he could set a precedent here? Get his name in the history books?

'That's what went wrong, you see,' Conor admitted, peering over at Gary. 'I let her down after the miscarriage.'

Gary blinked. 'The miscarriage?'

'Didn't Neasa tell you?'

'Of course she did,' Gary lied, surprised at how hurt he felt. Why hadn't Neasa told him? 'Anyway, go on.'

Conor looked at Gary's fleshy, avid face and sobered instantly. This wasn't the kind of thing you talked about with total strangers, tanked up on beer. It had been the most vulnerable, hurtful time of their marriage and it was intensely private.

Conor had never encountered death before at close hand and it had terrified him. He was hurled into a pit of black thoughts about mortality and had ceased to see the point in any of it. He saw the dangers of becoming too dependent on someone who might so easily die. Look at the newspapers! It happened every day! Women and men were killed in car crashes, in fires, in domestic accidents. They were drowned, murdered, or they died of illness. Women even died in that most natural of human activities, childbirth. Not many, it was true. But women still died. It was in the pregnancy book in the chapter on complications.

Conor felt so overwhelmed by morbidity that on some days he could hardly speak to Emily at all, much less connect with her.

Her feelings seemed a much simpler affair to him. She grieved openly and copiously and wanted to talk endlessly. Insisted upon it, in fact, as though her way was the only way of dealing with things. But she'd already had experience of the process with her father's death, and seemed to know instinctively what to do, which was to seek support. And so her need for him was suddenly huge and desperate, a need that she had never really had before. He was unprepared and unpractised and, anyhow, was in denial. He felt like he was choking. He reacted in a knee-jerk way by rationalising, by offering her logic.

She believed that he was not as affected as her and there were accusations that he had not wanted the baby in the first place. At the same time the understanding was very clearly there that this event had happened primarily to Emily. Which it had, of course, in a physical sense.

Conor was very confused. He needed to talk but couldn't, and anyway, it seemed that Emily's feelings were more valid and that he was merely there to support her, as always.

He couldn't. He did not know how to deal with her pain. He had not seen this side to bubbly, optimistic Emily before and it was disconcerting. Certainly, his old ways of bucking her up didn't work now. He felt that he was abandoning her at her most vulnerable time. They were on wholly new territory and both of them were treading on minefields. Conor felt that every time he opened his mouth, or kept it closed, he let her down.

He knew he had. He saw it every time he looked in her eyes, and he couldn't bear it. But she did not end it, as he feared she might.

Instead she moved on. She started to enjoy her work again, and to smile, and to make friends with total strangers. Conor took his cue from her and pretended that he had moved on too.

It was around that time that Ffion Rivera made her little joke. And two months later, Emily got pregnant again.

'Will we go to Milo's?' Gary asked, without any heart. He really was very upset with Neasa. Oh, he was all right for sex, but could not be trusted with confidences. Hell, she'd only told him about Emily and Conor *after* she'd made that phone call to Germany. It was like his opinion didn't really count for much.

Sometimes, he felt a bit like . . . well, like a toy!

'No, I'm a bit tired,' Conor said.

'Me too. Knackered.'

Both of them stood awkwardly and quickly. Gary was glad to leave and Conor was glad to see him go.

Emily was not in her bed.

'She never is,' Nurse V Mooney said with a disapproving sniff.

Neasa had come up against bigger and better than Nurse V Mooney. 'Where is she so?'

'I couldn't tell you.'

'You do try and keep tabs on the patients?'

Nurse V Mooney's eyes narrowed a little. 'We stopped chaining them to their beds a while ago now.'

Neasa gave a frosty, I'm-going-to-sue look. 'I hope for your sake she hasn't done anything stupid.'

After combing all the wards on the floor, Neasa was getting worried. But Emily wouldn't do anything rash. She was pregnant, right? Neasa suddenly remembered the picket line outside the hospital. Surely to God she hadn't got dragged into that?

'Oh, hi, Neasa!'

Neasa whirled around to find Emily cradling a tiny baby, cooing and smiling beatifically.

'Isn't she just the most beautiful little thing you've ever seen?'

Neasa peered at the baby suspiciously. 'It's not yours, is it?'

'God, no. It's Cathy's. She let me hold her for a while. Isn't she just lovely?'

'Lovely.' It wasn't true that all newborn babies looked exactly alike. This one was particularly ugly, with a big thatch of coarse hair and a face that was all bent sideways.

'Forceps delivery,' Emily murmured, and Neasa swallowed hard.

'Let's go and talk,' she said firmly,

'But I've only just got her,' Emily said.

'Now.'

Neasa watched as Emily reluctantly turned and handed the baby back to a big, rough-looking woman, the kind who wouldn't mind giving birth in a cowshed. The woman tucked the baby under one oxter and pressed a crinkled sheet of paper into Emily's hand.

'Good on you, girl.'

Neasa wondered if Emily had got involved in running some kind of underground tuck-shop or something.

She waited until they were in the murky visitors' room before asking.

'Oh, it's just a petition,' Emily said, offhanded. 'To stop the hospital closing. I've been getting a few signatures.'

Neasa sighed. Only Emily could get dragged into revolutionary activity during a personal crisis.

'Look, Emily, I rang that place like you wanted me to.'

Emily looked at her with those big, trusting eyes and Neasa's heart broke. But she told Emily about the hotel, the receptionist, the fax, Room 134 and Mary Murphy.

'I just hate being the one to tell you this, Emily,' she finished, illustrating this by letting two big fat tears slide down her face.

'Oh, Neasa.'

'No, really, I wasn't going to tell you at all. I didn't know what to do,' Neasa cried.

'It's all right, I already knew,' Emily said.

'Did you?' Neasa said hopefully.

'Yes.'

Neasa was greatly relieved not to be the bearer of horrible news. Belatedly, she remembered that she was supposed to be consoling Emily.

'Anyway,' she said quickly, rooting in her bag and taking out a draft separation agreement. 'I'll act for you, of course. For free. By the time we're finished with that bastard he won't have money for condoms, never mind hotel rooms.'

Emily looked at the separation agreement for a moment. 'Neasa, I'm not filing for separation.'

Neasa understood. 'Sure, you probably want to wait until you get out of hospital. But I'll have him out of the house by then. Don't you worry about that. I've already made arrangements to have the locks changed first thing in the morning. And maybe we should go for a barring order too?'

'He's not going to be leaving the house, Neasa.'

'Okay,' Neasa said more slowly. 'A mistake, in my opinion. You know the rule – never, ever give up the marital home. I mean, where are you going to live?'

'I'm not going to be leaving the house either.'

'Right . . .' Neasa said eventually. 'This could bugger up visitation rights – you know, for the baby. If you're both living in the same house.' Her face cleared. 'Unless, of course, you took one floor each. Now, that might work.'

'It's a bungalow,' Emily reminded her.

Neasa lost patience. 'What the hell are we going to do then? As your solicitor, you've left me with very few options here!'

Emily knew that Neasa would think her terribly weak. 'I know. But the fact is, I'm not going to do anything.'

'You have to do something!'

'Why?'

'Why? Why? Because that big shitty bastardy cheat of a two-timing fucker did the dirt on you! Betrayed you! Humiliated you! Let you down!'

'There's no need to rub it in.'

'And you're just going to let him get away with it?'

'Neasa, I know you're on my side here—'

'Too bloody right I am!' Neasa was very upset. 'Are we just going to let these kind of men make fools of us time and again?'

'No, of course not—'

'Should they not be punished in any way?'

'I suppose—'

'So what's all this "he's not moving out" shit? Emily, have you no dignity?'

Emily had known that this would be difficult. 'It's not about dignity. Look, I have things to think about. A lot of things. And I'm not going to do anything rash.'

Neasa looked at her. 'You're going to stay because you feel you ought to. Aren't you? You're going to stay because of the baby.'

'The baby is a consideration. Of course it is – I wouldn't be much of a person if I didn't think about the baby!' But Emily did her best not to get angry, because she knew this whole thing was more about Neasa than herself. 'But the baby isn't everything, Neasa.'

'Don't tell me you still love him?' Neasa asked in disgust.

'I don't know what I feel about him right now.'

Neasa stood, looking on the verge of more tears. 'I really think you're letting yourself down, Emily. If I were in your shoes, I wouldn't put up with it. I'd have too much self-respect.'

And she jerkily left the visitors' room, taking the separation agreement with her. Emily took a deep breath and let it out slowly. She had expected much of what Neasa said, but not all of it. Something must have happened with Gary. From the smell of Neasa's breath, she'd had more than one gin and tonic.

But Emily had once had the same ideals as Neasa, hadn't she? They all had, Jackie and Deirdre too, on those drink-fuelled nights down in Milo's. They were very young back then, of course, and single, and had had very high expectations of men in general, and potential husbands in particular. There had been an unofficial list of Necessary Qualities which had included intelligence, a sense of humour, earning power, sexual prowess, middling-to-good looks, a hairless back, some cooking ability (though Neasa pointed out that this wasn't absolutely vital if he had the earning power to take them out for meals instead) and a car. Most important, he had to be desperately, desperately in love with them. Crazily. Suicidally, even!

Because what could possibly go wrong if he was mad about them? And as for infidelity? Ooooh! Out the door! This very instant, without even a coat on his back! Whatever else happened, they wouldn't stand for that kind of thing, they would hiss venomously. If he even looked too hard at another woman, he was in grave danger.

At this point, Neasa would go to the bar to refuel with four pints of Heineken.

But as they got older, and the men they went out with were invariably and heart-breakingly lacking in most of the above-mentioned qualities, the girls had come to expect less. Not that they ever admitted this in their nights in Milo's. No, they made excuses for their men instead. 'But he's very good with the garden,' they would sincerely explain to each other. 'And he's mad about me.' At this, the girls would shrug, nod grimly, and agree, 'Well, I suppose if he's *mad* about you . . .', whilst pulling faces behind their hands.

In the end, only Neasa had shouted 'No compromise!' and would view the others' relationships as though they were odd, unnameable matter in a Petri dish. Emily hadn't been offended. It was all subjective. At the end of the day, love was a peculiar thing and there was no accounting for taste.

They had all held firm on the infidelity issue though, and Emily acutely felt the pressure now To Do The Right Thing and kick him out, if only to show the girls and everybody else that she was no pushover this time. She hated herself for always caring so much what other people thought of her.

Not that she had ruled out a separation agreement by any means. In fact she was giving it a lot of thought. But there were long-term implications of any action and Emily knew that she must continue to resist the temptation to do something in the heat of the moment.

Everything had been thrown to the four winds. How she would piece things back together she did not know. And Conor was only a part of this.

She stood and tidied up the visitors' room. As an afterthought, she ripped down the defaced vaccination poster of the baby and put it in the bin. Then she opened a window and let some fresh air in.

Her little ministrations didn't make a whit of difference. It was still a nasty, grim room. What this room needed, she thought, was to be blown sky-high and rebuilt again.

The vindaloo appeared to work. Trish went into labour that evening, very fast, and was carted off to Delivery immediately, smiling between the pains.

'I'm delighted,' she kept saying. 'Delighted.'

'Good girl, Trish,' Nurse V Mooney said in satisfaction. Not that there was anything wrong with being induced; it was just always nicer to get off the starting blocks by yourself. 'I'll ring Aidan,' she promised.

'Oh, no need,' Trish panted. 'I'll have had it by the time he gets his mother over to look after the rest of them.'

After she was gone, Maggie came over and huddled on Emily's bed.

'Do you think she'll get to the epidural in time?'

'I don't know,' Emily admitted.

'I tried to book one, you know,' Maggie said. 'But they told me that you can't book epidurals in advance.'

Maggie was very fearful about the whole thing. She was a severe asthmatic and had been hospitalised after a particularly frightening episode. She would not be going home until she had had her baby, due nearly three weeks before Emily's.

'Put it down on your birth plan that you want one,' Emily advised.

'I have, in big red letters,' Maggie said, chewing her

lower lip nervously. 'I've put it down on Tiernan's as well.'

'Tiernan has his own birth plan?' Emily enquired, after a bit.

'Oh no, just a copy of mine. In case it gets lost,' Maggie explained. 'We want to be absolutely sure that everything goes the way we want.'

It seemed a bit rigid to Emily but she said nothing.

'How long will Trish be in, do you think?' Maggie asked now.

'I don't know,' Emily said. She wished that Maggie didn't think that she was the font of all wisdom. If she only knew.

'I got all my relatives to sign the petition for you, by the way,' Maggie said.

'It's not my petition,' Emily explained again.

'I don't want to go to Cork.'

'Of course it would be nice to have our babies here, but I don't suppose we've much choice,' Emily said.

'Tiernan can't drive,' Maggie blurted. 'Well, he can, but he's been banned.' She didn't elaborate on why. 'I'll never see him when they move me to Cork!'

'There are buses and trains, Maggie – he hasn't been banned from those too, has he?'

'We don't think so,' Maggie said doubtfully, leaving Emily to wonder further what Tiernan had done. 'When I get an attack, he's the only one who can calm me down.' And she started breathing very fast.

'Now relax, Maggie,' Emily said sternly. 'You've

rakes of relatives. Can't one of them drive him down?'

'Oh, they're always visiting all right, but they're not dependable,' Maggie said darkly.

Cathy and Petra arrived later, having heard the news about Trish. Cathy brought a two-litre bottle of Coke and a family bar of Cadbury's chocolate.

'Tuck in, girls,' she encouraged. 'Once you start breast-feeding, the fat will fall off you.'

Petra glowered. Lies, damned lies. She'd put on a stone for every child she'd had, despite breast-feeding every last one of them until they were a year old.

'I suppose that's the end of the bridge tournament,' Cathy said. No one was sorry.

Cathy and Petra were much more sanguine about Trish's labour than Emily and Maggie, the first-time mothers. They dispensed advice liberally.

'You see, nobody tells you what labour is really like,' Cathy said candidly, and proceeded to do so in gory and bloody detail. Maggie's face got whiter and whiter as Cathy talked about membranes tearing and placentas that wouldn't come out, but most about the excruciating, horrifying pain of it all.

'They don't want to frighten you, you see,' she finished up cheerfully. 'They fill you with shite about how it's just like bad period pains. Well, if I had periods like that I'd shoot myself. No, girls, don't be fooled by that kind of talk. I was fooled on my first one. And do you know something? I was raging that nobody had told me what it was really going to be like.'

Emily tried to lighten the mood for the sake of poor Maggie. 'Maybe it's a conspiracy.'

'I'm inclined to think so,' Cathy said seriously. 'Because if girls and women were told how bad it really was, then there's no way they'd get pregnant. And the human race would die out.'

She had obviously given this a lot of thought.

'So I've decided that I'm not colluding in the conspiracy any more,' she declared. 'I'm not telling other women that labour is grand, that it'll all be worth it when you look at the little fecker's face. Well, girls, don't be fooled by that either.' She looked at them darkly. 'I often think that children aren't worth the bother at all. And I don't mind saying it either.'

'So why did you have two of them so?' Emily felt she had to ask.

'My husband wanted four, and two was the compromise,' Cathy said evenly. 'I've done my bit now and that's that.'

'You might soften and have another in a year's time,' Emily joked her.

'I don't think so. I'm sending him for the snip next month,' Cathy said, and roared with laughter. Everyone else laughed too. But nobody doubted that she was serious about this as well.

'You'd have thought we'd have had news by now,' Maggie said, desperate to get onto less bloody ground. She must review her birth plan at the first opportunity. 'She's been gone nearly two hours.'

'All in good time,' Petra said, and she and Cathy exchanged knowing looks.

There was still no news after another hour. Cathy and Petra gave up and went back to Elizabeth's Ward. Maggie stayed perched on Emily's bed, her little pixie face anxious.

'Maybe her placenta got stuck,' she said.

'Don't believe everything Cathy tells you,' Emily advised.

'It wasn't fair to frighten us like that!' Maggie said. 'Now I won't be able to sleep a wink!'

'It probably won't be as bad as she says,' Emily said, trying to sound authoritative. 'Anyway, it's different for every woman.'

'I don't know,' Maggie said doubtfully.

'Look on the bright side,' Emily cajoled. 'At least we've been warned. And now we can prepare ourselves better for the big day, right?'

'You're right,' Maggie said, looking greatly cheered. She reached over and rummaged in her locker. She took out her birth plan, her red pen and went to work, her brow furrowed in concentration.

'What are you doing, Maggie?'

'I'm asking for more drugs during the labour. You know, in case the epidural doesn't work.'

'Oh, Maggie.'

'I heard a story once about a woman who had an epidural,' Maggie said darkly. 'And only her left leg went numb. She didn't get back the use of it for six months.'

'Who tells you these things, Maggie?' Emily said impatiently.

'Supposing that happens to me? What use is a numb leg to anybody in labour?'

'It won't happen,' Emily said with a sigh.

'I just don't want to leave anything up to chance, that's all,' Maggie insisted, turning a page in the crumpled birth plan. 'You know, I think I might get Tiernan to type this up.'

Nurse V Mooney came in later and went to Trish's bed. She took Trish's washbag from her locker.

Maggie bounced up in excitement. 'Did she have her baby?'

'She did,' Nurse Mooney said without looking at them. Emily watched as the nurse pulled out Trish's suitcase from under the bed and started to pack her things into it quickly.

'Is she all right?' she asked.

'She is,' Nurse Mooney said. 'We're just moving her to a post-natal ward.'

'Can we go down to see her?' Maggie asked. 'Just for a minute?'

'No, she's exhausted, and her husband is in with her.'

Maggie was indefatigable. 'Is it a boy or a girl?'

Nurse Mooney looked tired. 'A boy. Look, the baby died, girls. So don't be sneaking off down to see her. She's very upset.'

She saw their faces and came over. 'It's very rare these days, but it does happen. There was nothing

211

anybody could do. Now don't be worrying that anything is going to go wrong with your own. It won't.'

Later, Emily and Maggie dragged Maggie's locker into the middle of the ward and pushed their beds together. Maggie said she didn't want to sleep on her own. Then they pulled the curtains around on Trish's bed because they couldn't bear to see it empty. They got into bed side-by-side. They did not pay any heed to Nurse Mooney's advice not to worry. They were only in this place because something had already gone wrong.

Emily lay awake in the dark and knew that Trish too was lying awake in the dark, in the room they'd put her on her own, where there would be no other pregnant women or babies to upset her further. She would be fretting because the baby had been a mistake, convinced that it had sensed that it was not wanted in the first place. She would be going over and over possible things she had done wrong. She would be searching for someone to blame but there would be no one. She would be in shock, that numb half-awareness that the thing you dread most has actually happened. 'Emily?' Maggie turned over in the dark. 'Are you crying?'

'No, no,' Emily said. How could she explain that she was not crying for Trish but for herself?

'It's all right,' Maggie said. 'I'm crying too.'

And she curled into Emily's back for protection.

They hadn't even told anybody that Emily was pregnant that first time. Bad luck, they'd declared. They would wait until they'd passed the three-month mark;

they would hold off until they got the first scan. When Emily lost the baby, there was no sympathy or support because nobody knew. Emily and Conor only had each other.

Conor had not really accepted that the baby had existed in the first place, Emily believed. There was no little scan picture, and Emily hadn't even had a bulge. His sorrow was a private and closed affair.

Emily in turn had felt that her depression and sadness was unwarranted, that she was being over-emotional and dramatic. Eventually she learned to hide her grief. Eventually she learned to deny her own feelings.

Maggie had fallen asleep. Emily lay there letting the honest tears fall and she felt very high up on the hospital bed, like she was floating, free.

Part Two

'Morning, Emily.'

'Oh, hi, Maureen. Don't tell me that rasher is for me.'

'It is. And I done you a sausage as well.'

'You're an angel!'

'Only don't let Maggie see. She'd be foaming at the mouth.'

'Of course I won't,' Emily assured her. Maggie was on a strict diet supervised by a nutritionist. Apparently animal fats exacerbated her asthma.

'Slip it into a butty,' Maureen advised. 'And tell her the smell is in her imagination. Most things are anyway.'

Maureen didn't have much truck with Maggie's breathlessness and wheezing. But then Maureen managed to smoke forty cigarettes a day without a bother in the world.

'Any luck on that job?' Emily asked.

'No, but I've got an interview with that other crowd you were telling me about. Are you sure it's all right to use your name?'

'Absolutely. I did some work for them last year. They owe me one.'

'I'll get some severance pay from here. I suppose that'll keep me going for a while,' Maureen said optimistically.

Emily ate her rasher as she watched Maureen plonk down a big pot of tea and some toast onto the table under the television. There was only Maggie and Emily left in Brenda's Ward now. They were officially the longest serving patients in the hospital and the catering girls had taken them to their hearts – well, Emily anyway – slipping her chocolate biscuits and extra cups of sweetened tea when the nurses weren't looking. Emily reciprocated by helping them set up for breakfast at six every morning. Now that the baby had dropped in readiness for the birth, it was lying firmly against her bladder and she was up most of the night running to the loo. That's when she wasn't sitting up fighting heartburn. Who would have thought, looking at those glossy pictures of smiling, placid women with tanned, swelling bumps, that the reality was so uncomfortable and distinctly lacking in dignity?

'Right. I'd better go feed the other animals in the zoo,' Maureen said, and off she went, cackling as though she'd made a great joke.

Maureen did such a useful job, Emily often thought, keeping everybody in the hospital alive with Weetabix and fish pies. Not that her fish pies were anything to write home about – Emily had once found a whole fish head on the end of her fork, complete with staring eyes – but what Maureen did was essential. Not like selling hilly farmland and crumbling old houses, and passing them off on the public as 'prime grazing lands' and 'stunning period havens'. In the office, Emily had been particularly good at overlooking a property's bad points and finding superlatives for its few miserable assets. But there was nothing surprising about that really.

There was Vera now, bustling up to the nurses' station and taking out her pen. She would record the night's happenings, who had been poorly and who had not. In a minute she would come around to do blood-pressure readings and take temperatures in her calm, unflappable way. Vera Mooney and Maureen would be able to look their Maker in the eye and say that they had used the talents he had given them to the best of their abilities.

The most Emily would be able to stand over was a handful of glossy sales brochures, and say that she had used her talents to fill the coffers of Crawley Dunne & O'Reilly. And not one of the partners had made the five-mile drive from Paulstown to visit her in three long weeks. Except for Gary, of course. For the entire visit, he had held himself as though he were an official ambassador.

'Place isn't the same without you, Emily. In fact, it's a shambles.'

Big, fat lies. Neasa had told her that Creepy Crawley

had calmly divided out Emily's unfinished files to everyone else. They took it in turns to make the coffee. Nobody had yet discovered the wire in the photocopier that only Emily knew how to jiggle to make the damned thing work, but someone had found that if you kicked it, it worked just as well.

Emily found it chilling how dispensable she really was. And so very hurtful. She had never viewed her place in the world before with such clear eyes, and found it so wanting.

Not that she had ambitions towards brain surgery or running soup kitchens. And someone had to sell land, after all. It was a well-paid job and many envied it.

But, oh, those migraines she would get on Friday nights. That ache she would have in her cheeks from smiling like an idiot all day long. And that heavy feeling on Sunday evenings, knowing that another week was starting where she would beaver away in her office, patting herself on the back for working through lunch. As if anybody cared. As if anybody even noticed.

She had thought herself so full of possibilities once. It was a long time ago, admittedly, and much of it could be attributed to teenage hormones. But sitting in a steamed-up classroom while a teacher droned on, Emily would stare out the window at the hockey pitch and wish that she could be done with school and get out there and start her life. She could do anything she wanted, be anybody she cared to be. And she would go home that evening and diligently do her homework, as if this were her passage, her entrance ticket to all the world held.

Even then she had not broken the rules.

'Do you ever wonder sometimes what she's thinking?' Karen said out at the nurses' station.

Vera Mooney said nothing but she watched Emily Collins through the door very carefully. She wanted to be sure that Emily was not becoming institutionalised. Oh, laugh if you like, but Vera had seen it happen to others, and in a very short time too. They frantically did crosswords and watched Sky News, but eventually the boredom got them down, and the sheer frustration of having no control over their own lives. The outside world receded on them very quickly and visitors would suffer through an exact account of what they'd eaten for tea, and what they had chosen for tomorrow's tea, and the snoring patterns of the other occupants of the ward. It was worse for pregnant women. The endless waiting often drove them mad.

Emily Collins was waiting all right. For what, Vera wasn't sure. It was like she was doing a gigantic multiplication sum in her head, one that occupied her wholly and endlessly. Vera rather hoped that she solved it before the baby arrived.

Vera, like Emily, was running out of time. St Jude's Ward had closed yesterday. It meant that Bernie and Yvonne and the rest were free to do picket duty, but it was another nail in the coffin. They had no hope now. All they could do was give one last dying kick.

'Have you written up the notes for Mr Dunphy?' she enquired of Karen.

'Um, no.'

'Well, do it then.' Just because the hospital was closing on Monday week did not mean they should slack off.

Vera went into Brenda's Ward and sat on the end of Emily's bed. Emily was cleaning out her make-up bag, running a cotton bud around the rims of tubes and powders.

'I don't know why I'm doing this,' she told Vera cheerfully. 'It's not as though I ever put any on in here.'

'It's the nesting instinct,' Vera said wisely. 'If you were at home, you'd be defrosting the fridge or spring-cleaning cupboards that you hadn't opened in years. Most women go mad cleaning just before they're about to give birth.'

'And you did it twice,' Emily said, marvelling.

Emily already knew that Vera had two girls. She knew a lot of things about Vera that Vera had never intended to tell her. She had a way about her that had you spilling your guts.

'Any more pains?' Vera asked, strapping a pressure cuff on Emily.

'They were pretty bad earlier,' Emily admitted. She was getting preparatory contractions thick and fast now. Some of them really hurt, and Emily wished that Cathy had not told her that they were child's play compared to the real thing. Emily had been practising her breathing techniques recently, and then remembered that Cathy had told her that she'd be lucky if she were able to breathe at all.

'Well, only three weeks to go now,' Vera said. She looked at the dial on the pressure cuff. 'You'd want to think about getting that baby bag sent in.'

The words were carefully chosen. The husband's absence had been noted up and down the floor. There had been only two visits in three weeks. Something was up there all right, but it was not Vera Mooney's place to speculate.

'I will,' Emily said.

'Mr Chapman will be here this afternoon,' Vera said.

'Oh, right.' Emily was unfazed. Mr Chapman came up every week, sometimes twice, to see her.

'He wants to do a scan, Emily. What with the pains and the bit of blood you had yesterday, he needs to check the condition of the placenta.'

'It was only a little bit of blood,' Emily said.

'All the same.'

'And what if he finds something?'

'Look, I can't really say. I'm not a doctor.'

'Ah come on, Vera. You know more than most of them.'

'I don't want to go pre-empting Mr Chapman,' Vera insisted primly.

'He'll do a section, won't he? If my placenta is malfunctioning.'

'That might be a course of action he would consider.'

'Oh, Jesus.'

'Now don't go upsetting yourself,' Vera said sternly. 'You're into your thirty-eighth week. All that baby is doing now is putting on fat, and it can do that just as well on the outside.' She stood. 'And it'll be lovely to see the baby on the scan. You should be looking forward to it.'

Vera left. Emily had to fight the urge to scuttle down in the bed and pull the covers up high over her head. She deeply resented her little bubble being so rudely burst with talk of caesareans and scans and placentas. Could she not be left in peace until she reached her fortieth week, or even longer if the baby decided it was happy where it was?

It had been funny, these past few weeks. They reminded Emily of the retreat she'd been dragged to by her mother years ago, to some holy house in the West. It was a proper retreat, with loads of suffering and praying and starvation, not one of those namby-pamby ones where everyone took it in turns to cook gourmet dinners before massaging each other's inner child. No, this was the genuine article, involving barefoot hikes up Croagh Patrick on nothing more than a cup of tea and a slice of Brennan's bread. Talking was forbidden, the better to help you focus on what a sinner you really were. Then four hours' sleep before a dawn Mass and a couple of rounds of Hail Mary's. Emily had thought it a total waste of time, except for the fact that she lost two pounds. But then she had looked at the faces of the other survivors. Past the paleness and exhaustion, there was a kind of hard-won peace and she was almost sorry that she hadn't made more of an effort.

Martha's had been a retreat of sorts too. There were rashers and sausages in Martha's, of course, and talking was not forbidden. But there was plenty of suffering and lots of time for contemplation. At the end of the day, Emily hadn't climbed any mountains, literal or metaphorical, and come down the other side shouting, 'I've solved it all, yippee!' She hadn't solved much at all. There had been no epiphany, worse luck, just endless grappling and searching and questioning, with the occasional foray into steam-filled classrooms for a little light relief.

The truth was that Emily did not know where she was going. But she had seen very clearly where she was coming from, and that was something. And it wasn't good enough any more. It had never been good enough to begin with, but she had nobody to blame for that except herself. For accepting, endlessly accepting.

Conor had been restrained. He seemed to sense that if he pushed things any further with her, it would backfire badly. He had left her alone, only to ring up once and anxiously ask whether Gary had been on to her in any legal capacity. Emily, mystified, assured him that he hadn't. Conor had seemed very relieved. Emily had always thought Conor despised Gary and was surprised to learn that they were obviously pally. Another side to Conor that she had never seen before.

She had phoned him a few times herself, to keep him in the picture about her health. And she had asked him to come in twice. This was out of necessity. She'd needed clean underwear and pyjamas, and the charger for her mobile. They'd managed by talking about the baby and her medication and the dogs. He had stayed less than twenty minutes both times and she had been grateful.

She rang him now and told him about the scan. He said he would come in.

She got out of bed and went to take her morning shower. Today, she found that her anger was less. Today she would talk to him.

Creepy Crawley came up behind Neasa in his usual stealthy way. God, that *hair*. She had it in a French plait today, which showed off her very fine, long white neck. Creepy imagined himself taking off that little bow at the bottom and unravelling the plait, twist by twist, inch by inch, and he was nearly undone.

Rumour had reached his ears last week that Neasa Martin and Gary O'Reilly had something going. Apparently it was common knowledge. The depth of his upset had surprised Creepy. *Gary*, who always reminded Creepy of a side of beef. Neasa had gravely disappointed him. Surely she deserved a man of intelligence and culture, a man whose knowledge of wine extended beyond red and white? It must be a momentary lapse, Creepy decided. Gary had just not taken no for an answer. The partners had already discovered that Gary did not understand the meaning of a lot of words, including 'paperwork', 'desk-bound' and 'middle-management'. He still thought he could drop everything to go off and close an exciting sale, not realising that it was now his job to select the person who would close the exciting sale. Still, he would learn. There was plenty of time yet before he started getting a slice of the profits. A rather small slice.

Neasa would most probably be at the partners' dinner on Friday. Creepy would see to it that she was sitting by his side, and at the far end of the table to Gary. A woman of her taste would quite easily spot the difference.

'Neasa?'

'What! I mean, can I help you, Mr Crawley?'

Neasa was working on a particularly difficult sales contract for a farm, and was bogged down in meaningless phrases such as 'heretofore assign' and 'decree unto the vendor'. She had a huge urge to draw a red line through the whole lot and write at the bottom, 'I'll give you my land if you give me your money'. They shouldn't have opened that second bottle of wine last night.

Gary had noticed her discontent of late, especially when she went around the house shouting, 'It's all a load of bollocks.' Sweetly, he had bought her a box of chocolates and some new silky underwear, and told her that her feelings would pass. At least he'd noticed, she reassured herself.

Creepy Crawley held out a letter as though it contaminated him. 'This arrived this morning. I was wondering whether you knew anything about it?'

Neasa saw that it was addressed to Emily.

'I didn't realise we were opening her post,' Neasa said. The letter had 'Private & Confidential' written on the top. The envelope would have had the same.

'Well, we have to, now that she's gone.'

'She *is* coming back,' Neasa pointed out mildly.

'Of course she is,' Creepy said quickly. 'How is she, by the way?'

'As well as anybody can be after three weeks in hospital.'

'Yes, yes,' Creepy said quickly. He didn't want to get into any talk about babies or labour. He was about to have his lunch.

The letter was from the Health Board. It was regarding the petition Emily had sent in.

'I have no idea what they're on about,' Neasa said primly. This was perfectly true.

'We don't want to get involved in that kind of thing,' Creepy said dismissively. He had private health insurance and a very good car to take him to Dublin should anything ever go wrong.

'Of course we don't,' Neasa soothed. 'To be honest, I think that hospital is getting to Emily. All that time on her hands. Anyone would go a bit cracked and start up petitions. Why don't you leave it with me?'

'All right,' he said reluctantly. 'And maybe you'd tell her that she can't be using our headed notepaper and name to back this petition thing.'

'I'm sure she didn't mean it like that,' Neasa assured him.

He went off. Neasa scrutinised the letter. How Emily had sent the thing off to them in the first place was a mystery. It wasn't as though there was a post office on the ground floor of the hospital, or indeed any typing facilities.

Emily was running away, Neasa knew. She didn't want to deal with the real issues and so she had latched onto this petition thing as a distraction. Hadn't Neasa's grandmother got very obsessive about her pension book as death stared her in face? It was pure escapism, as clear to Neasa as the spots on Gary's chin. Oops. Where had that come from?

On cue, the door to Emily's office opened and Gary came out. His tie was loosened and his shirtsleeves rolled up. This was purely for effect, of course, to give the impression that he was working so hard that he was actually letting off steam. He came over.

'I'm going out for a sandwich – want to get one and go back to Emily's office?'

Gary was annoyed that he'd said 'Emily's office'. It was his now. But everybody else persisted in calling it Emily's office too. It was most irritating.

'I'll pass,' Neasa said regretfully. 'I'm taking a late

lunch – I want to pop over and see Emily this afternoon.'

Gary was secretly relieved. He'd been working like a dog all morning and was totally knackered.

'Why don't you go to Milo's with the lads?' Neasa suggested.

Gary didn't really want to go to the pub. It was impossible to do any work after three pints of Smithwicks. The bottles of red wine every night were killing him too. But Neasa never seemed affected at all, and he just looked wimpish in comparison. He felt that any attempt to cut down on his consumption would be noted and chalked up against him as some kind of black mark.

'I don't think any of them are going,' he hedged.

'They are. Annabel told me.'

'I don't think I could be bothered,' he said quickly. He didn't want her thinking that he would be flirting with Annabel, the new temp in the secretarial division. He had looked at her once. Just once, when she had handed over a file. It seemed the polite thing to do. But Neasa had noticed, and he had never looked at Annabel since, to the point of directing any enquiry to a point two feet above her head. He seemed to be watching his Ps and Qs all the time recently.

'Go and have a few pints. I'm busy here,' Neasa said in a voice that brooked no argument. She wanted to read the letter from the Health Board.

'What's that?' Gary enquired.

'Oh, nothing,' Neasa said quickly. For some reason, she didn't want to tell him about the letter. It wasn't that she didn't trust him. She was just afraid that he might, well, sneer. Unless letters contained very large cheques Gary didn't have an awful lot of interest. She had a suspicion that he might find Emily's petition funny.

There she went again, Gary thought, holding things back on him! Oh, she could talk for Ireland over those bloody bottles of red wine, leaving no stone unturned when it came to stories of her childhood, her adolescence, her whole bloody life. When she was drunk she tended to repeat herself, which became terribly tedious, but he still listened! But he had noticed that she didn't discuss things like Conor's affair with him any more, and had been very unenthusiastic when he'd told her about his idea to secure Conor visitation rights to his unborn child. Had nipped it in the bud, actually. And he only trying to help!

Neasa saw that Gary looked a bit down. Probably because she hadn't agreed to sex and a sandwich in Emily's office. But it just wasn't that exciting any more now that it was actually Gary's office.

'Creepy wants to know whether I'm bringing someone on Friday night,' Gary said.

They were having a sort of official swearing-in dinner for Gary and all the partners and their other halves would attend.

'Oh, Gary, I don't know.' The thought of it made her

ill. She would have to get very drunk.

'Something better to do?' he asked lightly, but there was an underlying edge.

'Sweetness! Don't be ridiculous. It's just that it'll be full of stuffed shirts.' She hurried on, 'Except for you, of course. Let me think about it.'

Gary wasn't happy, she saw. She smiled brightly. 'Tell you what. Why don't we have a big romantic dinner tonight? With loads of wine and candles and I'll fill a big bubble bath for us later and we'll use that new thing you bought in that sex shop?'

'Great,' Gary said.

'Great,' Neasa echoed.

Mr Gerald Chapman set off from Cork at twenty past one. He would have to drive hard and fast if he were to make his two o'clock appointment in Martha's. The traffic was terrible out of Cork, which only added to his black mood.

Killian, his seventeen-year-old son, had arrived home last night sober. This had immediately made Mr Chapman suspicious. The boy had stood in the living room, head hanging, and told them that his girlfriend was pregnant.

'Oh my God,' Hannah had moaned. 'How could you do that to poor Deirdre?'

It wasn't Deirdre. It was a new one, apparently. Andrea. She was sixteen.

'I'm very sorry,' the little sod had said to Mr Chapman

beseechingly. Because somehow, his father would sort it out. He always did.

'Don't worry, son,' Mr Chapman said calmly. 'I'll deliver it for you.'

The boy was aghast. 'But we can't have it. I mean . . .'

'You mean you don't want it,' Mr Chapman said. 'Why didn't you think of that before you went sticking your little willy into a schoolgirl?'

'Gerry!' Hannah was horrified.

'No, Hannah.' Mr Chapman had never been angrier. 'You make a mistake and so you think you can have an abortion just like that? Like you were buying a fucking CD in a record shop?'

'Gerry, stop it now!'

He didn't even want to think of the irony of it. An obstetrician who couldn't teach his own son the basics of birth control! And now a young girl's whole life ruined. Children, bearing and rearing children. It was obscene. Mr Chapman felt as responsible as if he'd impregnated the girl himself.

Killian was looking at the floor, as though waiting for Mr Chapman to tell him that he was going to indefinitely suspend his pocket money. What was the point in talking to him about courage and responsibility and the value of human life?

'This is your mess, Killian,' was all he said. 'I wash my hands of it.'

It wasn't that easy. Andrea, it transpired, was the daughter of Cork Councillor Henry Maher. Councillor

Maher rang Mr Chapman later that night and left him in no doubt about his feelings on the matter. Andrea was sitting her Leaving Certificate next year, and she hoped to go on to veterinary college, and what was Mr Chapman going to do about *that*?

'It isn't a decision for us to make,' Mr Chapman said strongly.

'Bollocks it isn't,' Henry Maher said. 'She only turned sixteen a week ago. You *are* aware of the law on statutory rape?'

There was a meeting of the clans scheduled for Thursday evening. The outcome was inevitable.

And now there were more problems with Cork. They had just taken receipt of an extremely expensive piece of equipment for the paediatric intensive care unit, afforded by the cost-cutting measures of closing Martha's. Wonderful, except that nobody was trained in the use of the damned thing. It was sitting there in its packaging while staff they couldn't afford to lose went off to find out how it worked. It looked like his fault, of course.

The pickets were out in force outside Martha's, forcing him to slow to five miles an hour. Not that anybody dared to stick a placard against his front window. They contented themselves with stony glances, as though the hospital closure had been entirely his decision.

And there was Emily Collins going around gathering signatures for a petition. His one and only patient in Martha's. That had raised a few sniggers in the staff canteen.

Let them keep Martha's. He didn't bloody want it.

Full of self-pity, he marched from his car and inside.

Emily had her scan at five past two.

'Oh, look! A hand!' she said. She couldn't help herself counting the fingers, and was grateful that her baby had the correct number, plus the requisite thumb.

Mr Chapman saw her doing this. 'Obviously the baby is so big now that you'll only see bits and pieces of it on the scan,' he murmured, lest she accuse him of mislaying most of her baby. He had gone over her file and discovered she was a solicitor. Of all things.

'And the nose!' Emily marvelled. It was very cute and button-like, at least as far as she could tell. The picture was fuzzy and close-up.

She turned her head. 'Conor – why don't you come over and have a look?'

But Conor was no longer hanging back there by the wall. He was right behind Emily, looking at the scan. Emily found herself a bit taken aback that he had not waited for her permission.

'I take it you don't want to know the sex?' Mr Chapman enquired.

Emily was a bit torn. Part of her would love to know. She felt very strongly recently that it was a girl, even though they'd bought all yellow Babygros in case she was wrong. But she wasn't. A mother knew these things.

'I don't want to know,' Conor said quite definitely.

'I suppose not,' Emily said.

'Best to keep it a surprise,' Mr Chapman agreed, manoeuvring carefully over Emily's greased belly. It would be just his luck to inadvertently reveal the baby's genitals. It was a boy in any case.

Now he was concentrating on the placenta. As far as he could see, everything was intact. Good. They would be able to leave the baby alone for a while longer.

He snapped off the monitor and checked his watch. If he left now he would make it back in time to talk to Marion Spencer in Cork. She would know all there was to know about adoption. He wanted to be able to offer as many options as he could to Henry Maher and his daughter Andrea. But he knew that he might as well be talking to the wall.

His disillusionment wrapped itself around him now familiarly.

'What do you think?'

'What? Oh, sorry.' There was Emily Collins, eager for information about her baby. He gave himself a little shake and put on his professional face.

'We're not looking at a section right now,' he declared. 'If there's more bleeding, I'll have to reconsider.' He busied himself with her chart, adding as an afterthought, 'The medical term for the bleeding is antepartum haemorrhage.'

'Yes, I know,' Emily said.

'Oh. Right.'

He had been prepared to leave it at that. That was all

most people wanted to know anyway. The minute you started to get into unpronounceable names, they backed off. But she was waiting.

'Well, you see, there are three reasons why there might be blood.'

'Yes,' Emily agreed again. 'But they're quite rare, aren't they? When the placenta starts peeling away and that kind of thing?'

Those nurses must have been filling her in. Half of them believed they knew more than the doctors. 'Ah, yes, but that's only one reason. The other reason is when the placenta is positioned low. Which yours isn't.'

'That's right,' Emily said encouragingly, and Mr Chapman had the bizarre feeling that he was a medical student again and that she was putting him through his paces.

'The third reason is that the blood mightn't be placental at all, but has come from a urinary tract infection. Which you don't have.' He went on fast before she could get her spoke in again. 'So I'm inclined to think it's none of these things, and that in fact it was simply the loss of the mucus plug that often happens after the thirty-sixth week and which is perfectly normal.'

'That's what I thought,' Emily said with relief. When Conor had brought in her clean clothes, she'd had him bring all the medical books in too and had read them cover to cover, even the boring technical bits. And it was very interesting really, all that was happening to her body. She felt much less afraid now that she knew exactly what to expect. She wished she had read much more after the miscarriage. It would have helped to know that there were medical explanations, and she would have felt less like it was all her own fault.

'Anything else you'd like to know?' Mr Chapman asked warily.

'No, no, that's fine, thanks.'

He was relieved. Some of these people read so much that they became self-styled experts in their own condition. Not that Mr Chapman was against information. He was just against too much information in the hands of lay people.

He put away his bifocals. 'So we'll leave the baby where he is,' Damn. 'Or *she*, of course. I always call babies him.' Shit. Now he was a sexist. He cleared his throat loudly. 'We'll be moving you to Cork at some point today or tomorrow.'

Best to have Emily Collins where he could see her, for a number of reasons.

'Oh,' Emily said. For some reason she thought that Cork would never happen. She felt safe here in Martha's. She knew all the staff. She trusted them.

'Martha's is closing on Monday week anyway,' Mr Chapman said crisply. He shot her a look to let her know that he was on to her and her petitions.

'Will you be there for the caesarean?' Conor finally spoke and Mr Chapman jumped. He'd forgotten all about the husband. Jesus, was he a solicitor too?

'I never said there would definitely be a section,' Mr

Chapman said quickly. 'It's just a possibility. There is no reason why this shouldn't be a natural birth.'

'The delivery then, whatever. Will you be there?'

Mr Chapman was neither contractually nor legally obliged to be there for Emily Collins' labour, even though she was paying him as a private patient. Most times he did attend the labour of his private patients, of course, but there were some instances where he could not. If he were sick, for example; if he were delivering another baby; if he had family circumstances or if he were on holiday. There was any number of reasons why he did not attend births.

But he knew that if Emily Collins were to go into labour at four o'clock in the morning on the top of a mountain, he would feel obliged to be there.

'Yes,' he said heavily.

Emily and Conor did not go back to Brenda's Ward. Instead, Emily led the way to the visitors' room. She switched on lights and the heater, and closed the door. She wished now that she had not been so excited and vocal during the scan. She felt as though she had given something away. She resented him again, for robbing her of some of the joy of their baby.

Choosing a seat was a minefield. If she sat opposite, it would look like she was going to attack him. Side-by-side was out. In the end she chose a chair at a right angle to him, with a large, shabby armchair between them as a buffer.

She resisted the urge to fill the silence with words. It

was such an effort that she had a pain in her throat.

'So, Cork today,' Conor said, as a fairly harmless opener.

'Yes,' she agreed. 'I need the baby's bag. And my own bag.'

'Of course.' He nodded vigorously. 'I'll bring them in straightaway.'

'Tomorrow or the next day will do. If you want to come and see me in Cork.' She didn't want to encourage a flood of visits until they knew where they stood.

'If that's what you want.'

He didn't go on any more about practicalities. Instead he looked at her directly.

'How have you been?'

'All right, I suppose.'

Conor himself didn't look too rough at all, she suddenly noted. Not thinner or older or paler. In fact, he looked a bit too healthy and bright-eyed for someone who should have been sitting at home applying a rod to his own back. His fingers were tapping his knees in some silent tune, and she felt obliged to say, 'How's the job search going?'

'Oh, I've got some weekend work in Baccaro's.' Baccaro's was a restaurant two streets away from St Martha's. It was a very upmarket restaurant, but still a restaurant, where his music would compete for attention with *penne napoletana*. He must hate it. She found that she didn't feel too sorry for him.

He stopped tapping his fingers on his knee. It was a

nervous thing, she realised. 'Emily, I wish I'd never done what I did. It was awful and I'm truly sorry.'

She said nothing.

'But I can't keep saying sorry.'

'You've hardly said it at all,' she pointed out. 'Twice, actually.'

'Is that all?' He seemed genuinely puzzled. 'I keep having these conversations with myself, you see. Well, with you. Well, not *actually* with you, because you're in here . . .'

'I know.' She'd had many imaginary conversations too. Most of them had been blue.

He looked at her. 'Do you think there's any way we can move on?'

'We haven't discussed the affair yet, Conor.'

He seemed a bit puzzled. 'What do you want to know?'

'I don't know . . . why you did it, I suppose.'

'Emily, it was the most stupid thing I've ever done in my life. I was a fool. That's the only excuse I can give you.' He seemed to think that this was a satisfactory response.

'Come on. Surely there was more to it than that, Conor?'

'Look, do we really need to go backwards here? It's history.'

He was making her feel unreasonable. But she persisted anyway. 'I really feel I need to know what happened.'

He shrugged. 'We were going through a rough patch. You and me. I gave into temptation. It was stupid. Simple as that.'

She saw that she was not going to get anywhere. Perhaps he hadn't figured it out for himself yet.

'I want to put all that stuff behind us and make a fresh start here, Emily.' At least he'd declared his intentions. 'What do you say?'

She looked at her slippers. The bunny ears were sagging sadly from all the wear and tear.

'I don't know. I feel now that I wasn't getting what I wanted from us. I wasn't happy, Conor.' She felt she'd hurt him more with this statement than she'd been hurt by the affair. It wasn't intended for that purpose.

'Well, at least you're being honest,' he said, after clearing his throat.

'We have to be, Conor.'

'It's the talking thing, isn't it,' he said. 'I can go to lessons, you know.'

She realised that he was having a little joke, and was amazed at his audacity. Then she found herself smiling. His dry humour had always appealed to her. She didn't go so far as to joke back, though.

'We don't seem to connect any more,' she said. 'Not really.'

A small silence followed this. Conor eventually looked up.

'We did once.'

'I suppose we did. But everybody makes the effort when they're dating.'

'The whole thing didn't collapse the moment we walked up the aisle,' he said.

'Well, no, of course it didn't. It was more like a dry rot.'

'It was the miscarriage, Emily.'

'No, it was earlier than that.'

He seemed quite annoyed. 'You can't negate our whole past because I had an affair.'

'I'm not negating it.'

'You are. You make it sound like you were suffering in silence for years.'

'Conor!'

'What, can I not have an opinion because I'm the one who had the affair? And martyred you even more?'

Emily was furious. 'I am not a martyr!'

'If you were so unhappy, why didn't you say something?' Conor was red in the face now. She couldn't remember ever seeing him like that. 'Why are you telling me now that you were unhappy, making me feel like a fool?'

He felt like a fool? Emily was so angry that she could hardly speak.

'I didn't know I was unhappy!'

'What do you mean, you didn't *know*?'

She was momentarily blind-sided. 'I *did* know, I . . .'

'But you just didn't want to say anything about it? You expect me to understand your unhappiness by osmosis?'

This was shockingly unfair. 'You're my husband! If you'd bothered to open your eyes every once in a while, you might have seen!'

'No, Emily,' he blurted. 'Take some responsibility for once in your life.'

'*What*?' She stared at him, round-eyed. 'I'm sick of taking responsibility! I take responsibility for every bloody thing that ever happens within a ten-mile radius of me!'

'But not for your own happiness! You blame me instead!'

She stood up and left. Just like that. She slammed the door behind her – she, who had never slammed a door in her life.

Her slippers slapped loudly and violently against the polished floors of Martha's. She didn't ever want to see him again, ever ever ever! Who was he to sit there and dissect her, to batter her already ailing self-esteem? But that was typical of men who had affairs, wasn't it? To blame the wife. 'Oh, the pressure she put me under! Couldn't keep that one happy. I might as well go off and shag someone else. Someone easier.' He could talk about responsibility? He couldn't even take responsibility for his own actions!

She slowed down. She had to: she was out of breath. The baby's weight pressed heavily down on her, dragging her, and she wished fiercely that all of this was over.

'You're looking well,' Neasa said.

'You're not. Sorry, sorry, sorry. I just meant you look tired.'

'Oh.' Neasa wasn't a bit pleased. She and Gary hadn't even had sex last night. She watched as Emily turned over in the bed.

'God, you're huge now,' she observed. She might look tired, but she would never let herself get into *that* state. 'Mind you, I've seen your ankles worse.'

Emily seemed to be looking at some point over Neasa's head. She wasn't herself, Neasa knew.

'Has someone been saying bad things to you?' she enquired suspiciously. That Conor yoke had been in. Neasa knew, because she'd seen his car in the car park. Since this whole thing began, Neasa had only met him once. They'd run into each other in the chemist's, where Neasa had been buying a bumper pack of condoms. Conor had been buying maternity pads. She had contented herself with a 'Ha!' before walking out.

'No, no,' Emily said.

Things had been a bit tense since Neasa had accused Emily of letting Conor walk all over her. Neasa had regretted her words afterwards. She'd meant them, of course, but that didn't mean she couldn't regret them.

'How's Gary?' Emily enquired, not giving a thing away.

'Oh, great! Fine. Not a bother.' Two could play at that game.

'What's wrong, Neasa.'

'There's nothing wrong. Oh, how do you always know when something is wrong!'

'Except in my own case,' Emily pointed out.

'That's true,' Neasa said. Her lower lip quivered. 'It's horrible! It's not that Gary and I aren't in love – we are. But somehow it's gone a bit funny and forced.'

Emily listened sympathetically. She'd been down this road many times before with Neasa.

'Has he done something?' she asked, bracing herself. Still, nothing could be worse than the cross-dresser.

'That's the whole point – he hasn't. He's being as good as gold. He even came back from the pub at lunchtime after one pint. One pint! He said it was because he missed me.'

'So what's the problem?'

'I don't know!' Neasa wailed.

Emily sort of did, by looking at Neasa's hair. It was in an elaborate French plait. It looked terrifically sexy and must have taken her a good hour this morning to do. This was on top of the immaculate make-up job, the buffed nails, the polished shoes and the matching underwear. Neasa was the only woman Emily knew whose bra and knickers always matched. Things must be bad if she was resorting to French plaits.

'Maybe you need to relax a bit more with each other,' she suggested.

Neasa thought this was a bit rich coming from someone whose husband had recently strayed. There was relaxing, and there was letting things go to the dogs altogether.

'I refuse to let romance die,' she declared proudly.

'Indeed, and we could all take lessons from that,' Emily said. 'But maybe you're afraid of looking past that in case . . .' Well, in case she discovered that Gary was horrible. 'In case you mightn't be all that suited.'

Neasa sat up straighter. 'We are. He's exactly what I want in a man.'

Not 'I love him', or 'I'd die without him'.

'I don't want to state the obvious, Neasa, but none of them are perfect. Neither are any of us.'

'Speak for yourself.' She sighed deeply. 'And now there's this dinner thing on Friday.'

'Oh, yes.' Once upon a time, Emily would have gnashed her teeth in anguish at the thought of Gary O'Reilly sitting at the partners' dinner when it should have been her. Now she just felt sorry for him.

'Gary's afraid that if he doesn't produce someone, they'll think he's gay. He'd be very upset.'

Emily imagined that gay people would be more upset.

'Why don't you want to go?'

'My private life is my own.' Well, it was. She didn't understand why Gary had such a bee in his bonnet about making it 'official'. It was like some kind of rite of passage for him. The car, the two mortgages, the partnership, the public girlfriend.

Which was ridiculous, Neasa assured herself. Gary loved her for herself, just as she loved him for himself. She supposed she would have to go. Maybe Gary would be less tense if they were out in the open.

Emily winced and clutched her belly.

'Jesus Christ!' Neasa stood, flapping. 'Will I call a nurse?'

'No, no, it's just a preparatory contraction. There. It's gone now.'

How could Emily be so calm? When a big lump of a baby was going to force its way out through a very small place in the near future?

'Are you not nervous at all?'

'Yes.'

'Take whatever they'll give you,' Neasa advised.

'It's not so much about the labour.' Emily looked at her. 'I don't think I'm going to be a very good mother.'

'Oh, Emily.'

'No, I'm not just saying it.'

'But they sleep all the time,' Neasa said reassuringly. 'And then you just have to feed them and change their nappies occasionally. It's a piece of cake.'

Emily didn't look convinced.

'I'll even help,' Neasa offered generously. Just so long as she wasn't left alone with it. She wouldn't know what to do if it started crying or something.

'I just don't feel ready,' Emily said.

Neasa resisted the urge to point out that it was a bit late in the day for that.

'I feel like the baby's going to look at me and expect me to be brilliant and capable and know everything and I don't know *anything*.'

'Um, yes, I can see how you might feel that way,' Neasa said, who didn't. 'But the baby will love you anyway, Emily.'

'Why?'

'Why? Because you're its mother! It won't be able to help loving you, even if you're a totally crap mother!'

'And that's supposed to be good enough?'

Neasa was raging. That Conor again! Imagine having an affair on Emily, and then turning around and putting notions in her head that she was going to be a terrible mother!

'Emily, you are going to be fine. Trust me. You have loads and loads to give a baby.'

'We'll see,' Emily said.

Neasa clearly didn't understand. Emily wasn't sure she did either. But she had this sudden fear that she was not yet a grown-up. Not really. How could she be entrusted with a helpless infant when she wasn't a proper adult herself?

She felt that Conor, this afternoon, had inadvertently shone a spotlight into her soul and illuminated some nasty, mould-covered part of her that had been left festering for years. This mouldy thing, far from lying forgotten and benign, had actually been very busy undermining all her efforts, and laughing in the face of her hard work. It played jokes on her when it came to partnerships and promotions, and would occasionally tease her when she lay in bed at night wondering why things weren't as great as they looked on the surface.

She had thought it was merely her capacity to accept. It was much more sinister than that. It was putting her own needs last. And it had spread its tentacles into every single aspect of her life, blighting it.

Her stomach churned and jarred, mixing with her heartburn, and she burped.

'Excuse me.'

She felt a bit better now.

'That's disgusting,' Neasa said.

'One of the joys of being pregnant,' Emily said. 'You'll know all about it some day.'

'I will in my swiss. Oh, here,' she said, rummaging in her bag and taking out the Health Board letter. 'This came today. I didn't know you were writing to Health Boards.' This was said a bit accusingly.

'Yes, well, I just sent it in. No point in it lying around here.'

The letter thanked Emily for her concern, assured her that it was aware of the community's upset, but regretfully informed her that there was no other course of action open to them at this time.

'They don't even mention the petition,' Emily said.

'Actually, they do. Up there under "subject matter",' Neasa pointed out helpfully. 'They've probably filed it away in a deep dark drawer.' She might as well have added, 'Under Earnest but Useless Efforts'.

She tossed the letter into the bin by Emily's bed as though it were not worth the paper it was written on. The action annoyed Emily.

'At least I tried.'

'Well, yes, of course you did,' Neasa said, with no great conviction.

'What do you expect me to do? Go out there in my dressing gown and march up and down with the nurses?'

'I don't know what you're getting all defensive for,' Neasa huffed. 'You've done your bit. Leave it at that. I would.'

'You wouldn't have bothered doing a petition in the first place,' Emily pointed out.

'Of course I wouldn't. Those kinds of things never get results,' Neasa said, inadvertently annoying Emily more. Emily knew now that Neasa had not really been surprised that Emily had been passed over for the partnership at work. She'd been outraged all right, but only because Emily was her friend, not because she'd believed there had been a miscarriage of justice.

Emily felt very small and insignificant and powerless now. She did not particularly like herself.

'You know, Neasa, I'm tired. I might go for a bit of a sleep.'

'Me too. Oh, not here. I'm going home. I've a bit of a head on me. They can take half a day's holiday off me if they want.'

'Things that bad at the office?'

'Worse. Everybody's working so hard, there's no crack at all,' Neasa complained. And she had promised Gary a romantic dinner tonight. She would have to wax and shave everything, paint her nails and touch up her false tan. She sighed. Men had it so easy.

Nurse Christine Clarke came in as Emily was nodding off. She was covering for the day girls who were marching outside, and hadn't slept in thirty-six hours. Her blonde curls drooped sadly.

'Emily, are you not packed?'

'What?'

'The ambulance is waiting to take you to Cork. I thought somebody would have told you.'

'No,' Emily said, sighing as she sat up.

'They don't actually have a bed for you in an antenatal ward,' Christine said apologetically. 'But you'll be moved at the first opportunity.'

'And where exactly are they putting me in the meantime?'

'I don't know. You'll have to check when you get down there. Probably in a general ward or something. You don't mind, do you?'

It was the last straw. The very final straw, in fact.

'Yes, I do bloody mind!' she exploded. 'I'm a pregnant woman. I'm not going to be stashed in a corridor while they wait for someone to die before a bed becomes free!'

Christine burst into tears, her fatigue getting the better of her.

'I'm sorry,' Emily said miserably.

Christine turned and left, still sobbing. Emily buried

her head in her hands. The nurses here were so kind and nice; they didn't deserve to be shouted at. Well, Christine was a bit of a tit, but it wasn't her fault Cork had no beds free in the antenatal wards. Neasa always said that it was a sign of a very weak person when they were nasty to people who couldn't be nasty back. Not that that had ever stopped her.

Vera Mooney arrived in, in her civvies. Her nose was pink from walking up and down outside.

Emily sank down further into her dressing gown. 'Vera, I'm very sorry – is Christine all right?'

'Oh, fine. What's the problem? You don't want to go to a general ward?'

It seemed very small and mean now, and Emily felt like she was disrupting everybody's plans. But she was going to stick to her guns this time.

'I'd just rather not be moved around all the time, that's all,' she said apologetically. 'Especially in a strange place.'

'Quite right too,' Vera said. 'So will I send Liam and Joe away?'

It *would* be Liam and Joe. They were probably eating egg sandwiches and bitching about her right now.

'It's up to you, Emily. I'm sure they'll have an appropriate bed free tomorrow.'

Emily was relieved. A day wouldn't make any difference to anybody, would it?

'I'll wait if that's okay,' she decided.

Vera went and Emily snuggled down in her safe,

familiar bed and slept for four hours solid.

Conor was still sitting in the visitors' room. He saw little touches here and there that had Emily written all over them: fresh flowers in a vase, for example, left behind by some patient. The out-dated and crumpled magazines on the three-legged coffee table were arranged attractively, and two mismatched cushions had found their way onto the threadbare chairs. Give her another couple of weeks and she'd have repainted the entire hospital in a nice warm peach and added dado rails.

The house was wilting without her. Oh, everything was clean and tidy – he made sure of that. But the place had a stale, unlived-in feeling, like the heart of it was missing. Even the dogs – his dogs – looked at him accusingly, wondering how he had managed to mislay Emily. They'd been lucky to get any dinner at all that day.

He could not believe he had lost control like that, and said all those things. He could not remember the last time he had raised his voice. It always seemed to him such a weak thing to do, to go spilling feelings and emotions, giving away some percentage and diminishing your own position in the process.

It had been the shock of the discovery that she had never really been happy. Well, maybe not never. But from early on, much earlier than the miscarriage which he'd thought was the root of all their problems.

Or liked to think, anyway. It was such a neat thing to pin it all on, like those disappointed looks in the years before had counted for nothing. But nobody likes to admit that their deepest, unspoken fears were true all along – that really, he wasn't enough for her and never had been.

He thought again about that big handsome man at the wedding. He remembered his laugh, a booming, merry noise that had rang out across the bar. He remembered the look on Emily's face as she had watched the man.

He remembered also the look on Pauline's face when, meeting her for the first time as Emily's new boyfriend, Conor had tried to explain that he was a musician. Further intense questioning had forced him to admit that he was a pianist, to be precise. It seemed futile to explain to her that his real interest lay in the area of composition. He might as well have told her that he hoped to land on the moon.

Emily had assured him afterwards that Pauline's reaction didn't matter to her. And Conor had thought that it didn't matter to him either, but he remembered his sense of pleasure, of victory, the day he won a position with the orchestra. Emily was not now engaged to some hippy musician, but to a concert pianist. Take that, Pauline. Emily had been pleased too. Pleased and proud, and he had basked in it.

He promised himself back then that he would not lose sight of his ambition; that he would continue to write his own music. And he did, initially. But gradually his time and belief was whittled away until he stopped altogether. And he didn't want to do anything to rock the boat. He didn't want to do a single thing that might put Emily off him.

He wondered now whether he had tried too hard at the beginning. Had she got the whiff of a desperate soul, a man so in need of her that he would do anything to keep her? And he had thought he'd masked his feelings so well behind his veneer of cool reserve.

And he was still doing it to this day. He was much better at it now, of course, after years of practice. You'd be hard pushed to know whether a heart was beating at all underneath the urbane exterior. And he got away with this kind of behaviour, this kind of withdrawal, because he could. Emily's niggling and nagging and disappointed looks were quite easy to ignore. She wasn't one to push herself forward, and he had taken advantage of that. Preyed on it, even. All that shit she took from Crawley & Co. The liberties Liz and Pious Pauline took. Emily swallowed it all because she was good and kind and she always thought of others before herself. It had been easy to offer her less than the best.

Conor had never thought of himself as innately selfish but realised with a shock that he was sounding perilously like it.

And now there was a baby on the way. It would not be so easy to offer it less than the best. As the time grew closer and closer when he would hold his baby daughter or son in his arms, Conor felt more panicked. He had up to now vaguely thought that Emily would cope for both of them. She was so warm and so giving; she would be able to do it for him too, wouldn't she?

But the grim reality of visitation weekends was rearing its head. Conor might find himself quite alone with a baby, a child. And no Emily to help him, except to say to the child when she collected it on a Sunday night, 'Don't mind your Da. He loves you really. He's just not great at showing it.'

Nurse Christine Clarke went out onto the picket-line in a foul mood. To make matters worse, it was raining and she had no umbrella. Her mascara streaked down her cheeks sadly. Nobody bothered to tell her.

'That high and mighty cow won't go,' she said venomously to Karen.

'What high and mighty cow?'

'Emily Collins. Gave me loads of grief just because there was no bed free in antenatal in Cork. Refuses to go until they find her a proper bed.'

How Christine wished that St Martha's would close and be bloody done with it! She was going on two weeks' holiday to Ibiza before she started in Limerick, and had bought several little string bikinis in anticipation. She fully intended to give nurses an even worse reputation than they already had.

'Those private patients, they think the health service belongs to them.' Karen said in commiseration. 'Here,

Darren, did you hear that Emily Collins is refusing to go to Cork?'

Darren told Alice from Jude's Ward. He got a bit mixed up about the bed situation.

'What, she wants to bring her own bed with her?' Alice asked. This was a new one.

Darren wasn't really sure, but he didn't let on. Some of the girls could act very superior, like he wasn't a proper nurse just because he was a man. Oh, the sexist stories *he* could tell. 'It's nothing to do with beds,' he said loftily. 'She just won't go.'

When Alice told Bernie, she didn't mention anything about beds.

'She was behind that petition, you know,' Bernie said, excited. 'She must be upping the anti.'

Alice was still a bit doubtful. 'You'd never think it to look at her.'

'Isn't she Liz Clancy's sister?'

'*What*?' Alice hadn't known this.

'Oh yes,' Bernie said grimly. 'Hard as nails, that lot. I wouldn't mess with any of them.'

Tanya from Casualty had been biding her time. 'She's a solicitor too. Did you know that?'

'What?' The girls didn't.

'Crawley Dunne & O'Reilly. They'd buy and sell your mother. She'd know all the tricks.'

Bernie was nearly tearful. 'Isn't she great? We always said this campaign would go nowhere until the patients got off their arses and did something.'

The bed issue was by now totally forgotten, and Christine Clarke, the only one who knew exactly what had happened, left the picket-lines and went home. Vera Mooney had already gone ages.

'What has the board of management said?' Geraldine from catering wondered.

It transpired that they didn't know and a great wave of excitement swept through the picket-lines.

'This'll rock the boat,' Alice declared, delighted, as someone went off to make an anonymous call to the local radio station.

Emily heard them before she saw them.

'*Robbie!* Where did you get that syringe? Give it to me this *instant*.'

In they trooped, Tommy, Robbie, Mikey and Bobby, with Liz bringing up the rear in case one of them tried to escape. Willy was strapped to Liz's front as usual. He didn't seem to have grown or progressed at all in a month and Emily wondered whether that sling might be constricting him.

'Hi, Emily.'

'Hello,' Emily said. She felt better after her sleep.

'Not disturbing you or anything?'

'Not really,' Emily said, watching as her beans on toast went cold. 'Hi, boys!'

They stood in a semicircle at the bottom of her bed and looked at her with a mixture of fascination and horror.

'Are you going to die?' Bobby eventually asked.

'Bobby! Honestly, Emily, I don't know where he gets these things.'

'It's all right, Liz.' Emily remembered asking her mother about birds and snake skins, and she gave Bobby a special smile.

'I'm not going to die, Bobby.'

'Oh.' He looked very disappointed and turned his attention to her locker instead. 'Can I have a grape?'

'Ah, yes, of course you can.'

The rest of them took this as their cue, and descended on her locker like a swarm of locusts. Emily watched as grapes, chocolates and bottles of 7UP were devoured at speed.

'Those grapes, they have seeds in them,' she warned Liz.

'It'd take more than a few seeds to kill them,' Liz said rather gloomily. 'Boys! Take them over to the table.' She sat in the chair by Emily's bed. She didn't sigh today. 'I've tried to explain to them that you're having a baby. Poor Mikey and Bobby are too young, of course. But Tommy! Do you know what he said to me, Emily?'

.'What did he say to you.'

'He said, I suppose Auntie Emily and Uncle Conor had sex then. Sex! He's six years old, Emily!'

Emily laughed. Well, it *was* funny, a little bit. But Liz was annoyed that she wasn't taking it seriously. She puffed up further. 'And do you know what Myra Byrne heard some lads talking about in the school yard last week?'

'What?'

'Blow-jobs!' Liz hissed. 'She didn't know what they were on about at first – they were just talking about BJs. BJs, Emily! But she put two and two together. She's very sharp, is Myra.'

Indeed. She'd given a few of them in her time, according to local lore.

'I'm going in to talk to Mr Harrington. First thing tomorrow,' Liz declared. 'I'm not having that kind of filth coming into my house.'

'They're going to pick it up anyway, Liz. You can't really stop them.'

'Quite the expert now,' Liz said a bit loftily.

Emily threw her eyes to heaven. 'No, I'm not an expert, but I'm going to have to contend with the same thing myself in a couple of years' time, and I'm entitled to an opinion, aren't I?'

'Well, yes, of course you are,' Liz conceded. 'So, how are you?'

'All right. They're trying to find a bed for me in Cork.'

'Oh, that place is a right mess,' Liz said, as though she'd just come from there herself. 'Can't cope with the amalgamation at all, for all their guff. Poor old Larry Power was sitting in Casualty for three hours yesterday.'

That was pretty par for the course in any hospital, Emily thought. The noise level from the other side of the room dropped dramatically. The boys had put the television on and had found a cartoon.

'How are things at home?' Emily asked.

'Grand, why wouldn't they be?' Liz said.

'Well, you know – Eamon, the bank situation.'

'I don't know why you have to keep bringing that up, Emily.'

'What? I wasn't—'

'We're sorting it out,' Liz announced.

'Good,' Emily said tightly.

'He's made an appointment to go in and see the bank manager and the accountant and work out a system of repayments.' She looked at Emily. 'If you could believe a word out of the mouths of any of them.'

So, she knew about the affair. Emily was only surprised that word hadn't got around sooner. Liz shook her head vigorously from side to side now. 'I don't know. I just don't know.'

'Neither do I,' Emily agreed.

'At least it wasn't with some local one,' Liz said in commiseration. 'That was the only good thing about Eamon's mess – he doesn't owe money to anybody in the town. At least we know there'll be no gossip about either of them on the church steps on Sundays.'

Eamon and Conor had finally found common ground, unbeknownst to themselves.

And so had Emily and Liz, sitting there counting their blessings and telling each other that it could have been worse.

'I don't really want to talk about it, Liz,' Emily said.

Liz was hurt. And she after confiding in Emily and all! But that was typical of Emily. She'd encourage you to go on about yourself, and then tell you nothing at all about her own situation. She could be very selfish that way.

'Mammy's heard. She's worried,' she said, a bit superior. Liz had kept her own problems within the four walls of her house, and not bothered Mammy with them.

'Yes, well, Mammy's not married to him', Emily said and she didn't care if she sounded heartless.

'Anyway, I told her to stop dropping around shepherd's pies to that fellow.'

'Conor,' Emily said in a voice that invited no further comment on the subject.

The boys were bored with the television now and were jumping up and down on the two spare beds. Bobby was making a tent with the sheets and pillows. Vera would go mad.

'You did great work on that petition,' Liz said eventually.

'It wasn't too hard. People were in and out of here all the time.'

'Oh, can't you just take a compliment, Emily?' Liz said irritably.

'You're absolutely right,' Emily said. 'We don't pat ourselves on the back enough, you and me. We should blow our own trumpets every now and again.'

261

'I suppose.' Liz looked doubtful at this.

'No, really, we're brilliant.'

Liz threw back her head and laughed. She looked younger. 'I wouldn't go that far, Emily.'

'I would. Why not?' Emily smiled too.

'Despite the odds,' Liz added.

'Despite terrible odds. We should look at ourselves in the mirror every morning, like they tell you to do in those self-help books, and tell ourselves that we're magnificent.'

'Eamon would think I was mad if he found me talking to mirrors.'

'Eamon hasn't a leg to stand on.'

The nice moment was broken by a wail from the corner. Tommy was suffocating Bobby with a pillow.

Liz sighed and stood. 'I don't suppose I'll see you again. Not if you're down in Cork. I could try . . .'

'No, really, Liz. Maybe when I have the baby.'

Liz fidgeted with her bag. 'If you want to come and stay in our house when you get out, you're welcome – if we still have a house, that is. You could have Tommy's room. He can sleep in with Bobby and Mikey. It wouldn't be the quietest place on earth, but just until things settle for you . . .'

'That's very good of you, Liz. I'll keep it in mind.' Emily was touched. She wouldn't in her wildest dreams go and stay with Liz, but that wasn't the point.

'Right, well, good luck with everything.' Liz rounded the boys up with a bellow, and went off.

Emily thought about getting out of bed and packing her things for tomorrow. But the effort was too great, and she was having those pains again. Her breasts were also leaking; her pyjamas felt damp. She'd never heard of that happening to anyone she knew and she was mildly embarrassed. But her books informed her that it was perfectly normal.

At least something was. She felt that she and Conor were at a crossroads, and that things could go either way now. And it wasn't just on her part, either. She had not seen him like that before, like he had lost control. It was that stranger in him again. What had he been like with Ffion Rivera? Had he shown her hidden depths that he had withheld from Emily? Emily felt robbed, cheated.

Too much had happened for them to go on in any previous capacity. They would have to rebuild from the ground up.

Emily wondered now whether it was really possible to change. For *anybody* to truly change. All the magazine articles and self-help books assured you that it was. A simple quiz first to diagnose how hopeless you really were, then ten revelatory tips which could be applied in any order, followed by a paragraph on how great you should feel now that you were actually somebody else.

But what about things that were so ingrained, that underpin your entire life, things that form the essence of yourself? Even if you did manage to change those parts of yourself, was it a constant battle to maintain it?

Would you live your life as though it were one long, miserable calorie-controlled diet?

And if it were hard enough for one person to change, how did two people in a flawed relationship change in perfect synchronisation? Especially if they didn't know what it was about them that the other person *wanted* changed? Would it require endless, heartbreaking effort? Would the relationship become not one of spontaneity and joy and love, but gruelling hard work?

People in so-called happy relationships were very fond of saying 'oh, you have to work at it', as though it were yet another chore to do at the end of a long, hard day. Emily did not live in never-never land like Neasa, but neither did she want to become one half of those tight-faced couples who were together for all they were worth, but would really be much happier on their own. Or possibly with a small dog.

Neither was she afraid of hard work. Indeed, she loved hard work, was too fond of it really, as though it were an end in itself. But not this time. She would not waste her precious energy unless her conviction was there. And that's what it came down to at the end of the day.

She wondered whether Conor was thinking these things right now. It was odd, the way they'd always had of thinking exactly the same thing at the same time. Emily used to laugh and think it meant some kind of spiritual bond. Now she was inclined to think it was just coincidence.

Maggie came in, pink-cheeked and breathless.

'Are you having an attack?' Emily asked warily. Maggie's asthma attacks always frightened the life out of Emily. All that wheezing and gulping, and Maggie's hands would claw at the air as though she were trying to gather it up. The attacks had become more frequent recently as Maggie's due date approached fast.

'No, no.'

'Pains, then?' Maggie had been having a lot of pains. Everyone expected her to have her baby any day now.

'The girls were telling me!' she said in a rush. 'About you not going to Cork!'

'Oh, yes.' Had they nothing better to be talking about?

'Well, I think it's great,' Maggie declared.

Emily wasn't sure why. 'I'm going in the morning, Maggie. They just haven't got an appropriate bed.'

'Oh, they're desperately trying to find one. That's what the girls said. They'd nearly chuck someone out onto the streets to get you a bed!' Maggie was triumphant.

'I don't want them to chuck anybody out onto the streets.' Jesus, hadn't she enough on her conscience?

'I've decided that I'm not going either,' Maggie declared.

Emily roused herself from her cosy cocoon of sheets and blankets. 'What are you on about?'

'Well, the more the merrier,' Maggie said. 'They won't be able to ignore a sit-in.'

Emily thought about this for a minute. Then she laughed. Maggie was a desperate eejit sometimes.

'What?' Maggie asked, understandably hurt. 'I know I'll probably go into labour any minute, but I could sit-in until then, couldn't I?'

'Maggie, I'm not starting a sit-in,' Emily explained patiently. 'I just didn't want to go to a general ward, that's all.'

'But it's on the radio and everything.'

'What?'

'On LKR fm. Everybody heard it.'

'Everybody' was the thousand or so citizens who tuned into LKR fm on a regular basis. Emily imagined Conor listening to this, slack-jawed, and she laughed again.

'They didn't actually name you,' Maggie said stiffly.

Emily found she was a bit disappointed. Anyway, Conor didn't listen to LKR fm. He was an RTE 1 man, with occasional forays into the classical stations.

Maggie was looking at Emily as though Emily held her future in her hands.

'You do a sit-in if you want, Maggie.'

'I can't.'

'You can. You obviously feel strongly about it.'

'I thought you did too.'

'Well, I do . . . look, I've kind of made a promise to myself, Maggie. I'm not taking on other people's problems any more.'

Spoken aloud, this didn't sound half as noble as it did

in her own head. Maggie obviously thought so too.

'That's very convenient,' she said.

Emily felt annoyed again, like people were constantly pricking her with little needles.

'I did the petition,' she said.

'This is just a bigger petition,' Maggie reasoned.

'It's not. This is different. It's taking on something we know nothing about,' Emily argued fiercely.

'It's scary,' Maggie agreed.

'Aren't we scared enough? Aren't we about to have babies?' Emily pleaded. 'Haven't we pre-eclampsia and wheezy lungs?' Not to mention broken marriages.

'I can't do it without you,' Maggie said stubbornly.

Why was Maggie looking at her like she was some kind of leader? A hell-raiser, even? She giggled again.

'I don't know what you find so funny about all this,' Maggie said, miffed.

'You're right. It's not funny at all,' Emily said, sobering. 'Especially when they drag us kicking and screaming from our beds and cart us off in wheelbarrows.'

'They wouldn't do that,' Maggie said confidently. 'Think of the publicity!'

Maggie was speaking like one who had spent most of her life in the trenches.

'And what happens when we have our babies? Are we going to continue to sit in then?'

'Oh, Emily, don't be so negative!' Maggie almost stamped her foot in frustration.

'I'm being realistic. Now go away, Maggie.'

★ ★ ★

Neasa had spent most of the afternoon beautifying herself and preparing the romantic meal. She'd even cooked it this time, instead of opening a jar of Dolmio. She'd bought four bottles of good red wine and put so many candles in the living-room that there was a very real possibility of a house fire. Tonight would work, she resolved fiercely, and made a head start on the wine. Alcohol always added such a nice rosy glow to things.

Gary arrived in from work at half past seven. He'd been working later and later this past while, much to his chagrin.

'Hi, darling,' Neasa said, floating up to him on a cloud of Obsession.

'Those fucking pricks,' Gary raged, storming past her.

Neasa took a moment to regain her balance. 'What's happened now?'

'You'd know if you hadn't skived off this afternoon,' he said sourly.

Neasa decided to let this one pass.

He threw off his coat. 'You know the way we're nearly out of headed notepaper in the office?'

'Oh Gary,' she commiserated. 'Don't tell me they've put you in charge of stationery too?'

Gary's job these days seemed to be less about making sales and more about ordering paper clips and mending photocopiers. He'd even taken to making the coffee.

'Actually, yes,' he admitted. 'But it's not that. I was supposed to get my name on that headed notepaper,

268

Neasa! As a partner! They said they would change the name of the firm when I was promoted! They promised!'

Neasa told herself that he only sounded childish because he was upset.

'So what's the problem?'

'Well, my surname is O'Reilly, isn't it? They already have an Ewan O'Reilly!'

'Hmmm,' Neasa said. She could see their problem. Crawley Dunne O'Reilly & O'Reilly didn't have a great ring to it.

'I suggested that they put my name first,' Gary said. 'You know, O'Reilly Crawley Dunne & O'Reilly. But bloody Ewan didn't want my name first, said that I was the newcomer and so I should go last! So now *he* wants to go first!'

'So it would still be O'Reilly Crawley Dunne & O'Reilly?' Neasa asked carefully.

'Exactly! But this still wouldn't do him. Oh no!'

'How about Crawley Dunne & O'Reilly Times Two?' Neasa tried to coax him out of his black humour. He was unamused.

'Now Creepy suggests that we leave it the way it is, that we can both share the O'Reilly! I'd like to see *him* sharing his name! And that Daphne one sitting there muttering that they wouldn't have had this problem with Collins.'

Neasa was getting a headache. 'Why don't we have some food? It'll take your mind off it.'

It did not. All through Neasa's superb prawns with

feta and olives, Gary went through every possible permutation. He wrote various combinations down on a paper napkin while his wild fruit crumble went cold. It was like an elaborate pick and mix at the sweet section of the cinema, only minus the fun. Neasa knocked back red wine and watched silently.

Eventually he looked up. 'I have a solution.'

Thank Christ. 'What?'

'I'll have to change my name.'

He was joking, surely. But he was not.

'Gary, it's your *name*. Your identity. How can you change it?'

'Deed poll,' he said. 'Now, what would I call myself?'

Neasa watched as he took a fresh napkin and came up with all kinds of unlikely surnames for himself: Gray, Greer, Gilmartin, Gunne, Garland. Garland?

'I'd quite like it to start with a G. Alliteration and all that,' he told Neasa. 'But not something like Glitter, obviously. That would be silly.'

'Very,' Neasa said thinly, reaching for a fresh bottle of wine and taking it into the living-room. She would get very drunk tonight.

Gary was on her heels. 'Gary Gilmartin has a good ring to it, doesn't it?'

Yes, if he were a porn star. The scented candles dotted around the room gave off such a strong whiff that Neasa began to feel sick.

Gary finally realised that he might be banging on a bit. And Neasa was all dressed up too, he noted rather sadly. Suspenders and all, he could see the telltale signs under her clingy dress. Sex would be on the agenda later on so. 'Experimental' to boot, if some of the items he'd seen in the fridge were anything to go by. Once, just once, he would like to flake out in front of *Friends*. But she had already opened the bottle of wine.

He bit back a yawn. 'What would you like to talk about, darling? Childhood memories? Deepest insecurities? Hopes and expectations?'

'What would *you* like to talk about?' Neasa asked.

Gary wanted to talk about his new name some more, but this wasn't appropriate he knew. He was also rather worried about the way the radio in his BMW kept switching channels without warning. But this was too lightweight for the third bottle of wine.

Then there was the way Annabel's breasts always seemed to spill out over the top of her bra. Phil reckoned that her bras were deliberately a size too small. But this was yet something else that could not be shared with Neasa. He tried to think of a Deep and Meaningful topic of conversation but couldn't. Fuck it, he just wasn't a Deep and Meaningful type of guy!

Gary wondered when he could become himself with Neasa. Because *nobody* was themselves at the beginning of a relationship. They were always somebody else; mysterious, witty, sexy, and never suffered from flatulence or bad hair days. But with his other girlfriends, Gary had gradually relaxed into himself, and had been able to break wind again. There was no relaxing with

Neasa. It was all a terrible strain and he sometimes wondered whether she was worth it. But of course she was; she was the kind of woman who usually dumped Gary when she found out what he was really like.

She was a catch all right. The other lads in the office looked up to him because they all unofficially knew he was sleeping with her. She never slept with them, and wasn't likely to do so at any time in the future. She always looked terrific, and hadn't put on a single pound in all the time they'd known each other. Some of Gary's past girlfriends had let themselves go disgracefully once the first flush had passed. About the time he started to fart again, now that he thought about it.

Sex, he thought with a sigh, dragging himself to a sitting position on the couch. Sex would keep her happy.

My God, Neasa was thinking. Was it possible that they hadn't a single word to say to each other? How could this have happened? Even with the cross-dresser, the sexist, the chat-room junkie – all of them – she'd always had something to talk to them about right up until the horrible moment of revelation.

With Gary, there was no horrible moment of revelation. Just a slow, merciless disclosure of mildly offensive parts of himself. But nothing that Neasa could really put her finger on. Nothing that couldn't be overlooked in the name of *love*. She was being too perfectionist, she told herself fiercely, that had always been her problem. This time, she must not jump ship. She must rescue the situation. She threw back the last of her wine and turned to him rather desperately.

'Will we have sex? Mad, wild, brilliant sex?'

'I was about to suggest the same myself,' Gary said, opening her bra with one hand. Neasa had always found this extremely sexy. Now she wondered just how many bras he had practised on to become so good.

'I'll just move over . . .'

'No, no, I'm not that heavy, am I?'

'Not at all . . . there we go. Oops! Sorry, did that hurt a lot?'

'I'm fine, honestly. But if you'd take your hair out of my mouth . . .'

'Sure, sorry . . .'

The couch seemed far too small. But they pressed valiantly on anyway, ignoring the fact that there was a perfectly good king-size bed over their heads.

'Come get it, Tiger,' Neasa said huskily. This usually drove Gary wild.

'Miaow,' Gary said, sounding more like a puny kitten than a jungle animal.

Neasa decided to take the initiative, and jumped on him. She sashayed and squirmed and shimmied for all she was worth. It was quite some time before she realised that there was a problem.

'Um, I think I'm more tired than I thought,' Gary muttered.

'Of course, and all that wine doesn't help,' Neasa soothed. 'Do you know what's wrong?'

'What?' Gary asked, slightly alarmed.

'Over-use,' Neasa said, and they both laughed: a funny, forced laugh.

Gary was absolutely mortified. Him! Failing to perform! What the blazes was going on?

Cheeks hot, he struggled out from under Neasa and put the offending article firmly away. He could not look at her.

'You know, maybe I'll go home to my own place. Get a good night's sleep.'

'Not a bad idea,' Neasa said too readily.

Jesus Christ, she was thinking, did he not fancy her any more? Was she not being exciting and innovative enough? But how much more innovative could she get without it becoming illegal?

'Goodnight, sugar.'

'Goodnight, sweet pea.'

They must be using the last of Martha's budget on the heating, because Brenda's Ward was boiling that morning.

'Open a window, Maggie, would you?'

Maggie looked balefully over. 'Do it yourself, you bitch.'

She was sulking.

Emily sighed and threw back the covers. Her belly looked absolutely massive this morning; it was blocking out half the light. And the baby was thrashing about fiercely, making the entire thing lop from side to side violently. It was a struggle to keep her balance as she sat up. Now, how to get down from the bed. The floor looked very far away.

'Get Vera, would you?' she asked Maggie.

'Will not,' Maggie sang.

God, she was in a right old snit this morning. She was knitting with grey wool. A barbed wire fence, now that Emily looked closely. Maggie was such an amateur when it came to sit-ins. They'd cut through that in no time.

Emily tentatively reached down with one toe for the floor, but no joy. She would have to slide down farther. But still there was no floor. She peeked down, saw that the floor was a good hundred metres away, and screamed just before she tumbled off the bed and into the abyss.

'Rise and shine, girls.'

Emily woke sweating, her heart pounding crazily, to see Vera at the end of her bed with the pressure cuff.

'You'd better give me a minute,' she advised Vera. No sense in alerting the emergency caesarean team for nothing.

'Bad dream?' Vera asked sympathetically, making for Maggie instead.

'Nothing I haven't had before.'

But she'd never fallen off a bed until now. A crane, yes. Cliffs and mountains regularly. And she'd once fallen off the roof of the Department of Justice. That had been the night before her final law exams. All her classmates had fallen off the top of the same building, she had later learned; the pavement beneath had been littered with the corpses of nervous law students. It had been a routine fear of failure dream before a big event. The next one they could expect was before their first day at work, they'd reassured themselves. After that, the night before they signed for their first mortgage, and then when they got married, or divorced. Really, it was quite a convenient way of anticipating big events, somebody had argued. He'd wanted to be a barrister.

Emily's fear of failure dreams never quite worked that way. She would get one in the middle of a tedious, boring week, with nothing more stressful than Christmas on the horizon. Or sometimes after Liz or her mother had called around, or when Conor was more withdrawn than usual. But usually when nothing at all was happening and her life was on a steady plateau. When she was plodding along as usual, keeping her head down, and not offending anybody.

The would-be barrister would tell her that she was about to have a baby and her marriage was floundering, and it was a wonder she hadn't fallen off the bed twice.

Well, the baby was going to get out of her one way or the other, and it was a bit late to be worrying about her marriage failing, and what would he have to say to *that*?

But he had been a very intelligent young lad and Emily didn't discount his opinions entirely. What *if* those mid-week dreams had been a premonition? A kind of elbow in the ribs to wake up and look around her?

Or just to stop being afraid.

She was, she decided, going quite mad. Next she would be looking for black cats in the hospital corridors.

Maggie's blood pressure was up.

'Now, what's all this?' Vera said sternly. 'Have we been getting ourselves all riled up?'

'Yes,' Maggie said meekly.

'And you due any day,' Vera scolded her.

'Sorry.' And she looked over at Emily as though it were all her fault.

'I haven't done anything,' Emily clarified. This was quite true. She had absented herself from the ward last night, and any more talk of sit-ins. Nobody had bothered her in the visitors' room, not even her mother, who apparently had been in after hearing some nonsense on a local radio show.

Vera descended on Emily with the pressure cuff.

'That's the best I've seen it in weeks,' she said. 'Any more bleeding?'

'Not a single drop.'

'Mr Chapman will be delighted.' This was said rather tongue-in-cheek. Apparently when Mr Chapman had been told that Emily Collins hadn't arrived as scheduled, he had said some colourful things.

Vera finished making her notes. Maggie was looking avidly on. Vera reached out and smartly pulled the curtain around Emily's bed, shutting Maggie out.

'I believe there's some misunderstanding about Cork,' she said with admirable diplomacy. 'Some of the girls think that there's a sit-in.'

'Apparently so,' Emily agreed. 'Maggie too.'

'Yes, well, Maggie.' Vera left it at that. 'Anyway, I wouldn't worry. It's a silly rumour as far as most people are concerned.' She didn't feel it was necessary to name names. 'I'm only asking, Emily, because they've found you a bed in Cork.'

'That was fast.'

'Indeed. Apparently one just turned up.'

'In an antenatal ward, I take it?'

'Oh, better than that. You've got your own private room.'

'Well, well,' Emily said slowly.

'They've also generously offered to waive whatever extra cost is incurred if your medical health insurance doesn't fully cover a private room.' Vera was looking studiously at her shoes. 'The thing is, they can't hold on to this room for you forever, for obvious reasons.'

'I'd need to go today then.'

'This morning. In fact, Liam and Joe can take you right now.'

'In a luxury ambulance with a free minibar,' Emily said.

'Not quite,' Vera said. 'It's up to you.'

Vera transferred her attention from her shoes to the hem of her uniform.

There was no shame in going to Cork, Emily knew.

And Vera, bless her, would put paid to any more conjecture about sit-ins. And Cork was obviously going to treat her very well.

And really, Emily thought, she probably would have gone if they hadn't tried to buy her off. Or bully her, to be more exact. She felt like they had flicked on her Code Red switch. Up to recently she hadn't even had a Code Red switch, just a little button that made her nod and smile.

'About the baby,' she said. 'Would it be safe here? Would I be safe? Medically speaking?'

Vera didn't look insulted, which was even more to her credit. 'You're certainly safe until the hospital officially closes on Monday week. I honestly don't know what will happen then. It'd be your responsibility to decide after that.'

Emily nodded. 'I wouldn't anticipate all this taking much longer than Monday week anyway.'

Vera showed a careful interest. 'Oh?'

'I don't have a time frame yet, but I'll let you know.'

'And, ah, what would I tell the board? And Cork?' Vera enquired.

'Just that I'm occupying my bed until further notice.'

'Certainly,' Vera said briskly, and left.

Maggie poked her head around the curtain immediately.

'Well?'

'Well what?'

'Well are we sitting in or not?'

'Maggie, I'm just staying for a few days in case anything can be done about this place.'

'Great! I'd better go and tell Dee down in Elizabeth's Ward.'

'Dee?'

'She said she would sit in too. And Laura. And possibly Mary.'

Mother of God. Maggie had been busy last night.

'Obviously, I'll hang in there for as long as I can,' Maggie promised. 'But I've had more pains, Emily. I think today could be the day!'

She scurried off.

Emily contemplated ringing Conor to let him know that she wouldn't be going to Cork just yet, but it was only ten to eight. He wouldn't even be up yet. She'd ring him later on today.

She knew she was making excuses. She just didn't want to tell him about the sit-in. He would think she was being silly and emotional, and letting herself yet again be dragged into things that really had nothing to do with her.

She didn't think he would believe her if she said that, this time, she wasn't.

Conor had got up very early. He'd showered and shaved and put on good clothes. He'd even polished his shoes. He felt like he was going to an interview.

Now he gathered a few things for himself, clothes and toiletries to do him for a couple of days. Billy

Middlemiss had a flat in Cork near the hospital. He was going to be away for a few days and had told Conor he could stay there. He would drive back up for his weekend work in Baccaro's and straight back down again to be by Emily's bedside.

He had to put his things in the huge suitcase, where they rattled around rather morosely, because Emily had his Manchester United bag.

Then he collected the baby bag. They had packed it together, discussing endlessly the number of nappies, Babygros and vests they should take to the hospital, and carefully marking things off in a highlighter pen against a list they'd been given in antenatal classes. This list conflicted in many key areas with the list their baby-book featured. One would sternly warn you to take only the bare necessities, while the other would remind you not to forget a baby blanket. This immediately raised the question of whether the hospital did not provide baby blankets, and if they didn't, did they also not provide baby mattresses, sheets, a cot even? Ridiculous, really, but how were Conor and Emily to know these things? They had argued back and forth, packed and re-packed five times, ooahed and aahed over the tiny Babygros and it had been lovely.

Emily's bag had taken even longer to pack. It wasn't as though they had spare breast pads hanging round the house, or disposable underwear for that matter. Conor had actually thought the disposable underwear was a joke, until Emily had come home triumphantly from Mothercare with two packets of the things. Conor had spent an hour one evening making nametags for the bags: 'Emily Collins' and 'Baby Collins'.

Emily had joked that it was a shame that he didn't have his own bag.

They hadn't quite finished the packing before Emily had been carted off to Martha's. Conor had looked up the list and had got the last few bits in the chemists, including maternity pads.

He unzipped Emily's bag now to put them in. He found a plastic bag on the top marked 'Food'. Mystified, he opened it, and two Mars bars tumbled out, along with crisps, energy drinks, Nutri-grain bars, and those chocolate-covered peanuts he liked.

Didn't she know they would feed her in the hospital?

He consulted the list again. And he saw that she had ticked off in highlighter pen, 'Snacks for your birth partner during labour.'

They were for him. She would not be allowed to eat anything during labour in case of emergency surgery. But she hadn't minded about that, she had thought about him and the fact that he might feel like a bite to eat while she writhed in agony beside him.

'Oh, Emily,' he said.

He did not know if he would be there for the birth. He wanted to, very much, and he felt he had a right to be there. But birth partners were there to support and encourage and whether Emily thought he could give her that was up for grabs. Or whether she wanted him to. She might just want to ring him afterwards and he would traipse in like any other visitor to see his daughter or son.

He sat on the bed with the two bags either side of him and the big suitcase at his feet and he had a pain in his chest.

He would go to Cork and stay until he had worn her down. He'd worked out all his arguments last night; there were so many reasons for staying together, even apart from the baby, and he would give them to her one by one. Emily often caved in to his logic. Probably because she was usually put in the position of looking illogical, he realised now.

But if he could at least persuade her not to make any final decisions about the two of them, to give them a breathing space. He was trying to buy time.

He hadn't got beyond that, really. He knew there was a leap required on his part but he didn't know how to make it. He did not want to pretend that he had mutated overnight, or that he had seen the light. Nobody could do that, except born-again Christians, and Conor didn't believe in God.

But he did believe that the situation was very dangerous right now. Apart from anything else, the baby, when it came, would rightly demand all their time and energy, and there would be nothing left over for anything else. More importantly, the hurtful things that had been said yesterday had opened gaping wounds, and he felt that if he did not move now, immediately, all would be lost.

He picked up the suitcase and bags and went out to the car.

Some of them in Cork thought it was quite funny. A gang of pregnant women holed up in Martha's! What were they doing, holding a couple of breast pads out the window with 'No' written on one, and 'Surrender' on the other?

All the management had to do was threaten to withdraw the epidural. They'd cave in fairly quickly then. Or close the sweet shop on the ground floor. They wouldn't last long without chocolate.

Mind you, it wasn't a bad idea as ideas went. Nothing guaranteed to embarrass the politicians more than the prospect of women dropping babies on the pavement outside. It could set their entire equality drive back a good ten years.

But the general consensus was that nobody would do anything. Let them sit in Martha's. Let them have their babies there. And then just quietly close the place down when they had all gone home.

Secretly, a lot of them in Cork had wanted to give the Health Board a good boot up the arse for years and were quite envious that somebody had finally had the guts to do it. They didn't want Martha's patients in any case; they were already overworked, underpaid and disillusioned. In the meantime, it was certainly entertaining to watch the show, and it passed the time nicely in the canteen.

Mr Chapman did not go anywhere near a communal eating area that morning. He did his usual rounds, delivered two babies, met with his junior doctors and gave no indication at all that he even knew what was going on in Martha's. And if he did, that he didn't care.

He very much cared, because he had been taken for a fool. Last night, Martha's Board of Management had said nothing about a sit-in. They had just insisted that Emily Collins be given an appropriate bed. Mr Chapman had spent an hour reviewing charts to see who could be discharged as quickly as possible. In the end, Duggie Moran had found a couple of patients who were outstaying their welcome and they had been dispatched. Then, a quick reshuffle of beds until a lovely, big private room with a fresh coat of paint had been secured. And then Hannah informs him that it was on the radio that there was a sit-in!

Hannah played the radio a lot these days. It helped to drown out the screaming matches between Mr Chapman and Killian. Mr Chapman had done his level best to show the boy that there were other ways of dealing with this.

'We've decided, Dad,' Killian kept saying. 'We've decided, okay? Will you just stop pushing!'

Mr Chapman had made a big effort to calm down. 'Killian, I understand that for certain people, abortion is the only option. But it isn't for you and Andrea. You have supportive families. We'll help you every step of the way. I promise.'

He was holding out his hand in a way he never had to his son before.

But Killian just shook his head again. 'It's for the best.'

'The best for you, you mean. It's the easy way, Killian, the cop-out!'

Killian had looked at him very coldly. 'This isn't your decision.'

'I'm just trying to stop you doing something you may end up regretting for the rest of your life!'

'You are not. You're just trying to control me, like you try to control everybody!'

Mr Chapman started now as Duggie Moran banged into his office without even knocking on the door.

'Aren't they right bloody bastards? To keep you in the dark like that?'

Mr Chapman sensed that Duggie's sympathy was manufactured. He was loving this, but then again he had always been pathologically jealous of Mr Chapman's standing in the medical community. Duggie Moran knew as well as Mr Chapman that this was a no-win situation. What was Mr Chapman supposed to do? Go up and drag Emily Collins out to his car and drive her down here? Or go up obediently to see her as he had done thus far? Whatever way he moved, it would look like he was taking sides.

They were all watching this one very carefully. And him.

On the face of it, Cork's management was very laid-back about it all. All new patients from Martha's catchment area would still be coming into Cork's system on Monday week as planned. The sit-in was Martha's problem, not theirs, they declared.

And Mr Chapman's, because she was his patient.

'Do you know what I'd do?' Duggie said.

'What would you do, Duggie.'

'I'd go up and induce her on the spot.'

Mr Chapman found jokes of this nature distasteful and very disrespectful. But that was young consultants for you. In it for the money, half of them, he often thought. What happened when you had all the money you could ever need or want? What were you in it for then?

'Either way, I'd check my medical insurance if I were you,' Duggie advised.

What was the point? Mr Chapman already knew that his medical insurance did not cover Acts of God. Or Acts of Emily Collins.

'You've eaten all the caramels,' Karen said crossly to Darren.

'I have not! I always eat the strawberry ones that nobody else likes! And the bloody coffee ones!' Darren was very indignant. 'Tell them, Vera!'

Vera just continued with her notes.

'I like the coffee ones,' Christine interjected.

'Since when?' Darren said a bit spitefully.

The supply of Roses had abruptly dried up as ward after ward in Martha's had closed down. Now you couldn't find a box for love nor money, and tempers could flare quickly and violently over the last few chocolates that nobody had previously wanted.

'You shouldn't be eating them anyway. You're not even supposed to be working today!' Christine returned triumphantly.

This was true. Martha's should have been down to a skeleton staff. But Darren had received a phone call asking him to come and do a day shift on his day off. Vera had been asked to stay on after her night shift was over. It was a mystery.

But not to Vera, who chewed imperceptibly on a caramel. The board of management were avoiding any knee-jerk reaction to the sit-in. Someone very sensible, probably the Health Board's legal team, had advised them not to give the patients any cause for complaint about neglect or coercion. Under no circumstances were emotions to be riled further.

So they laid on extra nursing staff. Extra catering staff too. Mr O'Mara and Mr Dunphy were both on call, and the equipment in Delivery had received an unscheduled service that morning. Even the heating in the place had been turned up, lest the patients might want to complain about the cold. No, Vera thought, there wasn't a hospital in the country safer than St Martha's right now.

Maureen huffed past pushing the lunch trolley,

leaving an unusually delicious aroma in her wake.

'Chicken chasseur,' Christine said, tight-lipped. She had been down in the kitchen earlier. 'They're giving them fecking corn-fed chicken chasseur! And look at the muck we're still getting in the canteen!'

'What, has she demanded special menus?' Karen wanted to know. She wouldn't put anything past Emily Collins any more. And to look at her you'd think butter wouldn't melt in her mouth.

'The food is a management decision, Karen. You know that,' Vera said mildly. If it were up to her, she'd give Emily and Maggie and the whole lot of them caviar and champagne.

'What are they going to do about them?' Darren wanted to know, round-eyed.

'I hope they're not thinking of staying open until they all drop their sprogs,' Christine said, peeved. 'I'm going to Ibiza Monday week.'

'That's the spirit,' Karen said disparagingly.

'They haven't done anything yet,' Vera clarified.

This worried her. There had been no attempt to talk to the women. Apart from laying on extra services, the management was proceeding with its daily business as though the sit-in didn't exist. Indifference was often the death of strikes and protests, Vera knew. Even the local radio station had cooled off a bit, when they couldn't get any juicy quotes from anybody in authority.

The national media had yet to display any interest. There had been so many strikes and protests in the public sector in recent times that it would take something special to make them notice *this* one.

Still, Vera though hurriedly, fair do's to the girls. Fair do's to Emily Collins in particular. At least she tried.

'What are we supposed to be doing exactly?'

'I don't know, do I!' Maggie returned a bit impatiently. 'Sitting in!'

Dee, Mary and Laura had come down to Brenda's Ward, and they were all perched uncomfortably on the end of Maggie's bed.

'Does it mean literally?' Dee wanted to know, trying to stretch out her legs. Maggie's bed wasn't big enough for four pregnant women. And that Laura one was hogging more space than she was entitled to. Just because she was expecting twins!

'We *are* breaking for lunch, I hope,' Laura said. 'I'm starving.'

'I want to go to the loo. Am I allowed?' Mary wanted to know.

'You'll have to ask Emily,' Maggie returned testily. Honestly! All the griping and grousing, and they were only a few hours into the sit-in! Maggie had expected it to be much more exciting and glamorous, which is why she had gone around the rest of the wards with a rallying cry: To Brenda's Ward, everyone! The sit-in starts there! Up the revolution!

But now that they were all there, it was a bit of an anticlimax. At the very least they'd expected some men in suits to come in and threaten them. Maybe even a solicitor or two. Maggie had angled the bed towards the door in anticipation. But nobody came except Vera, who said it was handy to have them all in one place for blood-pressure readings. Mr Dunphy's arrival had caused a bit of excitement. Dee, his patient, was not in her bed where she was supposed to be. But he just said it was good to see her up and about and left. Just like that! Dee had felt very slighted.

'At least they know we mean business,' Maggie said valiantly, trying to rally the troops.

'I suppose,' Dee said doubtfully. 'Oh, scoot over, Laura!'

'It's a waiting game,' Maggie persisted. 'They'll have to do something eventually.'

'Like what?'

'I don't know!' This was Emily's department! Maggie was only second-in-command. It wasn't fair to leave her to field all the questions like this! But Emily was over in her own bed, with that Neasa friend of hers. Chatting away like she hadn't a care in the world – and the sit-in crumbling all around her! (Maggie's pains yesterday had turned out to be indigestion and she was very cross with the world in general.)

'Mick down in Vincent's Ward thought he might join us,' Mary offered.

'Great, we can do with all the support we can get,' Maggie said, relieved.

'But he changed his mind.'

'Oh.'

'Said he wouldn't be comfortable around pregnant women.'

'This isn't a pregnant-women-issue,' Maggie said with a sigh. 'It affects everybody!'

'But we're the only ones sitting in,' Laura pointed out.

'And we need to up the anti,' Maggie decided. If Emily wasn't going to bother her barney, then Maggie would have to.

'What'll we do?' Dee asked.

'Well, we could start refusing food.'

'It's chicken chasseur today.'

There was a small beat.

'We have to think of our babies,' Laura said.

'Oh, we do.'

'Absolutely! We can't be refusing food.'

Maggie thought again. 'In prisons they refuse to wash.'

Dee wasn't enthusiastic. 'Is it fair to do that to the nurses?'

'Not really, I suppose,' Maggie reluctantly conceded. 'Maybe Emily will have some ideas.'

They all looked over at Emily, who was drinking a nice cup of tea and obviously telling Neasa some very amusing story.

Dee, Mary and Laura exchanged little looks. They couldn't quite credit that Emily Collins had started this in the first place. She wasn't a woman to be taken very seriously by the management, in their opinion. No, they wouldn't be at all surprised if this sit-in was a flash in the pan and would all be over by tea. Which was salmon en croûte with new potatoes, according to Maureen.

'She'll think of something,' Maggie repeated strongly, seeing their faces. They were underestimating Emily. In truth, Maggie's faith in Emily was slowly eroding, but she bravely hung on to her loyalty.

In the meantime, she hoped that Emily would finish up with Neasa soon. She was dying to go to the loo too.

'Until someone comes up with an idea, will we have a game of bridge?' Dee suggested.

'Ooh, let's.'

'You see, I had this dream.'

'Really.'

'I fell off the bed.'

'That's very interesting, Emily.' Neasa smiled kindly, much the way she had done for a whole week while her grandmother had rambled on in the hospice. Neasa wondered whether she should buzz for a nurse, or a psychiatrist or something. Poor Emily had tipped over the edge this time.

'It *is* interesting, isn't it?' Emily ruminated.

'And now you want to take the Department of Health to court,' Neasa clarified.

'Not actually the Department of Health,' Emily said. 'Just the regional Health Board.'

'Oh, well, that's all right then,' Neasa said.

'And I suppose Martha's Board of Management. You'd have to include them.'

'Why not? How about the Minister for Health himself?'

'I don't know . . .'

'He might feel left out.'

'You're not taking this seriously.'

'No, I'm not. Because you're fucking bonkers!'

Emily wasn't offended. 'The sit-in isn't going to achieve anything, not really. We have to decide this thing one way or the other.'

'We?' Neasa said incredulously. 'Don't include me in this!'

'Hangover?' Emily asked sympathetically.

'Well, yes, absolutely wicked, but I'm still in possession of all my faculties. Which you are plainly not!'

'You haven't even listened to it all yet.'

'I don't want to!'

'It's quite simple, Neasa. I just want a judicial review of the decision to close.'

Neasa laughed.

'It's just a matter of filing a motion,' Emily insisted.

'Which you want me to do,' Neasa said.

'Well, obviously, I can't,'

'Obviously.'

Emily looked as though it were utterly reasonable that Neasa would take herself off to the High Court and lock horns with the Department of Health and Children.

'Emily, I'm sorely tempted, but I don't happen to have a spare fifty grand sitting in my bank account to pay the costs.'

'Don't be ridiculous,' Emily sniffed. 'We could do it for half that. Less if we're not paying solicitors' costs.'

'No.'

'Oh come on, Neasa! You know you'd love to go to the High Court.'

'Of course I would! I've never been in the High Court! Well, only as an apprentice. But that's not the point.'

'Remember how we always wanted to sit at one of those tables at the front, behind the lads in the white wigs?'

'Stop it, Emily.'

'Leaning over to whisper instructions every now and then?'

'Shut up!' Neasa clamped her hands over her ears. But Emily wouldn't let up.

'And then we'd walk out onto the steps of the Four Courts just in time for the six o'clock news, and say—'

'My client has no comment at this time!' Neasa shouted. 'I remember, okay!'

'So will we do it?'

'No! I don't even care whether the hospital closes or not!'

'That's beside the point. I care enough for both of us.'

Neasa looked at Emily as she reclined in bed, balancing a cup of tea on her big bump, her swollen ankles propped up on a pillow, and she wondered how it was possible for somebody in this condition to look dangerous. But Emily did. Not in a Gary kind of way – she could never hope to look like Jaws in a million years. It was more a quietly determined I-just-might-scratch-you kind of thing.

Maggie waddled past, carrying her own roll of Kittensoft toilet paper.

'Is it all right if I go to the loo?' she asked Emily anxiously. 'I don't want anyone to think I've left the sit-in.'

'Absolutely, take all the time you need,' Emily assured her.

'And can we break for lunch? It's chicken chasseur and the girls are very excited.'

'Eat away.'

'Oh, and Tiernan will be in later to join the sit-in. He'll have to leave, of course, when visiting hours are up, but every little helps.'

'It does,' Emily said. She turned back to Neasa. 'Well, what do you think?'

'I think,' Neasa said sarcastically, looking at Maggie's retreating back, 'that you need all the help you can get.'

'If you don't have anything positive to say, then just go,' Emily said shortly, surprising Neasa. How come Emily could get so fired up about hospitals closing when her relationship was in an even worse state than Neasa's? After last night's fiasco, Neasa had finally realised that there was something dreadfully wrong with her and Gary. Really, any sensible person would finish with him. But she did not want to admit defeat yet – she *couldn't*. This time, it would be like finally conceding that she was a total failure when it came to men. They would time and again let her down and she might as well throw her hat at them all and dedicate herself to her career or something worthy like that. God knows she'd ignored it for long enough.

'I'll do it,' she told Emily grudgingly.

'What?'

'I said I'll do it.'

'You don't have to, Neasa.'

'I do. For my personal growth,' Neasa said rather piously.

'Crawley Dunne & O'Reilly will have a fit.'

'They'll probably fire me.'

'I don't want that to happen.'

'Why not? I do,' Neasa said cheerfully.

'And Gary mightn't like it – him being on the other side, so to speak.'

'He'll be fine,' Neasa said hastily. She had been too embarrassed to tell Emily about Gary's name-change. It made him sound like such an eejit.

'Just so long as you don't fall out over it,' Emily said anxiously.

Neasa gave a rather lean smile. 'No danger of that at all.'

'Maybe you should think about it.'

'Jesus, Emily, I've just agreed! Are you trying to talk me out of it now?'

Emily might look dangerous, but she still had a way to go yet, Neasa thought.

'Does Conor know about this?'

'Sorry?'

'He doesn't then.'

'I don't see what it has to do with him,' Emily said rather defensively.

Neasa had no intention of defending Conor – that pig – but found herself doing it anyway. 'He might feel he has a right to know. And you don't want to make things between you any worse. Or maybe you do, I don't know.'

'I've already tried. His phone is switched off,' Emily protested. This was true, but it sounded very lame. 'Oh, look, we had a huge fight yesterday.'

Neasa nodded wisely, satisfied with this explanation.

Emily did not tell her that they were on the brink this time. And that Emily had not yet decided what to do. Maybe this sit-in was her way of avoiding the issue. But it wasn't going to go away. She knew that. Right now, though, she felt she had nothing to go back to the talks table with. Compromise wasn't the issue. They would each have to offer new parts of themselves and Emily hadn't found hers yet.

The porter in Cork was not well paid. Or at least not well paid enough to listen to gossip. He knew nothing about any sit-in and informed Conor that, according to the computer, Emily Collins should be in Room 2b on the fourth floor.

Conor took the stairs, weighed down by the two bags. He'd also bought a bunch of flowers. Nice ones this time – white roses, Emily's favourite. She'd carried white roses the day they'd married. Oh Lord, would she think the flowers were some sledgehammer attempt on his part to remind her of what they'd once had? He stuffed them into a wastepaper bin on the first floor.

No, words were needed now, not things, he thought, as he rounded the steps onto the second floor. He was going to come clean with her – totally clean. He would tell her about his love for her, that he would die if she left him. She must be left in no doubt about the depth of his feelings for her.

He was running up the steps now, unaware of the bags banging painfully against his ankles. He would tell her about his feelings of insecurity and inadequacy, his fears and anxieties, the whole bloody lot!

His new impulsiveness had come to him in the car, when he'd been rehearsing his logical arguments for them to stay together. And they had sounded so tight-arsed and pompous and dreary – anyone in their right mind would run a mile, screaming for a divorce. So he had thrown the lot out and decided that he would speak from the heart for once in his bloody life. He had nothing to lose and everything to gain.

The third floor now. He barely slowed, taking the

steps to the fourth floor two at a time. He felt that if he paused for breath he might get cold feet and say nothing useful at all. He had to take the risk. He just had to.

Panting and excited, he threw open the door to Room 2b. And that was where the confusion kicked in. The woman in bed was quite insistent that she was not Emily Collins and, indeed, she didn't look anything like her. Her husband strongly backed her up. Conor was ejected from the room, bag and baggage, and trailed down to the nurses' station, deflating rapidly.

In another startling twist, it was revealed to him there that his wife was actually part of a sit-in in Martha's.

'Oh, yes, of course,' Conor said, as though he'd merely forgotten. His face felt very hot. He was as surprised as if they'd informed him that she'd just given birth to triplets. He wanted to ask whether they were sure they had the right Emily Collins, but was too embarrassed.

'Right, well, good luck,' he said inanely, lifting the two bags and feeling more ridiculous than he ever had in his whole life.

'Conor?'

Jesus Christ, he wasn't going to run into one of the neighbours, was he? He was not in the mood.

It was Mr Chapman, looking very belligerent. He peered at Conor over the top of his bifocals.

'This is most unorthodox. Most unorthodox.'

'It is.' Conor looked belligerently back. Even bloody Chapman was in on this.

'As her consultant, I have to strongly advise against this course of action,' Chapman boomed, taking a step forward.

'Really,' Conor said, also taking a step forward. Sure enough, Chapman took a step back. One more step and they would be in a foxtrot.

Chapman looked at Conor's bags. 'What are you doing here anyway?'

'I came to see you,' Conor shot back.

'Ah.' Mr Chapman looked relieved. 'Maybe together we can sort this out.'

Conor didn't want to say anything in case he betrayed his ignorance of the entire situation. He just nodded.

'Is she intending staying in St Martha's until her baby is born do you think?' Mr Chapman wanted to know.

'Your guess is as good as mine,' Conor said honestly.

'Frankly, I'm worried about her,' Mr Chapman said, looking his most serious. 'The stress of this kind of activity isn't ideal for a woman with pre-eclampsia.'

'I don't suppose it is,' Conor said.

Mr Chapman was more relieved. Here at last was a voice of reason. Maybe this entire thing would be over today.

'It's rest she needs. And plenty of it.'

Conor just listened.

'She has to think of her baby,' Mr Chapman went on. '*Your* baby. And really, I can't be responsible for her when that hospital closes,' he finished up, shaking his head regretfully.

Conor looked at him. 'So you want me to talk her out of it?'

Of course Mr Chapman did, but it wasn't nice to hear it put so blatantly. 'Absolutely not. I'm simply urging you to assess the position responsibly.'

Conor looked relieved. 'Oh, that's fine. I thought for a minute there you were washing your hands of her.'

'What? I never said that. No, no, what I meant . . .'

'You'll still be coming up to see her then?'

'Of course I will!'

'That's great,' Conor said sincerely. 'I'll be sure to tell her that.'

Mr Chapman felt the situation had slipped entirely out of his control. Instead of nipping this thing in the bud, he had unwittingly become a party to her madness.

'So when will I tell her you'll be up?' Conor wanted to know.

'I don't know! Soon! I'll ring.' Mr Chapman walked away rather quickly. He felt the nurses at the station looking at him, and imagined that they were laughing behind their hands. And there was Duggie Moran, giving him that falsely sympathetic look again. And he after giving Duggie Moran hundreds of referrals over the years, all the overspill from his packed appointments book! And on top of it all, he had the Board of Management watching his every move over this sit-in business, like he was a junior doctor again.

He had no authority any more, no standing, not even with his own son.

He had to get out of here. He turned on his pager and left.

Conor wondered what to do now. Get his stuff from Billy Middlemiss's flat and go home, he supposed. Cap in hand, all his fine words like ashes in his mouth. He felt angry now for having got so heated and emotional, ready to spill his guts. He felt he had made more of a fool of himself than Emily had.

But wait a minute. Emily! His wife! Staging sit-ins and protests? The most she'd ever done in that field was refuse to cross the picket-line when the Dunnes Stores staff had gone out on strike.

Conor wondered wildly whether she had cleverly disguised an anarchic streak all these years. This wasn't outside the realms of possibility. He had read a biography once of a woman who had been a secret service agent for twenty years and all the while her husband thought she took in ironing. Emily had bought it for him.

But no, Emily was too much of a talker for that. They'd never trust her with sensitive information, knowing that she'd let it slip to the girls down in Milo's after two gin and tonics. And Crawley Dunne & O'Reilly would never give her time off for secret missions.

Conor shook his head, wondering why he was thinking these ludicrous things. It was just that the ground had been taken from under his feet by Emily's latest move. He was strangely hurt too, if he admitted it. He had thought that, like himself, she would be obsessed with the state of their marriage. Instead she was off doing something entirely different, to put it mildly. It was like she was steering away in another direction and leaving him behind, like so much baggage. The reality was that he was superfluous to her life really, and had been for a long time. And he had done it to himself by drawing a line in the sand that he allowed neither of them to cross.

He felt emotion rising in him again. He tried to rationalise it, to control it. But he couldn't this time. He picked up the two bags and went outside and to his mortification he was crying.

'Now, girls, watch carefully. This is how you change a nappy.'

Angela, the midwife, carefully picked up a plastic doll from the table. 'Remember, girls, you have to support the head. If you don't, this is what happens.'

And she let the doll's head flop backwards violently.

'Ooh,' all the women said, wincing painfully.

Angela held up a Pampers and looked at one of the new mothers. 'Now, Marie here has put her baby's nappy on back to front. No, no, Marie, it's all right. It's a mistake many of us make the first time out.'

And indeed Marie's newborn daughter looked perfectly happy in her back-to-front nappy.

'You'll get so used to it that you'll soon be changing nappies in your sleep.' Angela looked around at them leadenly. 'And you think I'm joking.'

Emily and Maggie tittered nervously. They were at the back of St Catherine's Ward along with Dee, Laura and Mary and, strictly speaking, shouldn't have been there at all. It was a class for the first-time mothers who had just given birth in the hospital. Vera had asked them whether they wanted to go along. Time seemed to pass very slowly on this sit-in. She'd assured them that their beds would still be there when they got back. After measured consideration, Emily had decided that they would go, even though they were the only ones there whose babies were still inside them.

'Cotton wool and water, girls, that's all you should use on newborns' bottoms,' Angela lectured. 'Any of those commercial wipes will take the skin off them.'

'Ooooh.' The women all winced again. Angela wasn't pulling any punches.

'I'll never be able to do that,' Maggie whispered, watching as Angela manoeuvred the doll around with speed, flinging its legs in the air, brandishing cotton wool, and finally holding up the doll to show everyone a perfectly applied nappy. It could have gone to a fashion show.

'There was no poo on the doll. I'd like to see her deal with *that*,' Emily whispered back encouragingly. As if Emily herself had ever changed a pooey nappy.

'Now, will we give her a bath?' Angela asked everyone.

'Let's!' the women squealed enthusiastically. Wasn't it marvellous that someone was actually showing them what to do?

While Angela filled a plastic baby bath with water – 'Half-full will do, girls, no sense in drowning the child' – Emily felt some of the other women casting curious glances her way, like she was an oddity in their midst. Here they all were, participating in the most momentous occasion in any woman's life, some would argue, and she was off organising sit-ins. Maybe some of them thought she wasn't maternal, not like them.

And a few of them were undoubtedly thinking that she was using her baby as a bargaining chip with the management.

Emily held her head high. She did not care what they thought of her. Well, of course she did. She was still *Emily* for heaven's sake. She cared very much. But the important thing was not to cave in to it.

Although she was wondering about the wisdom of the whole thing now. Still, most people who instigated a major High Court case would eventually see past the euphoria, she thought reasonably. Especially when they started questioning the cost of it all, the possibility of losing, the unwanted publicity, the wrath of the Health Board . . . Jesus Christ, she was mad!

'It's all right. It'll pass in a minute,' Maggie said soothingly, seeing Emily's face. Emily had had three panic attacks already about the court case, and Maggie had been very sweet about them. 'Look, she's taking the nappy off again!' she said, to take Emily's mind off it all.

'Now, girls, have the bath ready before you take all the baby's clothes off, you don't want it to freeze.' She picked up the doll. 'And remember, girls—'

'Support the head,' they chorused.

'That's it!' Angela was delighted. 'Now. Does anyone want to give the doll a bath?'

Everyone squirmed shyly in their chairs like they were back in Senior Infants. Then they all turned to look at Emily. Bloody hell, did they expect her to take the lead in every situation just because she had instigated the sit-in? She didn't even have a baby yet! She sat firmly on her hands, red-faced.

'Nobody ever looks at me like that,' Maggie said a bit sadly.

'Me neither,' Emily said. Up to now. It was very embarrassing, but it was also rather gratifying. Like she was someone to be reckoned with or something.

'Okay, girls,' Angela said. 'Watch carefully then. First you stick your elbow in the water to test the temperature. Lukewarm, girls, that's all the water should be. You don't want to burn the child alive.'

'Oooooh,' the women said, cringing. Several of them clutched their babies closer to their chests protectively.

'And don't be smothering it in any of those fancy bubble-baths either,' Angela said sternly.

Emily and Maggie looked at each other guiltily. Both of them had filled their bathroom cabinets with bottles of the stuff in bubbly anticipation.

'And a bath once a week or a fortnight is sufficient. There's no need to put yourselves and the baby through the torture every single night.'

That's what Liz maintained. Emily felt a new respect for her. She must ask her more about babies. Ask her properly, that was, not the grudging way she had done so far because she felt it was expected of her, and not really listening to what Liz had to say.

'Don't you wish you could take her home with you?' Maggie said, looking at Angela. 'She knows exactly what to do and I won't have a clue.'

'You will.'

'I won't!' Being around all the newborn babies was getting to Maggie, who was now officially a day overdue. This had not figured in her birth plan at all.

'We'll learn as we go along, Maggie,' Emily said sternly.

Emily herself didn't believe this for a second. How was she to remember all these things when the time came? Already she'd forgotten what Angela had said about the different types of milk formula. And there was that whole complicated business of sterilising bottles to come yet!

She found herself wishing very strongly that Conor were here. He would effortlessly memorise all these details, and calmly regurgitate them back at that crucial moment. Just as Emily was about to pop the baby into a boiling bath, probably. The problem was that you couldn't wing it with babies, and hope that you get it right; one badly sterilised bottle and you've given them a dose of gastroenteritis. How could she live with *that*?

She wanted him here to share the responsibility. It was too terrifying to contemplate being totally account-able for another person's life – a person who couldn't tell you whether they were sick or hungry or whether their nappy was just on back to front. And there were so many things that could go horribly wrong! Really, Emily thought, it was an act of criminal negligence to let women like herself and Maggie and Marie, total amateurs, waltz out of hospitals with defenceless babies. In any civilised society that cared for its young, babies would be brought up by professional midwives until they were about three while their parents did a compulsory MA in child-rearing. Then the child might at least have a fighting chance of reaching adulthood without being killed by gastroenteritis, or being drowned, or starved, or strangled by its own nappy.

When the call came through from Terry Mitton, Senior Counsel, Mandy at reception was totally ill-equipped to deal with it. No barrister had ever rung Crawley Dunne & O'Reilly in living memory. Nobody in the office even knew a barrister, although apparently Phil had met one once while visiting the offices of a proper solicitor. He had talked about nothing else for weeks.

'Hold the line, please!' she sang, before clamping her hand fiercely over the mouthpiece. What was she supposed to do now? 'Here, Gary? Do you know a Terry Mitton, SC?'

Gary stopped in his tracks. 'A senior counsel?'

'Yes,' Mandy whispered.

'He's lying.'

'No, he's not.'

Gary grabbed a copy of the Law Society Directory from Mandy's desk and thumbed through it. And sure enough, Terry Mitton was listed.

'What does he want?' Gary was nervous. Was it possible somebody was taking a negligence case against them?

'He didn't say,' Mandy said. 'Will I put him through to you?'

'Jesus, no!' He went on hurriedly, 'I mean, this is one for the partners.'

'You *are* a partner.'

Fuck. Gary didn't want to get into conversations with barristers. With his inexperience, he would be bound to make a balls of it. And he was already in the bad books with Crawley over the way the filing system had disintegrated into complete chaos. Crawley had actually said to him that it wouldn't have happened if Emily had been here! No, Gary had to avoid any more trouble.

'Phil, will you take a call from a barrister?'

'I will in my shite.'

'But you met one once.'

'I didn't *speak* to him.'

Gary was desperate now. Then Neasa came in from the loo. She'd talk the hind legs off any barrister. He was forced to look her in the eye, which he had been unable to do all morning. 'Neasa,' he muttered, 'would you take a call for me? There's this barrister guy on the phone—'

'Who?'

'Terry Mitton or something.'

'Of course I'll take it.'

'Great.'

'It's for me anyway.'

'What?'

Neasa looked at Mandy in despair. 'Did you not ask him who he wanted to talk to?'

'Um, no. I got such a fright . . .'

'Put him through,' Neasa barked, striding over to her own desk. Mandy, Phil and Gary looked after her in astonishment. What the hell was Neasa doing associating with barristers? More to the point, did the partners know?

Neasa turned her back on them and picked up the phone with admirable coolness.

'Terry. Sorry about that, I got delayed by a cosmetics company.' Well, she'd applied fresh lipstick in the loo. 'Now, what's the situation?'

Terry Mitton went on about making an application to have the initial arguments for a judicial review of the closure heard. That was the first hurdle. If and only if the judge thought they had grounds, then they would get their day in court.

'But first of all, we need to seek an immediate order to stop the hospital closing.'

'Go on,' Neasa murmured. God, he had a lovely voice. Like a big bar of Galaxy chocolate melted in the microwave.

Due to the urgency of the situation, Terry Mitton hoped to be heard in tomorrow's court proceedings. He would be faxing her a draft of his arguments later that day.

'Terrific,' Neasa said, forgetting all about his voice. She had a lovely, buzzy feeling in her tummy with the excitement of it all. Imagine, her involved in court cases and judicial reviews! It was even better than kicking German receptionists' asses. 'You might also mention the petition.'

Terry thought this was a great idea. The voice of the people, nothing like it! Hell, I'm good, Neasa thought. Of course, she had known this all along in a theoretical way. She just hadn't bothered putting it into practice until now. This really had been a great idea of hers, she thought.

'Will I be needed in court tomorrow?' she asked.

She would. Yippee. She must plan tonight what she would wear.

'I need to know for certain whether your client intends to go through with this. If I'm to issue proceedings to the other side,' Terry said.

He meant the Health Board, Martha's Board of Management and all other interested parties.

'Oh, she hasn't changed her mind,' Neasa assured him, hoping this was true. 'I was speaking to her only a second ago.' She'd ring her as soon as she got off the phone.

'Now, about costs,' Terry Mitton said.

'Ah.'

She had been prepared for a rather large sum, and admirably betrayed no shock when informed that it would be twice that.

'Sure, sure,' she said, acting as though he were selling himself cheap. Bloody hell, for that amount he should send a private plane for her in the morning. But it appeared that she would have to make her own way to Dublin.

When she replaced the phone, Gary was standing over her. She'd been acting hurt and confused around him all morning, but she didn't have time for that kind of thing now. There was work to be done.

'Well, Gary?'

'What was that all about?'

'Oh, I can't tell you right now,' Neasa said, very friendly. She would wait until the proceedings were issued before informing the partners that Crawley Dunne & O'Reilly were entered as the official solicitors. They'd lose a lot of face if they tried to weasel out of it. Of course, they might just show Neasa the door. Either outcome was a good one.

This really is the last straw, Gary thought. Now she wouldn't even share legitimate office business with him! And he was her boss, so to speak! He would force it out of her if he weren't so embarrassed about last night. At lunchtime, Dr Purcell had assured him that there was nothing physically wrong with him. The examination had been almost as mortifying, with Dr Purcell poking around down below while Gary looked desperately at the ceiling. Dr Purcell said that these things were most often stress-related and kept on and on about the health of Gary's relationship. Couldn't the man just give him a course of Viagra?

No. He could not. He advised Gary to go and talk to his partner instead. Talk to her? When she wouldn't even discuss work with him?

The more Gary thought about it, the more this non-performance problem was Neasa's fault. She expected everything to be so perfect all the time! Any man would wilt under the weight of her expectations!

Gary badly wanted to finish with Neasa before his self-confidence died altogether. But he couldn't now, not after last night. No, he would have to perform one last time, otherwise she might tell the whole office that it was over between them because of his impotence. Then he'd never get a crack at Annabel, whom he fully intended to hit on next.

'Will you come over tonight?' he asked, wheedling. He'd watch a dirty movie before she came, tank up on a few beers, shag her senseless, and then break it off. The relief, he realised, would be intense.

'I can't,' Neasa said regretfully. She had to do her nails, her bikini-line and polish her shoes for tomorrow. But really, she was afraid that if she went over, he would irritate her so much that she would end up breaking it off. It was inevitable, but she was just putting it off because she didn't want to look at where she was going wrong. 'I'm driving to Dublin early.'

'For what?'

'I can't say,' Neasa said again. 'But the partners' dinner is tomorrow night – we'll be going to that together, won't we?'

'I suppose,' Gary said unenthusiastically. He would have to wait until then. And it would be such a stressful event too, trying to impress Creepy and Ewan and Daphne with his choices from the wine list. It would be a miracle if he were able to get it up afterwards.

Neasa decided that she would give him the boot tomorrow night. She owed it to him to turn up for the dinner – he was counting on it. But that was it.

She felt the familiar crush of disappointment at having failed yet again. What was it about her that seemed to attract nothing but eejits and degenerates? Maybe it was something as simple as her perfume – she'd read a very interesting magazine article once on how human beings are sexually motivated almost entirely by smell. Was it possible that one little spray every morning could account for the shambles that was her romantic life?

She liked this idea – it was so deliciously simple – and thought about it some more. She might even change her entire image, and see what that brought her. Or maybe she was looking in the wrong place for The One. Could it be that he wasn't in Paulstown at all, but alive and well and living in Cork? She must extend her search immediately.

She felt much better now. Really, when you thought about it, she had simply been misguided in a number of key areas such as perfume and location, which were easily rectified. The One would turn up eventually, she had no doubt about it really. And she couldn't wait to be in love again.

The news of the application to put a stay on the closure of Martha's pending court proceedings had two direct impacts: it sent the Health Board into a spin and it got Pauline Ryan into her car during the hours of darkness. It took her half an hour to drive the five miles to Martha's, as she met ten oncoming vehicles and had to pull into the ditch as many times.

Emily sighed and put away her mobile phone as she saw Pauline coming down the corridor. Conor was not home, or at least he was not answering the phone. Neasa had pricked her conscience and she had wanted to tell him about the court case before it hit the local media. But he had been gone for hours and hours now. Despite herself, she was worried. You could set your watch by Conor. Where could he be?

'I hope you're happy with yourself,' Pauline said by way of introduction. She was wearing an extra crucifix today. She must be very upset.

'It's something that had to be done, Mam,' Emily said rather proudly. Her mother must have listened to the six o'clock LKR fm bulletin.

'I don't know how you can lie there and say something like that.' Pauline was aghast. 'And your own marriage in tatters, if what I hear is true!'

'Oh, all true, every word,' Emily said, although she wasn't quite sure what her marriage had to do with any legal action.

'And so you have to drag everybody else down with you?' Pauline demanded.

This was fairly vicious. So much for thinking that Pauline might be a little bit proud of the stand Emily was taking on behalf of the community.

'You can't go through your whole life taking things lying down, Mam.'

'Well!' Pauline looked at her like she had two heads. 'Try telling that to those children!'

'What children?'

'Tommy, Robbie, Mikey, Bobby and Willy! Who did you think I was talking about?'

'You've lost me now, Mam.'

'And they without a father now!'

Dear God. Had Eamon fallen into a cement mixer or something equally fatal?

'What's happened, Mam?' she asked in a weak voice.

'What's happened, says she! She who put Liz up to this whole madness in the first place!'

Had Liz finally lost the rag and *murdered* Eamon?

'Tell me what's happened!' Emily almost shouted.

'She's thrown him out! Oh yes. Just like that. Packed a bag for him and showed him the door!'

Emily was so surprised that her mouth fell open. 'Where's he gone?'

'A brother of his,' Pauline said sourly.

Emily tried to sort through the confusion. 'But . . . why?'

'Money, of course.'

'But she said they were sorting things out. That he was going to see the bank manager.'

'He went to see an auctioneer. He tried to sell the house to refinance the business, told Liz they could live somewhere smaller until things got better.'

Emily realised now that Pauline knew a lot more than she ever chose to let on. She had probably known about Eamon's money problems for ages but hadn't wanted to get involved. Had she also seen the cracks appearing between Emily and Conor, maybe even before they'd seen them themselves? Say nothing, that was another of Pauline's favourite phrases. Say nothing, keep the head down and be grateful for what you have.

'And now she's given him his marching orders. After you filling her head with nonsense!' Pauline said accusingly.

'I did not fill her head with nonsense.'

'Oh? Do you know what she said when I went over? That you told her to pat herself on the back. That she was marvellous!'

'Well, I suppose I did say that . . .'

'That she didn't take enough credit for what she did!'

'Yes, but I meant women in general—'

'And that Eamon Clancy dumped all the responsibility onto her and that if he wanted to bury his head in the sand, then he could do it somewhere else.'

'Now, I did not say that.' Liz had made that deduction herself, and an excellent one it was too.

'And now she has nothing!' Pauline finished up.

'That's ridiculous, Mam. She has self-respect, hasn't she?'

'Self-respect!' Pauline wasn't just a pre-feminist, she was a pre-pre-feminist.

'Mam, you wouldn't want her to stay with someone who couldn't face the music, would you? Come on. That's no life for anyone. Or for those children either.'

'Children! *Children!* And your own with no father and it not even born yet!' Pauline was almost screeching now.

'Keep your voice down, Mam.'

'I will not keep my voice down. Who are you to tell me to keep my voice down, you little pup? And you bandying your business all around Paulstown, like you're someone to look up to! Mistresses and petitions and court cases! Oh, yes, I heard about that too!'

'Stop it, Mam. Now!'

Pauline did stop. She put her hand up to her crucifixes uselessly and let it drop again. She was crying, Emily saw. That generally tended to happen when you've spent your whole life toeing the line and the shit still hits the fan. Emily finally had something in common with her mother.

'It'll be all right, Mam.'

'How can it be all right?' Pauline cried. 'Two of you with broken marriages, six grandchildren deprived of good, stable homes.'

'With cowboys and adulterers,' Emily said.

'Nobody would have noticed if you hadn't gone poking your nose in!' Pauline bawled inconsolably. 'I only ever wanted the two of you to be happy.'

'Were you happy? With dad?'

'Don't try that with me, Missy. Who are you now, Dr Anthony Clare?'

'Were you, Mam?'

'Your father was the most inoffensive man God ever put on this earth! You couldn't dislike him!' Pauline shouted, with the air of one who had spent many years desperately trying, but had given up and spent her life with a man she merely liked. Pauline cried harder now at the waste of it all.

Emily let her. She didn't feel particularly good about reducing her mother to tears. But anybody who lived life by a collection of hoary old sayings would some day get a rude awakening.

Pauline eventually looked up, red-eyed.

'I suppose you have it all worked out. You'll get that solicitor's office of yours to file for a divorce and get maintenance for that child, and you'll be as happy as Larry.'

'I thought you wanted me to be happy?'

Pauline just didn't want to believe that people could be happy outside the system. If that was the case, what had she been going to Mass for all these years, and attending the funerals of crusty old feckers that she didn't even know? Her reward was supposed to be at the end of it all, and now here was Emily sitting up and telling her that all her little insurance policies were null and void.

She looked a bit bitter now. 'I hope you can explain yourself to that child inside you.'

'I'll certainly do my best,' Emily said.

Pauline had one more crack. 'He's not a bad man, you know,' she said defiantly. 'Conor. I don't care what you say, he's not a bad man.'

'He certainly isn't,' Emily agreed, peeving Pauline further. 'And I'm not filing for divorce.'

That really took the biscuit, Pauline thought darkly. She goes and smashes everybody else's comfy little world for them, and then goes back to exactly that herself! Talk about the cat that got the cream!

Pauline drove home in the darkness in a rage, forcing three cars, a truck and a tractor to drive up into the ditch.

Ever since LKR's evening news bulletin, the nurses' station outside Brenda's Ward had been a hotbed of intrigue and gossip.

'Go home, Christine,' Vera commanded.

'I will not.'

'And you too, Darren. Your shift finished three hours ago.'

'So did yours,' Darren retaliated.

Nobody would go home. They were all waiting to see what would happen next. Apparently there had been an emergency meeting of the hospital board an hour ago. Someone said that a legal team from the Health Board had shown up too. But nobody told the nurses anything, as usual. They didn't care. Weren't they a mere thirty yards from the centre of all the attention, and she sitting up in bed in Brenda's Ward playing cards? For once, the nurses had got it from the horse's mouth.

'Isn't it delicious,' Christine sighed. 'I've never been part of a court case before.'

'You're not part of it,' Karen said. 'It's Emily Collins' case.'

'It involves the whole hospital,' Vera said diplomatically. 'I think we can all consider ourselves involved.'

This was just like *ER*, Christine thought, Ibiza all but forgotten. Maybe she would be called to give evidence. Wouldn't that be something?

'Right, girls and boys,' Vera commanded. 'Empty your pockets.'

'What?'

'This is going to cost money. And, as we're agreed that we're involved, we should contribute.'

'Oh.' Christine wasn't sure she wanted to be *that* involved. But she stumped up five pounds anyway. Darren only had two pounds fifty on him. Karen wondered if she could get a sub, otherwise her contribution would be a bus ticket and a half-eaten packet of Polos.

'Right, well, thanks anyway,' Vera sighed. She would put in fifty quid herself. It was the very least she could do for Emily Collins – that and bring her extra cups of tea and bonus diuretics. Emily had had her blood pressure read four times in the last hour too, and a thermometer had been popped into her mouth every time she drew breath. Everybody was taking extra good care of their champion. Nothing could be allowed to happen to her. At least not on *their* shift.

'She's being very cool about it all, isn't she?' Darren said, and they all peered in the door of Brenda's Ward at Emily Collins. Maggie and Dee and the rest were perched on the end of Emily's bed. Bridge, again.

'She's that type,' Christine said. 'She's a solicitor. She probably files court cases every morning before breakfast.'

Only Vera could see Emily's fear. It wasn't belligerence or a need for attention or even a huge belief in Martha's that was driving her now, but personal factors that Vera could not even guess at.

Not that Vera was overly concerned. She wouldn't

mind if Emily Collins was in this purely for compensation. Let her have it. The important thing was that this closure would not go unchallenged.

Here came Conor Collins now, walking towards them with two bags. He nodded at them all curtly and went into Brenda's Ward.

'I think he's gorgeous,' Karen offered.

'So do I,' Darren agreed.

'He's after having an affair,' Christine said airily.

'What?'

'Someone was saying it in Milo's. With another opera singer, apparently.'

Vera looked up sharply. 'Since when did we go discussing patients' private business?'

Well, all the time, actually. But the girls and Darren knew when not to cross Vera.

'Now. Everybody who is not on shift is to go home this instant,' Vera ordered. Herself included. She wanted to see whether the national media was picking any of this up.

'Will we go to Dublin tomorrow?' Darren asked impulsively. 'And sit in the High Court?'

'Let's!' squealed Christine.

'We are all down for shifts in the morning. Nobody is going to Dublin,' Vera said sternly.

Conor peered at the piece of toilet paper Emily had handed him.

'What does "posset" mean?'

'Posset?' Emily peered too.

'It sounds like a small animal.'

'Oh, it's nothing to do with animals.' Emily was quite definite about that. She searched through more of the shiny, hard toilet paper upon which she'd made notes at Angela's class. 'Oh, here! It's when a baby pukes up some of its milk. Apparently, that's the baby's way of sorting out an over-full stomach.'

'No Rennies then,' Conor said.

Emily laughed. It sounded a bit incongruous. She stopped. 'Where were you all day, Conor?'

Conor did not tell her he'd been to Cork. He couldn't. 'I just had a few things to do.' He looked at her. 'As indeed you had yourself.'

'Yes,' Emily said. She didn't make any further explanation, just looked at him a bit defiantly.

'You've taken on a lot there,' Conor just said.

'I know, but Neasa will be doing most of the work,' Emily said. She gave a little defensive laugh. 'I just have to pay for it.'

She waited for Conor to say something very practical and very sensible, and therefore very soul-destroying. Reason was anathema to the idealism of sit-ins and court campaigns.

'Well, do what you have to do,' he said. 'You will anyway, whether I agree with you or not.'

'I did try to ring you, Conor,' Emily said, feeling very guilty now.

'After the event. Oh, look, it doesn't matter, Emily.'

He could not let her see just how much it mattered. Instead he went on quickly, 'I'm moving out.'

'Sorry?'

'Out of the house. I'm going to rent out on the Cork Road. It's just two miles from home – obviously I want to be near to you and the baby when you get out of hospital.'

Emily was totally shocked. She had not seen this one coming. Somehow she had thought that it would be her call.

'Why?'

'Why? Because things are wrong, Emily. You're not happy. I'm not happy. What's the point in bringing a child home to that?'

Emily's face felt a bit numb. He had organised all this and she hadn't even made any decisions yet! How could he have swung so quickly from wanting to move on to wanting to move *out*?

'I'm not even in the house – why can't you stay there for the moment?' she asked, hoping it didn't sound too desperate. This was too sudden, too severe.

Conor shook his head impatiently. 'That's just a half-measure. And I'm sick of half-measures.'

'So what are you saying? You're leaving me? It's over?'

'Sorry, I don't think I've made myself clear. I want us to start again, Emily. Independent of the baby. That's why I'm moving out.'

He seemed very definite about this and Emily would

do no more pleading with him to stay. She wondered how or when the tables had turned.

'So what are we going to do, draw up a little roster of times when you'll come by and see the baby?' She sounded a bit brittle.

'I certainly want to do more than just see the baby,' Conor said. 'Just because I won't live there doesn't mean I'm not going to get involved in looking after it.'

'Very noble,' Emily said. 'And what about me? Do I figure in this at all?'

'Well, we'd have to work something out there too. If you want to.'

'You mean, like, we'd meet up for *dates*? Oh, Conor, please!'

'You were the one who said the problems went right back,' he pointed out. 'So maybe we need to do the same.'

'I think you're being very simplistic,' she said. 'We can't make it all candlelight and roses again, Conor, however much we want to! That time has gone!'

'I never mentioned candlelight and roses.'

'But you think it can all be worked out by you running off.'

'I am not running off.'

'You are! Like you always do! Only this time you're actually moving out as well!'

Conor looked a bit tired. 'I don't blame you for thinking that. But that's not what I'm doing, Emily.'

'Really.'

'I'm moving out because before we know it, you'll be home with the baby, and we'll be too tired and stressed to think about anything else, and we'd just find some acceptable way of living together without sorting out anything really because it would just be easier.'

Emily took this as a direct insult. 'You mean I'd find it easier!'

'I might too.'

'But you really meant me. Well, let me tell you, my days of putting up with the second-rate are well and truly over!'

She hoped that this sounded very decisive and dramatic.

'Good,' Conor said. 'That goes for both of us.'

So now he thought *she* was second-rate? It was a wonder he didn't piss off to Australia or somewhere.

'There's a pair of us in it, Emily.'

'No, there is not. I didn't try and solve the problems by having an affair.'

Conor gave a small sigh. 'You see, this is what I mean. You're still angry. I'm still feeling guilty. There're all these feelings going around that are not going to be resolved while the baby possets in the background.'

He had a point and she hated him for it.

'What are we going to do, hire a baby-sitter while we go off and discuss feelings?'

'That's obviously something we'll have to think about.'

'They don't grow on trees, you know!' She flung

herself back in the bed and looked at him belligerently. 'And you're not a bit frightened that once we start living apart, we'll find that we like it better?'

'That's a possibility,' Conor said.

'And it's a risk you're prepared to take?'

'Yes,' he agreed, annoying her further.

She would not let him see her own anxiety. 'Are you sure now that you wouldn't like an open relationship while we're at it?'

'Oh, Emily.'

'Mind you, I don't know where I'd get time for other men, what with trying to keep a newborn alive, having meaningful discussions with you, and finding my waist again. All on my own!'

'You won't be on your own.'

'I will be! You've just said it! You're leaving me to cope on my own!' She blinked a bit fast. 'Look, this is a stupid idea, Conor! I need you back in the house when I come home!'

She had laid herself on the line. Conor said nothing for ages.

'For practical things, Emily. That's all.'

'Yes, for practical things!' She didn't want to get beyond this, she hadn't sorted out her own feelings yet. 'They're legitimate enough when I'm about to have a baby!'

'Okay,' Conor said. 'If that's what you want.'

'It is,' she said, less sure at his sudden capitulation.

'And neither of us will ever know whether we stayed

together for any other reason except practicalities,' he finished.

There had to be a catch of course. Blast him anyway for being one step ahead. Emily tried to fight it, but hadn't she already come to this impasse herself? Whether they loved each other enough at the end of the day?

'Oh, go then!' she said.

He told her that he would be moving out the day after tomorrow. Then he asked when he might come in and see her again. Like he was making a confounded date! Like this whole ridiculous nonsense had already started! Emily had presented him with the back of her head and he had left.

She seethed for ten minutes and then it came to her. Of course! It was so obvious! He was calling her bluff! By declaring that he was moving out, he was hoping to make her all jittery and insecure, fearful that she would actually lose him and that really, everything was fine and she'd only been pulling his leg about being unhappy. It was the oldest trick in the book!

The trouble was, Conor wasn't one for calling any-body's bluff. He couldn't even pull off a simple joke with any aplomb. He always ended up letting the punchline slip halfway through.

He really was going to move out.

Emily felt angry again. How come he had ended up in the driving seat? She'd love to be able to announce she was moving out! She still might! Why not? Why should she sit around the house waiting for a visit from him? With the added confusion of whether he'd come to see her or the baby? She'd be a nervous wreck!

Deep inside was an insidious feeling of relief. She could go home when all this was over and not be hurled into more drama. She would have enough of that, what with sterilising bottles and changing nappies. No, let him move out! She needed her 'space' too!

'What's wrong?' Maggie arrived back from walking the corridors in the hopes of bringing labour on. 'Did they not give us a spot in tomorrow's calendar for the hearing?'

'I'd like to see them try,' Emily spat. 'And it's not a "spot", Maggie, like we were entering a karaoke competition. It's called a listing.'

'So we have one?' Maggie asked doggedly. All her relatives would be asking when they came in later and she had to be sure to give them the latest facts. Apparently, Maggie's Aunt Amy's lodger's best friend worked in RTE. They were trying to get him to give the campaign a plug. He only worked on *The Late Late Christmas Toy Show*, but you never knew.

'Yes, we're listed for tomorrow afternoon, Maggie.'

Maggie hugged herself with excitement and wasn't even put out when Emily declined a game of bridge and said she was having an early night.

The next morning Creepy Crawley was forced to share the lift up to the third floor with two pregnant women.

He coped by pressing himself as far into the corner as he could, and keeping his eyes firmly on his shoes. They were highly polished and perfectly matched his intimidating three-piece suit. The last time he'd worn this suit was two years ago, when he'd gone to visit his wayward nephew in the local garda station over that nasty drunk and disorderly business.

The lift stopped and he elbowed his way out ahead of the pregnant women. The heat and the whiff of antiseptic made him reel, but he bravely headed for St Brenda's Ward. He wished now he'd thought to bring flowers or something. That would have been a good touch. You'd have thought Daphne Dunne would have suggested it, her being a woman. Not that she ever behaved like one. The language out of her this morning! F-ing this and f-ing that! And some B words that Creepy had never even heard before. Ewan seemed to know what she was talking about and had joined in with a few choice words of his own, most of which also seemed to begin with F and B. Oh, and one with a W. Now that Creepy thought about it, that one had been directed at him. It was most unfair. Just because he slobbered all over Neasa Martin didn't mean he had an obligation to know what she was up to all the time. No, that was Gary O'Reilly's department. Or Gary Gilmartin, as he'd taken to calling himself. There was no way *that* would end up on the headed notepaper.

Gary hadn't been invited in to the meeting. Not because of any conflict of interests, what with him apparently dating Neasa. He just never seemed to have anything useful to contribute. He would just join in the f-ing and b-ing because everyone else was doing it.

It was silly anyway, Creepy thought, to go losing the head. Reason was what was needed in this situation. Reason and tact and persuasion. Hence his presence in Martha's this morning.

'Emily! There you are.'

'Oh, hello, Charles.'

He was a bit taken aback. She never called him Charles. It was Mr Crawley to his face, or Creepy behind his back. And she didn't even bother to sit up in the bed.

'Just dropped by to see how you are,' he lied, trying out a big smile.

'Well, you can see for yourself,' Emily said, patting her belly.

Indeed he could. In fact, he had never seen anything like it, except in a documentary about sea lions. But her face looked the same, thankfully. He would be fine if he focused on that.

'And, ah, how long to go now?' he asked jovially. He knew that this was the kind of thing you should ask pregnant women. That, and had she thought of any names for it yet. Then maybe round off the conversation with a little joke about how she would have her hands full. Most of them just wanted you to notice that they were pregnant, Creepy believed, as if it had never happened to anybody else.

'Three weeks, minus a day or two,' Emily said.

'Well, well,' Creepy said meaninglessly. 'I always think Michael is a nice name. Or Jennifer, or Alan for that matter. Something sensible. You don't want to go lumbering it with something trendy like . . .' He couldn't think of any trendy name except from a song which had been playing on the radio on the way in, 'Fatboy Slim.'

'That isn't a name we're considering,' Emily assured him.

'It won't thank you when it gets teased in fourth class.' Creepy said this rather bitterly. Fourth class was a period in his life he would rather forget.

If Creepy got any more transparent he would disappear altogether, Emily thought. She wondered now how she had felt any loyalty towards him or any of the rest of them. But they thrived on people like her, vultures preying on hard-working moles desperate for a word of praise. Dangling partnerships in front her nose like a carrot in front of a donkey.

Emily wondered how she had got into this whole animal-comparison business. It was just that Creepy looked so much like a pig this morning, or a snake in the grass. Possibly he had been genetically modified to combine both.

'I suppose you're here about the hospital closure.'

Her directness momentarily flustered Creepy. This wasn't like Emily at all. Still, he supposed that they had them all on drugs in here. 'It has only come to our attention that we appear to be involved.'

Terry Mitton SC had called this morning to see if Neasa was on her way to Dublin. She was, and Creepy had taken the call instead. Imagine his surprise.

'We don't specialise in litigation, Emily,' he said gravely. 'We're in conveyancing.'

'Right,' Emily said slowly, as though she hadn't spent six years taking two percent on Creepy's behalf. 'So I'm on my own, in other words.'

'No no no no,' Creepy said, when he actually meant yes yes yes yes. 'It's Neasa we have the problem with really. She should have informed us.'

'And instead she's on her way to the High Court right now,' Emily said cheerfully.

Creepy gave an involuntary shudder at the mere mention of the High Court. 'Yes, and frankly, we feel it is not our place,' he said, unsmiling.

Emily looked at him pleasantly enough. 'It's my fault. You see, I didn't think you'd mind representing me, after me working so hard for you all these years.'

Creepy was ready for this. 'Absolutely.'

'With very little reward,' Emily added.

'You *did* get that bonus we credited to everyone's account only last week?' he enquired with a smarmy smile.

'You know what I mean, Charles.' Her expression was flat and unyielding, and Creepy's Joop! deodorant started to experience its first real pressure. Maybe he should have sent Daphne in. Emily's hormones had obviously done something horrible to her, and Creepy was not an expert in this field.

He cleared his throat. 'Funny, we were just reviewing the partnership situation earlier. And I'm delighted to be able to inform you now that you're up for a partnership.'

'I've been up for it before,' Emily said.

'No, I mean you've got it this time. Or, you will in due course once we've ironed out any misunderstandings.'

Emily had to resist the urge to spit on his three-piece suit. Honestly, was the whole world out to compromise, pressure, coerce and generally screw you over? What had happened to all the nice, decent people? Had they become part of the screw-you brigade because that was the only way to protect themselves?

Emily resolved that to become hardboiled was even worse than being a pushover. The prospect of living her life like she was on a survival course was too bleak, always looking over her shoulder for the Creepies of this world. Surely it was possible to be nice and still avoid being screwed?

'If Crawley Dunne & O'Reilly wants to back out, then fine.' She didn't lower herself to refer to the partnership. She just let him see from her face exactly what she thought of him, what she'd always thought of him behind that supplicant smile. 'I'll find someone else to represent me. There are plenty of them out there. I'll file for a change of solicitor in the morning. Now, if you don't mind, I'm going for a nap.'

Creepy found himself back on the corridor, scarcely able to credit that he had been dismissed. He should feel triumphant really. After all, he had got what he wanted, which was to be shot of this, with no fuss. And he hadn't even had to admit that there was no partnership. He'd made it up on the spot. Daphne and Ewan would be delighted with the outcome, and they could all go on selling land with gusto.

No, there was absolutely no reason at all to feel a bit, well, sneaky and sly and low.

Which he was, of course – it was just that nobody had had the bottle to point it out to him before. And Emily had always been so nice, too. That's what was so disappointing about this whole thing. Where were all the nice people gone, Creepy wondered?

'Save Martha's!'

'We say NO to closure!'

'Save Martha's!'

'We say NO – mind that bloody placard, Darren, you've snagged my tights – to CLOSURE!'

'Sorry. Save Martha's! We say – oh look, here comes Chapman – NO to CLOSURE!'

The band of protesters outside Martha's, its ranks swollen twenty-fold with news of the court case, stopped to gawk in the window of Mr Chapman's car. He eased indifferently past them as though they were a flock of stray sheep. Then someone actually planted herself in front of his car. Mr Chapman's foot never wavered from the accelerator, and the protestor was forced to dive to one side or else lose a limb.

'Save MARTHA'S!'

'We SAY NO TO CLOSURE!' they screamed after him.

Yes, well, it wasn't up to them, Mr Chapman thought, and a jolly good thing too. He swung into a disabled parking space at the doors of the hospital and sat there for a moment.

He wasn't due to see Emily Collins today. But management had let it be known in their inimitable fashion that his presence was necessary at Martha's. He had coldly asked them whether they believed Mr Dunphy and Mr O'Mara, Martha's consultants, couldn't take proper care of her. On the contrary, they had insisted. But nobody wanted to ruffle any feathers what with the High Court hearing this afternoon. Check her out. Best be on the safe side.

It was as though Emily Collins, by her own actions, had ceased to become a patient for whom medical care was her basic right. She was now a political agenda and medical care would be dispensed accordingly. Plenty of it, it was true, but this was not a situation Mr Chapman was at all comfortable with. It only served to highlight for him how skewed his path had really become.

He had spent the morning arranging to abort his own grandchild. Henry Maher had informed him that his daughter would not be picking a clinic out of a UK phonebook and going over on a cheap flight like she were some little scrubber. Mr Chapman would use his contacts to get her the best doctor, the best clinic. Mr Chapman would also pay all expenses.

He had done it all, even booked the flights. Two return tickets. If this was what Killian wanted, then he would damned well go over with her. He would not shirk *that* responsibility. They would take a week off school, the pair of them, on sick notes which Mr Chapman had also organised.

Hannah had said this morning that he must make the peace with Killian, that the boy was genuinely affected and that he needed their support. Mr Chapman had not even said goodbye to him as he was leaving.

News of the application to keep Martha's temporarily open spilled into the car from the radio. All the Cork radio stations were carrying it. Whether a full judicial review of the hospital closure would be granted would not be known until a later date, the newsreader informed him.

If they got an order to keep Martha's open, they wouldn't be hearing about it on the Cork radio stations. No, they'd be looking at it on the bloody RTE six o'clock news.

Something caught his eye and he looked up. There was Emily Collins in the window above, gesticulating wildly down at Mr Chapman. Good God, what on earth was she doing?

She mouthed something at him, desperately.

'What!' he shouted, as though she could hear him.

She pointed again, face growing more and more pan-icked. Was the woman in labour or something? Then she shut her eyes in resignation just as Mr Chapman was pitched forward in his seat. What the hell . . .?

It took him a moment to realise that he had been rear-ended. Or, more precisely, that someone had backed into his stationary car. The person didn't even notice. He heard a crunching of gears and the offending car moved off smoothly. Behind him, the protesters broke into laughter and a round of applause.

'I'm terribly sorry,' Emily said again. 'It's just that she's not used to driving at night.'

'It isn't night,' Mr Chapman pointed out testily. 'It's three o'clock in the afternoon.'

'She shouldn't really be on the roads any time after lunch,' Emily confided. 'Is there much damage to your car?'

'I haven't looked yet.' He had. The rear fender was dented, and the H on his customised number plate, CHAP, had been damaged. Now it read suspiciously like CLAP. He watched Emily Collins closely now for signs of amusement, but could find none.

Emily felt awful. Pauline hadn't even called by expressly to see her. Oh, no! She'd been dropping Paddy Byrne and Mrs Conlon down to the gates, because they'd wanted to join the protest and neither of them could drive – not that Pauline could either. Pauline had called up to see Emily as an afterthought.

'I'll get her insurance policy number for you.' Emily was anxious to make amends.

'That won't be necessary,' Mr Chapman said stiffly. The last thing on this earth he needed was more legal wranglings with the Collins clan. He would pay for the damage out of his own pocket. And if Emily Collins ever became pregnant again, or if any of her extended family became pregnant, or indeed any friend or remote acquaintance or even a pen pal of hers, Mr Chapman would see to it that his books were full.

He really was decent, Emily thought, not to try and claim for the damage off her poor mother. From the look on his face earlier, she'd thought he might even try and press charges.

'Take it in cash then,' she said.

'Sorry?'

He watched, astounded, as Emily took out her wash-bag, unzipped a little pocket inside and held out a bundle of cash to him.

'There's about two hundred pounds there.'

'I don't want it,' Mr Chapman blurted. Like a lot of rich people, the sight of cold hard cash embarrassed him, even though he gladly took large amounts of it in cheque form.

'It's Mam's anyway,' Emily insisted. 'She gave it to me to buy something for the baby.'

Mr Chapman felt even more embarrassed. Now she was taking the food out of her child's mouth to give to him!

'It's not necessary,' he said again, face hot.

Emily looked at him to make sure he was serious, before putting the money away. 'That's very kind of you.'

'Don't mention it.'

'So long as you're sure,' she said earnestly. 'I was just thinking earlier, there are so many people out there ready to do you over. I just didn't want you thinking that me or my mother is one of those people.'

Mr Chapman had rarely seen an expression of such utter sincerity, and it unnerved him further. And on a solicitor, too.

'Let's get on with the examination, shall we?' he said quickly, before she could make him feel any worse. At least no doctors or interns or nurses or anybody else was looking over his shoulder. He would not countenance it after his spectacular humiliation at Emily Collins' mother's hand. And that porter, Tommy or something, had had the audacity to tell him that he shouldn't have parked in a disabled space in the first place. And now he felt bad about that too!

He cleared his throat loudly. 'Any more bleeding?'

'No.'

'Any pains?'

'Just the usual.'

'Any discharge?'

'No.'

'Anything unusual at all?'

'Well, I have been feeling a bit breathless.'

Not so breathless that she couldn't instruct a solicitor, Mr Chapman thought, feeling a bit feistier now.

'That's usual. The baby is crowding your internal organs due to its size. And also the extra weight you're carrying makes your heart and lungs do more work.'

He reviewed her chart again. Her blood pressure was stable. Her urine had been clear for weeks now. Even the puffiness had gone down. She had colour in her cheeks and the baby was kicking away like a rugby player. Far from this ridiculous campaign increasing her stress levels, he would go so far as to say that she was thriving on it!

'What do you think?' she asked anxiously.

What Mr Chapman thought was that she should be discharged right now. She didn't need to be in hospital. She should be at home, taking it easy and waiting for labour to commence naturally.

He should just walk out to the nurses' station and tell Vera Mooney to send her home.

He was her consultant, wasn't he? He had the authority to do it! And he would stand over his decision, which was medically the right one. Her chart said so. It would back him up every inch of the way. In fact, she could have grounds for complaint if he *didn't* discharge her.

And that would be the end of the sit-in. The rest of them would fall like dominoes. The whole court action might even run out of steam. Get her home in front of the telly and away from the frontline and her cough would soon soften.

Of course, she might refuse to go. But it was one thing to refuse to be transferred to Cork; another thing entirely to refuse to leave a hospital after she had been discharged. Taking up precious resources, beds and money when she didn't need them. Wait until the papers got hold of *that*.

It would be one great weight off Mr Chapman's mind, one way of getting some control back in his life.

She was waiting for his prognosis, her little heart-shaped face anxious and open. Imagine, a woman like her, thirty-seven weeks pregnant, standing up to the might of the Department of Health and Children! How could she hope to win? It was preposterous. Really, he would be doing her a favour in more ways than one.

He wrote the word 'discharge' on the bottom of her chart and signed his name under it. Or at least he tried to. His hand refused to wield the pen. He was afraid that if he persisted, his hand would write something like Homer Simpson, the star of Killian's favourite TV show which blared through the house every evening, setting Mr Chapman's nerves on edge. It had not been on this past week, Mr Chapman suddenly thought.

He fumbled with his pen again, and it slipped from his fingers to the floor.

'Are you feeling all right?' Emily prompted eventually, concerned.

Mr Chapman looked at her with dislike, sick of her concern and her sincerity, sick of her bloody morals, when he had left his behind in some locker room many years ago out of necessity and was now trying to recapture through his son.

In a temper, he picked up the pen and drew a sharp line through the word 'discharge'. Fine! Let her fight the fight if that's what she wanted! Let her see that she was up against a system that was as unyielding as it was archaic! He would like to see what illusions she had left *then*. Oh, they had all been there, every last one of them.

'I'm keeping you in, okay!'

'Um, okay. Is anything wrong?'

'Wrong? Ha!' He made an effort to lower his voice. 'No. Nothing wrong. Just for observation.'

'Okay.' She gave him a crooked little smile. 'Although it would have been quite nice to go home.'

Mr Chapman's eyes popped. Honestly! There was no pleasing some people!

'I'll see you Friday,' he said grimly, and stomped out.

She was really starting to like Mr Chapman, Emily decided. He was a stuffy old stick, granted, and she had been dreading what he might say about the sit-in and court case. But he had behaved very professionally about the whole thing. And he had been very sweet about the car business. It just went to show that once you got to know people, they were generally very nice – unless they were Creepy Crawley or Daphne or Ewan or Eamon Clancy or Nurse Christine or Gary or any number of others, of course. No, she was glad now that she had held onto her optimism despite everything.

She reached for her mobile to ring Conor and fill him

in on Chapman's visit. After all his talk of 'starting again', there hadn't been a peep out of him for a whole day. He was probably busy moving the TV and stereo and cappuccino-maker and most of their furniture into his new residence on the Cork Road. Just so long as he left the electric kettle. She would need that to make bottles for the baby, Angela had said. That's if she didn't get the hang of breastfeeding. It had been fairly hammered home in antenatal classes that this was the best for the baby, the implication being that women who didn't at least try were denying their child a higher IQ. But Emily and Neasa and every other person of their generation had been reared on SMA. If you thought about it, the whole Celtic Tiger economy was *built* on SMA. And Soda Stream after that.

'Hello?' Conor said.

'I don't know if I'm going to breastfeed,' Emily informed him loftily.

'Emily?'

'Of course it's Emily. Anyway, have you any objections?' she said in a voice that defied him to have any.

'Well, I hate to point out the obvious, but they're your breasts.'

'I'm glad we agree on something.'

There was a suspicious thud in the background.

'Are you moving the TV?' she asked.

'What? No. I'm in the attic.'

'What are you doing in the attic?'

'Pottering.'

'Nobody potters in the attic.'

'Looking for things, then.'

Emily looked at the phone as though it were his face. 'Conor,' she said, 'my trust in you has taken a severe battering. Now we can talk about starting again all we like, but if you don't make some effort to win my trust back, then you'd better extend your lease on the Cork Road.'

A small silence. 'I'm sorry. You're right. I didn't tell you because, well, it's stupid.'

'Tell me anyway.'

'I'm looking for that music score.'

'What music score?'

'Um, the one I wrote myself.'

'I see.'

'Tried to write. It's not as though I *finished* it or anything. I just thought of it yesterday and . . . well, I decided to look for it. That's all. Anyway, I can't find it, so it doesn't matter.'

'Have you looked in that box over by the water tank?' Emily enquired eventually.

'The box the stereo came in?'

'No, the foot-spa box.'

'I didn't know we had a foot-spa.'

'We don't – oh, look, it doesn't matter. Just try it.'

She heard him picking his way carefully across the attic beams. They'd never got around to laying down a floor. She hoped he wouldn't put his foot through the ceiling of the baby's room. Now she heard him opening the box.

'It's full of birthday cards. My God, Emily, from when you were twelve!'

Emily maintained a dignified silence. Conor kept nothing. He even threw out *The Sunday Times* on a Monday morning, when there was reading in it for the whole week.

'There's my bicycle light!' he marvelled. 'I've been looking for that for years!'

Emily did not know how his bicycle light had ended up in the attic and she wasn't about to get into it now. He said nothing for a minute.

'Conor?' she asked impatiently.

'Sorry, Emily . . .' He seemed very preoccupied.

'What have you found now?'

'Nothing,' he said. 'Anyway, here it is. The music score.'

'I told you,' she said, quietly triumphant. You see, there were advantages to being married to someone like her after all.

She could hear pages turning. He would be wearing his funny I'm-in-music-mode expression. Well, this time she wouldn't be excluded.

'What did you want it for?' she asked.

'I just had this idea that I might, you know, finish it.' He sounded embarrassed again.

Emily thought back to the time when Conor used to compose music. Somehow he never seemed to get anywhere with it. Then the steady job with the orchestra came along and he stopped writing altogether.

'And why don't you?' she asked.

'I don't know . . . I don't even know why I'm digging this stuff out.'

Maggie drifted past with her Kittensoft toilet roll. Emily turned away. Somehow this seemed very intimate.

'I suppose like yourself, I've been doing a lot of thinking about everything really,' Conor eventually said. 'And maybe I was stuck in a rut with the orchestra.'

Mary Murphy popped unbidden into Emily's mind, brandishing her violin victoriously. Emily took the violin, broke it smartly over her knee, and handed it back. Now go away, Mary.

'I thought you liked the orchestra,' she said.

'I did. But maybe I'm tired of playing other people's music.'

She could hear him sitting down. She too lay back on the pillow.

'Finish a piece then,' she said.

'It's not as simple as that, Emily. I mean, I don't know if I can. I don't know if any of it's any good.'

'It is good. It's great.'

'Yeh.' He was brushing her off.

'What, just because I'm not a music buff doesn't mean I can't tell good from bad.'

'Emily, you like Country and Western.'

'You've just never listened to the lyrics,' she said huffily.

'And I've heard your music. I know it's good.'

'When have you heard it?'

She didn't want to tell him about standing outside the living-room door on Saturday mornings while he practised. On some Saturdays he wouldn't practise at all; he would play something she had never heard before, with frequent stops in the middle, and she would know it was his own stuff.

'You're right, Conor. I haven't listened to it because you've never played it for me,' she said instead.

'You never asked,' he said back.

'My mistake.'

'Mine too.'

There was a funny little silence now. Conor eventually cleared his throat.

'All the baby's things are in that box, Emily.'

'What?' She wanted to make him say it, to acknowledge it.

'The first baby's things.' A beat. 'Our first baby.'

'Yes. I wanted to put them away before this baby arrived. There's not much.'

Just a few Babygros bought in the hot excitement of that first pregnancy, a cuddly toy, and pair of tiny white socks that had made her heart feel all funny.

'I didn't want to use them for this baby. It didn't seem fair to it, like it was being forced to carry baggage that had nothing to do with it. But it didn't seem fair to our first baby to put its things away in the attic like so much rubbish, like it never even existed. And it did, Conor.'

She wondered was he holding those things now. She thought he might be.

'I thought it would be better if I were strong,' he said eventually. 'Or at least looked to be strong. I thought it wouldn't be much help if I went to pieces too. It didn't work, did it?'

'No. For either of us.'

'Emily? Are you all right?'

'Yes, fine.' She was probably better than him right now. 'What are you going to do now?'

She was half-hoping that he would say that he would jump in the car and come and see her.

'I don't know. I suppose finish up here and start moving my things out.'

'So you're still moving out.' She felt a bit flat.

'Emily, you're much better at all this stuff than me.' She knew what he meant, not that she would agree with him. She was just farther down the line. 'I don't want to rush in there and get it wrong.'

'Okay. If that's what you want.'

They said goodbye and Emily hung up and she felt less angry, less bewildered than she had in weeks.

The outcome of the court application came via an unusual source.

'I hear on the radio that you won,' Eamon Clancy said, his jolly red face not in the slightest bit jolly today. 'Again.'

'Just the once,' Emily clarified. 'It's only the first stage of a long, drawn-out procedure.'

'You know what I mean.'

'I'm afraid I don't, Eamon.'

He waved a sheet of paper in her face. 'What's the meaning of this?'

'What is it, Eamon?' she asked calmly. A vein throbbed wildly in his forehead and she was afraid it might burst. Still, he was in the right place.

'It's a demand for maintenance!' Eamon shouted.

People seemed to come into this hospital and shout at her a lot, Emily had noticed. Her advanced pregnancy didn't seem to put them off at all. To stop any more hysterics, she whipped the piece of paper from him and perused it.

'It's a demand for maintenance.'

'I know it is. I just said it is!' He looked at her maliciously. 'You've some nerve. But you were always like that. So superior, with your fancy job and your fancy piano-playing husband, looking down on the rest of us, like builders are the scum of the earth or something!' He waited for her to contradict him and was eventually forced to move on. 'And now you're drawing up maintenance demands against me!'

'It's actually Liz who wants the money, Eamon. Not me personally. I just looked after the paperwork. In fact, I didn't even do that, for obvious reasons. I believe Phil in the office handled it in the end.'

'Well, here's what I think of your maintenance demand!' And he tore it in half, something he had obviously been anticipating most of the day.

'Oh stop it,' Emily said, tired of him now. 'How do you think Liz is supposed to feed and clothe those boys?'

'She can do it for less than three hundred and fifty pounds a week!'

'Eamon, those boys go through five packets of cornflakes a week!'

'Don't talk to me about cornflakes,' Eamon said grimly. 'Don't talk to me about twenty-five litres of milk! Or ten pounds of bananas, two big bags of potatoes, twenty-one yoghurts – but Mikey has decided he likes yoghurts again, so that'll go up to twenty-eight a week now!'

'Twenty-eight yoghurts a week?' Emily was shocked.

'Not to mention the sixty-three nappies a week Willy and Mikey go through between them,' Eamon went on heatedly. 'And the seven night-nappies Bobby still needs. Do you know how much a nappy costs?'

'Ten pence?'

'*Ten pence!*'

'Um, fifteen, then.'

'Twenty-five pence apiece! That's what a nappy costs, unless you go for those own-brand ones – and to be honest I wouldn't advise you to because they're not as good and you only end up forking out at the other end for detergent to wash soiled clothes.'

'Ah, thanks, I'll bear that in mind.'

'Anyway, don't you be telling me how much it costs

to rear a child, because I know,' he said, hitching up his jeans belligerently. Like most other builders, the waist-band periodically slid down to settle somewhere around his knees. Emily wondered whether there was a special store that only builders shopped in.

'Sorry, Eamon, I didn't mean to . . .'

'Don't try and tell me only women *really* know about rearing children!'

'Yes, you've made your point.'

Satisfied that he had, he went on, 'Hasn't the cost of them five fellas been on my mind ever since the business got into trouble? What was I supposed to do? Throw up my hands and say, "Ah well, it didn't work out. Sure we'll have to make do on the dole?" And they roaring and shouting for fuckin' Teletubby videos and trips to McDonald's and I'm supposed to tell them that I can't afford it?' He took a few quick breaths. 'I couldn't tell her – Liz. Jesus Christ, how do you tell your wife that you can't support your family any more?'

Emily felt uncomfortable in the face of his emotion. Eamon, the hard man. 'You're going to have to involve her. Make decisions together.'

'Give up on the business, you mean.'

'That's a matter for the two of you.'

She didn't want to be dispensing advice to Eamon, as though she were a raging success in the marital depart-ment herself.

'Can't you talk to her or something?' Eamon asked.

'No. I can't.'

'As her solicitor. You could advise her—'

'No! Do your own dirty work, Eamon!' She moved on swiftly before he got all testy again. 'Anyway, I'm delighted you called around.'

'You are?'

'Yes, I was wondering what kind of a price you could do me to lay an attic floor?'

'What?'

'Our attic floor at home. I'm looking for an estimate.'

Eamon was very taken aback.

'And no cutting corners, Eamon, not like the last time.'

'I didn't cut corners!'

'You didn't level the ground under the patio properly either. Two of the stones are very uneven already.'

Eamon scratched his head. 'They weren't uneven when I laid them.'

'They're uneven now. And I don't want my child going head over heels on its tricycle when I let it out to play.'

'God, no. Of course not,' Eamon said quickly.

'There could be a terrible accident.'

'There could. There could. I'm sorry about that, Emily.'

'Will you have a look at it?'

'Of course I will! Straightaway.'

'No rush,' Emily said generously. 'Any time in the next few days is okay.'

'You can count on it,' Eamon said fervently. 'And I'll bring you in that estimate tomorrow, okay?'

'Just drop it by the house, Eamon,' Emily said hastily. 'Whenever you're doing the patio stones.'

Suddenly he was very suspicious. 'I don't want any handouts, you know. You and Conor throwing me a bit of work out of pity.'

Emily sighed. 'Do you want to do the job or not? Because I can go to Paudie Coyle instead.'

'That cowboy!' Eamon exploded. It appeared that even amongst cowboy builders, Paudie Coyle was in a league of his own. 'He'd skimp on the wood so much that you'd be falling down through the cracks.'

'Kind of like my patio stones then.'

'I said I'd sort that out,' Eamon said, and stomped out.

Emily felt quite proud of herself. At least now he would lay the attic floor on time, and they wouldn't be waiting nine months like they had for the patio. Imagine, after all these years, she had finally learned how to deal with builders.

'Oh my God!' she suddenly squealed.

Maggie looked up from her birth plan, which she had been studying in an effort to work out why she was overdue. 'What? What?'

'I nearly forgot! We got the order to keep Martha's open!'

'Oh my God!' Maggie squealed too, jumping up and down like a lunatic and clapping her hands. Emily was a bit worried that her waters might break.

'Not permanently, Maggie,' she hastily clarified. 'We still have to apply for leave to seek a judicial review, and only then is the real fight on—'

Maggie didn't care. 'We won! We won!' And she went galloping out to the nurses' station to break the news.

Emily watched the rejoicing from her bed. She knew that they all thought it was down to her, and it was in a small way. But she just wasn't the type of person who enjoyed being in the limelight all that much. And really, she thought, there wasn't a damned thing wrong with that either.

Neasa wore a pink, shag-me-now dress to the partners' dinner. But she balanced it out by wearing her hair in a chic, tasteful roll and not a scrap of make-up except for lip-gloss, which she touched up now in the restaurant loo. She didn't bother twisting this way and that in front of the mirror, searching for cellulite or unsightly bulges. She was one of those rare women who loved every single inch of her body. No, given the chance, she often thought modestly, she wouldn't change a single thing about herself. Well, there was the naturally dull brown hair, but why whinge when the supermarkets were stacked high with black dye? And if some part of her happened to displease her some day, she would just go and get it straightened, or pumped up, or sucked out, or cut off. Cosmetic surgery easily tipped the pill as the best thing that ever happened to women in her opinion. And she wouldn't go around spouting that nonsense about how she'd had her boobs or nose done so that she would feel better about herself, and upping her self-esteem. Hell no, forget that PC shit. It was all about sex, and bettering the odds for *more* sex, at the end of the day. Anybody who said otherwise was deluding herself.

Back at the table, Creepy almost did himself an injury in his enthusiasm to hold out her chair for her. On her other side, Ewan O'Reilly placed her napkin on her lap and patted her knees rather slavishly.

Opposite Neasa, Daphne Dunne picked up where she had left off five minutes ago. 'A great win for you, a great win,' she repeated again, her bulbous eyes glazed from champagne.

'For us *all*, Daphne,' Neasa said sincerely. She felt a bit superior because she'd put away twice as much champagne as Daphne and didn't look remotely stupid on it.

'No, credit where credit is due,' Ewan boomed. 'I was just saying earlier that we don't always show our firm's talents to their best advantage. Crawley Dunne & O'Reilly could have a great future in litigation.'

'No, *I* said that, Ewan,' Daphne interjected strongly. 'Why should we be stuck selling marshy land when there are people crying out to be represented in court?'

'You've had some interest then?' Neasa enquired.

'A bit,' Creepy said, guarded.

Regina in the office had told her that the phone had

started to hop the minute the word filtered down about Neasa's triumph. The firm was already considering two substantial actions against insurance companies, a contested will, a red-hot negligence claim and two criminal defences. Not that they would touch the criminal stuff. Criminals generally didn't have the kind of money that Crawley Dunne & O'Reilly would be charging.

'I believe you were on LKR fm, Ewan,' Neasa simpered. 'Talking about Emily's action.'

'Oh! That! Very embarrassing. To be honest, Neasa, I was just winging it.' He had adored every minute of it. They'd had to cut him off in the end due to time constraints.

Neasa smiled around at them all as though she loved them, and then got the boot in. 'I take it we can ask Emily not to file that change of solicitor motion then?'

Daphne, Ewan and Creepy looked at each other as though they had been caught smoking behind the bike shed.

'That was a misunderstanding, Neasa,' Creepy eventually muttered.

'That's not what she told me.'

Daphne shot Creepy a filthy look before planting her two dimpled elbows on the table and pitching forward into Neasa's face. She tried to look confidential.

'We were worried about her taking on something like this when she's so pregnant. That's all.'

Neasa had a great urge to tell them they were right fuckers and that she would rather eat swill out of a trough with a crowd of pigs than dine with them tonight. But she wasn't that drunk, and sometimes there were advantages to be gained by not always shooting her mouth off. She'd learned a lot from Terry Mitton SC this afternoon. In fact, she felt that she had matured quite a bit by the whole experience.

'Emily's very hurt and annoyed,' she said, and this was the truth. 'She refuses to withdraw her application to change solicitors.' This wasn't true at all.

She waited now until she saw them trembling.

'In fact, she's found a solicitor who will do it for nothing just for the publicity.'

This was a total whopper altogether.

'We can do it for nothing,' Daphne eventually said.

'We'll waive all costs,' Ewan butted in quickly.

'She did give us six years of service,' Creepy said. As usual, everything he said to Neasa managed to sound vaguely sexual.

'But there's Terry Mitton's fees. And all the court fees,' Neasa said bluntly.

'They've offered to pay those?' Daphne closed her eyes in pain. That would put a dent in her partner's bonus. A minor dent.

Neasa was about to give a little speech about what a fantastic cause it was, and how the community would respect them for standing up on their behalf, but rightly suspected that this would only weaken her argument with them.

The partners shifted and looked at each other in

anguish. Eventually Ewan spoke.

'I think we can do that. Can we, Daphne?'

'I think so, Ewan. Do you think we can do that, Creepy?'

'Charles. Yes, I think we can. What do you think, Neasa?'

And they all looked at her.

'Let's do it,' she said magnanimously, and they all felt great.

'Oh, look, your glass is empty again, Neasa. I'll order more champagne,' Daphne twittered.

They fussed and fretted and fawned over her, and she let them. It was Emily really who should be basking in the adulation. But in her absence, Neasa might as well enjoy it. And in fairness, she had spared Emily the hassle of selling her newborn to pay the legal fees.

'Now, do tell us all about your day in court,' Daphne insisted.

'Oh, do,' Creepy said, wiping away drool with his napkin.

Neasa proceeded to do so with gusto, giving herself a rather more central role than she'd actually had.

At the far end of the table – at the *unfashionable* end – Gary watched her give forth with a mixture of rage and jealousy. This was his dinner! His inauguration! And he was being upstaged by his own girlfriend!

Not that anybody knew she had come as his partner. He'd even been denied the chance to parade her as his appendage, the only reason he'd wanted her here in the first place. No, she had been personally invited by Creepy and the partners because of her victory in the High Court, and had come under her own steam. Not as anybody's girlfriend. It was enough to make him puke up his wild-mushroom tartlet.

Well, he wouldn't even shag her after this! She didn't deserve it! And let her put around rumours about his lack of libido! He'd have sex with Annabel on the photocopier at the first opportunity and send around copies of the event over the internal email. Then everybody would know how great he was.

The partners boomed with laughter at the top of the table, and Gary's rage and insecurity grew. She had stripped him of everything, he believed, even his masculinity! And now she was coaxing the partners down the road of litigation, when Gary was firmly a conveyancing man. If she had her way, he'd be reduced to making the coffee. Which he already did, he realised with a dull shock.

'Would sir like black pepper?' the waiter asked.

Gary looked up coldly. 'Sir would like black pepper when and only when his steak arrives rare as ordered! Not burnt to a crisp!'

He had meant to sound authoritative and experienced. He just sounded loud and ignorant, and the table fell silent. It was the wrong thing to have done. Again.

'Actually, I don't mind having well-done steak,' Neasa said casually into the void. 'Why don't we just swap plates?'

It was accomplished in ten seconds and everyone nodded in approval at her diplomacy. Gary stared at his plate, disapproval crushing him. And his steak knife and fork had gone with his steak down to Neasa, and he had none. He couldn't bear to draw attention to himself again. He would have to eat his dinner with a spoon, like he was a child.

She had done her best to spare him embarrassment, Neasa thought a bit self-righteously. He might at least have shot her a grateful look. But then again, she wasn't paying much attention to him. And he was staring at his plate, looking very sour and down, and nothing like the love of her life.

She felt guilty, which was most unlike her. She would probably break his heart later when she told him it was all over. He was still in love with her, that much was plain.

But what else was she to do? He was not The One. She couldn't imagine now how she had ever thought he was The One.

Terry Mitton had asked her out. Not blatantly, there was a certain professional code to be observed. He was as gorgeous in the flesh as he'd sounded on the phone. Maybe a bit short at five-foot-nine, but she charitably decided she could overlook that. And so intelligent and cultured, and he filled his white wig wonderfully. He had hinted at lunch. She hadn't said yes, of course. Best not look too keen. But she'd go. It was a little secret she'd been hugging to herself all evening.

Oh goody. Here came more champagne. She must take another trip to the loo first. This pink dress did not look its best on full stomachs or full bladders.

She met Gary coming out of the Men's.

'Enjoying yourself?' she asked kindly. She would be very mature and nice about all this.

'No,' Gary said shortly.

'I know,' Neasa said sympathetically. 'Daphne can really go on when she's drunk, can't she?'

'I wouldn't go pointing any fingers there, Neasa, if I were you.'

Oh dear, he was going to be difficult about this. Still, she must soldier on.

'Maybe we could have a drink together later,' she said. 'At my place.'

'No thanks.'

'We need to talk, Gary.'

He fixed her with a really nasty look and she was a bit surprised. 'Fine,' he said. 'How about nine o'clock in the morning? I'm free then.'

Neasa gave a little laugh. 'Nine is a bit severe.'

'And you'll be struggling with a hangover.'

'I should think we all will after tonight, Gary.'

'But you have more practice than most.'

What was his point here? She started to get a bit annoyed. After she had made the effort to be so civil, too! Still, she reasoned, he could probably see the writing on the wall and was desperately trying to avoid the issue. Well, Neasa was not one for avoidance, no sirree.

'I don't think we're all that suited, Gary,' she said bluntly.

'You've got that right,' Gary said, rather stunning her. 'I don't know what would keep you happy. Fucking Superman.'

He looked very vicious now and Neasa was wary. 'If you feel like that, Gary, maybe we should call it a day.'

Gary stuck his big fleshy face into hers. 'You got there a split second before me, babe.'

Neasa's mouth fell open. 'Don't call me babe!'

'Why not? I can say what the hell I like now you're not like a stone around my neck. Fuck, I feel reborn!'

Neasa looked at this foul-mouthed, sweaty, vicious creature in front of her and it finally hit her. 'My God. You're a creep.'

'I know! I'm a total creep!' Gary cried with relief. 'That's what I've been trying to tell you all along! But would you listen? Oh no! You thought I was Mother Teresa with sex thrown in!'

Neasa felt a bit sick. 'You fooled me.'

'Yeh, well, you fooled me too.'

'I did not!' Neasa was outraged. 'How have I fooled you?'

'Mind you, it took me a long time to see it,' Gary went on slowly. 'Because you do it so well. You don't even see it yourself, do you?'

Neasa felt afraid. 'Go away, Gary.'

'You're a fucking lush, Neasa.'

She laughed very loudly. 'Oh Gary. Take your

wounded male pride and piss off.'

Gary looked at her with a funny expression. 'I'd be delighted to. I'm not looking for true love at the bottom of a bottle.'

You'd have thought Neasa would have come in this morning, Emily thought crossly. Their quick phone conversation yesterday afternoon had covered none of the juicy details of the court appearance. Neasa had rushed off to get ready for the partners' dinner, leaving Emily to find out this morning from the *Examiner* that the application for leave to seek a judicial review of the closure of Martha's had been set for Monday week, due to the urgency of the situation. Still, it was the weekend. Neasa was probably in bed with a hangover and Gary.

'This doesn't happen in John Grisham books,' Maggie said, cross too. Tiernan's relatives had started ringing up in droves to see had she had the baby yet. She felt the pressure mounting on her. And not so much as a twinge.

'Yes, well, this is reality, Maggie,' Emily said tartly.

But there was a bit of a sense of anti-climax in Brenda's Ward, and indeed, across the hospital. The euphoria of the win had gradually worn off, especially when it had sunk in that they really hadn't won anything concrete at all. Martha's would stay open, of course, until this thing was decided. That was something, Emily supposed.

'Does this mean we're not doing a sit-in any more?' Maggie wanted to know.

'What?'

'Well, if the hospital is staying open . . .'

'I don't know, do I?' This constant questioning was getting on her wick.

'You'd have thought they'd have given us a bigger piece in the *Examiner*,' Maggie added, further peeved. They'd got four column inches on page 5. 'They don't capture any of the emotion of the thing!'

'At least we got covered,' Emily said shortly. Maggie expected miracles! Emily wished that Maggie would have her blasted baby and stop driving them all mad.

Maggie rooted in her locker and looked up at Emily accusingly. 'Have you been using my toilet roll again?'

'I have not been using your toilet roll.. I wouldn't dare.'

'That's not fair! Aren't I always letting you use my Sure?'

It was like they were eighteen again and sharing a cramped flat, with all the attendant squabbles and minor irritations. Maggie's toilet habits and the way she picked at her teeth after meals were greatly getting on Emily's nerves. Emily, of course, couldn't see anything about herself at all that might annoy Maggie. Apart from borrowing her deodorant, which was such a minor offence! But that was Maggie for you.

'I'm going for a walk on the corridors,' Emily said loftily.

'Go then! It might improve your mood.'

The corridors were depressingly familiar. Emily looked in vain for a stray wheelchair. She'd had a ride around in one yesterday just for something different.

She walked on fast, edgy and impatient. The baby insistently jabbed at her ribs, and she suddenly felt sick and tired of being pregnant, of carrying this lump around day and night. She looked down balefully at her belly. Oh just come out and be done with it!

The intense desire that the baby would stay safe inside her forever had gone, she realised. There was still that anxiety over the unknown, and the fear that a newborn naturally brings with it, but something had changed. Emily found that she wanted the challenge. She was restless for it.

It wasn't just the baby. Martha's had been a sanctuary of sorts, affording her security and refuge at a time when she had needed it most. But that had changed now too. *She* had changed. There was a great urge in her to take back the reins of her own life.

And she couldn't. Take the court case. Here she was dependent on Neasa to do the job for her, while she waited in vain for her to drip-feed her information!

And Conor was moving out today and there wasn't a damned thing she could do about that either. This enforced separation was rapidly turning into a great disadvantage. It was leading them down the path of action, not discussion.

She felt a great pressure to do something concrete too,

instead of waiting here passively for his next move. But what could she do? Threaten to break her waters?

It was all most unsatisfactory. And here she was, back at bloody Brenda's Ward again! Even the hospital corridors seemed to have shrunk.

'Emily?' Maggie called.

What was she going to accuse Emily of stealing now – her 7UP? It had been flat anyway.

'Come here, quick! Look!' Maggie was pointing out the window.

Emily reluctantly joined her at the window. 'What is it now, Maggie – oh!'

Both of them hung on the windowsill looking down.

'And it's raining and everything, aren't they great?' Maggie cried. 'That'll show the *Examiner!*' Laura was coming out of the loo in the corridor. 'Laura! Come in here and see this!'

Dee followed fast and they all huddled together at the window looking down.

'Who are they, RTE?' Maggie asked, breathless, as the camera crew down below moved a few feet to the left of the entrance, where the nurses and locals walked up and down with their placards.

'I don't think so.'

'It is. That's Charlie Bird!'

'It's not Charlie Bird.'

'It is! I'd know him anywhere!'

'He's under an umbrella. You can't see anything.'

The umbrella moved slightly.

'I told you it wasn't Charlie Bird! It's a woman!'

'Sweet Jesus! It's Marian Finucane!'

'Maggie, would you shut up. It's not Marian Finucane. Marian Finucane is radio.'

'David Davenport then,' Maggie said valiantly, refusing to accept the fact that it wasn't RTE.

Laura had great eyesight and it was she who spotted the letters TV4 on the side of a microphone.

'Oh. Still, isn't it great that we're getting the coverage?'

'Absolutely, even if it *is* in Irish.'

The crew below moved another few feet to the left.

'They're trying to get some of the protesters into the shot,' Maggie said.

'And the sign for St Martha's,' Dee said expertly. They all watched a lot of news on the TV in this place. 'Would you look at that Christine one elbowing her way to the front of the pickets!'

'She's putting on fresh lipstick!'

They all groaned.

'Oh, what's she saying?' Maggie strained to see as the reporter below turned to the camera and her lips began to move.

Laura's expert eyesight again came in handy. 'She's saying that they're going to have to wait until the pissing rain stops.'

'You can make that out, even in Irish?' Maggie was very admiring.

Emily ignored their chatter, peering down. The protesters on the pavement outside, sensing a media presence, had gone rather shy and embarrassed, apart from Christine. There was a lot of giggling and awkward wielding of placards at any rate.

'Save Martha's!' they squeaked, looking at the ground.

'Oh come on! Give it more gas! We say NO to closure,' Emily muttered restlessly. Where was Vera when you needed her? She'd fire them up!

Now the camera crew were packing up and retreating to a car until the downpour passed. It mightn't take much to make them leave altogether, Emily thought grimly.

She turned to the women.

'I think we should go down,' she said.

Predictably, they thought she was mad.

'Why not?'

'Well, um, because we're pregnant?' Laura hazarded. In fairness, she was having twins.

'So what? Does that mean we're incapable of walking up and down for a few minutes?' Emily felt a bit giddy now, like a prisoner about to make a break for freedom. 'Come on, girls. We're the main players here! Why should Christine hog the limelight?'

'Vera would never let us,' Maggie said, worried.

'Vera need never know.'

'I think you're insane,' Dee said bluntly.

'She hasn't been herself today,' Maggie explained to Dee.

'None of us are ourselves!' Emily returned sharply.

'We're like a crowd of battery hens cooped up in an incubation factory!'

'That's a bit harsh,' Laura said.

Emily's frustration spilled over. 'I certainly find it harsh to be stuck in here for weeks on end because somebody put me in a little category labelled "at risk"! Our entire regime revolving around producing safe, healthy babies, like there was nothing more to any of us! And there is!' She belted her dressing gown tightly. 'I'm going down there, and I don't care what Vera or the consultants or the management or anybody else says! Neither do I care whether any of you come with me!'

She told herself afterwards that she certainly *would* have gone on her own, but it was a great relief all the same when Laura blurted, 'Feck it. Wait for me. I haven't had a breath of fresh air in weeks. I feel like I'm going to explode.'

'I don't suppose there's any *law* against it,' Maggie added reluctantly. 'I mean, they can't stop us.'

'Stop us? I'd like to see them try!' Dee said indignantly.

They all wanted to come now, of course.

'Maggie, there's no time for make-up.'

'It's just a bit of powder. I've a big nose. I don't want it accentuated on television. And I might go into labour after all the marching, you never know. I want to look okay.'

Dee and Laura hurried off to change into fresh night-dresses. 'I've egg down this one,' Laura explained. Even Emily succumbed and exchanged her bunny slippers for the sensible navy 'official' ones in her maternity bag.

At last they were ready, and there was a lot of nervous laughter as they hurried down the corridor in a little clump. At the nurses' station, Nurse Karen looked up suspiciously.

Maggie called urgently, 'Susan's gone into labour down in Elizabeth's Ward.'

Karen went scurrying off in the opposite direction, and they all looked at Maggie, greatly impressed by her cleverness.

'There's more to me than babies too,' she said loftily.

At the end of the corridor, they piled into the lift.

'Sorry, you'll have to take the stairs, Laura.'

Laura lumbered off unhappily, supporting the twins with her hands. As the lift descended, they hoped that Tommy-the-porter was on one of his innumerable fag breaks, and wouldn't catch them.

He was, and reception was empty. They slowed down now, less sure as it appeared that nobody was going to stop them at all.

'Are you sure this is a good idea?' Laura ventured.

Emily stepped forward and threw open the front doors of St Martha's.

'It's freezing!' Maggie squealed. Emily didn't find it cold at all. It was crisp and clear and fresh, apart from the diesel fumes from the road and the stench of something unmentionable from Maureen's kitchen, and she lifted her face to it.

'Right. Are we ready?'

Without waiting for a reply, she went. The first step was the hardest. Then she was off, marching right down the middle of the car park. Her nightie was flapping around her ankles, her slippers slapping in puddles, and she was smiling.

'Wait for me!' Maggie was the next to take the plunge, and she scuttled after Emily, puffing asthmatically. Emily looked back to see Dee and Laura bringing up the rear, their bellies swinging in unison.

'Hi, Tommy!' Emily sailed past him. His cigarette fell from his open mouth to the ground.

It started to drizzle slightly again, but Emily didn't care. Her dressing gown fell open and she didn't care about that either. Let people stare. She was only pregnant.

'Emily, you're going too fast for Laura.'

'Oh, sorry.'

On they marched towards the entrance gates. At the picket-line, and she saw somebody notice them, and nudge her friend. More people turned towards them. Emily rounded the bend towards the entrance gates smartly, the women flanking her now. An approaching car was forced to stop, or else drive through them.

'And what are you looking at?' Dee enquired of the driver belligerently as they strode past.

'Isn't this marvellous?' Maggie cried, whooping loudly. She even forgot for a moment that she was overdue.

The chanting at the gates petered out as more people

turned to look. Emily saw with satisfaction the TV team in the car sit up and look out. They'd get out for this one, rain or no rain.

Now they were approaching the entrance gates, and they slowed. There was dead silence as the protesters were confronted by the sight of four pregnant women in their nighties and slippers. The protesters shifted uneasily; had they come to give out to them about the noise?

'Oh, hello, Mrs Conlon,' Emily called.

Her next-door-neighbour peered back suspiciously. 'Emily?'

'How's the kitchen extension coming along?'

'Um, they refused planning permission.'

'That's an awful shame,' Emily lied cheerfully.

Nurses Christine and Darren stepped up quickly.

'Are you looking for Vera?'

'No, no, we're joining the protest.'

Christine and Darren looked at each other blankly. This wasn't allowed. This exact situation wasn't covered in their nurses' handbooks, of course, but they just knew it wasn't allowed.

'Have you checked with any of the doctors?' Christine finally asked, hoping to shift the responsibility onto someone else.

'Oh Christine, are you going to give us your placard or not? You can share with Darren.'

Nurse Yvonne from the now-defunct Jude's Ward muscled forward. 'Here. You can have mine.'

'Thank you,' Emily said.

'And will someone support Laura here?' Yvonne said crisply. 'Just to take some of the weight.'

Old Reggie Dwyer and Yvonne's husband Bill found themselves squiring Laura. She thanked them profusely and their cheeks pinkened with pride. The rest of the protesters weren't quite sure how to respond to the new arrivals. Then the doors of the TV4 car flew open. Everyone turned to look.

'Save MARTHA'S!' a lone voice at the back of the crowd shouted.

That did it. With a shuffle and a squeak, the protest started again with new vigour, bearing Emily, Dee, Laura and Maggie off down the pavement in its midst.

'We say NO to CLOSURE!' Maggie yelled, losing the run of herself altogether.

They marched for twenty minutes before a member of management was sent out to politely inform them that if they wished to continue, then they would have to discharge themselves from the hospital for legal reasons.

Liz looked different.

'Have you done something with your hair?'

'Washed it,' Liz said.

And unless Emily was very much mistaken, Liz was wearing make-up. Just a scraping, mind, but the last time she'd seen Liz made-up was for Willy's christening ages ago.

'Is that a new coat?'

'You're so nosy, Emily! I've had this coat ages, I just never wear it. Beige shows up every speck of dirt, and with that lot . . .'

She jerked her head towards the five boys. Willy was out of his sling and lying on one of the spare beds, while the other four took turns trying to pull him off.

'Are you sure he's . . .?' Emily asked.

'Oh, he loves it,' Liz said.

'We might be on the television this evening,' Emily couldn't help saying. TV4 had captured the whole lot. It had been exhilarating.

'Right,' Liz said with a modicum of interest, and Emily deflated. 'Eamon's coming over this evening to see the boys – I'll be hours getting everything ready. I won't have time to watch the television.'

'He was in here yesterday, you know.'

'I know. Funny how he goes to see you, not me.'

She looked very hard, and Emily could see how Eamon might find it difficult to admit failure to her.

'He says he wants to talk about the maintenance tonight,' Liz said tightly. 'Like I intend to blow it on myself! Like I live the high-life or something!' She jerked her sleeve up to check her watch, and Emily got the whiff of perfume. Perfume?

She looked more closely at Liz and detected an unmistakable air of excitement about her. This, combined with the clothes, the make-up, the perfume, raised her suspicions. Could Liz be up to something daft, like . . . well, Emily didn't want to imagine what.

Liz furtively looked towards the door, as though she were late for a rendezvous or something.

'Emily, I need a huge favour.'

Emily looked at her a bit nervously.

'I need someone to look after the kids for an hour.'

'What?'

'I know. I know. It's not ideal. But Mammy's had palpitations again. Mrs Spencer says she won't take them after the last time – her garden ornaments, remember? I'm really stuck.'

'Can't you ask Eamon?'

'No. I don't want him to know.'

What on earth was she up to?

'Why, Liz?'

'Look, it'd just be for a hour.' This wasn't washing, she saw. 'Oh, you're so niggly, Emily! I'm going for a job interview, okay?'

She looked very defensive. Emily was hugely relieved.

'Where?'

'Just back in the chemist. They're not really looking for anybody at the moment, they said, but they must have *some* work if they're going to interview me.'

'That's great, Liz.'

'It's not, I probably won't get it. I'll be too rusty after all these years.' She looked at her hands, which she'd tried to make presentable with moisturiser and nail polish.

'You couldn't get rusty rearing five boys,' Emily encouraged. 'All the organisation it takes! The hard work! The patience!'

'Well, patience . . .' Liz said doubtfully. 'They have a new computer system in there and all. I won't know how to work it.'

'Ask them to teach you.'

'You make everything sound so simple, Emily.'

'What do you want me to tell you, that you're wasting your time turning up at all?' Emily said loudly. She had that childish urge again to sit on her hands in case she ended up belting Liz. 'Well, by God, if I have to mind that lot for an hour, I'd like you to at least make a *go* of it.'

'So you'll do it?'

'I honestly don't think they'd allow me to look after five children in here, Liz.'

'They needn't know,' Liz pleaded.

'I really think you should ask Eamon. He'd be delighted that you've got an interview.'

'He won't be delighted. He'll just go on about the cost of childcare, and all the tax I'll have to pay, and what happens when the kids are sick – things I haven't even thought about yet because if I start on all that, I won't go at all.'

'He *is* very concerned about the kids, Liz.'

'Oh sure, the kids – but not me,' Liz said rather bitterly. 'He has no idea what it's like to be waiting around for handouts from him, while he plays the big man that we're all dependent upon!' She took out her car keys and closed her handbag with a loud snap. 'Willy has just been changed and fed, so he should be all right. There's books and jigsaws for the boys in the baby-bag, and if all comes to all, there's a big packet of buttons in the side pocket,' She whispered this bit. 'It'll be fine. I've warned them all to be on their best behaviour.'

The five boys looked over at Emily cannily, and she had that horrible feeling a fly must have when it comes up against a spider's web.

'Liz, I . . .' She looked at Liz's nervous, thin, made-up face, and she just nodded. 'Good luck.'

'Thanks.' Liz looked a bit awkward. 'You've been great about everything, Emily. I mean it.'

But lest Emily might get a swelled head, Liz turned away quickly, kissed all the boys anywhere she could reach, and left.

'Well, boys!' Emily said loudly. 'Will we play with a jigsaw puzzle on the bed?'

'I don't want to,' Robbie said at last.

'Of course you do!'

'I don't.'

The little shit. Emily could see disaster looming. 'Buttons,' she said loudly.

There were no buttons in the baby bag. Just a forlorn, empty bag. There was chocolate all over Bobby's face, and he smiled at Emily happily.

Neasa rose early as it happened. She put on the pair of old jeans that she saved for spring-cleaning and redecorating and she went straight downstairs. She had things to do today. The first port of call was the press under the kitchen sink, and a big roll of black bin-liners. Neasa always kept more bin-liners in stock than most people. But most people didn't have nine serious partners in four years and hadn't as much need for bin-liners. She started in the living-room. Into the bin-liner went the copies of Gary's *Law Review* that he had left behind on her coffee table, to be returned to him this morning. These were followed swiftly by two novels, his training shoes, a spare set of car keys, his Ralph Lauren facial moisturiser and a pair of boxer shorts she found behind the sofa. She was nothing if not thorough, and she worked her way around the room with the practised ease of one who had done this many times before.

She briefly hesitated by the CD collection. Had he given her *M People* as a present, or had he bought it for himself?

She couldn't remember, and chucked it into the bin-liner anyway. She always gave the dearly departed the benefit of the doubt. The cross-dresser had actually doubled his CD collection this way. 'It's nice to know that you're not bitter and twisted,' he had muttered, and Neasa had smiled understandingly. Little did he know. She just hadn't wanted to give him an opportunity to go ringing her up about missing possessions, thus dragging the whole miserable thing out a second longer than necessary. Onwards and upwards, that was her motto.

She didn't bat an eyelid as she progressed upstairs to the bedroom, where she efficiently packed up Gary's Hugo Boss underwear, two silk shirts, a pair of pyjamas that he had never actually worn, a five-hundred-pound suit and tie. Oh, and his condoms in case he might want to use one soon. She would strip the bed later and put on a very hot wash.

She sat down on the bed for a minute now, queasy, even though she'd eaten a big fry and taken three painkillers. She'd outdone herself last night. That'd teach her to get drunk on champagne, she thought cheerfully.

Still, it had been a great night. Terrific! Daphne and Ewan and Creepy had hung on her every word. And why not? If she played her cards right, she might be heading up that new litigation division Ewan had talked about over his third brandy. At least she thought it had been his idea. Things had been a bit of a blur at that point.

No, she had no complaints at all this morning. Apart from a hangover, of course, but she would bet that Daphne Dunne was sticking her head down a toilet bowl at this very moment. Gary would probably have ended up accusing *her* of being an alcoholic too had he not left straight after dessert.

'Poor Gary,' she sighed sympathetically. His own worst enemy really. He'd want to watch himself or one of these days someone would take a slander suit against him.

And, honestly, if anyone drank too much it was him – off to the pub at lunchtime three days a week with the lads! Neasa never went to the pub at lunchtime – how was *that* for a so-called alcoholic? Alcoholics went sneaking off to the loo for a quick nip from a flask in their handbags, for heaven's sake! They hid drink in toilet cisterns at home, and they ate Polo mints all the time. They couldn't hold down jobs, they messed up their relationships, and they were usually drunk by eleven in the morning. And, Neasa thought knowledge-ably, they nearly always had some big murky secret in their backgrounds that made them drink their heads off to escape it.

As if Neasa were like that! She did her drinking in public. Quite a bit of it, certainly, but she enjoyed it and there was nothing wrong with it. It certainly didn't affect her work or anything like that. And her past was gloriously free of anything remotely traumatic, apart from her grandmother's death, and she had come to terms with that.

'Oh, stop it,' she told herself brightly. There was no need to go rationalising and reasoning like this, like she had something to worry about. But it was natural to be a bit defensive when someone hurled accusations at you, however groundless.

Her stomach had settled a bit now, and she felt better. The problem with men like Gary was that they were misogynists at heart. They couldn't bear to see women doing as well as them or, God forbid, better. Their answer was to bring them down using any available means. And if they couldn't beat a woman fair and square, then they tried to plant insecurities in the hope that the woman might actually bring herself down!

He was a right pig when you thought about it. And she had been going to return his things to him very civilly, too! Well, not now. The charity shop in Paulstown would be delighted with his Hugo Boss underwear, one careful owner. They'd be delighted with the suit, the CDs, everything. Perhaps not the condoms though. She must take those out before she left. In fact, she might blow them up and hang them from the office ceiling, and tell everybody what a disaster he was in bed. She could plant insecurities too! And hers would actually have some foundations.

She put him from her mind clinically, and started to review her wardrobe. She had her big day in court coming up Monday week, not to mention the date with Terry Mitton. She could feel a shopping trip coming on. She couldn't embark on a new romance in old clothes. And, who knows, this could be The One. She had a feeling about this one.

Ten minutes later, she was in her car with her credit cards. Gary's stuff was in the boot. She would drop it by the charity shop on her way. She would need a big empty boot for all the new clothes she would buy in Cork today.

It was a dreary grey day but she put on sunglasses anyway. Her eyes hurt a bit. She'd take it easy tonight, maybe get a video and a Chinese or something.

The traffic was light in Paulstown. The charity shop was up on the right, past the traffic lights. She slowed and craned her neck to see whether it was open. It was. Good.

'Fuck!'

She didn't see a car coming from the left. She jammed her foot on the brake. So did the driver of the other car, and for a moment it seemed that they had stopped in time. But then Neasa felt the car rock as the other car touched off the passenger door. Terrific. Another hike in her insurance premium.

'Nice driving,' she said sarcastically, jumping out of her car and confronting the other driver, a man. The car had a Dublin registration, she saw. Fucking tourists.

'You broke the lights,' he said, looking a bit shocked.

'What? Don't be ridiculous.'

But he was right. Neasa felt a bit sick as she saw clearly that her light was red. The man had the green light.

'All right, sorry,' she muttered. 'Are you all right?'

'I think so,' he said.

Mortified, Neasa stomped around to the passenger side of her car and threw open the damaged door. She found her licence and insurance details in the glove compartment and thrust them at him.

'Here,' she said, wanting to get this over with as quickly

as possible. 'Obviously I'll pay for all the damage.'

'Shouldn't we wait for the police?' the man wanted to know.

Neasa rolled her eyes. Where did he think he was, Detroit? 'Listen, Frankie Noonan won't appreciate being called out because I jumped a light. Trust me on this one.'

'Oh. Right. It's just that my wife has already called them.'

'Fantastic.'

She was out of the car now, red-faced with anger, telling Neasa what a reckless driver she was. Neasa just stood there defiantly. Garda Frankie Noonan would sort them out. He hated Dubliners, even more than he hated Cork people.

Frankie Noonan didn't come. It was a guy from Mitchelstown. He was young and cocky and Neasa instantly disliked him. He walked dramatically around the two cars as though he were at a murder scene.

'Can you just take the details and let me go?' Neasa said loudly. He probably hadn't had as much excitement in years.

He dutifully stepped up and started to jot down details from her documents into his notebook.

'Headache?' he enquired, looking at her sunglasses.

'A bit,' she replied shortly, snatching back her papers. 'If you need to know anything more, I can be contacted at Crawley Dunne & O'Reilly. Solicitors.' She said this last bit rather loudly.

He was standing very close to her now and she didn't like it. This wasn't the time or the place to be making a pass at her. As if he had a hope.

'Were you drinking last night, madam?'

'Sorry?'

'Last night? Were you drinking?'

'I was out for dinner. I had a few drinks, yes,' she said, very patiently, as though he were a buffoon.

'Quite a few?'

'It was a celebration,' Neasa said tightly. 'Is that against the law, Garda?'

'Not at all,' he said. 'Drink-driving is, though.'

Neasa threw her head back in amazement. 'It's eleven o'clock in the morning! I am perfectly sober.'

'You won't mind doing a breathalyser test for me then.'

'Where's Mammy?'

'I told you a minute ago, Robbie, she'll be back shortly.'

'I'm thirsty,' Tommy announced.

'I'll ask Maureen for a jug of water. How about that?'

Tommy looked at her as though she'd offered him arsenic.

'Would Coke do instead?' Conor asked, miraculously producing a two-litre bottle from a large plastic bag.

The visitors' room experienced a brief lull as the boys guzzled Coke. Emily looked at Conor gratefully. He'd not only brought the emergency supply of buttons she'd requested but also Hula Hoops, Milky Way bars, Coke and apples. They hadn't touched the apples, naturally.

'Isn't it amazing all the same how quickly they can do those jigsaw puzzles?' Conor said. He had a thin sheen of sweat on his upper lip.

'It is. It is. And how they were able to take Bobby's tractor apart. All those screws, too.'

Emily had broken two nails trying to put the thing back together again.

'Still, only fifteen minutes to go now,' Conor said manfully.

Emily nodded optimistically. 'She might even be back earlier.' She looked at him. 'Thanks for staying on with me. I mean it.'

'Of course I was going to stay,' he replied softly, and she smiled. 'You shouldn't have to cope with that lot in your condition.'

Her smile disappeared. 'Oh, so you just stayed out of concern for the baby then.'

'Stop being so high-handed, Emily.' He looked at her. 'Just because you're going to be on the TV tonight.'

He gave her a dry look and she went a bit pink.

'So, have you moved out yet?' She tried to sound cool and unaffected.

'Took the last things over this morning. I've left the place clean and tidy and all,' he added quickly.

'Fine,' Emily said. You'd think he was just a lodger.

'And I've taken the dogs, of course.'

Emily was a bit taken aback. 'You've taken the dogs?'

'Well, yes, you mightn't be home for another month. And anyway, I didn't think you'd want to look after two dogs *and* a newborn.'

'Aren't you great,' she said colourlessly. Now she wouldn't even have the blasted dogs to talk to!

Conor shifted in his chair. 'Emily – don't touch that, Robbie – we've been over this. I thought we decided it was the best thing to do.'

'You decided.'

'You agreed.'

'Because you wanted your "space".'

'I think we both do.'

'People are always going on about "wanting their space". I often wonder what they do with it all,' Emily said sarcastically.

Conor seemed a bit puzzled too. 'Reflect, I suppose.'

'On the shoddy state of their marriages.'

'Something like that,' Conor agreed, smiling a bit.

On the spare armchair where they'd propped him between two cushions, Willy suddenly twisted his head towards them.

'Oh, look at him, Conor. He's all excited for some reason!'

His face was indeed very red. He fixed his gaze on the ceiling rather desperately, and gave a little grunt. The veins under his white skin bulged as he strained hard.

'Oh,' Emily said.

A whiff reached them.

'Yes,' Conor said, sadly.

Willy finished up, gurgled, and turned to look at Emily and Conor expectantly,

'I suppose we should change him,' Emily said eventually.

'We should. We should,' Conor agreed, fresh sweat breaking out on his upper lip.

They looked at each other blankly. Emily wondered if that midwife Angela was in the building.

'It can't be that hard,' she said sternly. 'I'll get the nappies. You lay him down on the floor over there.'

'Um, no problem.'

Emily rummaged in the baby-bag for supplies while Conor approached Willy with great care. After three attempts, he lifted the child off the chair, holding him out awkwardly so that his feet dangled in the air. Willy thought this was great gas.

'Will I support his head?' Emily asked anxiously.

'I think he's got the hang of his own head, but maybe to be on the safe side . . .'

It was with a great sense of achievement that they finally got Willy down flat on the floor. He looked up at them with great confidence.

'We'll have you done in a minute,' Conor reassured him. 'Right, I suppose the first thing is to take off his dungarees.'

This was quite a job given the number of zips, buttons and popper-fasteners. They peeled off the dungarees and found that his top was also popper-fastened underneath. Once that was pulled up, they were confronted with a vest with more of the things.

'He'd never get through the metal detector at Cork Airport,' Conor muttered.

Emily undid the last lot and finally he was down to his nappy. The smell hit them full in the face.

'My God,' Conor said. 'And look, it's leaked out.'

It had too. Angela hadn't said anything about leakages.

'We've plenty of wipes,' Emily said strongly. This was no time to go to the wall. If the boys over there sensed any hint of fear at all, they would run riot.

Conor surprised her by bravely reaching for the two sticky flaps on the sides of the nappy.

'I'm going in now.'

Emily giggled. But when he opened the nappy she had to turn away.

'How can something so small produce all that?' Conor said in wonder. He seemed to be enjoying this now.

'Wipe him, quick,' Emily said, handing over a bundle of the things.

Conor, with calm, methodical swipes, eventually managed to get him clean. Then he wrapped up the nappy securely and thrust it into the plastic bag he'd brought the Coke in.

'I'll dig a big hole when I get home and bury it.'

Willy was delighted to be without his nappy, and he kicked about enthusiastically.

'He's smiling at you, Conor.'

'I should think so too. You were useless.'

She knew his toughness was only a front. Look at the way he was tickling Willy's foot!

They put on his new nappy and spent ten minutes doing up all the popper-fasteners, zips, buttons and buckles again.

'We're old pros now,' Conor said. 'Ready for anything.'

She felt a great tenderness now as she imagined them with their own baby.

'Why can't it be like this all the time?' she asked suddenly.

'I don't know.'

'What kind of an answer is that?'

Conor looked at her, and it was with genuine curiosity. 'How did you think it *would* be? Marriage?'

'Faithful.' It was out before she could stop it.

'So did I.' He looked more puzzled than sorrowful.

'I expected friendship, the odd bit of passion and romance, companionship, sharing the same ideals with someone.'

'Yes.'

'I also thought it would be intimate and close.'

He nodded.

'So if we both expected the same things, what happened?'

'They're not our God-given right, Emily. They don't automatically come with the wedding package.'

'You mean I'm being unrealistic?'

'No, I don't mean that at all. I suppose it's a question of compromise.'

'So I can have the friendship and the companionship but not the intimacy and closeness?'

'No, I . . .'

'Well, I want those, Conor. I can get companionship and friendship from other people.'

She sounded very hard and unyielding. Conor sat up straighter.

'So you're prepared to give this a go, then?'

'I'm just saying—'

'No, you haven't said anything, Emily! Not a thing about a commitment to me or to our marriage. I'm the one who's been begging and pleading all the way along, for some little bit of reassurance or even the tiniest indication that you love me at all! Instead you draw up lists of requirements and demands, and I always seem to fall short.' He looked at her. 'Maybe I always have.'

Tommy looked over, alert to domestic dispute. He was used to it. When Emily eventually spoke, it was low.

'I'm the one who's had to get used to this affair.'

He looked impatient. 'I know that. But, God Almighty, are we going to have it hanging over our heads for the rest of our lives?'

'It takes time to deal with these things, Conor! We've hardly talked about it, even!'

'My affair?'

'Yes!'

'What's there to say? You want me to keep saying sorry, is that it?'

'No!'

'What then?'

'I don't know . . . if I had an affair, *you'd* want to talk about it!'

'I wouldn't,' he said very definitely. 'I'd want to put it behind us.'

Emily was very annoyed. 'That's very easy for you to say!'

'What is not easy for me is this constant limbo, with no light on the horizon at all. I don't even know if I'm going to be there for the birth of my own baby!'

'This, from someone who's going to be living in a different house when the baby comes home!' Emily hissed back, her anger bubbling to the surface.

'I do not want to live in a house where I'm merely tolerated. If and when I come home, it'll be because you want me there,' Conor said flatly.

'It's not down to me.'

'Oh come on, it is.' He looked at her oddly. 'You've always held the power in our relationship and I'm starting to think that you know it.'

'What? I do not!'

'Stop sitting on the fence then. Say you want me if you do. If you don't, then I'd appreciate it if you'd let me know as soon as possible so that I can get on with things.'

'Shut up! Shut *up*! We're on!'

St Brenda's Ward, packed to the rafters with nurses,

patients, visitors, doctors and Tommy-the-porter, went very quiet. You could have heard a pin drop as the newsreader on the TV looked down at them all sombrely.

'And now we're going to a special report on the increase in petrol prices . . .'

'Oh, Maggie.'

'Sorry, I thought we were going to be on next – how could petrol prices be more important than pregnant women in active protest?'

They obviously were, and everyone turned away from the television to pick up conversations left in mid-thread.

'*Avery*. What kind of a name is that for a child?'

'It won't thank her.'

The doctors were over by the door.

'Said he was out in his vegetable garden when he tripped and fell, and happened to impale himself on a carrot.'

'Was he the same fellow who was in Casualty last year after a similar accident involving a courgette?'

Tommy-the-porter was wondering about his future.

'It's night security work. There's a TV and a toaster and all.'

'God, I'd take it, Tommy.'

Over by Emily's bed, Neasa stuffed grapes into her mouth.

'It's a three-ring circus in here,' she said rather sourly.

'I know, but this is the only television left in the place

that actually works. And, naturally, everyone's excited.'

'I suppose,' Neasa said, very unenthusiastic for one who was actually representing the parties in court. She felt Emily looking at her.

'Look, Neasa, it's always hard when these things happen, but you'll bounce back. You always do.'

'I know. I know.' She didn't want the pep talk, but knew that Emily felt she had to say it.

'Just give it a bit of time. And anyway, from what you've said, it's probably for the best.'

'It is, definitely.' She tried to sound bright and normal.

'The office might be a bit difficult, but people forget very quickly, you know. There'll be new gossip in no time and nobody will give you and Gary another thought.'

There certainly would be new gossip, gossip that would eclipse anything that had gone before. Neasa couldn't even think about that right now. It was too awful.

'Neasa . . . you don't think you might be a bit unrealistic in terms of expectations?'

It seemed that Emily was determined to sort her out, she saw. She'd only come in to Martha's at all because she knew Emily would be expecting her.

'Yes, probably.'

'I mean, we'd all love for the honeymoon bit to last forever. It's exciting and great and passionate. But it's false too in a way. You don't really know the other person until it has passed.'

'The voice of experience.' This slipped out before she could stop it.

'Oh, go home and sleep your hangover off,' Emily said testily.

Neasa exploded. 'Jesus Christ! What is *wrong* with everyone! Well, I'm sick of it!'

And she stormed out, just as Maggie squealed again at the television.

'Emily! It's you!'

On the screen, Emily marched right up to the camera, her dressing gown hanging open to reveal her big round belly. And there was Laura, walking on her own despite the efforts of her two chaperones to contain her. Maggie was next, taking those little dainty steps and looking the picture of pretty motherhood. Dee brought up the rear, shooting a belligerent look out at everyone before marching on. They looked magnificent.

'My nose! My nose,' Maggie moaned.

'Nobody's looking at your nose,' Christine snapped. She hadn't been in the shot at all.

The reporter stood in front of the protesters now and did her piece. Nobody was listening. Everyone was busy picking themselves out in the background.

'There's Yvonne!'

'Oh, and look, Tommy!'

Then it was over and back to the studio. Vera started to clap. The whole ward broke into applause.

'Wasn't that fantastic, Emily?' Maggie swooned. Now

she really had one up on Tiernan's relatives. 'Emily? Where's she gone?'

Neasa looked up as Emily entered the visitors' room.

'Why can't you just leave me alone, Emily?'

Emily was hurt, she saw. 'If you want to be alone, why don't you just go home?'

'I'm waiting for a taxi,' Neasa admitted.

'A taxi?'

'Oh, look, my car's in the garage, okay? I had a bit of an accident earlier.'

Emily was all sympathy. 'Why didn't you say! No wonder! Jesus, are you all right?'

'Fine, fine.' She might as well tell her – she'd be asking her to represent her when it went to court anyway. She looked at her hands fiercely. 'I was arrested for drink-driving, Emily.'

She felt Emily sitting down beside her.

'I mean, it was all so stupid! I just had too much last night – I should have known that I might get caught.'

Oh, how she hated this hunched, defensive feeling, this knot of shame in her stomach. And Emily's disapproval hitting her like slaps. As if Emily herself had never got drunk and done something foolish in her life!

'It was a minor accident, Emily.'

'Stop it, Neasa!' Emily flared. 'This is drink-driving causing an accident. You're going to be banned. There's no doubt about that. And you'll be very lucky if you don't get a prison sentence. You know what Judge Morrissey is like about drink-driving.'

'He'll just fine me – anyway, I mightn't even get him.' Neasa was frightened now. 'Will you represent me? Please? I couldn't ask anybody in the office. I just couldn't.' If she still had a job there, that was.

'Yes,' Emily said, without putting her through anything more. Emily stood up to go and her upset with Neasa was clear.

'Emily,' she said after her. 'I would never get into a car knowingly under the influence. Come on, you know that. But nobody thinks they're over the limit the morning after. It doesn't occur to them.'

'I suppose not,' Emily said.

Neasa was relieved. 'I know I had a lucky escape. This'll teach me a lesson.'

'I hope so, Neasa.'

Neasa had that hot feeling in her face again. 'What's that supposed to mean?'

'Just that—'

But Neasa didn't let her finish. 'Jesus Christ! Just because you're pregnant and you haven't had a decent drink in nine months! Are we all supposed to go on the dry with you?'

'I'm not saying that—'

'But you're thinking it! You think I've got a problem with drink, don't you?'

Emily looked at her. 'You told me the truth about Conor when I asked you. So I'm going to tell you the truth. Yes, I think you drink too much.'

'Thank you very much for your truthfulness, Emily.

Now, if you don't mind, I'd like to wait for my taxi in peace.'

When she looked up again, Emily was gone. Neasa curled up on the shabby armchair and she was shaking.

Conor didn't come in the next day. Or the next. In fact, he did not come in that whole long week. He was waiting, obviously, for her to make her decision.

It wasn't that she didn't *want* to make that decision. Certainly she didn't appreciate being dealt an ultimatum, but she did not let her minor annoyance cloud the issue. And it wasn't that she did not have feelings for Conor any more. She did, and she admitted this now. In fact, she would very much like this whole thing settled and sorted. Like Conor, she too had felt the impatience and tension building in recent days. Maybe he was right. Maybe it was time to decide this thing once and for all.

But she still couldn't make that decision. Every time she tried to think about it, she was distracted by a nagging, persistent disquiet, a hangover from their row in the visitors' room. It was nothing that she could immediately put her finger on. It seemed silly, and she tried to figure out what it was that was bothering her.

Eventually it came to her. It was Conor saying that she held the power in their marriage and always had. This seemed to Emily to be so utterly off the mark that she couldn't even begin to make sense of it. Her, have power over Conor? The most self-sufficient person she had ever met? A person who gave her reassurance and support only when she begged for it? Now, who held the power *there*?

She could not understand it. And it continued to nag at her.

'The baby's heartbeat is fine,' Mr Chapman announced.

Emily looked down, mildly startled. She was so used to Mr Chapman now that she had completely forgotten that he was somewhere under her nightdress. She had to resist the urge to reach down and pat him affectionately on the head, like he were one of the dogs at home. She really had become very fond of him.

'That's great,' she said.

He straightened up and put away his stethoscope. Emily thought that he looked different. Tired or something. And it was Sunday and everything – you'd have thought he'd have taken the day off.

'And how are you feeling yourself?' he enquired.

'Oh, grand.'

'Good, good. Eating well?'

'Yes.'

'Getting a bit of exercise? A bit of fresh air?' He couldn't resist getting the dig in. It seemed that the whole country had seen the TV piece last week. The pressure on the Health Board and Martha's management had been building all week. The showdown was tomorrow morning in Court No. 3. Duggie Moran and the rest of them had organised someone to phone straightaway from the court with the outcome. Mr Chapman found that he did not actually care.

He really was taking this court thing badly, Emily thought, as he pushed up her nightdress another few inches and began to feel the baby's position with his hands. Emily had on a pair of pink knickers, quite racy really, but the supply of white nun's bloomers with the different coloured trims had rapidly dried up due to the lack of handwashing facilities in the hospital.

'The baby's head is fairly well down in the pelvis,' Mr Chapman intoned.

'When do you think it'll be born?'

'I never give predictions.'

'Oh.'

He proceeded to do so anyway. 'Your due date is not for another ten days. Women often go over on their first child.'

Mr Chapman felt he was acting out a part he had played hundreds, thousands of times before, that of the concerned professional who would facilitate a most momentous occasion in so many women's lives. Women who were at the end of the day strangers to him, and he to them.

Andrea had had her abortion on Friday afternoon. Not that Killian had phoned or anything. Mr Chapman had been reduced to ringing up Patrick Marcus, the contact of his who had carried out the operation. It was only out of concern, for God's sake, but Marcus seemed to think that this was a great invasion of Andrea and

Killian's privacy and had told Mr Chapman in no uncertain terms that it had nothing to do with him and that he had no rights whatsoever to any information. He had then hung up on a stunned Mr Chapman.

'Good luck,' he said to Emily unexpectedly now, and he meant it. But he saw that he had scared her. Consultants were supposed to pretend that luck had absolutely nothing to do with it; that medical science would win out at the end of the day.

'I'll call by Tuesday or Wednesday,' he said more briskly. Why not? He had already worked all weekend, just for something to occupy his mind. And at least she couldn't complain that he was neglecting her.

'Um, thanks,' Emily said to his retreating back. He was being very odd today. She hoped he would be up to it when her big moment arrived. Conor would go mad if he wasn't, and they after paying him a thousand pounds too.

That feeling of disquiet was back again the moment she thought about Conor. She considered picking up the phone and asking him to come in so that they could talk.

But, knowing Conor, he would not even remember the intricacies of their conversation. And if he did, he would tell her she was reading too much into things as usual. He would want to know whether she had decided to move on with him or not.

But they were good at that, weren't they? 'Moving on' without really resolving anything. Pretending that they had sorted things out when they hadn't at all, and off they would walk into the sunset until the next big crisis loomed and the whole thing would fall apart at the seams again. Probably permanently. Because each time they negotiated a crisis, they emerged weaker as a couple, not stronger. And if she picked up the phone to Conor and said 'yes' right now, she was continuing the whole sorry vicious circle.

'Emily?'

'Yes! Oh, sorry, Maggie, what is it?'

Maggie was sitting up in the bed, a mobile phone glued to her ear. 'Auntie Olive is going into the Four Courts tomorrow for the judicial review and she wants to know what the dress code is.'

'It doesn't matter – anything.'

'It doesn't matter, Auntie Olive, anything.' Maggie looked back at Emily again. 'Could you be more precise? She's only seen a courtroom on *Judge Judy* and she doesn't want to make a fool of herself.'

'Tell her trousers and a top.'

'Trousers and a top, Auntie Olive.' Maggie rolled her eyes. 'Would a skirt and a top do, Emily? It would. Great.' She listened for a moment then turned to Emily again. 'She said to tell you that you were fantastic on the telly last week, that it gave her goose bumps.'

It was quite amazing how many people had seen that piece of footage. Cards of support had been arriving in Martha's all week, along with letters and phone messages and even two bouquets of flowers. Oh, and one letter from a woman in the midlands who said they were a right bunch of hussies to be parading themselves in front of cameras in their condition.

'She's taking a whole gang up with her,' Maggie said, having dispatched Auntie Olive. 'She might even make a banner, she said, if she can find markers. Isn't she great?'

'Great,' Emily agreed.

'And there's Laura and Dee after holding on too,' Maggie said. 'You have to take your hat off to them.'

And she burst into tears.

'Maggie,' Emily said softly, used to this, 'I know it's hard going, but you have to hang in there.'

Maggie was now eleven days' overdue. And not a sign in the world of anything stirring, despite four vindaloos.

'I can't stand this, Emily,' she sobbed. 'There's something wrong. Maybe the baby is dead!'

'The baby is not dead. Didn't you hear its heartbeat an hour ago?'

Vera kindly put a stethoscope on Maggie's belly a couple of times a day to reassure her. Everyone was being very nice to Maggie at the moment.

'I'm going to ask to be induced,' Maggie resolved tearfully.

'Maggie . . .'

'I am! You can ask them, you know! You can tell them the mental stress is driving you mad!'

Physically, all was well. Excellent, in fact – Maggie

hadn't had an asthma attack in nine days. The irony of this was something she didn't appreciate right now.

'Maggie, give it another little while.'

'This wasn't supposed to happen, you know,' Maggie said, brittle. 'This wasn't in the plan.'

'Forget the plan, Maggie. Maybe the best thing is to relax right now.'

Maggie smiled bravely. 'You're probably right. It's just that I'm sick of this place. I want to go home.'

'I know. I know.'

'Half of me wouldn't mind if your friend Neasa loses in court tomorrow,' Maggie confided. 'At least Cork would be a change of scenery.'

Neasa had not been in to visit in a week either. She had phoned Emily twice to keep her up to date on the court action. Both calls had been tense and impersonal.

Emily hadn't pushed it. She felt too guilty in any case. Why had she not noticed what was going on with Neasa before now? How had she not seen through the smokescreen of her failed romances? Not that Neasa had propagated her own myth deliberately. Emily felt that she was genuinely stumped by her romantic disasters. But the men were more a symptom than a cause.

Impulsively, she picked up the phone and dialled Neasa's home number. She got the answering machine, even though she sensed that Neasa was nearby, listening. She left a short message anyway, to wish her good luck in court in the morning, and to thank her for doing this.

'Do you want a game of bridge?' Maggie wanted to know. She had not let the dwindling patient numbers in Martha's dampen her enthusiasm for bridge. Desperation had driven her to play a game with herself yesterday.

'No thanks,' Emily said. *She* felt cross now – cross and frustrated and irritated with things in general. And Conor in particular. She would phone him tomorrow, she vowed. She would tell him to come in and they would have a long chat about all the things that were bothering her. And he could stuff his 'decision'! She wasn't ready to make one yet.

Just before eight o'clock, Vera came in. She was on the night shift and was in uniform, but with a pink and yellow party hat on her head. It looked very incongruous.

'The staff are having a bit of a party down in Jude's Ward. Nothing too mad, no drink or anything like that. But we thought we'd like to mark the day.' She looked at Emily hurriedly. 'That's not to say that we're not confident about tomorrow. We are. And if we win, we'll be having another party. With drink.' She held out two more party hats. 'Anyway, the staff were wondering would you join us? And Dee and Laura too, of course.'

Emily shook her head. 'Ah no, Vera, it's a staff thing.' She did not think she would be much company.

'It's not,' Vera said firmly. 'It's a hospital thing.'

'Can we, Emily?' Maggie, as usual, waited for Emily's

permission to do anything. 'There's damn all on the telly.'

'Please,' Vera said. 'Maureen's made bean enchiladas and everything, from a proper recipe book.'

This was their way of saying thanks, Emily knew. She threw back the bed covers and put a smile on her face.

'We'd be delighted to.'

Damn Maureen and her bean enchiladas. Emily tossed and turned much of the night, fighting wind and horrible dreams. Then she would be assailed by interminable periods of wakefulness where she would fret about the court case tomorrow; the baby; Neasa's drinking problem. She even worried a bit about Liz and Eamon, and the five boys. Lest anyone feel left out, she spared her mother a quick thought too, and Mrs Conlon who apparently had launched an appeal against the planning permission refusal.

Maggie's deep and contented snoring filled the ward, and Emily wrapped her pillow around her ears, gritting her teeth. Maggie was fond of saying that nobody else ever complained about her snoring and that Emily was being over-sensitive. So, really it was all Emily's fault. It was funny how people could twist things to shift the blame onto someone else.

Conor jumped into her mind again, accompanied by that growing irritation. The more she thought about his assertion that she held the power in their marriage, the more it seemed like an accusation. Somehow or other she had created an imbalance in their marriage which caused Conor to be so upset that he had gone out and had an affair. That was the bottom line. That was what had been bugging her all week.

No wonder he hadn't wanted to talk about the affair! No wonder he'd hardly said sorry to her at all! He thought it was all her fault in the first place! Oh, he could deny it for all he was worth, but Emily knew.

Were it not a quarter to four in the morning, she would phone him up and demand that he get his sorry ass in here right this moment. She still might!

In the meantime, a mattress spring was digging uncomfortably into her hip. She huffed up onto one elbow, gave the pillow a good belt, shifted over six inches and flopped down violently again.

The force of her landing dislodged more wind and she felt a little ping down below. She expected relief.

It was not wind. She lay there for a moment, quite still, as a warm wetness spread over her thighs, soaking her nightdress. It felt like gallons, but it probably wasn't very much; she had read her books and knew what was happening. When it was over, she carefully got out of bed in the darkness, changed into a fresh nightie and went to find Vera.

'Well, it's earlier than expected,' Vera said.

'A little,' Emily agreed calmly.

'We'd better get you down to Delivery.'

'Sorry?'

'You need to be examined.'

'But I'm not even having any pains. Not proper ones anyway.'

'If your waters have broken at this stage, I'd say you're on the way,' Vera advised. 'The pains will probably start pretty quickly now.'

Emily was shocked, and hadn't the faintest idea why. She only had ten days to go. It was perfectly possible – indeed, highly probable – that she was in labour right now and would have her baby within the next twenty-four hours.

'I'll just get your labour bag,' Vera said, and went off.

Emily stood on her own in the dark corridor, her hands clutching her belly, amniotic fluid dripping down her legs. She calmly told herself that everything was going to be fine. Hell, the moment had finally arrived – she should be enjoying herself!

'Here we go.' Vera was back.

'Thanks,' Emily said cheerfully, and burst into tears.

Vera was very kind. She put an arm around Emily. 'What's wrong?'

'Nothing. Everything.' Emily couldn't explain her upset. She said the first thing that came into her head. 'I thought it was just wind. I ate loads of Maureen's kidney beans at the party.'

'So did we all,' Vera said grimly. The whole hospital had been suffering since. It would nearly make you wish for Maureen's lukewarm shepherd's pies made with cheap mince.

Tommy-the-porter loomed from around the corner,

giving Emily a fright. He was pushing a wheelchair.

'Delivery?' he said.

Emily felt fresh shock and panic rising in her. Maybe it was all those weeks and months of anticipation. When the event was finally happening, she couldn't quite believe it.

'Don't worry,' Vera said. 'I'll come down with you.'

Emily found herself folded into the wheelchair, her labour bag balanced on her knees. She clutched the straps fiercely as Tommy threw his weight behind the wheelchair. They eventually set off on his third attempt.

'Okay?' Vera asked, trotting beside the wheelchair.

'Yes,' Emily lied. She felt quite nauseous now, and Vera was right – the pains were getting noticeably stronger and more regular.

Down the dim corridors of Martha's they trundled, past the kitchen and the smokers' room and the visitors' room. Emily never remembered it being as quiet as this. Doors were dark and wards silent. But most of the hospital was closed. It was all a bit eerie and unsettling, and when Tommy broke into a coughing fit, Emily jumped.

'Are you okay?' she asked.

'Fine,' he said, and stopped to lean against a wall. Emily felt very much a burden, when it was obvious that he needed the wheelchair more than she. But eventually they set off again.

'Will I get one of the girls to ring Conor?' Vera asked casually.

Emily pretended to have a contraction to buy some time.

'Breathe through it,' Vera advised. 'You too, Tommy.'

After much huffing and puffing, Emily felt she had to give an answer. 'Ring him, but tell him there's no rush.'

Vera wasn't sure how to take this. 'The thing with first-time labours is that nobody really knows how long they will last, Emily. You don't want him to miss it, do you?'

'I suppose not,' Emily said reluctantly. She didn't know what she wanted. Someone she trusted, she supposed. Someone she knew. Someone with whom she wasn't extremely angry right now.

Ow. She had a real contraction now, a proper one, and it took her breath away. She hunched over in the wheelchair and she was shocked by the ferocity of it. Something primeval and brutal was happening to her body, something that she could not temper or stop.

When she could breathe again, she looked up at Vera grimly. 'Ring him and tell him to get in now.' By God and if she had to go through this thing for their first-born, then Conor would too. Every inch of the way.

They rounded a corner and the bright lights of Delivery burst out of the darkness. Tommy, seeing a fag-break on the horizon, picked up pace enthusiastically, and they crashed through the double-doors with great noise and fuss.

'Now, Emily, Jessica over there will look after you,' Vera said.

Jessica seemed a most unlikely name for a midwife. She sounded like she should be selling expensive lingerie. Emily had somehow expected all midwives to be called Emer or Maura or something similarly earthy and comforting.

'Hello, Emily,' Jessica said, stepping up. 'Again.'

'Um, yes,' Emily said. This was the same woman who had escorted her from Delivery that very first night.

Jessica looked at her keenly. 'By the way, Martina's doing very well. She had a baby girl. Just in case she didn't get a chance to ring you or anything.'

She was on to Emily all right. But she said it nicely. And Emily was very glad that Martina was okay. She had been thinking of her on and off since that night.

'Good luck, Emily,' Vera said.

'You're not going?'

'You'll be fine. You're with the experts now.'

Emily didn't want experts. She wanted people she knew and trusted. 'Vera,' she blurted. 'I'm afraid.'

'Of course you are,' Vera soothed. 'Every woman is when it comes to giving birth. But don't let the fright rob you of the joy of it all.'

Another savage contraction convulsed Emily. Vera was taking the piss, surely.

Vera waited until the contraction was over, then she patted Emily on the arm and left. Just like that! Oh, cheers!

'Now, Emily,' Jessica said brightly. 'Can you walk?'

Emily, not wanting to make a fuss, hobbled from the

wheelchair, still clutching her labour bag. Jessica tried to take it from her, but Emily held on tighter. People always seemed to be trying to take bags from her. She must be a pickpocket's dream.

'In here,' Jessica said cheerfully, throwing open the door to a labour room.

It was not at all what Emily had expected. She had been given the obligatory guided tour of Cork's labour facilities as part of her antenatal classes. The labour rooms there had been spacious and sensitively lit, with clever, abstract pictures on the walls and sophisticated new beds that went up and down and sideways and possibly inside-out at the mere touch of a button.

Martha's labour rooms boasted harsh fluorescent lights and peeling white-ish paint. The bed was mean and narrow and the medical equipment looked like it was on loan from a museum. The only picture on the wall was a discoloured diagram of what appeared to be the female reproductive system. Surely Martha's obstetricians and midwives already knew what this looked like? Emily felt her confidence dwindle further.

'Now, if you'd just pop up onto the bed,' Jessica said.

Emily was later to reflect that Jessica said 'pop' a lot. It seemed that Jessica had yet to learn that no woman in labour ever popped anywhere. They inched painfully, or they rolled agonisingly. They all *wanted* to pop, but very few of them ever did.

'If you could just let your knees fall apart,' Jessica instructed, pulling on white rubber gloves with much loud snapping. 'This won't hurt a bit,' she said with that rather irritating cheerfulness again.

Emily looked at the ceiling as Jessica did her thing down there. Now she was pulling off the gloves and peering up from between Emily's knees.

'Four!' she chirped.

Four? Four what? Emily's mind went blank. 'Oh, *four!*' She was four centimetres dilated. Already!

'You're doing pretty good,' Jessica sang. 'Keep it up!'

Emily's enthusiasm was dealt a brutal blow as a contraction sneakily pounced.

When it was finally over, she looked at Jessica, uncomprehending.

'It's terrible.'

'I know,' said Jessica, clucking.

'No, no, you don't. I mean it's *really* terrible.'

'You need to relax and breathe over it,' Jessica advised, and Emily wanted to hit her very hard. 'I'm going to ring Mr Chapman,' Jessica added. 'Let him know how you're doing.'

Emily was shocked. 'It's ten past four! I don't want you getting him out of bed!'

But Jessica was gone. It was a relief really to be spared her relentless cheer. Emily was left on the flat of her back looking up at the ceiling again. There was a big crack running across it and one of the bulbs in the fluorescent lights flickered ominously. A part of Emily still couldn't believe that this was happening.

Conor would be here very shortly. He was probably

in the car right now, driving down dark country roads. Would he break the speed limit for this one? She suspected he might. Well, he needn't expect a big warm welcome from *her*.

She wondered was the baby all right. She had not felt it kick or move at all in the past hour. Could it possibly be asleep? In the midst of all this madness?

'Please be all right,' she said, cradling her tummy and crying again, a little bit.

'Emily?' The whisper came from the door. And there was Maggie, in her nightdress and bare feet, peeking in. 'I woke up and you were gone!'

'Maggie!' Thank God – someone nice. 'Come in, stay with me for a bit.'

'I'm not supposed to be down here at all,' Maggie hissed, but skipped in all the same and huddled by the side of Emily's bed, round-eyed. 'Are you all right?'

'I've been better.'

Maggie squeezed her hand. Emily clung on to her, thankful for the support.

'Talk about timing,' said Emily. 'With the court case tomorrow and everything.'

'I know,' Maggie said. 'I don't suppose there's any chance you might be able to hang on . . .?'

'No chance at all.'

'I didn't tell the others you were gone into labour,' Maggie confided. 'I didn't want morale plummeting.'

'I'm going to have to ask you to take over the

campaign, Maggie,' Emily instructed. 'Just until I'm back on my feet.'

Maggie looked delighted at her new position of responsibility. 'I'll do the best I can,' she said bravely.

Emily shifted on the bed uncomfortably. The weight of the baby pressing down on her stomach was making her nauseous.

'Is it awful?' Maggie wanted to know in trepidation.

Emily looked at her worried little face. No sense in giving her a heart attack. 'Easy peasy,' she bluffed.

'Oh good,' Maggie said with relief. 'I knew that Cathy one was exaggerating. No pain threshold, that was her problem.' She reached into her dressing gown pocket. 'I brought you down a damp facecloth. It's not clean, but at least it's cool.'

'Lovely,' Emily said, as Maggie laid it on her forehead. It didn't help at all, but she didn't want to offend her.

Maggie took something else from her dressing gown pocket. 'And here's my birth plan.'

'What?'

'Well, you didn't do one in the end, did you?'

'Um, no.'

'So you can work off mine,' Maggie said generously, spreading the five densely-written pages along the side of the bed. 'Where do you want to start? The foot massage or maybe I could light some aromatherapy candles for you?'

'No candles, thanks anyway, Maggie. We don't want to set the fire alarms off and have to vacate the building.'

'That's true,' Maggie said reluctantly. 'We'll play some music instead. I brought you down the tape Tiernan made especially for me. It's ocean sounds. He managed to get the Atlantic *and* the Irish Sea, isn't he marvellous?'

'Marvellous,' Emily echoed weakly, as she felt another contraction come to life inside her. Surely it hadn't been that long since the last one? But it didn't matter. It was on its way and there was not a damned thing Emily could do about it. She gritted her teeth and cursed the universe.

Maggie was fiddling with an ancient tape machine in the corner. 'Imagine, you're finally going to have your baby, Emily! Isn't it incredible?'

'Yes,' Emily managed, as the pain spread out inexorably from the centre of her, eating her up.

'Have you thought of any names?' Maggie demanded.

'No . . .'

'You're hopeless, Emily! Anyway, never mind, because guess what else I brought down for you?' She reached into her bottomless dressing gown pocket again. 'My baby-name book! Let's start with A, will we? Girls first. Abigail, Adi, Agnes – imagine, *Agnes*! – Ailish, Amanda . . .'

Emily did not hear any more. She was in the throes of the horrible monster now. She tried to relax, to breathe above the pain like Jessica had told her to. And it didn't bloody work. She felt her fingernails sink into the palms of her hands as her whole body felt like it was mangling itself. Surely something was wrong? Surely human beings could not live through this kind of pain? Just when she thought she could not bear it any more, the agony began to subside, slowly. She floated back to planet earth again and her vision cleared. Maggie must be on to B's by now.

Maggie was not. Her eyes were like saucers and her face white as she stared at Emily. 'Golly,' she whispered.

'Sorry,' Emily said, feeling somehow that she had let Maggie down.

'Maybe you're just not relaxing properly,' Maggie ventured.

'I'm trying to.'

'You're not doing your breathing right, either.'

'I am.'

'No – sorry, Emily, but with all due respect you haven't been practising.' Maggie looked quite annoyed now. 'You can't expect to go into these things unprepared, you know.'

Emily wasn't sure where this was coming from. 'Maggie, shut up.'

'I will not shut up! You didn't even do out a birth plan!'

'I didn't want a birth plan.'

'Oh, you didn't *want* one! Of course you didn't. Not like the rest of us mere mortals!'

'*What?*'

A dam inside Maggie seemed to burst, and she looked at Emily with a mixture of anger and resentment. 'We're not all like you, Emily. Able to do it all –

the big lawyer career, the baby, filing court cases and staging sit-ins in our spare time. If anything goes wrong for you, you always have something else to fall back on. I don't!'

All this sounded very insulting. For two pins now she would tell Maggie to fuck off. 'Nobody's stopping you doing other things, Maggie.'

'But that's just it! I don't want to do anything else!' Maggie cried. 'I've never wanted to do anything except have babies.' She looked very defensive. 'Oh, I went to college. I even worked for a while. Went after the promotions and the company car, because you do, don't you? But what was the point? I'm not an achiever; I'm not brave; I can't change the bloody world; not like you.'

This seemed to Emily to be way off the mark. 'I never wanted to change the world either! If you must know, mostly I am terrified and horrified.'

Maggie dismissed this with a flick of her hand. 'And I endured it, you know, those awful dinner parties when people would ask you what you do, and the little embarrassed silence when you tell them you don't have a job. No kids and no job! What is she, lazy, or just stupid? And Wendy over there with three kids and she running Coca-Cola! But I didn't care that they wrote me off. Because I was waiting, you see, for the baby. That was my career, that was my purpose in life—'

'If you'd excuse me for a minute please, Maggie, I'm

about to have a contraction.'

'Oh, sorry, fire ahead.'

Maggie retreated as Emily went into a black hole again. Emily held on to her sanity by focusing on Conor's book *The Pregnant Father*, and how it had warned its readers to be prepared for foul language and mindless accusations during labour. But surely these were supposed to come from *her*?

When the contraction was over she clawed her way back up the bed a bit. Maggie took up immediately where she had left off, looking a little annoyed at the interruption.

'And then it happened, I got pregnant, and everything started to make sense. I thought, here is something that I'm going to be brilliant at. Here, at last, is something that only I can do! And look at me! I can't even go into labour on time!'

'Oh, Maggie.'

'I know,' Maggie said without rancour. 'And look at *you*, ten days early.'

She said this as though she had something to be jealous about! As if Emily were the be-all and end-all! Emily wouldn't feel quite so annoyed if she didn't feel so tired and, well, hungry.

'Get the birth snacks out of my labour bag,' she bluntly told Maggie.

'I'm not hungry.'

'For me, Maggie.'

Maggie was shocked. 'You can't eat! You're in labour!'

'I know, but I'm mad, me,' Emily said loudly.

'No,' Maggie said, firmly.

'I'll have to get them myself then,' Emily said, lunging for her labour bag and extracting a bag of cheese and onion Tayto earmarked for Conor.

Maggie moved with surprising speed and wrestled them from her. 'You might have to have emergency surgery! I'm sorry, but I can't let you eat!'

'Give them back!' Emily was furious now.

'It's for your own good!' Maggie said stubbornly. 'I'd expect you to do the same for me.'

'If you do not give them to me I'll . . . I'll . . . oh, just give them to me!' Honestly! Who would have thought being in labour entailed all this? She'd thought she would only be required to do a bit of puffing and pushing – not defend herself against all kinds of horrible allegations of competence and bravery and taking control of her own life. Maggie had some nerve!

She flung herself back against the pillows and glared at Maggie. 'I'm not what you think I am, you know!'

'Sure, whatever, don't get yourself excited,' Maggie said patronisingly – as though she hadn't started all this in the first place!

'I mean it, Maggie!'

'Of course you do. Will I wet your facecloth again?'

Emily gave up. Why was she fighting it anyway? Why all the defensiveness? Everything Maggie had accused her of being was, well, *good*. Was it so impossible to believe that everything she had gone through had changed her for the better? She might have a way to go yet, but why not take credit for a damned good start?

'Maybe I will have a damp facecloth after all,' she conceded with dignity.

'Good for you,' Maggie said, contrite now. 'Emily, I'm sorry for having a go at you. It's the last thing you need right now.'

'Your timing could be better.'

'It's all this waiting around for the baby to come,' Maggie confessed miserably. 'I feel sometimes I'm going mad. It's just getting on top of me, that's all.'

'That's okay, Maggie.' Emily could afford to be magnanimous now. Maggie had pointed out some useful facts, after all.

'What's going on here?' Jessica was back, and not pleased to find Maggie in situ, a torn bag of crisps in one hand and a dripping facecloth in the other. 'This is a restricted area.'

Maggie and Emily looked at each other, co-conspirators again.

'I'm Emily's birth partner,' Maggie loftily informed Jessica. 'Until Conor arrives.'

Jessica, despite appearances, was no fool. 'Patients are not allowed to choose other patients as their birth partners. For a variety of reasons.'

'It's my fault,' Emily simpered. 'I asked Maggie to bring me down a tape of ocean sounds.'

'She did,' Maggie lied vigorously.

'Right . . .' Jessica said reluctantly. 'Now, off to bed with you.'

Maggie nipped up to the head of the bed. 'You'll let us know, won't you, Emily? How it goes?'

'Of course I will.'

'Good luck,' Maggie said tearfully, squeezing her hand. 'Oh, and do you mind if I keep these crisps? I'm starving.'

'Out,' Jessica ordered, before hospital management got wind of this.

With Maggie gone, Jessica was back to her buoyant self, and she wasted no time in switching on machines and monitors, and producing a big black belt-like thing. It was an electronic foetal monitor, which she now strapped around Emily's midriff.

'Great,' Jessica sang. 'Now we're all set!'

Emily felt anything but set as another contraction began its vicious, insidious assault on her insides.

'Breathe, Emily,' Jessica reminded her, and did a few enthusiastic puffs to keep her company. 'That's it!'

Emily looked at her with dull eyes. 'Do you ever have a bad day?'

Jessica just made another note on Emily's chart. 'Why are you so angry, Emily?'

Before she could retort, Emily was sucked into the vortex of pain again. When she opened her eyes a little while later, Conor was standing at the end of the bed.

'Hi,' he said.

'Hello,' she said hoarsely.

They regarded each other in silence for a moment; her sweaty and grim-faced, him trying to look calm and collected but wearing mismatched socks. His eyes darted from the monitors and wires and back to her again. He looked pale.

'Where's Jessica?' Emily asked eventually.

'She went to get some ice.'

'Ice?'

'Apparently you wanted some in your birth plan.'

'That's not my birth plan. It's Maggie's . . . oh, it doesn't matter.' Briefly she wondered what Maggie had intended to do with ice. 'You don't have to stand all the way down there, Conor. I'm not going to start biting.'

'I know that. I just didn't want to crowd you.' He reluctantly advanced a few steps and maintained a careful distance at the head of the bed, throwing another look at the monitors and tubes.

'How are you?' he asked.

'I don't know. It's not so bad at the moment, but then again, I'm not having a contraction at the moment.'

'Would you like me to rub your back?' he offered, not sounding all that enthusiastic.

'No. I couldn't bear it, to be honest.' She felt that if anybody touched her now she would scream.

'Okay . . . would it help if I did the breathing with you when the contractions happen?'

'I don't think so,' Emily said, her irritation growing. He was quoting *The Pregnant Father*, chapter and verse.

And he might look a bit more excited about the whole thing! Sneakily, he had worked his way back to the bottom of the bed again.

'Eh, right,' he said. 'Do you want me to talk you through it? You know, give you encouragement—'

'Tell me I'm opening up like a fucking flower?'

He seemed at a loss. 'I don't know what you want me to do, Emily.'

'Have you no imagination, Conor? Have you no idea what I might need?' Here came another contraction. She felt it building up inside her like a small volcano. 'Or maybe you *like* waiting around for my orders, seeing as I'm the one in the saddle in our marriage, apparently.'

The last thing she saw was his confused face before she shut her eyes tight and went to battle with the contraction. It was a tough one, closing around her belly and chest like a vice, squeezing the breath from her lungs. She fancied that it was trying to kill her. Well, it wouldn't. She hung on grimly until it eventually ran out of energy and was forced to subside. Strike one to her.

'Let's go for a walk, will we?' Conor said, when it was finally over. 'Up and down the corridors.'

He had obviously given himself a little pep-talk while she had been in the throes. Get with it, man! At least *look* as though you want to be here!

'I don't want to,' Emily said baldly.

'You did when we talked about this at antenatal

classes. I distinctly remember you telling me that you wanted to walk.'

'You *would* remember that, wouldn't you, Conor? Isn't that just typical of you?'

He ignored this. 'Let's go.'

'I can't! Are you blind? I'm hooked up to that monitor!'

He gave the monitor another wary look as Jessica came back in. 'That thing isn't keeping her alive, is it?'

Jessica laughed heartily. She seemed to find everything hugely amusing. 'Not at all. It's just to keep an eye on the baby – which is doing fine, by the way.'

Conor seemed greatly relieved. 'So you might be able to unhook it? If we were to go for a walk?' He seemed very keen on this walk.

'Of course – we encourage patients to move around during labour,' Jessica chirped. 'Nothing worse than lying on the flat of your back waiting!'

'Absolutely,' Conor agreed heartily.

Emily looked from one to the other and at this moment she was hard pushed to decide whom she hated more.

'I want an epidural,' she informed Jessica.

'Yes, I think we need to look at some form of pain relief,' Jessica agreed. 'I'll tell the anaesthetist. He's down with Laura at the moment.'

'Laura?' Emily was floored. But it was twins: Laura had expected that she wouldn't go to full-term.

'And they've just brought Dee in as well.'

'Dee?' Emily was even more shocked. But Dee was a week overdue. Still, it was a bit disconcerting that the whole campaign appeared to have spontaneously gone into labour.

'And Maggie?' she asked.

'Oh, Maggie's still hanging in there.'

She would be hopping mad.

'Off you go,' Jessica said, throwing open the door to the corridor.

Emily wasn't that happy at being forced off her warm bed. But pride made her climb down all by herself, and take a few cautious steps across the floor. To her relief, she didn't faint and nothing fell out of her.

'Okay?' Conor asked, as she paused for a moment in the corridor to get her bearings. He himself looked a lot better now that he was out of that room.

'Let's go then,' he said briskly. He was definitely back to himself – ordering her about, acting like she needed him to wind her up and point her in the right direction!

'I want to be alone,' she said loftily, walking off ahead of him at a brisk pace.

She passed vases of flowers and dusty religious statues and a photo of a baby with a smiling face. The baby was lovely, and Emily realised with a start that this was what it was all about: the pain, the nausea, the foetal belt, the hormonal madness. It was all just part of the process of her baby being born. It was easy to lose sight of it.

She lost sight of it a moment later as another contraction descended. At its height, she didn't give a hoot whether she gave birth to a monkey; she just wanted it all to be over. Behind her, she thought she saw Conor put out his hand to support her, but she gathered her energy and set off again, leaving him behind.

Time ceased to have any meaning. She measured it by the number of times she passed the photo of the baby . . . twenty, thirty, then she lost count. Doctors and midwives swished by, looking over curiously – her huffing up and down the corridor with Conor trailing three feet behind holding Maggie's damp facecloth. She did not have the energy to care as contraction after contraction overtook her, each one worse than the last. In the middle of one, she thought she heard Dee cry out from a nearby labour room. She didn't have the energy to care about her either. It was every woman for herself in here.

At one point, she registered that the clock over the nurses' station said it was eight am. *Eight?* Could she really have been here nearly four hours? The clock must be wrong.

There was no respite at all between contractions now. Eventually she stopped walking altogether and leaned against a wall, red-faced. She felt like her body was defeating her. She could not see any end in sight; only more and more pain and she wanted to cry again.

Conor was waiting with a glass of iced water. 'Jessica said you could have this.'

'I don't want it,' she said, even though she did.

He put it down without comment. 'Would you like to have a shower? It might pass some time.'

'No.'

'Look, you can try all you like, Emily, but I'm not leaving.'

'What?'

'I am not leaving this place until my baby is born. You can like it or lump it.'

Emily's eyes popped. 'Just a second here, Conor. *I'm* the one in labour!'

'I think we're all well aware of that at this point. But that doesn't mean that I have absolutely nothing to do with it.'

'Your bit is done,' she said childishly.

'So I should bugger off and leave you alone?'

'If you like! If you want to know the truth, you're not much bloody use to me!'

He gritted his teeth defensively. 'You're never happy, are you? On the one hand, I'm supposed to be spilling my guts at every opportunity, confiding every last thought, hope and dream in you. But on the other hand, we don't want me getting *too* emotional, do we? Because I only exist in a supporting role, right? We wouldn't want me robbing you of your moments in the sun!'

'*What?*'

'You don't have a monopoly on feelings, you know. Just because people don't show them doesn't mean they don't have them.'

Emily opened her mouth to retaliate but ended up collapsing against the wall, huffing through a contraction instead. It was another brutal one. Through the mist of pain, she was aware of Conor hovering, his hands half-cupped in case she might topple over and fall. She would love to, and break his leg maybe.

Panting, she flung herself away from the wall and glared at him.

'You're doing it again! I can't believe you're doing it again!'

'What am I doing?'

'Coming up with reasons why you had the affair! First I'm a power freak, and now I don't take account of your hidden emotions!'

'Oh stop it, Emily.'

'No I will not stop it. You're blaming me!'

'I am not blaming you.'

'So why did you do it then, Conor?'

He threw up his hands in exasperation. 'What is the point of going over all this again?'

'*Again*? We've never gone over it! Not once!'

'Because it's history, Emily.'

'History? Like the miscarriage was history?' She ignored his face. 'Things don't become history just because you refuse to deal with them!'

'Fine! So what do you want to know then? Where? When? How many times? Was she any good?'

'Oh, shut up.'

'No! Just tell me what you want to know! If it means

so much to you, I'll tell you the whole sorry saga from the beginning to the end! Right here in the middle of the corridor while you're in labour!'

'I just want to know why!' Emily shouted back. 'Why!'

Jessica was hurrying up the corridor now, looking from Emily to Conor warily.

'Emily? The anaesthetist is waiting to give you your epidural.'

Thank Christ. She could not bear the agony much longer. She turned her back on Conor and hobbled off.

Back in the labour room, the anaesthetist was shifting from foot to foot rather impatiently. He wanted to go home.

They all had to wait while Emily had another contraction. Then Jessica said, 'I'll just do a quick exam first, Emily. If you'll let your knees fall apart again . . .'

The anaesthetist and Conor both looked studiously at the floor. But Emily did not care if she were on MTV.

When Jessica eventually looked up, her face was even more cheerful than usual.

'Eight!' she sang.

'Eight?'

'You're eight centimetres dilated! It must have been all that walking! Isn't it marvellous?' She looked as pleased as if it had all been her own doing.

The anaesthetist deflated totally. Eight centimetres! Someone might have let him know. Without further ado, he turned and left.

'Where's he going?' Emily cried.

'It's too late for the epidural, Emily,' Jessica said.

'It's not. It's not. I want one!'

'It will make things harder and longer for you. Come on, you're doing so well on your own. You're nearly there,' Jessica argued.

'I can't do it . . .'

'You can. We'll help you every step of the way.' She looked at Conor expectantly. 'Won't we?'

Belatedly he nodded. 'Of course.'

'I want Mr Chapman!' Emily wailed. He would get this baby out of her – she had paid him a thousand pounds. He would do what he was told!

'He should be here any minute,' Jessica soothed. 'But I'll give him a buzz on his mobile. In the meantime, let's try some gas again.'

'It doesn't work,' Emily said, rather self-pityingly. She'd already tried it and it had only made her want to vomit.

'Let's try again,' Jessica said firmly, helping Emily into a sitting position, and unhooking the gas mask. 'Actually, Conor, maybe you could help here?'

She held out the gas mask.

He was shocked. 'But I wouldn't know what to do . . .'

'It's quite simple,' Jessica said briskly. 'You're just going to help Emily to breathe through the mask, that's all, when you see a contraction coming. You'll see it on the monitor – the little green line, see?'

He looked at the monitor as though it might self-combust. 'Um, right.'

'Oh, look! Here's one coming now!' Jessica said with a jolly smile, and walked out the door.

There was a nasty little silence in the labour room except for the slight hiss of gas. And on the monitor between Emily and Conor, that little green line started to climb.

Conor couldn't take his eyes off it. Emily saw his Adam's apple bob up and down a few times violently. She saw panic in his face, and . . . fear?

'I'm sorry, Emily,' he blurted suddenly. 'You're right. I'm no use to you here at all.'

'Conor . . .'

'No, no, don't try to make me feel better. This is the moment when you need someone the most, and I'm just not up to it.'

'Conor; please . . .'

'Will I ring Liz? She'd come in.'

'Conor, just give me the bloody mask!'

'Oh, right, sorry.'

The green line on the monitor was nearing its peak now and Emily was engulfed again. Vaguely, she felt the mask press firmly over her nose and mouth, Conor finally springing into action. Then the pain obliterated any other thought. She thought she might have mentally said a Hail Mary at one point – she must remember to tell Pauline that. She would be delighted. But just when she thought it should have been over, it got worse. She had never known anything like it. Cathy, she screeched silently, I believe you.

At last it subsided. Slowly. She felt her dry lips fall away from her teeth again and she opened her eyes with an effort. The mask lifted from her face.

Beside her, Conor was terrified. His eyes were wide and wet and his face parchment white. Emily had never seen him like this before. She was worried.

'Conor? Are you all right? Are the tubes and things upsetting you?' Her pregnancy books had warned her to be prepared for all kinds of squeamishness and fainting from menfolk at this point. It was not a myth.

But Conor just kept staring. 'You're not going to die, are you?'

Emily knew that this was too serious to give in to any impulse she might have to laugh. 'I don't think so. I hope not. I think it's just labour, Conor.'

'You look so sick.'

'I *feel* sick. But they wouldn't have left us in here with just a gas mask if they thought I was in any danger.' She tried to lighten the mood, to take the strange look off his face.

'I'm afraid,' he blurted. 'I'm sorry. I know you don't need to hear this right now . . . I just wouldn't be able to cope without you, Emily.'

'Conor, I am not going to die. Can we please stop talking about me dying?'

But Conor kept looking at her as though she were on

her last breath. 'It's different for you. You'd be able to cope without me.'

'What are you talking about?'

'You always have. You've never really needed me as much as I need you. You've never *loved* me as much as I love you.'

'Conor, that's ridiculous!'

He seemed to think she was being facetious. 'Oh come on, Emily. It's always been like that! From the very first time we met, when you took pity on me—'

'What?'

He spoke very fast as though he were afraid he wouldn't get it out before she expired. 'It's true. And I was so grateful that I pretended to be what you wanted me to be, or what I thought you wanted me to be. But it was never equal between us, the love. Somehow I thought you would catch up with me. But you never did.'

'Gas!' she shouted, as another contraction snuck up on her. It was a nasty one, but she fought back as best she could, anxious for it to be over. She had barely drawn breath again before she turned back to Conor. 'How was I ever supposed to "catch up" when you always run away on me? A relationship isn't going to deepen if you always pull back!'

'I was trying to protect myself, Emily,' he said quietly. 'Hold a bit back. For the day when you finally realised that I wasn't really enough, and you left me.'

Emily's eyes could not get any wider at this point.

And she had thought he possessed no imagination? And all this time he had been indulging in conjecture and speculation and wild fantasies about her leaving him!

'And just in case I didn't get up the gumption to leave by myself, you thought you'd help me along by having an affair?' she asked incredulously.

'I was stupid.'

'Tell me something I don't know!'

He looked at her directly. 'All right. I was lonely.'

Emily felt a tightness in her chest. 'I think that's probably your own fault.'

'I know it was,' he said.

'Go on,' she forced herself to say. Well, she had wanted to know why, hadn't she?

'All right. I could talk to Mary like I couldn't talk to you because I didn't love her and it didn't matter.'

There wasn't a sound out in the corridor now. Even Dee had stopped her screeching.

'What did you talk to her about?' Emily asked.

'Not you. Not us. The miscarriage, a bit.'

'The miscarriage?' This hurt terribly.

'With us . . . you talk and I listen. I always feel you're the more important person in our relationship, so when something *does* happen, you get first dibs on attention.'

Emily felt terribly defensive. 'It's up to you to open your mouth a bit more!'

'I know that! I'm admitting that! But it's on your side too, Emily! You push and prod all right, but only when it's to do with you! Most of the time I feel I can't say anything because I'm supposed to be there for you to fall back on!'

'Rubbish!' Emily hissed.

But he was her plain-clothes garda, wasn't he? The voice of reason when she wanted him to be? And then she expected him to turn around and share with her, but only to a point that suited her. She certainly didn't want a man who went around the house gnashing his teeth, a man with emotional diarrhoea. It was a very fine line to ask anybody to tread.

Naturally, she didn't admit to this immediately. 'So while you were off talking to Mary, I had nobody to talk to!'

'I know. I'm sorry.'

She felt another contraction come to life. Well, she would have her say first. 'If you think *you're* afraid, Conor, I'm terrified! Terrified to ask for the slightest bit of support, frightened to look for anything at all for myself because you'll look at me like I should be on Prozac! It's no bloody wonder I've never been able to stand up for myself!'

Conor did not interrupt.

'I mean, look at you tonight! The very time I need you most, you're faffing around with damp facecloths and gas masks and you're just not going to muck in at all, are you? You're going to stand back and "protect" yourself, because you've got this ridiculous notion in your head about who loves who more!'

It did sound ridiculous, and Conor smiled a bit. Emily would have too, only that out of the corner of her eye, she saw the green line on the monitor rise and rise, and the pain became bad. She hurried on.

'So the upshot is that you're afraid and I'm terrified, is that it?'

'Yes,' he agreed.

'How on earth did we end up like this, Conor?'

'I don't know,' he admitted. 'I'm sorry, Emily.'

'I suppose I'm sorry too.' This sounded a bit too contrite. 'Even though I think you should have said something before!'

But he wasn't going to take this lying down. 'And so should you, if you felt you weren't getting what you wanted! There's no point in giving me those disappointed little looks when I don't know what the hell they mean!'

'You needn't worry on that score! I'm a different woman now, you know!' A woman in labour could get away with this kind of statement, she felt.

'So am I!' Conor retaliated. 'Or a different man at least.' He cast a look at the green line on the monitor. 'Emily, maybe you should have some gas—'

'Are you trying to avoid issues here?' she asked suspiciously, ignoring the pain.

'I am not! It's just that Jessica left me in charge of gas!'

'That decision you wanted me to make, Conor . . .'

'Why don't we leave that for the moment?' he said, looking worriedly again at the monitor.

'I can't make it. Not yet.'

'Yes, yes . . .' The green line merrily raced towards it peak. 'God Almighty, Emily, could we please concentrate on the matter at hand here! Use the gas!'

'You're just not going to stop, are you—' She was cut off mid-stream as the contraction finally hit her full-force. Her mouth fell open and she stared wordlessly, helplessly at Conor.

'Oh Lord,' he said, fumbling about with the gas mask. 'Hang on, Emily, hang on, I'll get this thing on you . . . damn!' He had somehow wrapped the tubing around his leg. He looked at Emily's stricken face, and she saw that fear again, that backing off when things got too tough, and she closed her eyes to him and lay frozen and alone as the contraction attacked.

She started to say a Hail Mary again. It was worth a try.

Then she felt a hand on hers; tight, reassuring. Conor. She opened her eyes briefly to see him close to her, his face comforting, or at least a good impression of it. His voice was low in her ear.

'Don't hit me,' he said, 'but maybe you should try doing your breathing.'

'Can't . . .' she managed.

'You can. You've been doing it all along. Come on. Just try. I'll help you.'

She did try, a little bit, expecting Conor to start puffing in unison. But he didn't. Instead he rubbed her belly, quite vigorously like the midwife had shown them in antenatal classes. She didn't know if it actually helped. But, on the other hand, it didn't hurt.

The contraction was at its peak now and she felt it slipping out of her control.

'Jesus, Conor,' was all she whispered.

He didn't really humour her at all. Instead he said, 'Just remember, Emily, you're eight centimetres. You're nearly there.'

He kept saying that over and over, that she was nearly there and that the baby would soon be born. After a while she started to believe him. It didn't get any easier but somehow it got more bearable. And he never let go of her hand.

That was the way Mr Chapman found them twenty minutes later when he swished in wearing blue scrubs and smelling of canteen coffee.

'Hello,' he said pleasantly.

They looked at him as though he were an intruder. Possibly they didn't recognise him in his scrubs. 'It's Mr Chapman,' he clarified rather sharply. And he after driving up from Cork too! Still, maybe they were annoyed that his predication of the birth date had been wildly off target. That would teach him.

But no, they gave him a cursory greeting before going back to their breathing, both of them very concentrated, very calm really. Mind you, she was huffing much too fast in Mr Chapman's opinion. They were trying to produce a baby here, not run a mini-marathon. He hoped she wouldn't ask to take the placenta home to bury in the back garden. He wouldn't put it past her.

'She's almost ten,' Jessica informed him crisply, after a quick exam.

Of course she was. He wouldn't be here otherwise. Like every other obstetrician, he only showed up for the grand finale.

'Okay, Emily, we're nearly there,' he said with his usual calm authority, snapping on gloves.

Two other midwives joined them now. Mr Chapman liked to think it was because they had heard he was here. It didn't occur to him that they had come for Emily, the woman who was fighting their court case for them in exactly one hour's time.

He had thought of the court case on the drive up. Cork's management would be raging that he had not thought to ring them up and let them know that Emily Collins had gone into labour early. But his first loyalty was, as always, to his patient. And anyway, it was in the hands of the courts now. His job was to deliver her baby safe and sound.

'Excellent,' he said, doing an exam. He felt the baby's head under his fingertips, round and hard, straining to get out. 'I think we can start getting ready to push, Emily. Jessica will tell you when.'

The place was suddenly a flurry of activity. Two midwives helped Emily into the birthing position, slightly hunched over with her chin tucked into her chest, and her hands clamped under her thighs. One of the midwives gave her quiet instructions on how to push – 'One long push down. Keep it going as long as you can, okay?'

Jessica took up residence in front of the monitor, watching and waiting. The fourth midwife was ready to assist Mr Chapman.

'Ready?' Mr Chapman said, throwing a detached smile at Emily and Conor.

They watched him with pale, tired, frightened faces. They looked very young, almost like teenagers, and for a moment he forgot that he heartily disliked the pair of them.

'It'll be all right, you know,' he said, kindly. The midwives looked up in surprise. He was not known for his bedside manner, and he felt a bit embarrassed now.

'Well?' he barked brusquely at them. 'How are we doing?'

'Here comes one now,' Jessica announced, watching the monitor. 'When I tell you, start pushing, Emily, okay?'

On the bed, with her arms locked around her thighs and stringy hair falling in her eyes, Emily tried not to panic. She turned to Conor who was practically on the bed beside her. He was mucking in so much that he was nearly crowding her.

'I'm afraid,' she whispered, as she felt the pain growing steadily stronger. 'I don't think the baby's going to be able to get out down there.'

'He will if he has my driving skills,' Conor reassured her.

'Here we go!' Jessica cried enthusiastically. 'Push now, Emily! PUSHHHH!'

And Emily did. She dug her chin into her chest and gave a long, hoarse shout as she squeezed downwards with all her might. Blood rushed to her head with the strain and she fiercely hoped that nothing up there would burst.

'Don't let up-don't let up-keep going-keep going,' Jessica chanted, her damned enthusiasm strangely infectious now. Emily did as she was told and kept going.

'That's it, Emily! You're doing brilliantly!' Good lord – surely that wasn't Conor shouting like he was at a football match? It was, and she bore down with all her strength one last time.

'All right. Well done. Relax, Emily,' Jessica said. 'Deep breaths.'

Emily fell back onto the pillows, exhausted, feeling that her whole face must be hideously swollen. But it was strange, this feeling of exhilaration and excitement.

Suddenly she was desperate to see this through, to hold her baby in her arms.

'Can you see it yet?' she asked Mr Chapman breathlessly.

'Um, no. It takes a bit more than one push.'

'Oh.'

But she didn't lose heart. When the next contraction came, she attacked it with all her might. The midwives all started braying again and the room rocked to the roar of 'Push!'. She was almost starting to enjoy herself.

It was a different story fifteen minutes later.

'I can't do it any more. I can't.' She was prostrate on the pillows, exhausted, sodden and defeated. Conor had used every last word of encouragement in his vocabulary and even Jessica was starting to repeat herself.

'Here comes another one,' Jessica said. But Emily went at the next contraction only half-heartedly, feeling that she had nothing left to give.

'You might need some help here, Emily,' Mr Chapman informed her, and she froze as she thought she saw him eyeing a large pair of forceps. Surely to God those things wouldn't fit inside her? And if they did, how would he get them back out again with a baby's head stuck between them?

Conor saw her face. His voice was for her only. 'Don't give up now, Emily. After coming all this way. You're on the last leg! Come on. I'll help you. Let me help you.'

'Here we go again,' Jessica announced.

'Are you ready, Emily?' Conor asked. 'Will we give it another go?'

She looked at him. 'Yes.'

'PUSH!' Jessica shouted.

Emily did. She felt she were going to split open with the effort but she kept on pushing, Conor bearing down with her, his hands on her shoulders, his voice in her ear urging her on.

Then, the magic words.

'I have the head,' Mr Chapman murmured.

'Ohmigod!' Emily squealed, beaming insanely at Conor.

'I know. I know. It's fantastic.' He smiled back almost as madly. 'Good luck.'

'Yes,' she said, and she went to work for the last time.

Down below, Mr Chapman didn't feel it necessary to give any running commentary. He had the baby's head in his hands now. Its eyes were scrunched up tight and the little mouth puckered in outrage, all ready to bawl the second it had the breath to do so.

Mr Chapman smiled although he was unaware he was doing so. Almost there. He had a shoulder out now. It was a fine big baby; he would put it at eight pounds or more. And boisterous. All that wriggling! He kept a careful eye on the perineum, but there was no sign of any tear. Good. There would be no need for any stitches at all.

The rest happened very quickly, and the same as it always happened bar the odd few cases. Another push and he had the baby out and he was holding him up to drain away any fluid from the respiratory tract, and he was saying those words, 'It's a boy'. Then he was cutting the cord and Jessica was helping to staple it and the baby, crying, suddenly opened his eyes and looked up at Mr Chapman in that blind way that newborns do. And Mr Chapman involuntarily thought of the grandchild he had been denied, the grandchild he would never deliver and who would never look up at him like that, and he felt bereft.

'Mr Chapman? I need to weigh the baby.'

'Of course.' Mr Chapman blinked and handed over the baby briskly to Jessica. He settled down to wait for the placenta to come out.

He never spoke during this because he wanted to give the parents some privacy as they met their baby for the first time. But he couldn't resist looking up to see Emily Collins bending over her bundle, shocked, exhilarated, uncomprehending. At least she was normal in that respect.

The placenta was taking its time. He checked his watch. Ten-thirty. Two things struck him: the court case would be starting about now, and Killian and Andrea had a ten-thirty flight back from London. He knew, because he had booked it himself. Andrea had insisted on travelling on a Monday morning, as though she were trying to fool people that she was a business-woman or something.

He knew that they would not survive this, Killian and Andrea. He had seen the first traces of blame in her face already. He doubted that Killian had any notion yet.

He found that he felt sympathy for his son, perhaps for the first time. Like most things in Killian's life, the break-up would come from left of centre and take him completely by surprise.

There was nothing Mr Chapman could do. His inter-ference was not wanted, even though he preferred to think of it as protection and guidance. Was this what parenting finally came down to, merely picking up the pieces? Good luck to Emily Collins. She would need it.

The placenta was finally out. He was finished.

'Let's have a look at the little fellow,' he said before he left, as he always did.

Emily Collins looked up at him with shining eyes and held out her baby. Conor Collins hovered protectively. Mr Chapman peered in at the little face and nodded. 'He's lovely. Well done.'

Emily Collins was tearful. 'Mr Chapman – thanks. You were marvellous.'

'My pleasure,' Mr Chapman said politely. He couldn't resist adding, 'And good luck in court today.'

'Um, yes.'

Mr Chapman left, followed by three of the midwives. Jessica pulled a blanket up on Emily.

'Thanks.' Emily smiled hugely at Jessica, her new best friend.

'I'll be back shortly,' Jessica advised. 'Then we'll get you moved down to a post-natal ward.'

Emily and Conor were left alone at last.

'Are you all right?' Conor asked her.

'Yes, yes,' she said impatiently. 'My God, Conor! We have a baby!'

And indeed they had. He was resting on Emily's tummy.

'Is he all right?' Conor ventured. 'Can he breathe, do you think?'

The baby was completely swaddled in a blue blanket, except for his face. His eyes were brown and were squinting against the glare of the fluorescent lights. Apart from that he didn't make a move.

'I think so,' Emily said, doubtful. 'You know, he's not at all how I imagined he would look.'

'Well, you thought he would be a girl, didn't you?' Conor said helpfully.

'So did you!'

'I said I didn't care what it was so long as it was healthy,' he argued. 'I hope he likes the colour yellow.'

'Look at all that hair, Conor.'

'What? Where?'

'Where? On his head!'

'Oh, right. Yes. I didn't think they grew hair until they got out. Still, it suits him, don't you think?'

They just looked and looked at this baby, not sure what to make of him, not sure what to feel at all. Emily, her exhaustion kicking in now, was just glad that he was alive and healthy and normal. And, really, he was beautiful.

'Isn't he?'

'What?' Conor said. He didn't sound himself.

'Beautiful.'

Conor looked down at the baby for a long moment, considering. 'He's all wrinkled,' he said eventually. 'He looks like a little old man.'

'Yes,' Emily agreed. 'My father.'

'I suppose we'll be calling him Robert so.'

'Only if you think he looks like a Robert.'

'He looks like a Robert.'

And it was decided.

Part Three

She saw them the minute she entered the church, huddled together on a seat at the back. Her heart lifted as she went towards them.

'Maggie!'

Maggie looked up, confused for a moment. 'Oh, Emily! Wow, look at your face! It's all gone down!'

'Thank you,' Emily said, not sure at all that this was a compliment. 'And Dee! And Laura! You're great for coming.'

'We wouldn't have missed it.'

It was marvellous to see them all again, and there were hugs and kisses and exclamations all round. They had all meant to meet up ages ago, of course, but between one thing and another . . .

'And you've brought all the babies!' Emily exclaimed. Four car seats were lined up on the pew in front. The babies were all magnificently decked out in Baby Gap and Gymboree. She hadn't seen any of them since they were newborns.

451

'Look at little Chloe! She's gone huge!' she swooned, leaning in to tickle Maggie's baby under the chin.

'That's actually my Regina,' Dee clarified.

'Of course it is,' Emily said, mortified at having offended two women in the one breath. But Dee said, 'At least you didn't think she was a boy. Most people do.'

And they all guffawed heartily.

'What did you call the twins in the end, Laura?' Emily asked.

'Baby 1 and Baby 2,' Laura sighed. 'We just can't make up our minds.'

'Well, come on then!' Maggie cried. 'Let's see the man of the moment!'

Emily shyly held out her own car seat. Robert was sleeping, a miracle in itself. She'd snatched the soother out of his mouth on the church steps and was glad now. None of the girls' babies had soothers. A lot of parenting books frowned on them.

'Look at him in his little white dress!' Dee said.

'That's actually a christening shawl,' Emily clarified, and they all guffawed again, even more heartily.

'He's gorgeous,' Laura chimed in magnanimously. 'He's the spit of you. The absolute spit.'

'Um, thank you,' Emily said awkwardly. She still found it disconcerting, this need people seemed to have to reassure her that the baby bore some resemblance to either of his parents. They would chop him up into parts, and insist that he had Conor's nose but Emily's eyes. It was like a kind of false flattery – as though either of them had had any control over the matter at all.

'Come on. Sit down, Emily,' Maggie urged.

Out of the corner of her eye, Emily saw Liz, Eamon and the five boys enter and go to the top of the church.

'I shouldn't really . . .'

'Just for a minute,' Maggie insisted. Emily squeezed in beside them, adding her car seat to the cluster on the pew in front. 'Tell us, are you expecting a big crowd?' Maggie wanted to know.

'No,' Emily admitted. 'It's all very last minute what with Conor going away tomorrow.'

'Of course,' Maggie said. 'We were thinking of having Chloe's christening on a Friday – you know, when most people are at work. Tiernan's relatives alone would come to two hundred and forty-three.'

'We're keeping it to a hundred,' Dee confided. 'A nice manageable number.'

Emily and Conor were only having forty people today, but Emily had been up since dawn disinfecting toilets and making interesting sandwiches in the shape of boats. She was exhausted.

There was a funny little silence now. 'Isn't it great that we're all together again?' Maggie heartily declared.

'Great,' the women all echoed.

'And we thought we'd never get out of St Martha's!'

'Well, *you* didn't, Maggie. Imagine, sixteen days overdue! It must have been a record!'

And they all laughed again.

Now that the formalities were over, the women got down to the real business. They huddled in together over the five baby car seats. Emily huddled in too. Wasn't it great to catch up with them all again?

'How is Chloe feeding?' Dee immediately wanted to know.

'Great,' Maggie confided. 'She's on juice and everything now.'

'Juice!' Laura cried. 'Baby 2 won't even drink water. But he's putting on weight really well.'

'Good for him! And how's Robert's cradle-cap, Emily?'

Emily wanted to tell Maggie to keep her voice down. Announcing it to the whole church! 'Fine. I'm massaging it with olive oil.'

'Olive oil?' Dee was disapproving. 'No, no, you need some of that special shampoo, Emily. That'll clear it up in no time.'

'Right,' Emily said, a bit stiff. She'd already tried the shampoo; half of Robert's head had washed away with the suds.

'And how's Regina sleeping for you, Dee?'

'Oh, great. We got eight hours of a stretch out of her last night!'

'Eight hours!' Everyone was very envious.

'Chloe only slept for six,' Maggie said.

'My boys went for five,' Laura said.

Emily said nothing. Robert had never slept for more

than three hours at a stretch since the day he'd been born two months ago. Maybe if he were a better sleeper Emily wouldn't look so much like a washed-out old rag. She wished now that she'd made more of an effort for today. She was wearing a loose-fitting outfit she'd already had in her wardrobe, which she had thought looked perfectly respectable. She just didn't have the energy to traipse down to Cork to scour the outsize shops with Robert in tow. She wished she had now. The girls all looked fantastic, like they were going to a wedding. Maggie's cream trousers still had the shop creases in them. And how come they all looked so *thin*?

On the pew in front, Robert stirred and started a low, lone whinge. Emily looked down at him, willing him to go back to sleep. He cried quite a lot for no apparent reason, usually in the car when she was in the fast lane on the motorway. Or at night, just as she was falling into an exhausted sleep. She would strip him down and look for signs of rashes or stray nappy flaps, but there would be nothing. Up and down they would walk on the landing, him grief-stricken and her guilt-ridden that she did not know what was wrong with him.

'Maybe you should pick him up,' Dee eventually said. Emily's face felt hot at the implication of neglect.

'He sometimes settles on his own,' she said defensively. It was true.

He didn't. His whinge changed into a cry.

'Now, now,' Emily said, furiously rocking the car seat. She was aware of the girls monitoring the situation closely, hoping against hope that Robert didn't wake up their own babies. Laura had started to rock the twins a bit nervously.

More embarrassed, Emily reached down and undid Robert's harness, and scooped him up from the car seat. She took off his little white christening hat and the shawl. He was probably boiling, that was what was bothering him.

'So tell us, Laura, are you breast-feeding the twins?' she asked brightly, bobbing Robert up and down with an air of nonchalance. Shut up now, Robert, she pleaded. After all I do for you, give me a fucking break.

'Oh no,' Laura declared, looking shocked. 'Nobody could manage that. Besides, it gives Mark a chance to get involved.'

No wonder she looked so bloody fresh if the husband was doing all the work.

Robert's face grew redder and redder as he looked at Emily pathetically. She saw Conor's family, seated near the top of the church, turn around with concern, and she teetered between mortification and total sympathy with Robert. Did he have a dirty nappy? A quick sniff told her no. Tell me what's wrong with you, she begged him.

'Poor Robert!' Maggie said, awkwardly. Dee and Laura exchanged looks. Chloe, Regina, Baby 1 and Baby 2 slept on angelically.

Robert's heartfelt wails filled the church now, and everyone looked distressed, apart from Liz's five boys who looked down avidly. Emily craned her neck for Conor. Where the hell was he? She bitterly regretted her airy decision that they should drive to the church separately. After all, they lived separately. Both of them were very careful not to lose sight of that.

'Do you think maybe he's hungry?' Dee ventured, rocking her own silent, gorgeous daughter.

'I fed him an hour ago,' Emily said stiffly.

But, on cue, he started rooting around her chest to find a nipple. He was starving.

'Oh!' Emily said. 'Look at that!'

And indeed they did, the whole damned congregation now, including the priest who had ambled out to prepare the readings. She felt watchful eyes on her as she tried to hitch up her top and open down the flap on her maternity bra without dropping Robert. It was hard enough to do in the solitude of your own home, never mind in front of a bloody audience and God.

What she really wanted to do was go out to the car and feed him there. But the girls would probably think she was acting like breast-feeding was something to be ashamed of. But she just didn't feel competent or confident enough just yet to whip them out wherever she happened to be. And they were her *breasts* at the end of the day, a private part of herself. She didn't feel they had become any less private just because she was breast-feeding.

Robert, sensing a good nosh-up on the way, grew frantic now, clawing at her skin with his little fingers.

She turned away from the watchful eyes and hiked him up under her jumper. For once, he latched on immediately and closed his eyes in bliss. She always liked this bit. It was the one time he made her feel really useful, and she wished that she were alone with him to enjoy it.

'There's a restaurant in Cork that doesn't allow breast-feeding at the table,' Dee announced. 'When I rang to make a booking, I asked.'

'Disgraceful,' Emily muttered.

'Maybe we should boycott it,' Laura declared.

Emily didn't have the energy to boycott anything. How come Maggie, Dee and Laura were coping so well? Did they just have easier babies?

Emily felt guilty now for heaping the blame for her own shortcomings onto Robert, and she hugged him closer. She would try harder. And she would *never* be caught again wearing her dressing gown at three o'clock in the afternoon.

Robert's guzzling sounds filled the church, or so Emily thought anyway, and he was taking twice as long as he usually did. Maggie, Dee and Laura occasionally clucked benignly, and checked every now and again to see how he was doing.

'There! Isn't that better?' Dee said to Robert as he eventually finished up and Emily sat him upright on her knee. Raging, Emily patted his back rather harder than usual, and he gave a huge burp. At the top of the church, Tommy and Robbie broke into loud sniggers.

Eamon roundly clipped them around the ear. Robbie started to cry.

Emily felt fresh sweat break out under her armpits. This day was turning into a disaster.

'I was reading a new report that said formula could well be better for children in the long run,' Dee offered into the silence.

'Is that a fact,' Emily said tightly, regretting even inviting Dee. Inviting any of them! But they had all been so close in Martha's, sisters-in-arms, taking on the world together. Giving birth together. Dee had even had a look at Emily's perineum after the birth to tell her what the damage was. And now look at her – at *all* of them – sitting there prim and superior! It was like they were strangers.

Suddenly, Dee's immaculately made-up face gave a violent twitch. Her eyes screwed up uncontrollably and she started crying. Really crying, sobbing, and a thin keen of despair came from her mouth.

Emily was so taken aback that she just gawked. So did Laura and Maggie. The rest of the congregation pretended not to notice.

'I tried to breast-feed. I wore the nipples off myself,' Dee sobbed. 'After two weeks she was nearly dead with starvation and the district nurse said I had to go on formula.'

Maggie and Laura didn't seem to know what to say. Emily stepped in, strongly. 'You really shouldn't take the breast-feeding thing so seriously, Dee. She looks great on formula. Doesn't she, girls?' She looked hard at Maggie and Laura for a bit of support. She was getting the strong whiff of pretence all around. Well, bugger that. 'Come on. It's hard work,' she declared. 'We all know it's bloody hard work.'

'Thank you, Emily!' Dee cried. 'And everyone expects you to be so fucking happy all the time! Derek coming home from work and wondering why I'm not grinning from ear to ear with joy when all I've talked about for the past three years is having a baby!'

Laura's composure disintegrated even more rapidly. 'And they try to help, don't they? To make the dinner, to pick up some of the filthy laundry off the floor, but that just makes you feel like you've been sitting around on your arse all day long!'

They seemed to have forgotten entirely that they were in a church.

'And the visitors!' Maggie chimed in avidly. 'All Tiernan's bloody sisters who keep telling me to get the baby into a routine. A routine! And there's me sitting on the couch hoping they won't stay long enough for me to offer them coffee, because I haven't made it to the shops for milk because she's puked once and poohed twice before we've even made it to the car and I just don't have the energy left!'

Emily sat back and let them have their say. They were dying to. Honestly! What a crowd of ninnies they all were, herself included, trying to put up a good front, trying to be superwomen!

Dee had stopped crying now, and went on in a low, ashamed voice. 'Sometimes I hate Regina. Sometimes I wish she had never been born. That sounds terrible, doesn't it? If the district nurse knew I was thinking these things, they'd whip her away from me and into care.'

She didn't hate her at all. That was obvious from the way she was cradling her so protectively. Laura and Maggie put their arms around her to comfort her.

'It's just that you can't imagine life going on and on like this,' Emily said sensibly. 'No sleep, no life outside the house, nothing in common with your friends any more who come over to tell you about their nights out and who's shagging who in work. And they coo over her and rock her and tell you how lucky you are. Then they hand her back and go off to join the real world,' she finished up.

Dee and Laura and Maggie looked up, their perfect mascara a bit streaked now. 'You've had those days too?' Maggie asked incredulously. *Emily?* Surely not!

'I've had those *weeks*,' Emily declared.

'Oh thank God, I thought I was a freak,' Dee shouted happily, and the priest on the altar looked down sharply. 'I even thought I might have postnatal depression,' she went on, quieter.

'So did I!' Maggie exclaimed.

'Me too!' Laura added.

By the time the front pews of the church had filled up, the girls were smiling again, and handing around tissues, and promising to phone each other up, day or night, whenever they felt like chucking their babies out the window and opening a bottle of vodka.

'Not that I'd ever do it, not really,' Maggie anxiously clarified, looking around the church as though she expected a district nurse to be eavesdropping, ready to root out dissident mothers.

'Oh, me neither,' Dee agreed very quickly. 'And I didn't mean that thing I said about slipping her Valium.'

'Of course you didn't.'

That peculiar tension, the awkwardness, had disappeared, and Emily felt herself relax for the first time all day. She looked at Maggie and Dee and Laura as they fussed over each other's babies and she loved them all over again.

She put back on Robert's christening hat and the shawl. He gazed up at her intensely, unwaveringly. For all her inadequacies, he seemed to find her irresistible. When she picked him up, he would instinctively cuddle into her. His eyes had started to follow her around the room, and when she spoke, he would look in the direction of her voice.

Nobody had ever loved Emily like that. Not Conor, or Emily's own mother, or anybody else in the world. It made her feel very humble.

It also aroused a fierce feeling of protectiveness in her. Murderous feelings, even.

If anyone even told Robert to feck off, she was

scared that she would pounce on them and strangle
the life out of them with her bare hands. It was as if
she had turned into one of those primitive creatures in
a David Attenborough nature documentary, fighting
tooth and nail for the survival of her cub. With minor
differences of course; she did her foraging for food at
the baby fruit-juice section of the supermarket, and
Robert's most predatory enemies would probably be
found at the local crèche.

Robert did a little posset now, and Emily admired it
before wiping it away.

On the altar, the priest looked at his watch and went
off to round up the lone altar boy. The service would be
starting soon.

'Listen, I'd better go on up. I'll see you afterwards,'
she whispered to the girls now.

'And we should have some news later on this afternoon. You know, about Martha's.'

Maggie, Laura and Dee barely looked up from their
babies.

'Oh, yes,' said Maggie, vaguely. Maggie, who had
marched up and down in her slippers in the rain;
Maggie who had mooted the idea of a hunger strike!
Now she was acting as though the battle to save the
hospital had been someone else's entirely!

But perhaps Emily felt the same, if she were honest
with herself. It all seemed so long ago. They were
different people now, with different battles. They were
mothers.

Behind her, the church door swung open and she turned around expectantly. But it was only her mother, decked out in a florid two-piece and a hat. Her rosary beads were already wrapped around her knuckles in anticipation of a good praying session. Some things never changed, although Pauline had cut back on the number of Masses she attended a week from five to two. She was still addicted to funerals, though, and rarely missed one.

'A great day, a great day,' she said, delirious at the prospect of welcoming another innocent soul into the Catholic fold. Conor had told her last week that they were considering an ecumenical service just to rile her up.

'I just saw Conor drive up,' she said, looking at Emily with that familiar disappointment.

'Good,' Emily said, wondering if Pauline would be able to contain herself, at least for today.

She wasn't. 'I just don't know what you're thinking of!' she said, shaking her head so violently that her hat slipped down over one ear.

'Yes, thank you, Mammy—'

'Isn't it enough that you have him living in a separate house? Do you have to drive him away to Belgrade too?'

'Belgium. And I'm not driving him anywhere. He wants to go.'

'And that child not nine weeks old yet!'

'Nine weeks and two days actually,' Emily said

proudly. 'Doesn't he look great?'

'Yes,' Pauline was forced to concede. 'But listen, about Conor—'

'You'd better go on up, Mammy. All the best seats are nearly taken.'

This had the desired effect. Pauline set off up the church at a gallop, lest someone usurped her from the position of honour in the front row. Now Liz was on her way down, dragging a red-faced Robbie by his blazer.

'I *told* you to go to the toilet before we came!'

'He can go in the bushes outside,' Emily said, trying to spare Robbie further embarrassment.

'And don't wet your shoes!' Liz warned, sending him off through the doors smartly. But she didn't look that annoyed. In fact, she looked great. Her hair was shiny and well cut, and she was wearing a lovely blue trouser suit that made her look very sophisticated.

'I hope Robert doesn't bring the roof down during the ceremony,' Emily whispered nervously.

'Not at all. And if he does, so what? They're used to it at christenings.'

Liz was being great these days. Emily didn't know whether it was the shared experience of motherhood, or whether it was down to Liz's new job in the chemist, which had given her great confidence.

Either way, Emily was glad for these brief interludes of companionship. Lord knows they didn't last long. This one didn't either.

'Tell us, are you going to keep paying rent on that

house, even when Conor's gone?'

'He *is* coming back eventually, Liz. And he'll be flying home some weekends.'

'I suppose.' Liz looked at her as though the pair of them were quite mad. Maybe we are, Emily thought. But everything had happened so fast. There was no time for dithering or indecision. In the end, it had been Emily who had made up their minds for both of them.

Liz leaned in now, and lowered her voice to a mere whisper. 'I know this isn't the time or place, but Eamon was wondering if you had any news for him.'

'I only filed for bankruptcy on Tuesday, Liz. These things take time.'

'But they won't take the house on us, will they?' Liz betrayed her worry now. 'I've read stories in the papers.'

'They won't take the house on you. But all his equipment and machinery will be seized to pay off the creditors. He probably won't have anything left, Liz. To start again with.'

Liz didn't seem too put out by this. 'No harm. Anyway – between us – he's been offered some work by Paudie Coyle.'

'That cowboy,' Emily murmured.

'Maybe he's a bit economical with his raw materials, but isn't that why he has a thriving business while Eamon's has gone to the wall? Eamon was too generous with his customers; that's what I tell him.'

Emily said nothing. The patio stones lay beautifully

now that Eamon had had another look at them, and you'd hardly notice the four extra ones that had been laid by the hedge at all, and that should have been laid in the first place.

'At least he has something lined up,' she told Liz.

'But he said this morning that he won't take it!' Liz said indignantly. 'Says he's happy at home looking after the boys, says he hasn't spent as much time with them in years!' And she rolled her eyes as though Eamon had lost his marbles.

'Well, I suppose you're earning now,' Emily pointed out.

'I know, I know, and it's good money too. And to be honest it's great to have a bit of freedom from the boys.' But there was something else bothering her.

'If Eamon doesn't mind being at home for a while, then what's the problem, Liz?'

'I don't know ... I feel a terrible pressure on me sometimes, with them all at home depending on my wage. What if I lose my job? What if my hours are cut? What happens then?'

'You've been there before, Liz, yourself and Eamon would cope.'

'Maybe ... I never thought I'd say this, but I feel bad now that I was so hard on Eamon. He was carrying the can the same way as I am now.'

'True,' Emily said. 'It's funny how things turn, isn't it?'

Liz looked around impatiently for Robbie, anxious to

get back to her seat before Emily got more philosophical. But she'd always been like that. You could be having a perfectly decent conversation and she'd get all airy-fairy on you.

'I hope I don't do anything wrong up there,' she told Emily nervously.

'Come on, Liz. You've been through it five times before.'

'Not as godmother.'

Christenings had always been a bit of a trial for Liz, because she'd had to go through so many of them, and towards the end had run out of suitable friends and relatives to prevail upon to be godmothers or godfathers. They'd had to resort to a second cousin of Eamon's for Willy last year, and she had turned up in a most unsuitable outfit.

But being on the receiving end of the dreaded request was very different. Liz was totally amazed that Emily had chosen her over all her legal colleagues and fashionable friends. She felt honoured, and had bought a new outfit especially for the occasion, and let Eamon gripe. Anyway, he liked the way she looked these days. He never said anything, of course, but he noticed all right.

'Robbie! Close the door quickly. You're blowing out all the candles! Emily, are you coming up to sit down?'

'In a minute,' Emily said.

She waited until Liz and Robbie went off up the aisle, then she picked up the car seat and went outside in search of Conor.

Honestly, wouldn't you think he'd have made the effort to be early? There was no sign of him, just a lone man walking up the churchyard towards her, tall and lithe. For a moment Emily didn't know who he was. He was wearing a very fashionable grey suit and tie, and a dazzling white shirt. His hair was very short and stylishly gelled and he bounded casually up the church steps two at a time.

'Conor?' She nearly fell over.

'What's wrong?' he asked, seeing her face.

'Um, nothing. You look . . .' She nearly said 'like a ride'. It was quite a shock to discover that she was still in possession of sexual feelings. She'd thought they had come out with her placenta. Even more surprising, it was Conor who had provoked them. Her husband, for God's sake. Surely this wasn't natural?

'You look very dapper,' she said, a bit embarrassed.

'So do you,' he said warmly. She was furious with herself all over again for not buying a new outfit, for slipping up on her diet. He was just being nice.

'I'm not late, am I?' he asked. 'I couldn't get parking.'

Emily looked suitably amazed. 'Most unusual for you.'

'I know. But I'm trying to stop being so predictable.'

'Really.'

'Mind you, I saw your car parked in the priest's spot.'

'Yes, well, I was just being assertive,' she said airily.

They joked quite a bit like this, about each other changing. Emily would sometimes roar at him to put the kettle on for a cup of tea, and tell him she was just making him aware of her needs. Both of them lightly accused the other of avoiding issues when it came to who would change one of Robert's pooey nappies.

These jokes were the only really allusion they made to that long night spent together in the labour ward all those weeks ago. They were both very raw yet, Emily felt, and she had no desire to go poking around again in the murky depths of their marriage. Besides, where would they find the time, what with feeding, bathing, burping, soothing and generally trying to keep Robert alive?

Emily did not think that it was necessary in any case. The admissions made that night, of fear and insecurity and loneliness, were things that surely only needed to be said once in any marriage. What they were dealing with now were the gaps that had been exposed, the struggle to find their feet once again. As themselves, and as a couple.

'How's my man?' Conor said, swooping down to pick up Robert. 'Jesus Christ, Emily, he looks like a girl in that dress.'

'It's not a dress. It's a christening shawl,' she explained patiently.

She watched as Conor tickled, nuzzled, kissed and pretended to drop Robert in a determined effort to make him smile.

'Conor, please, we don't want him to be sick.' But she only said it half-heartedly. She did not want to do anything to discourage this particular change in Conor. She never mentioned it at all, in fact. There were some things that they did not joke about.

She wondered did he even see it himself. He would be ringing the doorbell at nine o'clock every morning, shifting from foot to foot impatiently to be let in. Then he would get dug in straightaway with Robert, hoisting him up on his shoulder and taking him out to see the dogs. As if the child even knew what a dog was! Emily would have to fight hard to get a look-in at all. Then Conor would usually have the bonus of changing a dirty nappy. Conor loved dirty nappies. The whole cleaning process, the disposal of the nappy, the applying of Sudocream, the fresh new nappy, all appealed hugely to his practical side, his sense of enjoyment in a job well done, and he would positively glow as he descended the stairs with a spanking clean Robert.

Emily had not seen this side of Conor before. She would like to think that it was primarily to do with her. But it was Robert, of course. No one, not even Conor, could resist him.

'Is it time to go in?' Conor asked. The openness he'd displayed with Robert was gone now, and that careful, questioning look was back on his face. Maybe she looked at him that way too. It was like they both knew each other's frailties and failings now, and were trying hard not to touch on them.

Instead they delicately felt their way around things, through things, hopefully both moving in the same direction. Last week for instance they had talked tentatively about Conor's family, and Emily's family, and the place of fear and control in the backgrounds. That was how they were working it. It was a long, slow, intricate process, and it was a shame that it was about to be interrupted with this Belgium thing.

'It's five to one,' Emily said, checking her watch. 'I suppose we'd better head in.'

'Neasa's not here yet,' Conor said.

'She can't come, remember?'

'Oh yes, of course,' he said quickly. 'Still, I suppose you'll see her this afternoon anyway.'

The final judgement on the closure of Martha's would be announced today. Emily felt her place should be with Neasa and the rest of the staff in the office who had worked so hard on this case, even if it meant leaving the christening party of Robert halfway through.

'You'll be all right without me, won't you?'

'Stop fussing, Emily.'

Of course she was going to fuss! She'd never left Robert, even for an hour, since the day he'd been born! And in a house where a party would be in full swing?

'I'll manage,' Conor said, seeing her face. 'That's if your mother doesn't attack me.'

'She won't.'

He was unconvinced. 'She probably thinks I'm skipping town and leaving you holding the baby. Literally.'

'She's already accused me of driving you away.'

'Which you are,' he said, wearing that jokey face again.

'I am not.' Emily did not smile back. 'We've been over this, Conor.'

'And we both agree that the timing could be better. With Robert. With us.'

'And we both agree that this is an opportunity you won't get again,' Emily pointed out.

'There'll be other chances.'

But they knew that there was no guarantee. It was a fluke that Conor had landed the gig in the first place. Billy Middlemiss had seen the piece of music that Conor had dug out of the attic and had finally completed. Billy had connections in the film industry and Conor had received a call out of the blue on Monday last from the director of a European film just completing shooting in Belgium. The composer originally hired had left due to 'artistic differences' – would Conor be available to write the film score instead? The film was small and independent but a huge toehold into the business. And it was paid. It was also urgent.

'Do you want to do it?' Emily asked baldly. She did not need to remind him that the alternative was playing two nights a week in a smelly, smoky restaurant with no prospects and no hope.

She saw the hunger in his face, the need to strike out on his own, to fulfil some essential part of him. Hadn't she the same needs herself? She only understood now how necessary it was to be utterly selfish before there was any hope of making anybody else happy.

'Yes,' he said finally, but he didn't look excited, or pleased.

'We'll manage,' she said brightly. 'You'll fly back when you can and Robert and I will fly over and it'll be fine. And you'll only be gone a couple of months!'

But it all sounded a bit empty and second-rate, and Emily felt defensive. She was trying to do her best here; to keep everybody happy, even organising the christening at a moment's notice so that he wouldn't miss it! You'd think he'd look a tiny bit grateful that she was encouraging him to do what he needed to do!

'Robert might say his first word and I won't be there to hear it,' Conor hedged.

'Conor, rest assured, he won't be saying his first word for a good year yet.'

'Well, he might forget who I am.'

'How will he forget who you are when he'll be seeing you nearly every weekend?'

It seemed easier somehow to concentrate on Robert. Robert, after all, was a definite in the equation; neither of them was in any doubt about their feelings about him.

It was the 'us' that hung in the air between them. Just as the lack of a definite decision on Emily's part had hung in the air, for the past two months now. The decision had been made, of course. They both knew it, they were both working hard at those changes that needed to be made, even if all they could do at this point was joke about them.

'And when you come back, maybe you'll move back in,' she said quietly.

'Yes,' he said.

No bells rang. No fireworks went off overhead. Emily wondered why it all felt so flat. Like a compromise or something.

'It'll pass very quickly,' she said cheerily. 'You'll be busy and I'll be going back to work before I know it. The time will fly!'

'Yes,' he repeated, giving her another funny, disappointed look.

She felt very defensive again. Would he be any happier if she declared that she couldn't possibly live without him and that he must stay? Why could he not see, as she did, that if the balance in their marriage were to be redressed, they had to start somewhere?

'If you have a better idea, Conor, then I'd like to hear it.'

He hesitated. 'No. I suppose this is the best we can do for the moment.'

'Well, then,' she said. 'Let's go in.'

'I can't believe you didn't bring the baby!' Mandy at reception squealed.

'He just got christened. He's at his own party,' Emily said.

'Oh,' Mandy said, as though this were no excuse.

'Aren't you glad to see me anyway?' Emily enquired.

'I *suppose*,' Mandy said. Emily still looked very fat, she thought. 'Most people have gone to Milo's already to wait for the news. Phil got a new mobile phone just for the occasion!'

'Let's not get too confident, Mandy.'

'Everyone knows we're going to win,' Mandy said breezily, gathering her bag. 'Oh, and when are you coming back to work?'

'Who knows?' Emily said lightly.

Mandy left. Emily walked quietly down the deserted open-plan office for the first time in three months. They'd had a new carpet put down. And the broken photocopier had finally been replaced with a very swanky new one. Someone had put up a rota for coffee-making on the notice board.

She could not believe now that she had worked here for six years. Six years! A tenth of her life, if she croaked it at sixty. And now she felt a total stranger to the place, a misfit almost.

Just how much of a misfit became clear to her when she saw that there was a new nameplate up on the door of her office. It said Gary Gilmartin. Who the hell was he?

She peeked in the door, wondering what changes had been wrought in her little office. But the room was as sterile as she had left it, and even more devoid of personality. Not a single file was out of place, and the desk was bare except for a coffee-making rota.

She forgot about her annoyance now and felt only pity for this poor Gilmartin creature. Crawley Dunne & O'Reilly was leaving its stamp on him just as surely as it had on her. Only she had realised it before it was too late.

Neasa came in from the storeroom at the back. Her arms were laden with items of stationery.

'How did it go?' she asked immediately.

'Okay,' Emily said. 'Robert didn't cry at all. I left Conor in charge of them all back at the house.'

'I'm really sorry I couldn't make it, Emily.'

'I know, Neasa.' Emily checked her watch anxiously. 'I said I'd be back in an hour. Robert might need a feed . . .'

'I hope you're not going to be a pain in the arse about that child,' Neasa complained, hurling a stapler, a puncher and three new packets of floppy disks into a cardboard box on her desk.

'Don't those belong to Crawley Dunne & O'Reilly?' Emily enquired.

'Oh, they won't miss them,' Neasa said. She threw in some headed notepaper too. 'For my references,' she explained.

'I said I'd write you references,' Emily said.

'I know, and thanks, but to be honest I'd prefer to write my own.' Neasa now closed the top on the cardboard box and grabbed a roll of sellotape to tape it all up. She was leaving Crawley Dunne & O'Reilly today for good.

'Are you nervous about the decision?' she asked now.

'A bit. Are you?'

'Bricking it,' she said with her customary baldness. 'I'm kind of glad that I'm not in court when the judgement is handed down.'

She was trying to be brave, Emily saw. Crawley Dunne & O'Reilly had stabbed her in the back.

'They're spineless bastards,' Emily said quietly.

'Well, I wasn't a "suitable representative" for Crawley Dunne & O'Reilly in court,' Neasa said sarcastically. 'They were probably afraid I'd get drunk and make a holy show of them.'

'But to choose Gary to go up instead . . .'

'Emily, I don't care. I am so *over* Gary,' Neasa said plaintively. 'I was over him before I'd even finished with him.'

'True,' Emily said. 'So. Which way do you think it'll go?'

Robert had been one day and three hours old when the courts had handed down the decision that a judicial review would be held of the closure of St Martha's Hospital. Dee, Laura, Maggie and Emily had nearly burst their stitches, those that had them. Then the slow trawl through the courts of the actual judicial review, and now the final moment had arrived. At 3pm in Court No 5 Justice Patrick Leahy would seal their fate.

'I honestly don't know,' Neasa admitted.

Emily felt another nervous twinge in her tummy. 'At least we got this far,' she said stoically.

'Oh, don't give me that shite about how it's not about winning but about taking part,' Neasa said.

She would not understand that to Emily it was in a way. The court action might seem a bit removed from her now, but she had still fought the fight. That would be with her always.

'All set then?' she asked.

'I don't want to go over to the pub at all,' Neasa said gloomily. 'Could we not just wait to hear the news here?'

Gary was on instructions to phone Phil's new mobile phone the minute he left the courtroom.

'It shouldn't take longer than half an hour,' Emily told her.

'Half an hour is about all I'll last on bloody mineral water.'

Emily looked at her. 'How did this morning go?'

'Oh, awful,' Neasa said cheerfully.

'How awful?'

'Cringe-making awful. All these fecking eejits standing up and announcing that they were alcoholics – like none of us knew! Like it was some big surprise to us! And we all at an AA meeting!'

'So it wasn't worth missing my son's christening for?' Emily said lightly.

'I wouldn't miss a tea break for it,' Neasa declared.

She was deliberately making it out to be silly. She could not tell Emily the depth of her upset at being at one of the things in the first place. It was the last stop.

You really were an alcoholic if you turned up at AA meetings.

Maybe it would help her in time. But this morning she had been too embarrassed to do anything except lurk at the back of the room, looking at the door and waiting to see all the desperate, depraved alcoholics arriving in. After half an hour nobody arrived, and it slowly dawned on her that the alcoholics were already present; all those nice, well-dressed and educated men and women who Neasa had somehow presumed were the meeting facilitators. None of them looked any different to her. Or she didn't look any different to them.

'Did you talk to that bastard?' Neasa said, deliberately changing the subject.

Emily knew immediately to whom she was referring: Garda Andrew Mitchell from Mitchelstown, the arresting garda on her drink-driving charge.

'Yes, he's back from his holidays,' Emily confirmed.

'I hope he had a lovely time,' Neasa said insincerely.

'He did, actually, and he apologised for the delay in sending out a copy of your statement. But I have it now, and he'll let us know the results of your blood test as soon as he has them.'

'When do you think it'll get to court?' Neasa asked efficiently.

'Given the courts lists, not a chance before next year, I would say.'

'Next year!'

'It's usual, Neasa. I'm hoping it'll be heard within nine months.'

'Nine months of this hanging over me?'

'I know. I know.'

Neasa stopped her fierce sellotaping of the box. 'I really fucked up this time, didn't I?'

Part of Neasa's decision to move back to Cork City was the fact that she would almost certainly get the mandatory two-year ban for drink-driving, and she needed to be within walking distance of a job, or else near a reliable form of transport. There would be no spur-of-the-moment drives into the country, or trips up to see Emily. Everything would have to be planned and worked out and she would have no freedom at all.

'You still have the car until then,' Emily pointed out.

'I know. The law is gas, isn't it?' Neasa agreed. 'You get arrested for drink-driving but they'll let you merrily drive around for a whole year until it gets to court.'

'Be thankful for small mercies.'

They talked about the probability of her being banned quite a lot. They never talked about the other probability, which was that they might hand down a jail sentence. She might only have dented a bumper, but she had still caused an accident. In those first weeks off drink, when Neasa had literally sweated poisons from her system, she would have wild dreams at night about Mountjoy and porridge and slopping out in the mornings. And having to say to her new co-workers, whoever they might be, 'Cheerio now, I'm just off to do a three-month prison sentence. Keep my seat warm!'

It was just all so wrong. People like Neasa didn't get arrested. They didn't get hauled up before a court, and they certainly didn't go to prison. Their names did not appear in the court reports of the regional newspaper, in the same column as lunatics who had set their neighbours' noisy dog on fire.

'Come on, Neasa,' Emily said sternly, seeing her descent into depression.

'I know. I know. I'll probably laugh about it in two years' time.' She dumped the cardboard box onto the floor. Her desk was now completely bare and she looked at it for a moment. Emily thought that she was getting emotional.

'You're better than this place, Neasa.'

'Of course I bloody am,' Neasa agreed robustly. 'I don't know what I was hanging around here for anyway.' She moved on swiftly before Emily could say 'Gary'. 'Actually, I'm looking forward to setting up all over again in a new place.'

Where nobody knew her or anything about her.

It had been all over the office, of course. That little snitch Phil had been coming out of the chemist the morning it happened and had seen the whole thing. Some of her so-called colleagues had contented themselves with disgusted looks, like she was a mass-murderer or something. Others had confided that they regularly jumped into cars blind drunk but had never had the bad luck to be caught. On balance, Neasa preferred the mass-murderer brigade.

Neasa had never cared about other people's opinions. But that was when people's opinions of her had generally been great.

'Oh, here,' she said, taking a solitary document from her out-tray and holding it out.

'What is it?'

'The blueprint for the new litigation division. Creepy asked me to pass it on to you and get back to him with any comments.'

'What?'

'Didn't he tell you? Honestly! Well, you should be getting a phone call. He wants you to head up the new division, Emily.'

'Does he now,' Emily said slowly, leafing through the introduction. It was full of tight-arsed words and phrases, and everything was broken down into niggly headings and sub-headings. She felt the back of her neck tingle. A migraine.

'Gary's totally pissed off that they didn't ask him,' Neasa confided.

Emily closed the document and threw it back in Neasa's out-tray. There was a silence.

'You're not coming back here, are you?' Neasa said slowly.

'I don't know.'

'Come on, Emily.'

'My maternity leave isn't up for another three weeks, I haven't decided,' Emily insisted.

'If I were you, I wouldn't. They're a right bunch of fuckers.'

'They *did* pay all the court costs for me,' Emily said uncertainly. 'Although if we lose today . . . they might refuse point blank.'

Neasa smiled wolfishly. 'I already got them to sign a letter.'

'What?'

'You can thank me later,' Neasa said airily. 'Anyway, back to you resigning.'

'I haven't resigned yet.' Emily bit the bullet. 'Oh, all right! I've had a couple of people approach me to act for them. You know, after the publicity about the court case and everything. I could do it from home.'

Neasa shook her head, marvelling. 'You'd go into competition against Creepy?'

'It wouldn't be competition,' Emily insisted.

'They're setting up a new litigation division! I would say they'll look on it as a direct assault!'

'So what!' Emily said loudly. 'There's room in this town for both of us!'

It was a relief to say out loud what she had been planning for weeks. Or, half-planning. It was difficult to concentrate on a new career path with Robert puking in the background.

But being here today had only strengthened her

resolve. She could not go back to being a cog in the machine.

'You won't make any money,' Neasa said baldly. 'Not for ages and ages.'

'I know that.'

'Still, I suppose now that Conor is taking Hollywood by storm . . . sorry, *Belgium*.'

Neasa made no effort to conceal her ongoing dislike of Conor. Privately, she thought it was only a matter of time before he strayed again. Oh, once they got a taste for it at all there was no stopping them. Even after her own experiences, Neasa had lost none of her ability to spot glaring great faults in others, including addiction.

'So long as Robert has enough to eat, we'll manage,' Emily said.

'I'd wait until he's on solids before I go making any assumptions,' Neasa said darkly.

Belatedly she realised she was being a tad negative about Emily's new venture. And, really, Emily might do very well, given that half of the southwest now knew her name. Plus there was Emily's marvellous organisational abilities and the wad of start-up cash that must be lying in one of her savings accounts. Emily was a great saver. 'Do you need a partner?' Neasa offered magnanimously. 'I know I said I was moving to Cork, but I'll stay if you need me. We could call ourselves Collins & Martin. Or Martin & Collins, that has a better ring.'

'No, Neasa,' Emily said gently. 'Thanks anyway.'

'Just because I'm a lush doesn't mean I'm not a good solicitor!'

'You're an ex-lush, and yes, you're a marvellous solicitor. But if I'm going to do it, I want to do it on my own.' Emily hoped Neasa would understand. She didn't need the weight of another person's expectations on her. But her reasons were more selfish than anything. And she wasn't going to make any apologies about it.

'You're right. We'd probably end up killing each other anyway,' Neasa said, the idea already forgotten. 'Well, good luck to you.'

'Thanks.'

'Let's go,' Neasa sighed, picking up her cardboard box. 'I don't want that shower of bastards thinking I'm afraid to go into a pub or something.'

She was. She hadn't set foot in a licensed establishment in ten weeks, two days and ten hours. The lunch with Terry Mitton had been in a cheapish café that served no alcohol – Neasa had chosen it. It had been awful. He had been much shorter than he'd looked in his black gown and wig – five-seven at a push. Neasa had thrown back orange juice in the hope that it would loosen her tongue. But she found she had nothing to say, or at least nothing that sounded quite as devastatingly witty or meaningful as it did on red wine. And she couldn't stop noticing the hairs that protruded from his nose, or the way he kept going on and on about how his two properties had doubled in value in a year.

Reality sucked. It was grey and cold and depressing,

and she had no armour any more to protect herself from it. Who could blame her for wanting to dress it up a bit? Was there a single person out there who did not want to escape the daily toil that was work, dreary boyfriends and endless bills? Didn't half the population go to the pub on a Friday night to block it out with a few pints, to loosen up, just to have a good time? That was all she had done.

She had just wanted it to go on.

The boyfriends had gone with the drink. What was the point? She was sure she would eventually become sufficiently comfortable with reality to start dating again. But, by God, The One had better be something special indeed if she had to put up with him stone cold sober.

They stopped down by the front door of Crawley Dunne & O'Reilly. Both of them knew they wouldn't be setting foot in the place again.

'To victory!' Neasa shouted defiantly.

'If we win, I'm going to get pissed,' Emily declared. 'Oh. Sorry, Neasa.'

'Will you miss me?' Neasa suddenly asked, letting two big tears well up in her eyes. Surely she was allowed to be a bit mawkish at a time like this?

'Of course I will.'

'You're only saying that. You won't give me a thought now that you have Robert.'

'Robert only takes up ninety-five percent of my time, Neasa. I'll miss you the other five percent.'

'You won't. You'll be smooching with Conor,' Neasa said jealously.

'I can assure you that Conor and I are not smooching.'

'You can't pull the wool over my eyes – you've kissed and made up, the two of you, haven't you?'

'He's going to move back in when he gets home from Belgium,' Emily admitted.

'So it's all worked out okay in the end,' Neasa said.

'Yes,' Emily said, wondering again why it all sounded so bloody hollow. She was cross now at her own disillusionment. She had got what she wanted, hadn't she? She had dug deep and got to the truth. She had not taken second best. So what if it didn't come with streamers and party hats attached? The important thing was that after all the grief, she had emerged with her relationship intact.

It struck her now how workmanlike all this was. It was the old Emily, putting her head down, doing the hard graft, and expecting the rewards that came with toil. And she knew in a rush that part of her was still stuck back there, for all her new risk-taking and assertion. These she had saved for her career, for High Court cases, for Robert even, who required plenty of assertion and some risk-taking. But not for Conor. Not for her marriage.

Why was she so afraid of making that last leap? Part of it she knew was the aftermath of the affair. Trust was not a cheap commodity. But neither was passion, or impulse, or being in love again.

She thought of that last leap again. Maybe it was finally time to jump.

'Can I use your nappy-changing unit, Conor?'

'Of course you can,' Conor said benevolently.

'I thought I'd change Chloe before we turn the news on,' Maggie confided.

'Very sensible,' Conor said. 'And don't forget to wash your hands!'

'Oh now!' Maggie said, giggling as she disappeared up the stairs with Chloe.

Conor let his big, friendly smile slip. Maggie was the most irritating person he had ever met – bar Pauline, obviously, who was over there in the corner with the priest, talking some kind of shite about the Legion of Mary. Conor had not known the Legion of Mary still existed even. And Laura had just put *Den* 2 on the TV at full blast; *Den* 2, for two-month-old babies! How did Emily manage to surround herself with these kind of people?

Not that Emily was even here. She was in the cosy comfort of Milo's pub while Conor was standing in the midst of curling sandwiches and damp crisps, wailing babies and the smell of vomit. Tommy, Robbie, Mikey and Bobby were playing a very boisterous game of tag, and had knocked over Conor's mother twice. At least all his side had already left. The noise and smell and press of bodies had quickly become too much for them and they had strapped themselves into their big boxy air-conditioned cars with ill-concealed relief.

Conor's impatience wasn't just rudeness. In fact, he had been exceptionally pleasant and chatty all afternoon he felt. Beyond the call of duty, really. Beyond his own capacity for sociability, if you wanted to get down to brass tacks. He was making the effort. If Emily wanted him to walk on hot coals, he would do it. Even if she wanted him to be nice to Maggie . . .

But he just did not want this circus today; not when he should be spending time alone with his wife and child; not when he had a ten o'clock flight in the morning that would take him hundreds and hundreds of miles away.

'Conor! Is it okay if we turn the radio on?' Dee shouted over the TV. 'It's nearly four o'clock, they might have the results on LKR.'

You'd think she was talking about a football match. Conor wondered whether Emily knew the outcome already. He was surprised she had not phoned, especially as Laura, Maggie and Dee were waiting here for the news.

He found that he had a nervous feeling in his belly. He knew it was more than the outcome of the court case.

'Robbie!' Liz screeched out in the hallway, but it was too late. Conor heard the sound of something breaking. He did not particularly want to know what. Instead he picked up Robert, went into the kitchen and closed the door.

Peace, blessed peace.

'Will we make a cup of tea?' he asked Robert.

Conor and Robert often made tea together. It was a little ritual. They would play games around the kitchen as tea bags were sourced, cups put out and the red light on the kettle switched on, to Robert's never-ending fascination.

There were no games today. Conor was not in the mood. Neither was Robert. In fact, the child was looking up at Conor rather despondently, and Conor felt very defensive.

'I don't want to go to Belgium either, okay?' he told Robert strongly. 'It's all your mother's fault!'

Well, it was Emily who was churning out the logic this time, not him. She was the one holding up the pros and cons, refusing to let sentimentality or emotions cloud the decision. Conor found that he could not argue with her reason. Especially as she had just asked him to move back into the house upon his return. Just like that! No conditions, no begrudgery! In reality, Conor was getting everything he wanted, and more – a new career and a second chance at everything he had made a balls of the first time around.

So why wasn't he jumping around the garden?

It was probably the timing thing, he thought. Off to Belgium, when he had already missed out on so much by living in a separate house! Oh, he could kid himself all right – he would arrive here first thing in the morning and don his mantle of doting father, before becoming the concerned partner to Emily, making her meals and putting on washes, and engaging in a little marriage counselling when they were both up to it. Then he would go back to his house late in the evening, secure in the knowledge that he had not failed in his paternal and marital duties, while still managing to hang on to his bloody pride.

'I'm very sorry,' he told Robert now.

He felt he had let him down very badly. By his actions, by his affair, he had created a situation where he absented himself from some of the responsibility of bringing up his child.

He carried this responsibility around like a great weight on his shoulders. But he was not daunted by it, not crushed in the way he was when faced with the responsibility of marriage. From the day in the labour ward when Robert had been born, and Conor had eventually persuaded Emily to hand him over, he had not been afraid of him. They had regarded each other with a cool interest, or Conor liked to think anyway, and he had rather hoarsely promised Robert that he would look out for him, son. Well, it seemed the right thing to say at the time, and Robert had looked up at him with a grave acceptance.

Conor only learned afterwards that newborn babies couldn't see a thing farther than twenty-five centimetres from their own noses. But it didn't matter because by then, the pair of them were in cahoots. Conor had half wanted to keep the relationship on some kind of professional footing, with him taking care of the nappy changing and laundry loads while Emily did the cooing and kissing. But he had not reckoned on his own spontaneity, a character trait he had always regarded as a bit of a liability and which had always firmly been Emily's department. He had fought it at first and then, three days into his relationship with Robert, had held up the white flag and given in to it gracefully.

He would catch Emily looking at him sometimes when he was unashamedly romping with Robert, like today for instance, and he would remember their conversation in Martha's and he would feel embarrassed all over again.

She knew now. She knew what a small and fearful man he really was; a person with no real courage; a man who had only wanted to half-marry her in case he might have to expose himself. The result was that they had had the good times and the bad times, but none of it had been very good or very bad. It had been a grey way of living, really, antiseptic and passionless.

It could be put down to fear of intimacy, of course, and he was sure now that he suffered from this. But he had made no attempt to overcome it until she had forced him to that night, and that was where his courage had failed him.

But the miracle was that she still seemed to want him. She must love him on some level if she was prepared to work this out. This knowledge made him very conscious of what he had to do, the effort he had to make.

He could not take her faith and let her down all over again. And this time there was Robert to think of too.

He had started to offer small bits of himself; some of his family background, for example, certain episodes in his early career. He used events to reveal himself. He was not able to talk like he had talked in the hospital. Not yet. But he felt they had put their feet on the first rung of the ladder.

And now bloody Belgium in the morning. Still, maybe it would only be a problem if they let it become one. And they would still see each other every weekend, wouldn't they? He even wondered whether it might be a good thing at this point to have a little space between them. Would it be so bad to stop for some reflection?

The kitchen door flew open, startling him. It was Maggie, Chloe under one arm and an unidentified baby under the other.

'The news has just started! Quick!'

'Coming now,' Conor assured her.

But he stood there for a moment, slowly rocking Robert, and he could not hide from the fact that he was doing it again.

Belgium was a safety net for him. An escape route now that things between him and Emily were gradually proceeding to a point where he would have to divulge more of himself, make some emotional commitment once and for all, instead of just talking about it. And he was running for his life.

Lack of courage could perhaps be forgiven once in anybody's life, he decided. But not twice.

He turned and purposefully left.

The smell of garlic and herbs hit Emily the minute she walked in the door. She stood for a moment, bemused. The only time there had been a smell of garlic in the house in the last two months was when Conor got chips and garlic mayonnaise down in Mario's.

There were candles in the living-room. Lighted candles, that is. Emily couldn't even remember the last time they'd put a match to a candle.

The next thing she registered was that the stereo was playing: soft, jazzy stuff, romantic stuff.

The old ghosts came back to ambush Emily and she stood stock still in the middle of the living-room. Mary Murphy rushed into her head, as she did at odd times, no matter how Emily tried to banish her. Sometimes she wondered if she would ever truly go away. Would she be there between them always, like a decomposing body that wouldn't stay buried?

In the kitchen, Conor was turning down the heat on the stove, the baby monitor on the worktop beside him. The lights on it were rising and falling evenly with Robert's breath.

'You're late,' he said to Emily.

'Yes,' she said.

'Drunk?'

'No! Well, maybe a bit. Everybody kept buying drinks

because Neasa was leaving. And she only on water herself.' Emily looked around the tidy kitchen. There was no evidence that a party had taken place here earlier. 'I hope you didn't push people out the door, Conor.'

'I did not! Well, except for your mother, but she never leaves unless she's forced to.'

'I thought Maggie or Dee might have stayed on.' You'd have thought they'd have wanted to hear all the gory details.

'It's been a long day, Emily. And with all the babies . . .'

'I suppose,' she said, secretly glad that he had managed to get rid of everyone. 'How was Robert? Did he miss me?'

'He did.'

'How much? A lot?'

'Desperately,' Conor assured her. 'He's upstairs having a nap.'

Emily was relieved, and felt a bit guilty. But she had a few things to tell Conor. She didn't want to be distracted by Robert or anyone else.

'I'm very sorry, Emily.' Conor got in there first.

'I know.'

'We really thought you'd win.'

'So did I, kind of.'

'Is Neasa upset?'

'Well, we all were, for a while.'

'I know.'

There was an awkward moment where they both

made a kind of sympathetic move towards the other but neither of them went through with it and they both looked at their shoes.

Emily cleared her throat. 'So, um, what did they say on the radio? We couldn't get any sense out of Gary on the phone except that we'd lost. I think he was crying.'

'Just that Martha's would close immediately and that a request for an appeal had been denied.'

'Great,' Emily sighed. 'I couldn't admit it in the pub, but I couldn't bear an appeal.'

'They said that there would be a ruling on costs next week,' Conor added.

'Right.' Crawley Dunne & O'Reilly would be picking up the bill in any case. Upon news of the defeat, Creepy had immediately cancelled the tab at the bar and had left, green-faced, with Daphne and Ewan stumbling in his wake.

'Vera rang,' Conor told her. 'She said she'd call you tomorrow.'

Vera had no doubt been glued to the radio all afternoon as well. At least they'd all hung onto their jobs in Martha's for two months longer than anticipated, even if the hospital had been empty of patients at the end. Open, but empty.

'Do you think I might have a glass of wine or would Robert be pissed when I feed him later?' Emily wondered.

'I think you can chance it,' Conor said, pouring two glasses.

She held hers up in a jokey toast.

'To the campaign.'

'To a great fight,' Conor said quietly.

'Yes. It was worth it.' She took a big gulp of wine. She felt like a chapter in her life had just closed, leaving her with an unusual feeling of satisfaction, despite losing in the end.

She watched as Conor took the lid off a saucepan, threw in a handful of fresh herbs and stirred. It smelled gorgeous.

'Is this a sympathy meal?' she said lightly.

'No. It's just a nice meal. That's all,' he said evenly.

Hmm, Emily thought. Conor seemed a bit off tonight. At least, he wasn't participating in their usual jokey banter. He was stirring that pot very seriously indeed, his brow furrowed.

The thought of Belgium was probably putting him off. Not that there was anything wrong with Belgium per se – didn't they have the most divine chocolate there, wasn't that attraction enough in itself? But the reality of the flight in the morning was probably sinking in with him. She knew he desperately did not want to leave Robert. She hoped that he did not want to leave her as much.

It was time for her to put her cards on the table. She put down her wine and turned to him, already anticipating his relief and happiness.

'Conor,' she said rather dramatically, 'I've decided I'm going to Belgium with you. Robert and I.'

She wasn't prepared for the look of horror on his face. '*What?*'

He must not have understood. She repeated herself more slowly. 'I'm coming with you to Belgium. I've booked a flight ticket and everything.'

'Jesus Christ, Emily!'

'What?'

'I'm not going to Belgium! I rang them this evening and turned the job down!'

Now it was her turn to look appalled. 'Bloody hell, Conor! What did you go and do a stupid thing like that for?'

He looked all huffy now. 'Oh, *stupid!* Just because I decided that I should get my priorities right?'

'I don't believe this . . . why didn't you talk to me first?'

'Why didn't *you* talk to *me*?'

Emily threw up her hands. 'You see? This is just typical of the lack of communication between us!'

'I couldn't agree more!' Conor butted in. 'And now I'm stuck at home with no job and you're flying with Robert to Belgium in the morning!'

'Obviously I won't be using my ticket,' she said stiffly.

'Obviously. Sure haven't we got money to burn?'

Emily began to feel very stupid now, her great act of noble self-sacrifice thrown back in her face. In her head, she had fantasised that he would be overcome by emotion, possibly break down in tears, certainly sweep her into his arms and very probably try to make wild love to her on the kitchen floor (she would tell him that it was too soon, naturally).

But instead he just looked hot and cross and he was muttering something under his breath.

'Pardon?' she asked.

'I said, do you want penne or linguini with this sauce?' he repeated, louder this time.

'You know something, Conor? I really don't care,' she snapped, grabbing her wine and marching into the living-room. Only Conor could talk about pasta shapes at a time like this. How had she ever thought that things between them had changed? Fooling herself! She might as well give up now.

'Emily?' He had followed her in. Probably to ask how long he should boil the fucking penne for.

'Yes, Conor!'

'I'm sorry if I upset you. I wanted it to be a surprise. A nice one, I thought. I'm sorry.'

Emily immediately deflated at his honesty. 'I wanted mine to be a nice surprise too.'

'Yes.'

They looked at each other, awkward now.

'That was a pretty big thing,' she said. 'To give up your job.'

'Not really,' he said.

'Stop being modest.'

He looked at the tea towel in his hands and back up again. 'I just felt I hadn't done enough. I wanted you to know how much I . . . well, you know.'

'Thank you,' she said. 'I suppose I wanted you to know the same.'

There was a little silence; a silence coloured by hope and expectation and optimism. And Emily felt lighter as she turned to him.

'What about the job?' she asked.

'What about it?'

'Can't you ring them and say you want it back?'

'I don't think they'll give it back to me.'

'They would if you begged.'

'I will not lower myself to beg,' Conor said primly.

Emily picked up the phone and thrust it into his hand. 'Beg,' she ordered. 'I'll cook the pasta.'

Split Ends

Sarah Harvey

Grace Ellerington has met the man of her dreams. But her friends think he's a *total* nightmare.

When Grace and Stuart announce their engagement, Olivia, Tanya and Louis feel duty bound to save Grace from making the biggest mistake of her life. And they'll try anything to split up the happy couple – bribery, corruption, copious amounts of alcohol, kidnap . . .

Amid these high jinks, Ollie, who runs her own bistro in Battersea, finds herself at the mercy of a ruthless (though incredibly good-looking) property developer who's just threatened to put a rather large fly in her soup. And, to top it all, he happens to be one of Stuart's best mates . . .

Split Ends is a hilarious novel about the bonds of friendship and how to stretch them to their limits.

Don't miss Sarah Harvey's previous novels, *Misbehaving* and *Fly-fishing* ('enjoyable and escapist' *Express*), also available from Headline.

0 7472 6833 9

headline

Now you can buy any of these other bestselling
Headline books from your bookshop or
direct from the publisher.

FREE P&P AND UK DELIVERY
(Overseas and Ireland £3.50 per book)

Olivia's Luck	Catherine Alliott	£6.99
Backpack	Emily Barr	£6.99
Girlfriend 44	Mark Barrowcliffe	£5.99
Up to No Good	Victoria Corby	£5.99
Two Kinds of Wonderful	Isla Dewar	£6.99
Split Ends	Sarah Harvey	£5.99
Pastures Nouveaux	Wendy Holden	£5.99
Fast Friends	Jill Mansell	£6.99
Launderama	Sue Margolis	£5.99
A Minor Indiscretion	Carole Matthews	£5.99
Better than a Rest	Pauline McLynn	£5.99
My Favourite Goodbye	Sheila O'Flanagan	£5.99

TO ORDER SIMPLY CALL THIS NUMBER

01235 400 414

or visit our website: <u>www.madaboutbooks.co.uk</u>

Prices and availability subject to change without notice.

27/8